ANDRE

The author was born in Oxford in 1935, was a Colleger
at Eton, and completed his education at Harvard and
Cambridge, where he became a don. While still an
undergraduate, he wrote his first two novels, THE
BREAKING OF BUMBO and MY FRIEND JUDAS.
He has written many works of biography and social
history, but his major effort over the past twenty
years has been the completion of 'The Albion
Triptych' of novels, begun by GOG, first published in
1967 and MAGOG, published five years later. His
latest novel, KING LUDD completes his vision of the
true history of Britain from Druid times to the present
day. Andrew Sinclair is married to the writer Sonia
Melchett, and they have five children.

SUMMARY OF
THE ALBION TRIPTYCH

While the novel GOG deals with 1945 and the history of the struggle of the people against power in England until that year of the victory of the Labour Party, and the novel MAGOG deals with the history of power and its corruption in England from 1945 to 1968, the last novel of 'The Albion Triptych', KING LUDD deals with Gog's version of the history of the Luddites – the machine-breakers between 1800 and 1887 – and the mythology of communications from the age of the Druids to the dominion of the computers.

Andrew Sinclair

MAGOG

A John Curtis Book

First published in Great Britain in 1972 by Weidenfeld and Nicolson

Sceptre edition 1989

Sceptre is an imprint of Hodder and Stoughton Paperbacks, a division of Hodder and Stoughton Ltd.

Printed and bound in Great Britain for Hodder and Stoughton Paperbacks, a division of Hodder and Stoughton Ltd., Mill Road, Dunton Green, Sevenoaks, Kent TN13 2YA (Editorial Office: 47 Bedford Square, London WC1B 3DP) by Richard Clay Ltd., Bungay, Suffolk. Photoset by Rowland Photo-typesetting Ltd., Bury St Edmunds, Suffolk.

British Library C.I.P.

Sinclair, Andrew, *1935–*
  Magog.
  I. Title
  823′.914[F]

ISBN 0-340-50246-0

To my longtime and sometime companions,
Jackie, Nigel, Jana, Pat and Chas

In the beginning of Albion were Gog and Magog, brothers and enemies, the giants of the people of the white island. And in the beginning of London were Magog and Gog, set upon high to protect the power of the City of Mammon. And the brothers took up arms against one another, fight without end, amen. . . .

Gog

Power corrupts. Powerlessness corrupts absolutely.

Magog

1945

'On this day of real peace in our time . . .'

Magog put the raw steak on his left eye and winced.

'Let us give thanks to the Lord God of hosts . . .'

Was it worth sacrificing two weeks' meat ration to soothe a black eye?

'Who has brought us a great victory for the forces of democracy and Christianity . . .'

Did the blood on the steak really suck out the bruises?

'Let us pray to His mercy . . .'

And if it did, how could he cook and eat the steak, now contaminated?

'And ask for His continued blessing upon us . . .'

Magog tried the other station on the BBC. He had no better luck. They were singing hymns.

> '. . . *I will not cease from mental fight*
> *Nor shall my sword sleep in my hand*
> *Till we have built Jerusalem*
> *In England's green and pleasant . . .'*

Magog turned off the wireless altogether. Victory was a dull affair – and bad for morale. Better a good defeat to make the people buckle down to it. Worry was what kept a man at work, just as pain made him notice he was alive. The collapse of Japan was a disaster for the war effort. Back now to the slack and the slump and the strikes of muddling along in peace.

Magog walked across the yellow lions and stags that lay about the blue centre of his Persian carpet. The glance of his good eye slipped off the window-panes of his house in the Nash terraces – unseen through the glass, the trees of Regent's

Park beyond. Magog went through the door of his huge white reception room on the first floor, and down the wide stone staircase that led to the hall, then to the kitchen. Lilacs in purples and whites promised joy in the little garden between house and mews cottage at the rear; but Magog ignored them. He was trying to save food for the nation.

Carefully, Magog took a bottle of milk from the refrigerator and filled a glass. He removed the steak from his eye and dropped it into the glass, hoping that the milk in its turn would draw the poison from his bruise out of the meat, so that he could eat it. Then he tried to examine his eye in a small mirror that had once been used to advertise Edwardian corsets. Squinting over the girdled lady in her stays, Magog saw one eye lidded and the other eye still puffed and purple.

He would have to wear a patch.

He was not an obvious pirate.

As he turned to go and complain to Maire on the telephone, he saw that the steak had turned the milk purple. Pollution was spreading everywhere.

On the telephone, Maire was not sympathetic.

'I won't go out with a man who wears a patch. Everyone'd look at you.'

'Rather than you?'

'Men wear patches only to *drag* attention to themselves.'

'They may have lost an eye.'

'People might think you were a war hero. And you never left your desk at the Ministry. If you got wounded in the cause of duty, you'd get piles.'

'I don't have piles.'

'Then you haven't been working hard enough, Magog, have you?'

'Call me Magnus, please.'

'I'm sorry. I've been seeing so much of dear Gog lately. I've got used to calling you Magog . . .'

'Don't call me that.'

'Magog, you shouldn't have got in a fight with Gog.'

'He got in a fight with me.'

'Did you give him a black eye too?'

'Several.'

'So that's why he couldn't see his way home to his dear wife. He didn't get in last night.'

'Did you?'

'That's irrelevant. *He* should have. Where is he?'

'Gone off vagabonding again, I suppose. Do you really mind, Maire?'

'We'll have to catch him to certify him.'

'We'll hear from him in jail. He goes in for assault and battery.'

'Hitting your brother isn't assault. It's the family way of showing he loves you.'

'Don't say Gog's my brother.'

'But he is your brother. And the war's over, Magog. You can't tell lies and call it the national interest any more. It's terrible, but we'll all have to tell the truth now, and nobody will be able to bear it.'

Maire came round to see Magog that evening. She had come to celebrate or to annoy. She wore a long black dress with sequins sewn in a series of open compasses up to the level of her breasts, which were covered by an Arctic fox stole asleep on her shoulders. Above the fur, her full pale cheeks smiled with the joy of treachery in store. When Magog removed the fur from her shoulders, he found that her breasts were bare above the top of her dress, but that each nipple was covered with a black patch like the one he wore over his left eye. As Magog pulled back one of Maire's patches to see the whole of his mistress's breast, she pulled back his patch on its elastic, then let it pop back against the bruise on his eye.

Magog yelped.

'Tit for tat,' Maire said. 'That's for fighting my husband. Shall we go to dinner?'

In the black-market restaurant in Soho where those with connections could eat in a time before war, Magog found it hard to describe Gog's attack and his own flight through the cheering mobs of VJ Day in terms that were not humiliating. He tried to praise his own forbearance, decency, tact; but all the same, a defeat was a defeat. Gog might be mad, yet he had won the day. And Maire's malicious joy at the story added to Magog's sense of outrage. If he had been honest with himself, he might have admitted that exasperation was his chief pleasure in his affair with Maire; for she taunted him, flattered him, lied to him, destroyed him with the truth, gave him presents, looted him, kept him waiting, turned up unasked, seduced his friends before betraying them to him – and was always forgiven, as she was the best company in London. Yet Magog would not admit to all this. He was not honest with himself.

'It's a wise father knows his own child,' Maire said suddenly.

'What's that got to do with your mad bruiser of a husband?'

'It's a wise mother knows her child's father, too.'

'My dear Maire, you're talking nonsense and to yourself. I also happen to be here, you know.'

'I had to talk to myself,' Maire said with the honesty that was her guile. 'Because you were only listening to yourself. Justifying your cowardice in front of me so you could hear yourself explain how brave you were, when you weren't.' Maire paused, then said triumphantly as if she were explaining everything. 'I went and saw my darling Anne-Marie this afternoon.'

'Pleasure or professional? I suppose one Frenchwoman can only be diagnosed properly by another.'

'Seeing Anne-Marie professionally's always a pleasure. How can any woman have a male doctor? I mean, the instruments are bad enough, but in a *man's* fingers as well. They're stubby, hairy even, and inside you . . .' Maire wrinkled her sharp nose.

Magog looked down at his smooth fingers. He used hot wax on them. Maire liked that.

'Anyway, Anne-Marie examined me,' Maire went on. 'And there you are. Definitely yes. I must say, she was surprised. She's always called me the Impossible Machine. Too elegant to have proper functions.'

'Definitely what yes?'

'It's a wise father knows his own child,' Maire repeated.

'Good God,' Magog said.

'Is He?' Maire said. 'He'd better be better than men. They tell me that terrible bomb you dropped on Japan deforms the unborn.'

'That's a classified top secret,' Magog said.

'Not when I know it, it isn't. I suppose you want a monster for an heir.'

'How do I know it's mine?' Magog was luxuriating in his usual sense of moral outrage at Maire's sins.

'That's what I started by saying, only you were too stupid to pick it up. Another zabaglione,' Maire said, 'now I'm eating for two.'

'It might be Gog's or anyone's,' Magog complained. Maire waved a loose finger and a pale waiter materialized like ectoplasm from her medium's mouth.

'Another zabaglione,' Maire said. 'The gentleman would have ordered for me, only he seems to have something on his mind.' She smiled her sweetest smile at Magog. 'Do you have something on your mind?'

'A woman has to know who is the father of her child.'

'Tell that to a poor German girl after the Red Army has *liberated* her. What's she supposed to do? Say to her infant, your father's a Cossack brigade?'

'You have not been raped en masse.'

'Not this week,' Maire said, then leaned forward, her grey eyes luminous with false love. 'That's why *you're* father to my child.'

'You could say that to anyone.'

'Not to Anne-Marie, though she'd love to be.'

'To any man.'

'I could, couldn't I?' Maire laughed as the waiter materialized again with the glass of yellow froth, then vanished faintly beyond vision. 'How marvellous to revenge ourselves for our biology at last. Merde to Mother Nature. *Choose* the father of your child. Screw who you wish, then saddle the man of your choice with the brat. Why not?'

'Because it's not fair on the man.'

'What has ever been fair on a woman?'

'He has to support the child.'

'And who bears the child?'

'If a woman just chose a man, he'd have no choice.'

'Does a pregnant woman have a choice?'

'I absolutely refuse to play father to your bastard.'

'But it was you who made the poor mite a bastard, Magog. Just like yourself. With your brother's wife too.'

Magog became incoherent, then silent at this point, while

Maire ate her zabaglione. He knew she could not get away with it, but she would. For she always involved a man, even in her more casual couplings. She had the gift of conjuring up obsession from the barren. No man could escape it, however light his first step into her hug, however casual his first lying in her bed. Maire was an addiction, a vicious taste. She intensified every moment until life with any other woman seemed a succession of stale Sundays. Now with her, Magog even forgot to check the restaurant bill, and was overcharged.

Maire did not stay the night. She pleaded concern for the embryo life inside her and went off to rest. Or so she said. Naturally Magog did not believe her, naturally he telephoned her later at home, naturally she did not answer the telephone, naturally she would tell him she was already asleep, naturally she had gone to a party elsewhere, and naturally she was a liar. So naturally Magog began to reflect bitterly on the laws of love.

There are laws of love. A woman, given the chance to behave badly, will. A man, given the same choice, also will. If a friend is involved, the behaviour will be worse. If it is a best friend, the worst. If it is a brother or a sister, the very worst. Blackmail will win over trust, coercion over freedom, slavery over independence, deceit over frankness, drama over decency, betrayal over loyalty, jealousy over generosity, and all shall be excused, for all humans must play these little tricks to excite their copulations. These are the laws of love.

'I would rather hate her,' Magog said aloud, and could not.

1946

Magog watched Maire's twins being born. He wore a white gauze mask and was one among the worshippers at the ritual. He had sworn that he would not be there, but Maire had made him be there. She had said that men should feel the pain of childbirth too, and she had told him the story of a writer she knew who had pissed a clot of blood in sympathy on the birth of his first child. She did not expect such extravagance from Magog, but she did expect his presence. And he was there.

The twin girls were severed and tied and spanked and made to howl and washed and shown to the chosen father. Their red faces, shrivelled with pain, had nothing in common with Magog's image of himself in a mirror. Yet instinct was strong enough in him to feel something, pride or joy or mere approval that the human race was going on. At the sight of birth, it was enough to play the role of the father. No man could actually be a father. He was too detached.

Magog left the room, took off his gauze mask and white coat. 'I must go back to work,' he said.

'So soon?' a nurse said. 'It's a proud day for you.'

'England waits at my out-tray,' Magog said, smiling to show that he was not being arrogant. Yet he meant what he said.

Population increase was not always approved by the Ministry of Resources and Development. Magog's job as the youngest Assistant Secretary in the Ministry had once been to prepare for his Under-Secretary George Germain a list of national resources that might be exploited – if Britain ever paid off its war debts, which was not very likely. Should there be a period of expansion, more people might be an asset, even in an island of limited space. But at the moment, people were trouble to the poor welfare state, and more people were more trouble. Maire, of course, had to produce the most trouble for the future, twin girls in a time when mother nature was compensating for the war by producing too many male babies. What an opportunity lay cradled and waiting for the twins, what havoc.

Magog often thought the British would have done better to lose the war than win it. Then they would not have had the problem of disposing of its débris, which now took up most of the time of most of the Civil Service. They could have just got on with the job of reconstruction like the losers were doing. Instead, they had to act as a form of gargantuan police van and dustbin cart, disposing of tens of millions of displaced persons, lost hopes, broken homes, shifted frontiers, unwanted mandates, unwilling allies and plain military refuse. Magog's immediate problem was nerve gas.

'It might have been useful.' Germain sighed and tugged at his ginger eyebrow without success. 'Sometimes I think, Ponsonby, the whole of human progress has depended on manufacturing the useless object for the unnecessary occasion.'

'We could drop the gas in those pot-holes in the West Country and seal them off,' Magog said. 'Stop up Wookey Hole.'

'That's wasting a natural resource. The Welsh love pot-holing. You simply can't keep a good miner up. I mean, who else would submerge down a flooded cavity at week-ends and call it fun?'

'Depoison the gas?'

'Too expensive. Nerve gas, as you know, is dirt cheap to produce if you have the know-how. But it costs a fortune to liquidate.'

'We could give it as a war loan to our allies in exchange for powdered egg. Then it's their problem.'

'Today's ally tomorrow's enemy. It could be used against us. Without pride, I must confess our nerve gas is the best. And we'd have to spend another few million working out an antidote against our own stuff.'

'What are the French doing about their surplus gas?'

'Dumping it off Cornwall. Diplomatically speaking, we should riposte and dump ours off Brittany. But naturally, you do not officially *know* this. Your recommendation should only concern itself with our department's area of responsibility. Of course, if it so happens to coincide with Foreign Office recommendations . . .' Germain's voice tailed off. His hints usually ended in silences rather than suggestions.

'How long before the containers rust and gas the fish?'

'Not in the political lifetime of this Minister, nor of the next, nor of the next. And that is the Civil Service's definition of eternity.'

'Capability Brown . . .' Magog began. Germain sighed to hear him speak and finished off the sentence for him '. . . planted trees and made landscapes which only the great-grandchildren of his wealthy clients would ever be able to see, for we should all think generations ahead.'

Magog felt the righteousness of fatherhood in his voice. 'It is our duty, you know.'

'Our duty,' Germain said, 'is to get the Minister through the next Question Time in the House of Commons and to keep things running . . .'

'Running down.'

Germain ignored Magog. 'And incidentally, we may have time to develop something for somebody, but I doubt it, and so do you.'

Magog considered Germain, the pallor beneath the curious ginger hair, the web of weariness that the overworked war years had spun upon his skin, the stoop that the burden of his over-mighty head had yoked on his shoulders. He knew that Germain hid his real concern behind a professional scepticism, and yet . . . After a while, a pose held for too long stiffened the joints. The attitude became the attribute. The model became the statue. Germain had tried and failed too often to believe anything much could alter.

'Did you ever hear of the dogs abandoned on the island off Istanbul?' Magog asked.

'The war rather impeded my summer travels,' Germain answered.

'The Turks decided that there were too many dogs in the slums of the capital. So they dumped three hundred of them on a bare rock in the Bosphorus. Tourists are now shown the sight. There are two hundred and ninety-nine gnawed skeletons on that rock. Not a shred of meat on them. There is one perfect unchewed skeleton, that of the biggest dog, which didn't quite have the guts to gnaw its own legs before it starved. The Turks don't think there's a moral in the story, but they do think we infidels are dogs.'

'Three dogs rule the earth, America, Russia and we do. We may eat the rest, Ponsonby, but not each other.'

'Two big dogs rule,' Magog said, 'and one basset hound. We've chewed our legs at the knees to survive. We'll be eaten next. We haven't got the teeth left, only the bark.'

Germain sighed again. 'Then we'll just have to think, won't we?'

'What else have we got,' Magog said, 'except brains?'

'Nothing much,' Germain said, 'but we'll pull through like we always have. Now if you wouldn't mind drafting a minute about the nerve gas. We really will have to keep up with the French, you know. And historically speaking, the sea's far more our cup of tea than theirs.'

So Magog went back to his desk and considered the sea. Could it absorb the nerve gas as it had absorbed all human folly from the time that a thing with gills which would become man had first crawled from the surf? Though the sea was very large and very deep, surely its secrets were not beyond the scope of its perverse offspring? Magog knew that if he worked on the sea for long enough, he would be able to understand it. But working *on* it meant that he could not understand it. He would have to work in it, full fathom fifty and more, to begin to understand the undercurrents of the rollers. And it would be cold down there and dark down there, enough to crush his skull into his brainpan and his ribs into his lungs.

A man was not an eel now. He had to build bathyspheres and submarines, to get his own back on the ocean. About time too. The oceans had been pushing him about for too long. Taking up two-thirds of a crowded world. Storms and sea-sickness, wrecks and castaways, widows and lost empires. The oceans had a lot to answer for, and they had only just begun to pay their price to man. For they ignored him and he had to use them. They were indifferent to him and he had to value them. They were natural, but he was human and no longer shared his nature with the world.

Magog pulled his ruled paper across his desk towards him. He winced at the coarse stuff that the government inflicted on the best thoughts of its finest few, just to save a penny or two. He began to draft a recommendation that would probably become an order and then an action, because its prose would be carefully worded to admit many possibilities, yet only the one conclusion indicated by Germain. As that was the cheapest and most diplomatic solution, the Minister would not want to see an alternative presented. And good civil servants present mostly what the Minister wishes to see, or they will have to do it again. So Magog wrote:

Very broadly, the problem of nerve gas disposal is no great problem, if it is despatched with the maximum of speed and secrecy and the minimum of expense. It is generally felt to be correct that the disposal of the gas in the Atlantic Ocean is the least offensive solution to home opinion, which should be informed only after the disposal, if at all. In case of possible bad reactions in the future, the said stretch of the Atlantic should lie near the coasts of another country, although naturally in international waters for reasons of law. Costs will be depreciated if the said stretch of sea is not more than one hundred miles from Plymouth. The corrosion factor of the containers of the nerve gas is stated by the manufacturers to approximate to one hundred years, although exposure to salt and other marine elements has not been fully quantified and will cause additional expense to calculate (See Appendix A). The Government has its part to play in protecting the taxpayer from further burdens caused by our victorious national defence, yet it should assure the future of British children and protect the beaches of the South Coast, one of our most important undeveloped natural resources. The disposal of the gas containers more than twelve miles off the coasts of France or Ireland could in no way known to modern methods of research do foreseeable harm to this country . . .

After strong representations from the French, the nerve gas was dumped off the Irish coasts. The Irish had, after all, been neutral in the war. This was their punishment. And anyway, the Irish were Irish, weren't they? They had no power and they could not retaliate. Magog approved the decision. As always it was the most rational solution, and therefore the best.

'It may be holy water,' Maire said, 'but I bet it hasn't been boiled. It's full of germs.'

The newly-christened Rosa Ponsonby Griffin screamed at the cold and infectious touch of the cross. The priest gave her, wet on forehead and middle, back to her nanny, before drying his hands on his vestments. 'Next, please,' he said. A second nanny passed him Rosa's twin sister.

'This one's to be called Josepha,' Maire said. 'Ponsonby.' She smiled at Magog. *His* surname, not Gog's, her legal husband's. 'Griffin,' she added and smiled at Gog, looming on her other side. His surname, to make the child legitimate, not another bastard like Magog. Both men should be satisfied.

Neither was, but both were silent. Magog heard the priest intone, watched him dip his finger in the Norman font that looked like a quality bird-bath, and winced as Josepha howled even louder than her sister to receive her names, with the cold finger of Christ. She also protested in all the ways open to her. The priest again put aside the sopping bundle of old lace into the arms of the second nanny, and he washed his hands in the holy water to remove the smell.

'I'll change the water,' he said to Magog, 'and bless some more.'

Gog could contain himself no longer. He shambled forward, his loose limbs and bony head and broad nose and lips making him look like a peasant come to the wrong fair. 'That's not a washbasin,' he said. 'And you should be defrocked.'

Maire came up behind Gog, practised in control. She put each of her hands into the crook of his elbows to stop him making a lunge. Then she peered round Gog's arm at the priest. 'We all want to thank you so much for christening *my* two mites,' she said. 'Don't let us keep you, Father Malleson. I'm sure there's a burial waiting for you.'

'There is,' Gog said.

The priest muttered and moved away. He neither ran nor walked, but seemed to skim off footless as a vacuum cleaner under his cassock.

'Gog, you are a dear,' Maire said. 'You even make a boring christening ominous.' Then she led him outside the church before he could try to shatter the font with his fist.

In the impossible summer day, the bees were too fat to rise off the flowers on the graves. They lay back in their beds of petals, drunk or dead on sun and nectar. No drowsy buzz backed the birdsong. Pausing under the dog's teeth of the Norman entrance of the country priory, Maire and Gog, Magog and two nannies with the two babies seemed to stand in the jaws of another time. But the stone bite did not close on the sinners. It

gaped to see them walk out into the graveyard, unharmed.
Retribution had lockjaw.

'Gog,' Maire asked, 'what are you *doing* on that firth of yours
in Scotland? You can't farm lobsters. They're not housetrained.'

'Nerval used to take a lobster round on a ribbon,' Magog said.
'It shook hands with his friends. Soon they had claws. Which
was right, since they were critics.'

'We'll have to farm the sea,' Gog said, 'or we'll starve. The
people will have to learn. The abbeys used to have fishponds.'
His wave included the restored priory buildings that flanked the
old Norman church and now housed a Catholic sect, which had
not yet given up Rome, although Rome had given it up centuries
ago. 'Now we'll have sea-acres. Anyway, there's nothing for me
in the South. London doesn't agree with me.'

'I'm flattered you bothered to come down all that way,' Maire
said. 'You must still care.'

'At least you didn't try to put me in an asylum this time,' Gog
said. He blinked at the sun and screwed up his eyes.

'Those who choose to farm are classified as lunatics anyway,'
Magog said. 'Wanting to endure all that *weather*.'

'You notice the time of day up there,' Gog said. He opened
his eyes to look at his half-brother, haloed by the backing
brightness. Magog's skinny length and scythe of a nose made
the skin on Gog's knuckles itch with the hope of a punch. But
he remembered that he was on his best behaviour and turned
to Maire. 'You're always welcome up north,' he said, 'with Rosa
and Josepha.'

'I'm sure you find your shell-fish better company,' Maire said.
She fingered the pearl on the black velvet band round her smooth
black hair that made a helmet of darkness above her white face
and suit and lace stockings and glacé pumps. 'But I do hope,
Gog, you were pleased they were called Rosa and Josepha. I
know what those names mean to you.'

Rosa-Josepha. The blue and orange poster that used to hang
in his bedroom with Maire. Siamese twins joined at the hip, thin
girls with pouting lips and four bare legs that made them look
as if they were a beautiful stool supporting the immaculate curve
of their arms. Ah Rosa. Ah Josepha. They were the talk of Paris
in the Belle Epoque when Rosa married a Frenchman. What did

Josepha *do* in the nights? What did *he* do? What did the sisters do to each other? Nobody knew and the husband didn't talk. Rosa had a child. One early photograph existed of that christening. Rosa carrying the child in her arms. On one side of Rosa, her sister looking down fondly at the baby, her husband smiling at his infant, which he was to leave soon afterwards. Ah Rosa. Ah Josepha.

'You didn't have to call them that for me,' Gog said.

'It's a family name,' Maire said. 'My granny was called Rosa-Josepha. Really.'

Gog looked at his wife, brightly smiling in the sun. She winked. Because she hinted she might be telling a lie, she might well be telling the truth. Maire never liked anything in her past to be too certain, in case it might be used in evidence against her.

'Well,' Magog said, 'at least Rosa and Josepha are in the family.'

Gog turned and went over to the nannies. With a curious formality, he took each little girl and kissed her and gave her back to her keeper. They were quiet in his grasp, as though they already knew his presence. Then Gog turned and walked down towards the priory gate, where he paused.

'Must go,' he called back. 'I've an experiment hatching.'

'I love you,' Maire called back, smiling. 'The arrangements as before?'

'Yes,' Gog called. 'Plunder it all. Just send me the money I need for the sea farm.'

He walked off, head leading the way on hunched shoulders down the road. 'He's certainly disinterested,' Magog said to Maire. 'But then, men like that should never be entrusted with the responsiblity of riches.'

Public money, private money. Magog saw a difference. Public accounts had to balance down to the last farthing and the last re-used envelope. No matter if a wrong decision caused tens of millions of pounds to be spent on an aeroplane that was a dodo, a ship that was a diving duck, a scheme that was a dead turkey. As long as the pennies squared off with each other on either side of the ledger, as long as there was positive proof that no private corruption had taken place, then the Ministry and the

Civil Service could parade their integrity and pooh-pooh their incompetence. Money could be wasted in Whitehall as long as it was passed straight to the profiteers and did not linger in any pockets on the way. Then the final public accounts would be certified pure, and the public could never hold their fleecing rulers to account. Any Minister could beggar Britain, as long as he was honest about it.

Private accounts were not the same. There a man's duty was opposite. He was bound to preserve and increase his hoard by every legal means at the expense of the state. Where there was a loop-hole in the tax law, he was obliged to pour his money through the gap until the government blocked that particular breach and the tax accountants found another. This avarice was a man's duty because a good provider was bound to hand on as much as possible to his heirs. Now that Magog was possibly the father of Gog's twin daughters and certainly in charge of Gog's estate through Maire, he could justify his love of swelling up bags of money many times over. He was benefiting his brother, his brother's wife, her children – and only incidentally himself.

Money was easy to make after the war, if there was some money already in hand. Through Gog's indifference to spending and Maire's ability to tap other lovers for her extravagance, Magog found that his half-brother still owned some two hundred thousand pounds in different shares and bonds at the moment of victory. Even the unsaleable railway and coal mine shares were to be generously compensated by a Labour Government, which preferred to nationalize rather than expropriate, and was to provide new liquid capital for those who had so exploited the public services that these had run into the ground. With this compensation, Magog could buy oil shares, for oil would be consumed by more and more people. He could buy metals, for people had to use raw materials; he could buy shipping, for people had to carry raw materials; he could buy industrials, for people had to make raw materials into goods; he could buy stores, for people had to buy the goods they made; and he could buy electronics, for growth industries would grow, if people had a future at all. Magog would have bought shares in the activities of all the world, if he could. But he only had two hundred thousand pounds to invest, which was not enough.

There is a law about the rich. Whatever folly they buy will make them richer, as long as it is scarce. Magog, knowing this fact, appreciated that art which appreciated. For his labours in administering Gog's estate, he did not pay himself in cash, but in contemplation. Each month, the estate gave him a present, a Degas dancer here, a Renoir nude there, a small Corot for his lavatory wall, a Guardi bright with promise of Venice in case he felt desk-bound, a Tang horse for the alcove that had been a grate, and a Tiepolo sketch of heaven for worship from his bath. Touched by spring fever, he once took a gamble and used his fair dues from Gog's fortune to buy himself a Picasso portrait. It was crammed into his wall safe, because it really wasn't worth a look. Yet as a hoard against inflation – and tax free . . .

'But you never go to the galleries,' Maire said. 'Living painters are far more interesting.'

'In bed, perhaps,' Magog said, feeling Maire's bare flank against his thigh. 'But I believe in the test of time. It's absolutely discriminating. The lousy sells badly to posterity.'

'Do I pass the time test as a work of art?' Maire asked. She smiled and rolled over and put a breast on either side of Magog's right shoulder. Her belly lay in the hollow above his hip-bone. Magog could not stop a reflex action and he brought his left hand across to stroke her top breast and feel her nipple harden to his touch.

'You're timeless, Maire. Like any masterpiece.'

'I'd better be, since you're younger than me.' Maire bit into Magog's neck, at first softly, then harder and harder until he shook his flesh free. 'Or you wouldn't get given any more pictures, would you, for looking after my husband's affairs?'

'It benefits you too.'

'If it didn't,' Maire said, 'you wouldn't.' She rolled away onto her back. 'You should buy living artists.'

'My Picasso . . .'

'Unknowns.'

'If artists would kill themselves quicker,' Magog said coolly, 'they'd get more for their pictures. They wouldn't glut their market.'

Maire laughed.

'Then the only good art is dead art?'

Magog smiled and turned to lie on Maire, stopping her chat with his tongue.

1947

Big Ben froze up. Time stopped. It was the worst winter for sixty-six years. Britain's economy skidded to a halt, bare-kneed schoolboys skated on the streams, the national coal supply ran out, one of God's sparrows fell in flight and brained a housewife, the Central Electricity Board met by candle-light in heavy over-coats to work out that there could be no electric heat or light in homes for five hours a day. Magog got his first chilblain and found it uncouth, four and a half million people were out of work, Maire flew to the Bahamas on a USAF bomber with a USAF general to deliver one urgent letter requisitioning a suite for two for the duration of the fuel crisis, the trains did not run on schedule or at all, Gog's lobster spawn died, shepherds tunnelled through the snow to get hay to their buried sheep, and the Minister of Power declared that the Labour Government was prepared for anything except the weather. Those warm enough to cat-call were silenced by the announcement of a new government programme – recovery through austerity. The war was not over.

WE'RE UP AGAINST IT. WE WORK OR WANT.

Magog undid his trouser-band. Bad news, his paunch was growing. He then turned back to the layout of the poster for the official propaganda campaign to come. WE'RE UP AGAINST IT. We certainly were. His nostrils wrinkled at the stench of the paraffin stoves that he had had to commandeer for his office, to beat the fuel shortage. His brains clotted in the cold – that was a national emergency. WE WORK OR WANT. An ambiguous slogan. The problem was that the workers wanted things and wouldn't work for them. WE

WORK OR LACK. Right, but too old-fashioned. WE WORK OR WON'T. Nice on the ear and eye, but easily parodied to We Won't Work. WE WORK OR BUST. The best version, but American. The Americans had already taken everything Britain had to sell, pawn, pledge or lease. At least they might leave us alone with our version of their original language. WE WORK OR WANT. Magog knew that he should leave the slogan alone without his version of its original language. Perhaps the Minister had written it himself.

WE'RE UP AGAINST. WE WORK OR WANT.

Doing nothing about anything often worked best.

Magog did not know why he was there. Normally the reason for his invitation by the Steel Lord was predictable by the fish and incontrovertible by the dessert. But Magog could not find the reason in the seating at the dinner table. On one side of him sat the inconsiderable wife of some minor Minister – and Magog did not consider her. On his other side sat a sullen Jewish girl, Hadassah Radzen. Magog noticed particularly her eyes, so dark and large that the flesh seemed to be pulled down from their whites to her swollen mouth. She spoke little, burning in the hot silences of the young. She had obviously been forced to attend and had no mercy on her neighbours. Magog had no appeal to her. The judgement of the young is final until they age.

When the ladies left after the meal, a small man came to sit beside Magog. 'Doctor Radzen,' he said. 'You were sitting by my daughter.' His eyes were, indeed, also large and dark, but they seemed out of place below his baldness and above his beard, which failed to cover the pits in his cheeks and chin and neck. Magog thought that Radzen's hair must attract moths.

'Magnus Ponsonby,' Magog said. 'Your daughter didn't seem to want to be here much.'

'Have you a daughter?' Radzen said. 'I'm old-fashioned enough to tell her what's good for her to do.'

'I have twin girls,' Magog said and felt twice as good.

'Double trouble,' Radzen said and smiled. He passed Magog the decanter of port without taking any. 'What does a good father do when his twins fight each other? Double trouble.'

Radzen shook his head and said with artificial diffidence, 'Like Palestine.'

Magog knew now why he had been asked to dinner.

'I wouldn't call the Arabs and the Jews *twins* in Palestine,' Magog said. He passed on the decanter.

'Thousands of years of living together . . .'

'Living together, but very apart.'

'Living side by side . . .' Radzen smiled again. 'It makes for a community.'

'Not a connection by blood,' Magog said.

'A connection sealed by much blood, wouldn't you say?'

'The Arabs must be awfully surprised you've begun to fight back,' Magog said. 'After fifteen hundred years of knocking you about, here you are with the Stern Gang, an eye for an eye and a tooth for a tooth, battling them for Palestine. The sword of the Lord and of Weizmann. You shouldn't have blown up the King David Hotel, though. We can forgive you killing ninety of us, but not destroying our headquarters. It's bad form.'

'What are ninety dead beside six million?' Radzen asked. 'After all, it's better to die in a hotel than a camp.'

'All the same, have mercy on the poor old British bobby trying to keep order in Palestine.'

'First he should have mercy on us,' Radzen said. 'After Belsen, don't you think you could let the last of the Jews land rather than drown?'

'That's not my department,' Magog said quickly. 'I'm in the Ministry of Resources and Development.'

'We also wish to develop Israel . . .'

'Palestine surely.'

'Palestine,' Radzen said. 'One should not be premature.'

'Israel,' Magog said, 'that's a nice prophecy. But we won't give up our mandate.'

'We may take it,' Radzen said. 'But I came to ask your advice.'

'I wasn't asked here by chance,' Magog said. 'Hazard here is always planned.' He nodded at the Steel Lord, who was talking about Benin bronzes to a competitor. 'I never knew he was a Zionist. He's more British than we are.'

'We're very good at camouflage,' Radzen said. 'History has made us so.'

'And now, what do you want?'

'Two things. You are scrapping many obsolete things we would pay well for. Why waste so much of your labour when you need the money?'

'Guns, you mean. Explosives.'

'Human products that must be used in self-defence.'

'You might use them against us in Palestine.'

'Only for delivery when you have left Israel.'

Magog smiled.

'We won't go, you know.'

'Public opinion's against you.'

'Diplomacy makes public opinion. It is deaf to mobs.'

'Then you'll be getting a down-payment for nothing,' Radzen said. 'You must admit, that's a good proposition. Something for nothing. You don't study myth and history, do you?'

'That's my brother's lunacy,' Magog said. 'I mean Gog's.'

'In history we learn only this, the myth must work itself out. Therefore the impossible may happen. Israel has been a myth for two thousand years. Now Israel will be. So ten per cent down on a million pounds' worth of scrapped war resources – when you leave Palestine.'

'The Arabs won't like it.'

'Will they know?'

'One usually knows the make of the bullet which kills you . . . or your gravediggers do.'

'I've always admired the British,' Radzen said. 'Very realistic. Their only flaw as far as we're concerned is that they have always loved the Arab and tolerated the Jew. Which is actually better than anti-Semitism.'

'What about Disraeli?' Magog said. 'Who got us into the Suez Canal?'

'And what about Lawrence of Arabia?' Radzen said. 'If Disraeli is resurrected once more to excuse yourselves for doing nothing for the Jews, I shall believe in Lazarus.'

Magog laughed.

'What's the second thing you want?'

'We're landing two thousand of our people back in Israel every week. Don't go on with your farce of calling them illegal immigrants. Remember your Nelson, turn a blind eye. And you'll win another great victory without even a fight. We'll smash the Arabs for you.'

'We don't want the Arabs beaten by you. We've put a lot of money in the Arab Legion.'

'Come on.' Radzen's eyes were bright with truth or laughter. 'Divide and rule. The old British game. You don't have enough money to stop the Arabs from taking back all your vital oil in the Middle East. So let us beat them for you. Then they'll spend all their time and energy in trying to crush Israel. And they'll have to make a deal with you. They can't fight on two fronts at once, which means they'll have to tolerate the enemy at their backs. So you can exploit the Persian Gulf in peace, while we focus their rage on us and the Mediterranean. If you can't beat them, why not let us beat them for you? Let them hate us, not you.'

'It's a nice proposition,' Magog said, 'to pass the time after dinner.'

'You could pass it on,' Radzen said, 'to the right quarters.'

'I could,' Magog said. And, as if on cue, the Steel Lord rose from his chair. If he had seen Radzen nod that his mission was accomplished, Magog had missed the nod. Perhaps the only code was politeness.

'We shouldn't keep the ladies waiting,' the Steel Lord said.

Magog fell into his affair with Hadassah without warning. Later on, he could hardly tell how it had begun. Not during the frequent drinks with Radzen when Hadassah had come and gone on her own business, casual and inexplicable. Not during the short encounters, uneasy with silence, when Hadassah had come to Magog's house in Regent's Park, bringing a personal note from her father about the make and the quantity of arms. And not during their chance meeting in Whitehall, when Magog had hit against a trip-wire and exploded a hidden violence in Hadassah by the Cenotaph.

'What are our monuments to our millions dead?' she raged. 'Barbed wire, locks of hair stuffing cushions, teeth with gold fillings gouged out, finger-marks on the ceilings of gas chambers? Our mass graves are abattoirs, sheep-dips. Your men fought, they got marble. Ours didn't, they ate each other's shit. Not now. We fight. Without the old Jews and the crimes you did to them, there'd be no conscience in you. But with the new Jews, you won't get any mercy. We learned from you, force is all. We'll take what we want, no asking.'

And Hadassah did, one May day. Magog was walking with her across the fields of grass in the Park that were pushing their green advance over the bare patches made by the winter footballers. Ahead, across a canal, a big cat roared its hunger in the Zoo. Near them, a small boy flew a kite on a long length of twine until its little diamond hung high as a hawk. By the trees, a stolid girl archer planted her legs into the ground and slotted her arrow and aimed and sent the shaft through the distant straw so fiercely that its point came out a foot the far side. Hadassah turned and crooked her arm round Magog's neck and pulled him into a kiss. He had no time to think. Her breasts were hot puppies against his jacket. There was no backing from their teasing.

In bed, Hadassah was arrogant, and Magog felt like a serf. She took him when she chose, reaching her climax as quickly as she could, letting him get to his as best he might. If she wanted him, she would rip her clothes off almost on the elegant steps leading to his door and she would chivvy him upstairs to her lust. There was no time even to draw the curtains; neighbours with binoculars could see what they could see. If she didn't want him, she would walk out of the house or, if she stayed because she was tired or it was raining or there were no taxis to be had, then she would flop into bed as indifferent as a flounder. The trouble for Magog was that she always slept naked. Hard with want, he would lie between the black sheets and watch her make her breasts tight by raising her arms to brush the back of her long hair up and under. But when she lounged across to join him and he moved towards her and began to stroke her nipples to excite her in textbook fashion, she would turn away and be asleep in less than a minute. Magog found her rather animal.

Sometimes Magog insisted so much that he became desperate. Then, like any Levantine, she would be stimulated into bargaining, an art she enjoyed more than making love, which was a mere appetite. It would cost Magog two hundred sten-guns for Israel for a cold lay with a water-melon, two howitzers for a screw with a tepid couscous, and a light tank for a hot time in Jerusalem tonight. Once Magog traded a lease-lend destroyer for passion till dawn and, in his satiation, the navy of the new nation was born. He had to take a taxi to the office, but he also had to give Hadassah her due. She might love her country more than him, but she was a maid of honour. She would always keep her side of the arms deal.

So the power of his desire pressed Magog into weakness and he arranged for the date for delivering the weapons to the Jews to creep forwards. He justified his policy to the Minister along the lines suggested by Dr Radzen – the British need to create an enemy state on the Mediterranean to focus the Arabs' hate away from the Persian Gulf and the oil. 'We must not only back the powers that be,' Magog told Germain. 'We must also back the powers that will be. While we should officially flatter any present government to safeguard our interests overseas, unofficially we must back the chief group of rebels in case they become the next government. Anyway, the more powerful the rebels are, the more the present government will have to rely on us. And if we don't safeguard our future with the rebels, the Russians will get in first.' By this enlightened policy of supporting reaction and revolution simultaneously, Magog hoped to shore up the ailing British Empire for a few more decades. Weakness bred cleverness.

Magog sneered at the curious honour that seemed to corrupt the failed Cromwell of the new Labour revolution, Clement Attlee, the Prime Minister. A slight unmeritable man, given by history the unique chance of winding up the British Empire and its ruling class, he was so warped by Public School ethics and a sense of fair play that he could never match the ruthlessness of the aristocrats like Churchill. The old warhorse Winston would never have given away India without throwing away Africa as well; the second had, after all, been acquired to protect the first and ran at a loss. So the wreck of a sinking Empire was left to scuttle England's economy and a leaderless Europe was shunned to grope its way to its own grouping without England and the aristocrats were allowed to break out from their last moat to enjoy their riches for a few more decades and Clement Attlee would go down in history as a decent man – and the greatest

traitor to the opportunity of his time and of the class he claimed
to represent since Parliament cut off the head of King Charles.
The chance of change never repeats itself. The Labour revolution did not come. And Magog lay in bed in his Nash terrace
with Hadassah Radzen, who never missed a chance. But then,
Israel was hardly born, while England was a geriatric case.

'You are my India,' Magog said, partitioning Hadassah's thighs
with his right hand. 'My Pakistan.' His fingers plaited the hair
on her belly. 'This is my Hindu Kush,' he went on, his fingers
slipping down. 'This the Ganges of my desire.'

'Fifty mortars,' Hadassah said. 'And if you bargain, it'll be
fifty-five. Or you'll have to have yourself.'

'This is my Israel,' Magog said, now holding Hadassah's far
breast, 'and this the valley of Jordan.' His hand wandered on a
pilgrimage down one slope of skin and up another. 'And this
Mount Sinai, and I'm already out of my mind with temptation.'

'Sixty mortars,' Hadassah said. 'You'd better make up your
mind quicker, or the terms will get worse. That's dirt cheap to
occupy a bit of geography like mine.'

'Sixty mortars,' Magog sighed. 'You've the soul of a rug-
dealer, not John Donne.'

'Sixty-five mortars,' Hadassah said, 'to show you really love
me. What's five mortars between friends?'

'I really love you,' Magog said and moved his body to cover
her. But she elbowed him away, turning her rump to him so
that he found himself lying against the lovely Jericho of her back.

'And the mortar bombs,' Hadassah said. 'Ten thousand. That's
about a hundred and thirty per mortar. We'll always be in the
market for more bombs, which is good for your trade surplus.
And your bed.'

'You are my casbah,' Magog groaned. 'My souk, my dirty
deal, my Alexandria. Do you ever get enough weapons, so you
don't have to ask for more?'

Hadassah suddenly turned and began stroking Magog gently
between his legs. Her lower lip felt at his eye-lids. 'I love you,'
she whispered. 'For fifteen thousand mortar bombs.' She began
to laugh. 'Give, Magnus, give.' His mouth stopped hers and his
arms locked round her ribs to seal the bargain.

For once, the deal was not delivered. There was foreign

intervention. As Magog began his thrusting towards the soft core of Hadassah that he would never reach, he saw her gasp in surprise, not joy. A seizure seemed to grip her body as her face slackened. Her muscles set hard, her legs locked round him, he was caught in the man-trap of her embrace. His pleasure changed to pain as her thighs and heels tightened in a vice round his rump. Magog could not move at all.

'A gentleman,' Maire said behind him, 'should get up for one lady and get off another.'

'I can't,' Magog said. 'She's had a spasm.'

'Shall I call an ambulance?' Maire asked. 'Perhaps you need surgery.'

'I can't be carried into the streets like this,' Magog said. He bit at Hadassah's ear without any effect on her fainting. 'It'd be a public disgrace.'

'The Civil Service already is,' Maire said. 'I'll ring for the Red Cross.'

'No,' Magog said. 'Get some cold water. It may shock her conscious. You shouldn't come in here without knocking. I thought you were abroad.' He struggled in Hadassah's leg-lock, but it was useless. He was clamped groin to groin.

'You're a fool ever to assume anything with me,' Maire said. 'People always come home and always at the wrong time.'

'Get the water. I'm being crushed to death.'

'What a way to go,' Maire said. 'Most men would envy you.'

'Just get the water. It must be a fit of hysteria.'

Maire pulled back the sheet and took her time in studying Hadassah; Magog's body she already knew.

'Not bad,' she said. 'When she grows up, she might be competition. How much does she cost you?'

'Nothing,' Magog said. 'It's just young love. Get the water, for god's sake.'

'Nobody'd have you,' Maire said, 'if they weren't having something more for it. My dear Magog, power is your only aphrodisiac. You don't get us for your belles fesses alone.'

Maire put her hand on Magog's buttock and gave him a cruel pinch between thumb and fingernail. He yelped, writhed, stayed caught in his tender trap.

'Lay off, Maire. Get that water.'

'Just trying to break the block,' Maire said. 'But I see, you really do want her.' She walked away. 'I feel I'm one too many. I seem to be cramping her style.'

'Water.'

'Oh, go dig a pond.' And Maire left.

After quarter of an hour of struggling, Magog managed to topple himself and Hadassah from the bed on to the floor. The fall broke her rigor. She sagged free. Magog took some time to bring her round. She told him that she had spent two years hiding in a cupboard in Holland during the war, when any intruder might have been death in the shape of a Nazi bringing Dachau in his eyes. She didn't take people dropping in lightly. Especially when she was making love. Then she began to rant at Magog about Maire, because Magog had forgotten to mention his brother's wife was his mistress.

'I'm not jealous,' Hadassah shouted. 'But you gave *her* the key, not me. Can't you even be private in your own home?'

Then Hadassah said a great many wounding things not worth remembering, put on her clothes, and declared she was leaving for good. And did. Even though Magog had a hundred mortars and twenty thousand bombs labelled as bananas and shipped to Tel Aviv the following Wednesday as a peace-offering to Hadassah, he was not forgiven. She would only meet him in hotel rooms for half-an-hour in the afternoons like a professional. And in these brief business encounters, no love was lost and all love was.

Josepha lay on her back, kicking both her heels into the sand. Sea or sky had fallen into her eyes. Blues looked at blues, iris mirrored air. She laughed with the whole joy of the little child, too young to know that she and the world must always be separate. In her vision, she and the universe were one element of blue. She choked and waved her feet like gulls. Then she howled. Rosa was pouring sand into her open eyes.

'Can it be deliberate?' Maire asked. She was swabbing out Josepha's eyes with wet cotton-wool, taking infinite care to remove every grain. Maire enjoyed seeming to be a good mother so much that she often was a good mother. Anyway, it was the nannies' half-day off.

'At the age of one and a bit?' Gog said. He watched Rosa now putting sand into her bucket and taking it out again, totally absorbed and ignoring her crime of trying to blind her sister a quarter of an hour before.

'It's original sin,' Maire said. 'Father Malleson taught me that. And I said, Fine, if I was born originally sinful, then it explained why I had gone on the same way all my life.'

Gog smiled. 'Children aren't sinful or innocent. They just work out what they are born to work out. Only they can't give facile reasons like we can for doing what we are bound to. Children just do what they must. Words come later. Lucky them.'

In Josepha's red bucket, Gog had trapped a prawn. He watched the colour show through its transparent shape, as it searched round and round the rim of its encirclement. There were giant prawns in the Pacific. Why not here? Protein for more children. He must get back to his sea-farm in Scotland, experiment without end, amen.

'I do what I want to do,' Maire said. 'Keep still, Josepha, it's for your own good. I've always done what I wanted to do.'

'Then you're unbelievable, Maire,' Gog said. 'And indeed you are. Like most people, I just follow my fate. We do what the genes have laid down, and the runes. They conspire with luck and history to force us through the way of life we may think we have chosen. But we say we chose it merely because we weren't given any other choice.'

'Nonsense,' Maire said. 'If I'd left the sand in Josepha's eyes, she'd have gone blind. She's seeing because I didn't.'

'You couldn't have left the sand in her eyes, Maire. You're her mother. You had to save her sight. You must admit, you couldn't pour sand in her eyes yourself, though you could certainly snip off my balls.'

Maire laughed. 'I'll send for my scissors. So lovers can do what mothers can't?'

'Even lovers can only do what is in the terms of love. They can kill, create, mutilate, adore, torture, transcend their loves. But they can't ignore their loves. The charades of our behaviour are all set. Solemnly and stupidly, we play them out time after time. But because we don't know of the millions of other people who have played out the same charades through all time, we think we're fresh, original, clever, masters of our fate.'

Gog looked out across the wide sands of Tenby, as golden as the pre-war advertisements had always promised. The rusting barbed wire and the pill-boxes were temporary scabs on the haunch of the bay that contained its causeway and its island and its contented sea. The last trippers of October were almost lost in the sweep of the sand, which made a pygmy of anything that man could do.

'I'm mistress for anyone I choose,' Maire said stubbornly. 'All right, Josepha, go and play. Why don't you bash in Rosa's skull with your bucket? Be a good girl and give mummy something more to do.'

Josepha crawled over to Gog and grabbed at her pail, which fell on its side. The sea-water ran into the puckering sand. The prawn arched and opened by Gog's foot, arched and opened again in the wrong element. Josepha tried to put her finger on the prawn and failed. So she began crawling towards Rosa, making noises at nobody in particular. Gog watched the prawn dying because he could not be bothered to walk a hundred paces to the sea to fill the pail again.

'Your myth and your necessity, my dear Maire, is to go on from man to man, setting them at each other and the world on fire. And that's only one of the myths you have to work out. I've got hundreds of myths driving me on to actions I may regret. And Rosa and Josepha, why, they're just playing out a sisters' version of Cain and Abel. Only the Bible and the Greeks never dealt with the war between sisters, though they did set down most of the myths that our moralists and psychologists misuse on us. Martha and Mary! That's small beer to killers like Rosa and Josepha.'

'It's only a Welsh afternoon,' Maire said. 'Spare me the Celtic twilight.'

'Rosa had to put that sand in Josepha's eyes,' Gog said. 'She'll be trying to blind Josepha all her life. She already knows you love Josepha more because she's quiet and doesn't cry.'

'Just brats getting into trouble,' Maire said. She shivered as a cloud passed over the sun, and she pulled up the straps of the two little black satin sails that covered her breasts and made the initial of her name on her brown body. 'Let's go back into that damned hotel. They'll have to put a plaque to me in Tenby. To Maire Griffin, who actually had a holiday at home, to make her mad husband happy and to show the Welsh *she also cared.*'

'You were just mad with Magog,' Gog said. 'Finding him in bed with a young girl. There's nothing like playing the virtuous wife to rub guilt into the wounds of your lover.'

'Stick to your myths,' Maire snapped. 'And leave motives to me. You may have the Druids and fate, but we have Proust. Paris may not be much of a home town, but at least we Parisians know just where and why we're sticking in the stiletto.'

So Maire and Gog went to separate the twins from the sand and from their tangle with each other. As he rose, Gog stepped on the prawn, now dead. He was wearing shoes and did not even notice. When he turned away from the grey sea, carrying one of the twins on each shoulder, a sudden sun crept out behind his back and shone on the slate fronts of the Welsh houses, so that their blacks became a blinding bright. In that dark vision, now radiant, Gog blinked and wondered whether his conversation had been an illumination.

'I must say,' Merry said. 'That's a fine way to treat your mother. I am not a hawker or a circular.'

When Magog had seen the short man in the pink wide tie with black sideburns thicker than the grey stripes on his white suit, he had presumed that a spiv was going to sell him a gold brick. So he had slammed the door, only to find that he had left his mother on the far side. Out of the corner of his eyes, he had thought she was a rhododendron in full flower behind the spiv. Repeated hammering had made him open up again to discover Merry, fatter and more impossible than ever, dressed like a gauzy flamingo in scarlet chiffons that did nothing to hide her overweight. The man in the pink tie had a heavy list to port as Merry hung delicately on his arm.

'Come in, just for a moment,' Magog said. 'I'm sorry, but I was on my way out.'

'You're always on your way out as I'm coming in,' Merry said. 'You always were such a slippery baby.'

'I didn't think you held on to me for long enough to notice

before you got me adopted by the Ponsonbys,' Magog said.

'Now, now, no family in front of Maurice,' Merry said. 'He likes the niceties.'

''Onoured I'm sure,' Maurice said. 'As one dealer in 'ardware to another, 'ow's 'owitzers movin'? Slowish for the season, don't you think, though Lugers is a nice line if you can get 'em.' He winked at Magog. 'And you can get 'em. Bein' in government's the best racket of 'em all. Might 'ave a go meself one day.'

'The annual Civil Service examinations,' Magog said coldly, 'are very competitive, although anyone may try.' He turned to Merry as they stood in the high white hall in front of a Turner of a steamer in a storm. 'To what do I owe the pleasure of this visit, Mother?'

Maurice answered.

'Dossy Radzen tipped me the wink. Nice bit of tit, her. Got it made, ain't you, cocko? Where's the Scotch?' And he rolled up the stairs as if they were his own, pushing Merry ahead of him by the rump, although he would have done better in a landslide, should she have slipped. Fortunately, Nash had designed the stairs for hooped skirts; they accommodated Merry.

In the large drawing-room, Maurice put one leg up on the chaise-longue covered in Regency stripes that were put to shame by his suit. He waved the drink in his hand. 'Dossy did say as 'ow you 'ad a posh set-up. Your kid's done all right, eh Merry?'

'Magnus always could look after himself,' Merry said, 'though he never bothered to look after anyone else. And certainly not his mother. Unlike dear Gog.'

'Don't you mention 'im,' Maurice warned. 'If I ever meet 'im with me boys, I'll 'ave him done up.' He turned to Magog. 'Off 'is nut, Gog is. Three times 'e's ruined me, just as I was cleaning up a bit after the war. 'E'd better stay out of my way.'

Magog warmed slightly to Maurice, who seemed to be a shrewd judge of character. 'Gog should be in an asylum,' he agreed.

'So should we all,' Merry said. 'More hock, dear, it's delicious. So lucky we're occupying the Rhine these days. Who wants all that steel in the Ruhr so long as we can have the vineyards?'

Magog gave more drink to his mother. Her taste in men had always been execrable, but Maurice was her triumph. Perhaps she was merely moving with the times and found the war profiteers more lucrative than the gentry. More likely age had caught up even with her ample gifts, and she now only had class to offer her keepers, who might need her contacts on their way up. Yet Maurice was too dangerous, if he knew the Radzens.

'All them British lads still gettin' it in the neck in Palestine. It's a bleedin' shame, 'cos they're gettin' it from British bullets too. You'd think they was gettin' shot in the back by their own side, wouldn't you just?'

'Unfortunately we armed the Arabs in the war,' Magog said. 'But it's their responsibility whom they use the guns against, not ours. We merely supply, we don't pull the trigger.'

'I'm with you all the way,' Maurice said, though Magog winced to be included in such company. 'But Dossy says there's a bloke in the British government what don't mind givin' an 'and to the Jews. No cash neither, just kind. Me personally I got to 'ave dollars, or it's no deal, even for Dossy. Military metal what still fires is worth its weight in gold, though I'll settle for Uncle Sams. No quids. Betcha you 'ave to devalue the pound.'

'I'm not in the Treasury,' Magog said.

'But you are in the arms game, and didn't ought to be. And British guns is killin' British lads out in that there sand. Don't sound nice, do it? I mean, if their poor mums and dads got to know, it'd break their bleedin' 'earts. And if the government did, somebody'd get his 'ead broke.'

Magog looked at Merry.

'Do you think blackmailers make for happy families?'

Merry smiled fondly back at Magog.

'We aren't a family, dear, we're just a blood group. And as natural affection won't raise a penny out of you, I'll settle for extortion. Anyway, my love, business bores me. I'm just a poor simple spender on my way to a mad shopping spree.'

'Did I 'ear blackmail?' Maurice said. 'That's an 'arsh word for a polite request. Your Mum, 'oo is my light of love, 'as woken in me 'eart a desire I 'aven't felt since I was chuckin' bottles with the boys through the windows in Bethnal Green. When the bottles 'it me, I'd say – I'll 'ave some respect, if you please.

One day, I said, I'll be Lord Morrie of Bethnal Green. And then you'll 'ave some respect, or else.'

'It's quite out of the question . . .' Magog began.

'I ain't in an 'urry,' Maurice said. 'I know you can't put up frilly curtains in a day. 'Umble does it. I'll settle for Sir Maurice Mowler for starters.' He turned to Merry and smiled. 'And Lady Same.'

'Even if I took up the matter with the Patronage Secretary,' Magog said, 'to get you on to the Honours List, I'd have to give you a recommendation. And there simply isn't one.'

'Ain't there?' Maurice said and took a cheque out of the back of the rainbow handkerchief in his breast pocket. The cheque was made out for ten thousand pounds and was payable to the Labour Party. Magog felt a tinge of respect.

'That's a bit too direct,' Magog said, 'even if Lloyd George were still around. Those who want to buy honours make out their cheques to the Society for Promoting Christian Knowledge or for Saving Pit Ponies or the British Legion or something useful. And even then, the government is often less charitable than the donors. There has to be a special reason to get a title. It really is better to have done something for your country – like me.'

Magog handed the cheque back to Maurice. The paper seemed to pause in his fingers.

'I've never done nothing that wasn't for my country,' Maurice said, 'I'm still 'ere, ain't I? I haven't scarpered off to the Ba'amas to live it up as a tax dodge.' He winked at Merry. 'I can live it up 'ere nicely, thank you kindly. No, Morrie Mowler is staying at 'ome and what does 'im good does Britain good, and what does 'im proud Britain proud, and what's great for 'im is Great Britain. I'm a man of the people, Maggie me old, and what I get, everybody gets, in a manner of speakin'. It's like the pools, everybody's got a chance for the easy life. If I go up to the Lords, it proves anybody can, don't it? Social mobility.' Maurice smiled. 'That's what some geezer told me. They've always got fancy words to doll up a bit of push, don't they? Sir Maurice Mowler. It's like they gave that medal to all the people of Coventry because of bein' bombed. Give me a title and the 'ole country will feel, if that blighter can get one, so can I.'

'You're a true democrat,' Magog said. 'Look, my advice is, go to an elocutionist, support good causes, and run as Labour candidate for the London County Council in Belgravia. And for God's sake *lose* your political campaign – it's boring arranging dustbin collections for three years. And groom yourself a bit.'

'He does need a stable-boy,' Merry said dispassionately. 'But I'll see what I can muck out of him.'

'So it's in the bag?' Maurice said.

'I don't promise anything,' Magog said.

'If there's an 'oly 'ush over the arms for Palestine,' Maurice said.

'What arms?' Magog said and smiled.

'And if I made the cheque payable to cash,' Maurice said and altered it.

'What cheque?' Magog said and took it.

1948

Magog had a rule of thumb, which he called the Rule of the Creative Thumb – or the Jack Horner Principle.

> *Little Jack Horner*
> *Sat in the corner*
> *Eating his pudding and pie*
> *He put in a thumb*
> *And pulled out a plum*
> *And said, 'What a good boy am I!'*

So the nursery rhyme went on, so the Rule of the Creative Thumb was applied. In a committee, where common agreement was essential, everybody had to pull out their particular plum. If all did, each felt that he had contributed to the result of the whole, and given human vanity, each felt that his plum was the sweetest fruit in the pie. Much of Magog's time was spent in making deliberate errors or inappropriate wordings of his drafts for committees. He designed every mistake to appeal to the special knowledge of one of the members of each committee. Sometimes he thought he ought to underline the mistakes, for occasionally they were not spotted, and he had to say tactfully to the expert, 'I'm worried about paragraph twenty-two, sub-clause four. Perhaps you could spare me a little of your advice.' Then the expert would make his contribution in a lordly way, happy to be setting the record straight and a bright young man on the right road. Magog was rising fast, too fast, in the Civil Service. There was not a single civil servant who did not feel that he or she was the one person who had really helped Magog.

The committee had sat. Magog had got what he wanted. It also happened to be what most of the British people wanted. For the popular success of a policy would lead to the success of the Minister involved, which would lead to Magog's success. This time Magog had recommended that the prohibitive tax be dropped off Hollywood movies. The mob had its circuses again. Bread could wait.

'Dear boy,' Sir Hamish Gorder said, 'that was a masterly draft. Too bad you dropped that clanger about excise rates.'

'With you there to correct me, sir,' Magog said modestly, 'I need have no fear. Another sherry?'

Magog rapped the top of the wine-cask that served for a table in the discreet pub that the Civil Service patronized after committees. He pointed to the four empty glasses on the table, his own, Sir Hamish's, George Germain's and that of Mulcree, who had somehow joined the group as he always did, without an invitation, which he never had. Mulcree tagged men of power more closely than their own shadows, for he was always there, even in the dark. Envy was his energy, scandal his sense of smell. And he nosed after Magog in particular, as his only rival both senior and younger in the hierarchy. There must be a stink in that.

'The same,' Magog ordered.

'With the bacon ration halved and meat cut to a shilling's worth a week,' Germain said, 'do you think we can afford the bosoms of *Forever Amber*? On that big screen where a rump is two hundred times life-size, we'll have a food riot.'

'Men don't want to eat,' Magog said, 'if they can dream. And

what is more potent than a dream of lust? Who'd you rather
have, Betty Grable or dinner at Maxim's?'

'Both, dear boy,' Sir Hamish said. 'You should know from the
Civil Service, we do hate to have to *decide.*'

'Then have them in the right order. Hunger follows a lay.'
Magog grinned. 'So *Forever Amber* today and steak tomorrow.'

'Then why don't we import a cargo of real tarts?' Mulcree
said. Envy, not wit, edged his voice. 'By your logic, they'd be
more welcome.'

'If you know tarts who cost one-and-ninepence, I don't. At
that price, a cinema seat is more comfortable and less full of
clap. And we'd have to feed the imported tarts. And the factory
workers would never get to work, and then they'd be carrying
their balls in their hands. I tell you what, Mulcree, you go and
have it off with a granny standing under the railway arches and
we'll go and see Dorothy Lamour in her sarong on *The Road to
Ruin.* Then we'll swop memoranda. The best thrill wins.'

While Sir Hamish and Germain laughed, Mulcree bowed his
head in silence. He seemed to be looking for his hate like a
bright penny on the linoleum.

'It's odd to find you rate illusion so high, Magnus,' Germain
said. 'The sherry must be Plato in your skull. In a siege economy
like ours, you'd think we wanted only necessities.'

'Everything but,' Magog said. 'If you can't cure mass misery,
make men forget it.'

'The film industry will like your draft,' Mulcree said. 'Do they
know you? If not, doubtless they will get to know of your help
– and its price.'

Sir Hamish pursed his mouth as if the new glass of sherry set
in front of him had gone sour. Mulcree did not like to mention
the unmentionable.

'I read *Film Fun* myself,' he said, 'when I can steal it from
my grandchildren. My life's ambition has always been to meet
Laurel and Hardy. Goodness knows, sometimes I think all I
want in life now is a good laugh and a good shit. And I'd settle
for the laugh.'

'I like the early Keatons myself,' Magog said, smiling before
he turned on Mulcree. 'My knowledge of the screen world is
confined to seeing the best films. Dirty little pictures I leave to

dirty little minds.' He turned on to Germain, excluding Mulcree absolutely. 'Do you go to the cinema often? Winston Churchill once told me, he used to stop the war every night and watch an old film in his boiler suit. Only Smuts thought this was frivolous. But why not, Winston replied, there's always a war on somewhere.'

Germain laughed. 'At present there is fighting involving hundreds of millions in China, Indo-China and India, now we've gone. But that is on the other side of the world. There is also fighting involving millions in Greece, the home of liberty. But as we have recently handed over Greece along with our liberty to the Americans to look after, that's their problem. We are merely fighting in Malaya and Palestine and have committed tens of thousands of men there. Which is why we say the world is at peace.'

'I wish we'd leave Palestine sooner than May.' Magog said, 'now that the United Nations have decided on partition. It's not doing us any good with Congress. What can we do when the chairman of the House Foreign Affairs Committee is called Sol Bloom? And think of all those lovely billions of dollars of aid that General Santa Claus Marshall is waiting to give us, just to keep us from going over to Joe Stalin. Frankly, I'd rather be better off at home than love the Jews so much I had to overstay my welcome in Israel.'

'I thought you did love the Jews too much,' Mulcree said, 'after reading your memos on Palestine.' He turned to Sir Hamish. 'I'd like to find out more about how our arms are getting to the Stern Gang. People who arm our enemies should be in prison.'

'They should be hanged,' Magog said and stared Mulcree out until he dropped his eyes. The man had no evidence, only rumour. 'But there's a good case for arming our enemies when they are about to become independent and our friends.'

Sir Hamish smiled. 'You're too clever for me, Magnus. Or I'm too old.' In the stained-glass hanging light of the pub, his face was blotched in purple and red while shadows pulled down his nose and his eyes. 'It was simpler when we just armed our friends and sent the fleet against our enemies. We're such a little fox now, I suppose we have to get up to new tricks. But rather you than me.' He finished his sherry. 'I never thought I'd ever *want* to retire. But it's the right time, before the ship goes down, or becomes an eel.'

'We'll float,' Magog said, 'if we're smart about it.'

'At the height of the Boer War,' Germain said, 'a troop ship hit a reef off South Africa. Smartness had nothing to do with it, since it was a gale. Death was likely. The men were marshalled in ranks on the deck, and they obeyed. They stood to attention singing *God Save the Queen* as the ship broke up. Nature was not impressed. None survived.'

'It's a good story,' Sir Hamish said.

'An old story,' Magog said.

'A fair story,' Mulcree said.

'History,' Germain said. 'All three.'

'We don't like our terrorists,' Hadassah said. She yanked at the buckle of her webbing belt, then she swung it in her hand like a weapon. 'They give us more trouble than they're worth.' She took off her khaki trousers and lay back on the bed in her sodden underclothes. A wave of ammonia and sweat made Magog recoil, then move towards the bed. 'Still, you can't fight a moral war. Unless you look on.'

Magog picked up a towel and sat beside Hadassah on the bed and rubbed her down. There was no water in the taps. A shell had hit the main that supplied the hotel in Tel Aviv. A British shell supplied by Maurice Mowler.

'I met a friend of yours in London,' Magog said. 'Maurice Mowler.'

'When I was a Haganah agent,' Hadassah said, 'I wouldn't call the company I kept friends.' She smiled. 'Present company excepted, of course.'

'Of course,' Magog said, rubbing her breasts with the towel. 'Mowler tried to blackmail me. I don't think I'll keep my Civil Service job too long.'

'You're wasted there, anyway. Why don't you go in for robbing banks? More honest than taxation, and more fun.'

'My last consignment of small arms is at the docks,' Magog said. 'I thought I'd visit Israel to see if it got into the right hands. Do you know, they tell me there was a battle for it. Jew against

Jew. Your army had to fight off the Stern Gang to get it first.'

'What did I tell you?' Hadassah said. 'We don't like terrorists, even our own.'

'They'll end as old men on pensions,' Magog said. 'Heroes of Israel.'

He felt Hadassah suddenly shiver under the towel, as the sweat dried on her skin.

'Don't go on,' she said softly to Magog. 'Don't you think I'm scared too? Two thousand years we've waited and wept and prayed. Now we're going to have Israel back for ourselves. Suppose . . . just suppose we got it wrong? It's too cruel. After all that time, suppose we got it wrong?'

Magog held her hand in both of his. 'You'll get it right,' he said. 'You do know why Europe got it wrong.'

Hadassah's face was light with faith.

'I have stood in Jerusalem.'

Siege lay within siege lay within siege, as the Jewish Quarter died house by house. The last couple of thousand Jews were penned into an area a few streets wide. Fire on them was so heavy that they could move only through the catacombs and sewers. They were falling back on their last two strongpoints, the Ashkenazi and the Tiferet synagogues. Arab irregulars were swarming closer with their explosives, jacketed in the cast-offs of many Levantine wars, daggers in their belts, gelignite in their hands, lighters ready for the fuses to bring the Hebrew walls tumbling down. They had already shattered the dome of the Tiferet and opened caverns in its walls. The few snipers left in its rubble were being picked off by the Arab Legion, posted on the battlements of the Old City, laying down a covering fire. The green and checked cloths on their heads were flowers of death on the stone blocks.

'Three hundred yards. Top of the synagogue. Thirty yards left. Brown roof. Fifteen yards down. Courtyard. Five rounds rapid. Fire in your own time.'

The Sandhurst voice directed the volleys of the Legion, then choked.

'Jesus,' it said, 'Jesus.'

The voice died of wounds. Outside the walls of the Old City, some Haganah forces sniped and attacked, desperate to save the last Jews alive in Jerusalem. The Arab Legion faced both ways at the enemy within and without. But the Haganah detachments were also being encircled by closing Arab armies. Net over net over net over the Holy City.

Hadassah was too tired to despair. She had been fighting for three days and nights. She had killed two men and had never killed a man before. Her right cheek-bone was bloody and bruised from the stock of the Bren gun. The magazines were all empty. Her loader had tied in his guts with his shirt when a piece of mortar bomb had blown a hole in his stomach, and he wouldn't live more than an hour or two. There had been little firing in the night or at dawn. The defenders of the Jewish Quarter had little left to fire. And yet Hadassah could not believe that they had lost Jerusalem.

In the lull of that last morning, she watched the swallows diving and flickering, at truce now after the bombardments. Yet the birds were wise enough to wheel round the gaudy flags that flew above each coward embassy and trembling faith – the Union Jack, the Vatican ensign, the Ethiopian banner, the Stars and Stripes. Hadassah swung the barrel of her Bren towards the red, white and blue crosses of Britain and cursed that she had no bullets to rip the flag-pole down. Then below her sights, she saw two old rabbis picking their way through the hillocks of rubble. White flag, twin black carriers, white flag. We have lost Jerusalem.

Hadassah had to admit, the Arab Legion behaved correctly. The Legionaries cut out the men, collecting a bazaar counter of prisoners of war to trade in the final exchange of men when the fighting would stop. But they allowed the women and children to pick up their bundles and drag their way down the alleys towards the Zion Gate. Hadassah was among the refugees, hidden in a long dusty dress, a child on one arm – in the other hand, a parcel of prayer shawls and spoons and bowls and the text of Deuteronomy.

Then will the LORD drive out all these nations from before you, and ye shall possess greater nations and mightier than yourselves.

Every place whereon the sole of your feet shall tread shall be yours: from the wilderness and Lebanon, from the river, the river Euphrates, even unto the uttermost sea shall your coast be.

There shall no man be able to stand before you: for the LORD your God shall lay the fear of you and the dread of you upon all the land that ye shall tread upon, as He hath said unto you.

Behold, I set before you this day a blessing and a curse . . .

Beside Hadassah, an old man with earlocks below a flat black hat. He shook his head from side to side uncontrollably. Nay, nay, nay, nay, nay. He did not believe, he could not believe, as the final diaspora came to the Zion Gate to be scattered from Jerusalem.

The Haganah raged outside the walls. Volleys struck at the stones. Shrapnel wailed in the dark. The refugees fell to the ground, prayed, grovelled, to escape the avenging fury of their own.

Furthermore, the LORD spoke unto me, saying, I have seen this people, and, behold, it is a stiff-necked people.

Let me alone, that I may destroy them, and blot out their name from under heaven: and I will make of thee a nation mightier and greater than they . . .

The anger of the Haganah was spent. The last whine of metal thinned to no noise. Outside the walls, the army of Israel waited to take away its defeated. Inside, the Jewish Quarter burned in pillars of fire. The child on Hadassah's arm cried and, as she kissed away its tears, she found herself weeping. Under Zion Gate, Hadassah wept and despaired.

'What is Israel without Jerusalem? There is no Israel without Jerusalem.'

Then hoped.

'Israel shall have Jerusalem.'

Jerusalem came down in a dire ruin over all the Earth,
She felt cold from Lambeth's Vales in groans and dewy
*   death –*

The dew of anxious souls, the death-sweat of the dying –
In every pillar'd hall and arched roof of Albion's skies . . .

Gog looked up from William Blake's Prophetic Books towards
the roofs of Whitehall. Pinnacles and minarets, white spires and
grey curves made a Xanadu beyond the duck pond in St James's
Park. A vision of the East hovered over the tops of the summer
trees, the mirage of a magic palace. Yet below that canopy,
power. Whitehall might lounge beneath petty parasols and
pleasure domes on high, but it ruled much of the world – or
remembered it had and could no longer, but still had to interfere.
Gog knew the trouble was that Whitehall could not forget. For
the palace was built to be the crown of the First British Empire,
not the undertaker's top hat at the funeral of the Second.

By the lake, Rosa and Josepha were feeding the ducks. Each
of their nannies held a bag bulging with bread and cakes, while
the little girls screamed with scared joy and clutched at their
nannies' skirts and cast food from the bags to the ducks and geese
and swans that surrounded them in a quacking pandemonium.
Bolder and bolder, the birds beaked in. Rosa and Josepha were
hidden behind a hundred necks that waved and struck and hissed
as vipers. The birds ripped at the bags, burst them, made
two heaps of furious feathers over the bait, while the nannies
snatched up their yelling charges and ran for Gog and safety,
their stockings holed, one girl bleeding at the knee from a
razor-bill. There had been no such orgy for the birds since
rationing began.

Thin faces of envy were watching the riot of the birds. At
last, one fat lady, whose authority seemed swollen by austerity,
could stand it no more. 'It's a bloody shame,' she said. She
strode forwards and began kicking the birds aside with her
gumboots, which she wore even on that hot August day, just in
case. She snatched up two rock cakes and a half-loaf, getting
her knuckles pecked for her pains. 'I'll report it to the Inspector,'
she declared as she looked towards Gog, who looked away at
the trees.

The rest of the spectators dallied. Did they love birds more
than their own bellies? Certainly they loved birds more than
brats, for the British beat their children more often than they

starve their budgerigars or whip their dogs. So they muttered, ready to lynch the two-year-olds, but being British, they only muttered and kept the peace. By the time that a bent man sallied out to grab his share, the birds had scoffed the lot and were waddling apart, using their beaks like sickles along the ground to search out the last crusts.

'Report this, I will,' the fat lady said and put a whole rock cake in her mouth. She would have added, 'Bloody scandal,' only she might have blown out a crumb with her words. Another lady, disappointed at losing the food, made a mental note to report the fat lady also to the Royal Society for the Prevention of Cruelty to Animals. The war may have ended, but informers still felt their duty to inform. And there is no greater happiness for the English than when their pleasure is also their duty.

Gog closed the Book of the Four Zoas and shepherded the twins and their nannies back towards Maire's house. The people in the Park stared and pointed, but Gog was too big to meddle with, and the soldiers on the parade ground on the other side of Birdcage Walk didn't seem ready to march out of the peeling Palladian front of Wellington Barracks to deal with a monster so gorged that he could give his tiny ones bread to waste upon fowl. Yet the soldiers might have marched, if they had noticed Gog's line of advance. For ahead of him, gay and casual and distant, the royal standard flew above the dull stone hulk of Buckingham Palace. The King and Queen were home to tea with the Princesses, although nobody except their footmen could see them or their biscuits. Gog's eyes were big guns blazing down the palace walls to expose such luxuries to the people, while William Blake again sang in his skull as he swung his gaze down the Mall to the tall hope of Nelson's column, the maypole beyond the park trees smiling and dancing in the sun above the weary workers who slept on the grass of St James's, denying London.

> *England! awake! awake! awake!*
> *Jerusalem thy Sister calls!*
> *Why wilt thou sleep the sleep of death,*
> *And close her from thy ancient walls?*

Thy hills and valleys felt her feet
Gently upon their bosoms move:
Thy Gates beheld sweet Zion's ways;
Then was a time of joy and love.

And now the time returns again:
Our souls exult, and London's towers
Receive the Lamb of God to dwell
In England's green and pleasant bowers . . .

The Lamb of God that visited Maire in her garden came in the form of an Inspector from the Ministry of Food. Magog brought him out to her, as she rested herself in the orange seat that swung between the two cedar trees. Maire was wearing an extravagant version of the New Look. No padded shoulders nor wedge heels nor short cloth-saving skirts for her, but a full white satin dress down to her ankles rustling with black petticoats beneath, and black lace rounding out her breasts and shoulders, and her waist nipped in tight as a soldier's hug. The Inspector could not imagine how she might have dressed herself on her rations although clothes were not his line. Even so, the regulations flapped in his skull like lost laundry.

Take care of your 1947–48 clothing book.
To save paper it will have to last you two years.
The 20 yellow coupons on page iii of the General, Child's and Junior Clothing Books become valid on October 1st for the five months ending February 29th next . . .

Maire stretched out an ankle that turned the Inspector's mind on a lathe of beauty. Her black silk stockings were never made in this country and their import was banned by a Labour Government, fearful that luxury might corrupt the soul and the vote. The Inspector wanted to touch the stockings to see whether they were real, but he knew his hand would be jerked jumping jack up her leg by a force beyond resistance to the last soft down left off coupons in the age of austerity.

This is how they are made up:

16 coupons 'E' – value 1	=	16
1 set of ¼ coupons – value 1	=	1
2 token 'F' – value 1½	=	3
		———
		20

Do not cut any of the invalid coupons from the 1947–48 books.

They will be needed later . . .

'Some champagne for the Minister,' Maire said to Magog. 'And the grouse pâté – off ration.'

'I'm only an Inspector,' the Inspector said.

'And I'm clairvoyant,' Maire said, 'from my gypsy grand-mother. I can tell your future in the beautiful shape of your skull. What *power* . . .' She patted the orange seat beside her. 'Do come and sit down, dear Minister . . . the title merely anticipates the inevitable . . . Only the best ever visits *me*.'

The Inspector sat beside her, while Magog hurried off to serve.

'If I may be so bold as to say . . .' the Inspector began.

'Be daring,' Maire said, admiring the little round face set under a pair of round wire spectacles. 'I love Lochinvars . . . Rolands . . .'

'How could you afford such a super New Look? Two years' clothing coupons, I'd hazard.' Then, seeing Maire's icy stare, the Inspector hurriedly added, 'I'm not a snooper, just interested for my wife's sake.'

'Woman to woman,' Maire said earnestly, 'the secret is saving. Every coupon I can hoard goes into a special piggy-bank I call my Harrods. Scratch, scratch, save, save, it never ends.'

'Ah, but the end result is really worth it,' the Inspector was proud of his gallantry. He had a way with the ladies.

'If I had the time, dear Minister, I'd be the regional organizer for the Make-do-and-mend campaign. As it is, I'm still recuperat-ing under doctor's orders from my war effort.'

'What did you do?'

'Hush hush,' Maire said. 'So hush hush I don't know myself. But it was for the Resistance. I'm French, you know.'

'I might have guessed,' the Inspector said. 'The French have a *je ne say quoy*.' The Inspector knew phrases in fifteen languages, all of them indifferently. 'When I saw those stockings . . .'

'I must confess, those are a gift. You know what Frenchmen are. They came from a general I helped over the border at Biarritz,' Maire laughed. 'I must confess, silk lowers my resistance.'

Magog appeared with three glasses of champagne on a silver tray; by them, melba toast spread with pâté. The Inspector sighed.

'My goodness, I'd never believe there was a war on here.'

'There isn't,' Maire said. 'Only everybody else has forgotten how to live in peace. Thank you, Magog. If you could leave me alone with the Minister.' She took the Inspector's hand and guided it towards a glass of champagne. Her fingers were moths on his skin. 'We have important things to chat about.'

'Naturally,' Magog said, glad to escape from such a compromising situation. If the Inspector actually inspected Maire's house, what would he say to the six hundred cans of Virginia ham and Californian peaches hidden under the stairs? Magog was ashamed of Maire's squirrel mentality, but her failing was surely the temporary corruption of war. It was her business if she was a hoarder. He merely disapproved, but was too polite to refuse supper after supper at her table.

'When you, ah, stroll in that outfit in the streets,' the Inspector said, 'aren't you afraid other women will rip your clothes off like they did in Paris to that Dior model?' He smiled. 'And men, too.'

Maire gave her best company laugh, which always ended a little too abruptly to show pleasure.

'Women only want to lynch what they aspire to,' Maire said. 'In my humble way, I try to be a beacon of hope in these mean years. Somebody has to spend their time at the hard duty of personifying the promise of tomorrow in the rubble of today. If I didn't exist, dear Minister, who would believe that Easy Street was just around the corner, as the government is always promising? Soldier on, say I, to every woman – and you can be like me.'

The Inspector would have liked to have believed Maire, and her obvious sincerity touched his heart at the same time that the champagne was tickling his nose. So he sneezed into his hand, begged her pardon, put his palm to his breast to quiet his emotions and to rub off the snot, cleared his throat and regretfully set about his business.

'A complaint,' he said, 'my dear lady.'

'I have nothing to complain of,' Maire said. 'Life treats me very well, all in all. We always get what we give, don't you think?' She uncrossed her legs and smoothed her satin skirt between her thighs. The Inspector could not take his eyes from her fingertips that smoothed out a rut of delight in the sheen of the cloth.

'A complaint against you,' the Inspector said. 'I'm very sorry, but you know . . . duty.'

'Duty,' Maire sighed. 'Duty is getting dreary. Every day, more duty. Do you know, dear Minister, I'm thinking of giving up duty for Lent. Or for the duration of peace. We should make a self-sacrifice even now.'

'Three months' bread ration to the ducks in St James's Park,' the Inspector said gloomily. 'Forty witnesses. Fed to them by your twin girls, Miss Rosa Griffin and Miss Josepha Griffin, if I'm not mistaken.'

'You are never mistaken, dear Minister. Just merciful. I hope you are not going to put my tiny tots in Wormwood Scrubs. Though I must say, there'd be a little peace around the house.'

'The bread came from here, I presume, madame?'

'You presume too much, and I did think you were a gentleman.'

'Then where from?'

'They stole it, I presume,' Maire said. 'I simply don't eat bread. Loathe the stuff. And kids have sticky fingers. I once saw Rosa grab Nelson's Column, firmly believing she could carry it off.'

'Stealing bread is impossible these days,' the Inspector said, 'especially if you're two years old. All bread is eaten at once.'

'So it was,' Maire said. 'Those clever ducks ate all the evidence. So what bread?' She smiled and put her hand on the Inspector's thigh – to pick off a thistledown that had drifted there. 'It's a principle of English justice. You can't hang a murderer without the body. So what bread?'

'I'll have to ask the ducks,' the Inspector said and smiled. 'I'll examine their droppings and see if the cubic capacity has gone up.' The Inspector laughed. He passed for a wit in the group called himself.

Maire couldn't manage a smile.

'What price England,' Maire sighed, 'if we can't even give a treat to our feathered friends? I'm sorry, Minister, but I'm very religious. It was Saint Eustacia's Day.'

'Saint Eustacia's Day?' the Inspector said.

'Saint Eustacia. She was a Christian virgin who found herself suddenly surrounded by a horde of Attila's Huns with time and her on their hands. Just as they stripped her for their pleasure, the Virgin heard her prayers and took her up to heaven in the shape of a pelican. It's a miracle.'

'Saint Eustacia's Day,' the Inspector said, looking in his diary. 'I'm Catholic myself. I thought I knew all the Saints' Days, but not hers.'

'She's a Parsee saint,' Maire said sweetly and quickly. 'My dear mother was a Parsee, converted of course. Do you know, we worship birds so much that we leave the bodies of our dear departed to be translated to heaven in the beaks of sacred vultures. I saw my beloved granny go that way.'

'Your gypsy granny who can tell the future?'

'That's right, Minister. What's more vagabond than to fly to heaven on the wings of vultures? Do you wonder that I love birds so much? In each one, I see the soul of my granny.'

'You wouldn't be having me on,' the Inspector said sadly.

'Have *you* on?' Maire smiled. 'I wouldn't mind that at all.'

The Inspector finished his champagne and shook his head like a dog. His sense of the righteousness of things was disappearing fast. 'There'll have to be a charge,' he said. 'There has to be.'

'Minister!' Abused innocence made a schoolgirl of Maire's face. 'It's not like you.'

'It is, ah, it is,' the Inspector smiled at his own authority. 'It gives me no pleasure.' He grinned. 'None at all.' He positively snickered. 'I feel for you, but a job's a job.'

'Then I must protest.'

Maire opened the handbag beside her on the swinging seat

and took out a ration-book and a platinum lighter. She ruffled the dull coloured leaves of the book to let the oxygen in, then set fire to it. The paper was so dense that it refused to flame, then suddenly caught alight, so that Maire had to drop the blazing ration-book onto the silver tray on the ground to save her fingers.

'You can't do that.' The Inspector bent forwards to put out the blasphemy, then found himself scrabbling on all fours on the ground, his mouth on Maire's satin knee. Somehow, the seat between the cedar trees had swung away from him. He beat the abominable arson with his palms and scorched them for his pains. 'No, no, no, ah, no.' He got to his feet and had to brush the knees of the trousers of his last best suit before he could deal with the burning book, which now was merely embers on a discoloured rainbow of silverware. 'You can't do that,' he said. 'It's done,' Maire said. She stood up, queenly in her outrage. 'I would rather starve than be thought un-British in the country that took me in. When I have saved my rations crust by crust to give to the poor ducks – presented I may say to the King Himself for his war efforts by the grateful Canadian government.' Maire put a hand to her eyes for effect or for a tear. 'It's too much. I'll fast to death, then you'll be sorry.'

'It's another offence to burn a ration-book,' the Inspector said. 'It's government property and they cost one and tenpence ha'penny to print.'

'I'll burn myself next time,' Maire said. 'Suttee. On a pyre on my dead husband's grave. Twenty-two kills in the Battle of Britain till the Nazis killed him. Have you seen the plaque to George Griffin, VC, DFC and five bars, on Tower Hill?'

'Can't say I have.'

'It's by the Execution Block. Visit it next time you go to rubberneck.'

'You shouldn't burn your ration-book,' the Inspector said, 'even if your husband was a war-hero.'

'He stopped Hitler burning London,' Maire said. 'What's one burned ration-book against a city saved from the incendiaries?'

'I'll get you another,' the Inspector said. 'I shouldn't. I'll stretch a point and get you another ration-book. And we'll forget the bread for the ducks.'

Maire was radiant. She flung her arms round the Inspector and kissed him on both cheeks.

'That's a French goodbye,' she said. 'Did I foretell you'd be a Minister? *Prime* Minister.'

The future Prime Minister left shortly afterwards, not quite believing what he had promised. But his promise was his performance, and he knew Maire would keep him to it. Maire watched him go from the drawing-room window, bouncing with triumph, while Magog watched her.

'You can't always get away with it,' he said.

'I always do better than that, Magog dear. I profit from my sins as well as survive them.'

'You burned one ration-book and you got another. That's no profit.'

'The one I burned,' Maire said, 'was last year's – out of date. I'll get a brand new one. Darling, think of all the gastronomics ahead, when we add it to the fifteen ration-books I already have.'

'Maire, you're impossible. If you were Minister of Food, we wouldn't need one. There'd be no rationing left.'

'I'd rather be Marie Antoinette,' Maire said. 'All the Minister of Food can say to the masses is, Let Them Eat Snoek. Well, I say, Let Them Eat Steak.'

1949

The judge of the tribunal at Westminster was enjoying himself. His face made him look more of a clown than a Solomon, his nose seemed to swell with mirth until it was as big as a beetroot, his good cheer pulled his mouth up to his eyes instead of dropping it down in sentence. And he had something to mock. For the witnesses who were passing through the stand made powerful men look petty, businessmen seem bumblers, and civil servants appear to be waiters grubbing for tips under their desks. Quotas and rations, import licences and restrictions had confused the worlds of post-war London, so that the underworld had merged into the world of finance and government contacts. In the shuffle of places after the defeat of Germany, nobody cared too much where his neighbour came from, as long as he knew the right people. And for those who wanted to make money, the right people were the officials who could allow the import and export of everything from paper to ham pies. In a nation short of nearly everything, the hand on the rubber stamp was the emperor.

King's Counsel, who was examining the football pools' promoter in the witness stand, himself needed some help from the black market. He did not have a wig or a gown to his name because of the clothing shortage, and the cuffs and turn-ups of his suit were frayed at the edges. Yet his strong face dominated his fortunes as he demonstrated his circuitous craft, which ended where it had begun, proving nothing except his own cleverness.

'You thought the whole thing was extraordinary?'

'Yes, I did,' the pools' promoter said.

'Why was it that you thought it was extraordinary?'

'Well, the fact that *this man* knew so many people in high places.'

This man smirked in the dock. On his round and ready face, the smirk showed that he did know many people in high places. If this was his crime in the eyes of the tribunal, why, it was a crime that many people would consider a privilege.

'Well,' King's Counsel continued, 'why did that strike you as being extraordinary?'

'For the reason I have said.'

'What was the reason?'

'Well, it just struck me as extraordinary that he should know so many people.'

Magog joined in the laughter of the tribunal. He was sitting on the wooden benches and was waiting to be called to the witness stand. George Germain sat on his right side. 'Don't thank me, my dear fellow,' Germain had told Magog, who had expected to be deserted by all his colleagues when he was named in the bribery case. 'It's the done thing to back one's subordinates. Very old-fashioned I know, but there you are. I'm sure you'd do the same for me if I were accused of dipping my fingers in the public till.' Magog had replied that he would always back Germain, but he knew he would not have sat down beside his chief in front of the seat of judgement.

The pools' promoter was dismissed, Maurice Mowler was called to the stand. He strutted forwards, squat and cock-sure in his sky-blue suit with the padded shoulders, web-footed in his crêpe-soled shoes. He waved to Merry, who sat like an over-blown oriole in her bright-feathered hat among the journalists in the hall. Maurice might have been reviewing the troops, judging by his pride as he took the podium and swore to tell the truth, the whole truth and nothing but the truth.

'You know the defendant?' King's Counsel asked.

Maurice winked across at the round face of the accused, who shrugged at the acknowledgement.

''Ooever says 'e don't know 'im ain't been around where it matters,' Maurice said. 'That bloke was in and out of the 'Ouses of P. with 'is baskets of fruit like a ruddy Santa Claus. Often I used to say, they'll put you away, boyo, with a gallopin' case of the give-it-aways.'

'But surely the defendant only gave presents away to those who could give him back import licences for his clients?'

'If a pal gives you a bit of goods from the kindness of 'is 'eart, you might expect 'e might expect you to give 'im a bit of an 'elpin' 'and. It's only natural.'

'Then bribes were exchanged?'

'That ain't 'ow it's done,' Maurice said firmly.

'How is it done?'

'Well, in business, there's trust, that's what there is. You do a job and you gets your pay, or you do a job on 'im what won't give you your pay. But with government blokes, you give 'em somethin' just for the goodwill like, and then you sits and waits . . .'

Here Maurice half-turned and looked towards Magog, who did not meet his eyes. The memory of Maurice's cheque for ten thousand pounds made Magog look away towards Germain, who looked back at him in inquiry. 'You know the man?' Germain whispered. *'En passant,'* Magog replied.

'Continue,' King's Counsel said.

'Government geezers,' Maurice said, 'won't say nothin' for sure. They 'int that you'll get what you want, but all in their

good time. I've known young blokes become grandfathers waitin'
for their good time.'

There was more laughter and the smiling judge rapped his
hammer for quiet.

'I take it, then,' King's Counsel said, 'that you did see the
defendant giving gifts to officials in the Civil Service and in the
government?'

'I never seen nothin',' Maurice said, 'that ain't none of my
business.'

'And what precisely is your business?'

'A little bit of everythin',' Maurice said. 'You know 'ow it is.
A bloke 'as to scratch around to live in this wicked world. But
basically, I get what people wants to the people who wants
it.'

'Very commendable, I am sure,' the judge said, intervening.
'That means that you deal with government contacts yourself.
Could you name any names for the benefit of the tribunal?'

'I've got a rotten 'ead for names, Your 'Onour,' Maurice said.
'But faces, I never forget 'em.'

'You know the defendant,' the judge said. 'Do you know
anybody else in this room?'

Magog wished that he had remained outside in the lobby until
summoned to the stand. He was suddenly a child again, caught
lying. He prayed to be invisible, knowing that he was only too
plain to see.

'I know 'er,' Maurice said cheerfully, pointing to Merry. 'And
'im, that's 'er boy.' Now he was pointing towards Magog. ''E's
in the Civil Service all right. But though I'm a member of the
family, so to say . . .'

At these words, Magog could not keep a shudder from
showing. He saw Germain smile and he loathed him for it.

'I never asked Magog for nothin' that wasn't legit,' Maurice
said. 'Not your Morrie Mowler, what expects one day to be
sittin' in the 'ighest seats of the land . . . by your side, Your
'Onour, per'aps – no disrespect intended.'

'And none taken,' the judge said, happy at the colourful
success of the witness, which would mean even more publicity
for the tribunal and its good-humoured judge. He now turned his
eyes towards Magog. 'Thank you for being such a co-operative

witness, Mr Mowler. If I might call you again later, if necessary?'

'Any time, any old time, Morrie Mowler will be in to Your 'Onour.' Maurice positively beamed his good intentions.

'And if King's Counsel has finished his examination . . .'

King's Counsel bowed his head. He also scented bigger prey.

'Then perhaps we should call Magnus Ponsonby.'

As he took the stand and swore the oath, Magog felt himself tremble. But he knew that the mask which he presented to the world was as stiff and cold as always, fit for that conspiracy of British gentlemen which ensured anything unpleasant could be brushed under the mat with a casual aside or, even better, a mild joke. The magic of knowing the right words would work again on this occasion, since those born to rule always rose to every occasion.

'Were you ever, Mr Ponsonby, approached by the defendant in your capacity as Assistant Secretary to the Ministry of Resources and Development?'

'Never.'

'Have you ever seen the defendant before?'

'I may have seen him. But I have a bad memory . . .' As Magog now glanced at the round and undistinguished face in the dock, he gave a quick and secret smile that was almost a badge of recognition to those who knew . . . 'for the common and garden.'

King's Counsel smiled. He knew a fellow soul when he heard one speak.

'So you do not remember meeting the defendant?'

'I do not.'

'But you have met Mr Mowler?'

'I have.'

'In what capacity?'

'With my mother.'

'Did he give you anything or ask you for anything?'

'He has been generous to the family.' Here Magog looked across to his mother and saw her pleased expression at his public avowal of her. 'But I think I am conscious enough of my duty as a public servant . . .'

'Of course, of course,' King's Counsel's voice was syrup as he consulted his papers. 'I believe, however, that you were approached about the question of granting licences for a shipment of arms to Palestine.'

'Israel,' the judge said. 'It's called Israel now.'

'I stand corrected, Your Honour,' King's Counsel said. 'You did recommend the granting of those licences, Mr Ponsonby?'

Magog paused before replying. Mulcree must have informed on him. For a moment, Magog thought of telling the truth. But all history proved that the man who made a clean breast of anything lived dirty for all posterity.

'It is a matter of record in the department,' Magog said.

'Were you offered any inducement to make this recommendation?'

'None whatsoever.'

'Were you sympathetic to the cause of Israel?'

Magog turned to the judge.

'I fail to see the relevance of the questions, Your Honour. I presume even civil servants have the right to their private beliefs.'

'Not if these affect public policy,' the judge said. 'Continue.'

'You were sympathetic to the cause of Israel?' King's Counsel asked.

'Yes,' Magog said. 'I am.'

The truth stated with decency and dignity was the best gloss on a lie. The word of a gentleman.

'You were offered no *favours* for this?'

Mulcree could not have known about Hadassah, unless he had set Security onto Magog.

'None at all,' Magog answered.

'Mr Mowler apparently received licences for the shipment of arms to Israel.'

'Not from me. I do not have the power to issue such licences.'

Pass the blame on. Only a signature proved guilt, and Magog signed nothing that could be compromising.

'Surely you tried to influence the granting of these arms licences?'

'I have always and only,' Magog said in firm and sad tones, 'always and only tried to influence others for the good of my country.'

There was a pause after this statement. It was a good

statement. Somebody even clapped. The judge blew his nose in a red handkerchief. King's Counsel nodded. There was nothing more to say.

'Thank you for being such a straightforward witness,' King's Counsel said.

'I have tried to answer your questions,' Magog said. He turned to leave the witness stand.

'One minute,' the judge said. 'Tell me, do you ever find a conflict between your public life and your private life?'

'Every day,' Magog said. 'This is why the legend of Caesar's wife is so important for us. We must be above suspicion . . .' He paused to let his sincere expression change to that same secret smile . . . 'Or, at least, we should never mention it.'

The judge grinned, so did King's Counsel. They shared the joke.

'You are implying,' King's Counsel said, 'that because it is impossible by definition to corrupt a civil servant in England, the defendant is guilty only of boasting that he did.'

'As it is impossible to corrupt a civil servant in England,' Magog said, 'there is no tribunal as there is no guilty man as there could have been no bribe.' He looked at the nondescript man in the dock and smiled. 'Not only have I never seen the defendant before, Your Honour . . . I can see nobody in the dock at all.'

In the laughter of the tribunal, Magog knew that he was wholly acquitted.

Even so, Magog decided to resign. It was better to retire with honour before the evidence caught up with him. And the fields were greener in the private sector of the economy. The Labour Government was slowly losing popularity, since the British people could not understand how the country which had won the war should still be rationed, when defeated Europe was back to the free-for-all of eating what it could afford to buy. The capitalists on the home front were already licking their chops and planning for the future. Austerity was on the way out, opportunity waiting to leave his card in the hall.

The Steel Lord, mindful of Magog's services to Israel, offered him a job at £10,000 a year as liaison man with important clients.

Magog refused. Although there was security in steel, there was no risk and no possibility of fortune. So Magog dropped a few words about his help in getting the duty taken off the import of American films. The result was that a group of film investors and producers approached him to serve as their chairman and general adviser. Magog was made the head of the Film Production Finance Guild with offices in Berkeley Square (where nightingales never sang), with four secretaries (one blonde, one redhead, one brunette, one lilac in spring and russet-haired in autumn), with an expense account only limited by the utmost stretch of his guests' waistbands, and with a chauffeured Rolls-Royce that carried dark-glass windows, a dictaphone and an inbuilt wine bar. Now armoured, Magog could ride out to save the British film industry.

It needed saving. It always needed saving. It was the only industry that tottered on from crisis to crisis without an intervening year of equilibrium. At the moment, it was in a state of depression after high fever. The year before, the government had reserved nearly half the home market for British films. The result had been that every indifferent script kicking around London had been converted into a piece of bad film. Now that these films were being shown in the cinemas, the public was staying in the sunshine, or else going to see every American film that there was to see. A huge entertainment tax added to the ruin of the British producers and distributors. The government was milking the artificial cow it had created and even, like the Masai, was drinking its blood and capital. The result was that the cow was drained and half-dead. Nobody would give it any more cow-cake. With the cinemas mooing for good films from home, more than half the British studios were empty and half the film technicians on the streets.

It was a good situation for Magog. In the doldrums, any wind is a good wind. And Magog knew how to puff himself. He quickly created a feeling of movement around himself – not to be confused with progress. He set up an infinity of interviews, most of them to be cancelled at the last moment from pressure of work. He had his four secretaries typing memoranda on coloured paper that fell on the desks of the inert and the illiterate. His Rolls-Royce idled outside the offices, its engine ticking over as if permanently about to bear Magog away to a conference. He would rise in the middle of a meeting, whispering something about seeing the young President of the Board of Trade, Harold Wilson, or somebody so powerful that the name ended in a murmur. In appearance, Magog might have been off to visit God Himself. In fact, he would go off to his private telephone to talk to Maire. For their affair had bloomed again like a late rose.

Maire admired Magog's new style. She enjoyed being the centre of decoration of a world that admired set-dressing. She had an excuse for swank. Although she had never bothered about excuses, it was nice for her natural ostentation to seem like virtue. At the premières of films, when the women were overdressed, Maire would appear in a long black robe, her only ornament the silver-fox skin that hung its head and tail along her arms and drooped its belly down her bare spine. At a simple trade cocktail party, however, Maire would blaze in black sequins and white ostrich-feathers like some lost star of the twenties who had decided to dazzle our cold planet one last time. Maire was always out of place, yet perfectly at home in the admiration of the men who surrounded her. She never asked the opinion of a woman. She knew her whole sex was biased except for herself.

Maire was unusually flattering to Magog, even moderately faithful. Her total triumph over Hadassah, who had disappeared to build up some kibbutz in the deserts of Israel, had made Maire able to forgive Magog for his deviation towards the Levant. Always free to do what she wished, Maire had never allowed Magog the least freedom from her sudden incursions into his life. And now that he had chosen to make her his consort in the eyes of the film world, she felt such pleasure in Magog's company in public that she might have called it love in private, had she been younger. As it was, she gave herself so generously to Magog that he felt as cock-sure as any movie stud. This sexual arrogance combined with his real power made the starlets sidle about him like bitches round a post.

Maire encouraged Magog to make use of his opportunities. She really wouldn't mind, she said, if Magog had his little bit of fun on the side. What other man could resist it? But Magog was too wise to act on her compliance. He knew that, if Maire heard

of a peccadillo, she would use it against him to keep herself out
of his bed – even though she had recommended him to slip.
Women pimp for other women, so that men shall turn the other
women down to prove their desire for what they already have.

The charge of the Highlanders made the side of the mountain
shake. This was chiefly because the side of the mountain was
made of planks and brown matting. The Highlanders were not
that fierce either. Most of them came from the medical schools
of the London hospitals. They were better at using scalpels than
claymores. They certainly drew more blood with the scalpels.
Their claymores were made out of rubber. When they hit the
redcoats at the bottom of the mountain with their weapons, they
sprained their wrists with the bounce back.

'Cut,' the great director said.

Magog sprawled back in the canvas chair marked FANNY
BAGLE. The actual lady was being stitched into a dress made
of cultured pearls, specially cultured for this Scots history epic
– *Montrose Meets Mary Queen of Scots.*

'It's a historical impossibility,' Magog had softly complained.
'Unless Montrose got Mary's corpse to walk.'

'You'll see the lovers meet all right,' the producer had promised. 'So will fifty million members of John Q. Public breaking
down the box offices. What's history? Can fifty million paying
people be wrong?'

'Well,' Magog had temporised, 'I will say money is very
authentic.'

'And we can use the spare footage from *Bonnie Prince Charlie*
which is real production value,' the producer had said. 'History
is just a schemozzle. Who the hell can tell one lot of wild men
hacking each other into hamburgers from another lot of horrors?'

The great director thought he could, as he addressed the
extras.

'I'm all for time-warp,' he was saying in his soft voice, weary
with failed persuasion. 'I'm all for the eternal recurrence, infinite
rebirths, journeys into the past, a jump on to the bandwagon of
the ages. But get make-up to paint in the marks of your bloody
watch-straps. Highlanders told the time by sundials, and they
don't have any sun up there.' He turned to his First Assistant.

'Tell Central Casting I'm not accepting any more male extras under four feet tall with wooden legs and sixty-inch busts. This is meant to be the Charge of the Clans, not a Tartan Drag Fling.' He turned back towards the clansmen. 'Top of the slope, my darlings. We go again.'

As the extras slowly began to climb the false slope, occasionally rolling their eyes towards the great director in the hope that he would notice them and promote them to instant stardom, Fanny Bagle rattled forward in her gown of pearls.

'Angel,' the great director said, 'you look just like Cleopatra ought to have. Could you bear to get up there with the hairies and gently descend the slope behind them? Queen flanked by her faithful warriors and all that.'

'I might get lost behind the extras, my petal,' Fanny Bagle said.

'We'll hold you in centre frame and pan with you, darling. It'll be a great link shot.'

'A close-up,' Fanny Bagle said. 'I don't come down that death-trap except in close-up.'

'We'll do that next shot,' the great director offered. 'This shot relates you to the charge.'

'Have you *seen* them,' Fanny Bagle said, pointing a long red nail at the extras, going away followed by the make-up girls. 'Relate to them? Petal, that lot don't even have mothers. They were put together from the trims left over from the last Frankenstein.'

'Please, darling,' the great director said. 'For your audience. For your agent. For your piece of the box office. For me.'

'Medium close-up,' Fanny said, relenting. 'Hold my face and my corsage.' She looked down at her swelling breasts that made two delectable mounds under the spill of pearls. 'In medium close-up, my fans won't see me sprain my bloody ankle. And walking down slopes pulls up the bust. That's what my public wants if I can't be *speaking*. They want my quivering bloody boobs.'

'A medium shot, darling,' the great director said. 'Let's compromise.'

'I've already compromised,' Fanny said. 'Do I or don't I know what my public wants? A medium close-up.'

The great director appealed for help.

'Mr Ponsonby,' he said, 'what do you think?'

Fanny looked at Magog. Her eyes were an extraordinary violet and her skin had the satin flush beloved of beauty columns. She hung on the verdict of money like all three goddesses waiting for the golden apple.

'I think,' Magog said judiciously, 'that in the everlasting struggle between art . . .' he nodded towards the great director '. . . and the artist' . . . he smiled at Fanny . . . 'between the creators and the audience, there is a middle ground without compromise that is both beauty and box-office.' Magog smiled again to see Fanny's rapture at his mastery over language. 'A close medium shot would make everybody happy, if you, dear Miss Bagle . . .' Magog's fingers seemed to flutter over curves in air '. . . were to end close to camera, finding the body of your lover at your feet. You could then kiss his cold lips in very close-up. And cut to delirious applause.'

Fanny shook her head, stunned.

'Marvellous,' she breathed.

The great director did not like being replaced.

'Montrose doesn't die till the last reel.'

'He isn't dead in this battle,' Magog said. 'Her kiss brings him back to life again. Who wouldn't come alive if dear Miss Bagle kissed him?'

'Darling Mr Ponsonby,' Fanny said. 'You are a petal.'

'Why don't you take over the picture?' the great director said. 'I'll go and back a horse.'

'It was only a suggestion,' Magog said. 'Please feel perfectly free to disregard it. You have complete authority on the floor.' He smiled once more at Fanny as he rose. 'I must finish my discussions about the end money.' He looked at the great director. 'I do hope the picture is completed, don't you?'

The great director nodded and turned to his First Assistant. He knew the game. What is making a film compared with backing a film?

'A studio cart to push Miss Bagle's stand-in to the top of the slope. We'll block out a new angle. Montrose's stand-in to lie down in front of camera. He plays dead which isn't difficult for a layabout.' The great director slouched off.

'Thank you, Mr Ponsonby petal,' Fanny said.

'Thank me at dinner tonight,' Magog said.

'I'm on early call tomorrow.'

'We all need our beauty sleep,' Magog said. 'But sometimes we need to sleep with beauty.'

Fanny laughed as Magog left her. He would not keep his date with her tonight. His secretary would cancel the dinner at the last minute, mentioning a sudden conference with the Bank of England. Fanny would be piqued and waiting, ready in case something went wrong with Magog's affair with Maire. It was always good to keep a beautiful woman in reserve. A show of power was the ultimate aphrodisiac, especially if it was casually done.

As his Rolls-Royce took him back from the studio to his office, Magog dictated a memorandum to his board. In one hand, he held a microphone, in the other hand, a glass of Château Mouton Rothschild 1929. The great depression had, luckily, not affected the vines that year.

'I advise,' Magog said into his microphone, 'that *Montrose Meets Mary Queen of Scots* should be finished unfinished. Although four hundred thousand pounds have been invested in it to date, two hundred thousand more to complete it would be throwing bad money after worse. Enough footage has been shot to hack some sort of historical hundred minutes out of the material if we don't care about continuity, and who does? The remainder of this last week should be spent shooting Miss Bagle in a bath of porridge. We could have a tie-in with a breakfast cereal, which would help to sell our own product. (Baths of porridge were fashionable health cures in old-time Scotland and Miss Bagle's vital spots can be oatmealed out for the censor.) If the public doesn't go and see Miss Bagle in the mush and the altogether, I don't know the public. Every family that munches its breakfast bowl each morning will be in there, spooning her up.

'The Montrose principle should be applied immediately to the whole movie business. The way to get the film industry back to health is to stop making films. Let other countries make films and lose their money. We will show the films they make and take our cut. This will take the ice out of our price. Then let us make cakes, chocolates, commercials, good British things which we know how to make for a sure sale in the intervals. But no more films! By ruthless economy, we can save our cinemas. There will be something to show in them because there will always be foreigners stupid enough to risk their money in movies.

'The entertainment unions may be a little annoyed that we will not be employing their people. The answer is that they would be better occupied making tea-pots for export than having tea-breaks during the shooting of costly flops. It is not we, the producers and distributors, who have killed the British film. It is the greed of the technicians, the actors, the agents, and the directors. If they want to make films, let them make the money first. They will make it no longer from us.

'This is not a crisis of leadership, my friends. This is a crisis of followship. The film industry must learn to follow where we lead. Menaced as we are by a screen no bigger than a man's hand – Dare I use that dirty word, television? – it is our duty to stop making pictures in order to save the picture business. We must increase the price of seats and ensure that the money goes to our shareholders, for whom we hold an awesome responsibility. President Woodrow Wilson once declared: "Trade follows the film." Now I declare: "Trade follows the non-film." Let us sell cinema audiences pop-corn and ice cream. But let us waste no more money on making films. As one of the responsible custodians of the movie industry, I say stop! For god's sake stop the cameras turning! Only then can the picture business start again.'

When polished, it became a fine memorandum. Magog was proud of his command of the jargon of his new trade. He was giving his employers what they wanted to hear in words they understood, just as he had done in the Civil Service. And when the great J. Arthur Rank largely gave up making movies for making flour, Magog felt influential. After all, corn was better baked in loaves than processed in laboratories. Men had to eat before they could dream. Magog felt no twinge at the memory that he had said the opposite to Germain and the Minister, when he had helped to get the import tax lifted off American films. Arguments were, after all, conditioned by circumstances. In a free country, a man had the right to change his mind. It seemed odd to Magog that pig-headed men who stuck stupidly to one point of view were sometimes considered men of principle. The best principle was surely to accommodate oneself to the shifting realities of life. If politics was the art of the possible, then principles were the patina of the pragmatic.

On the great black blocks of granite that dammed the end of the loch, Gog stood by a steel tank of shrimp larvae. The embryos had been flown from San Francisco Bay by air freighter. The voyage of the shrimps had taken three days, although Sir Francis Drake had once taken more than a year in the *Golden Hind* to reach that Californian bay, when exploring in the other direction. Gog thought of the Elizabethan cockleshell as he briefly floated his metal ladle on the surface of the tank, then plunged it down to dig out another scoop of the larvae before dropping them into the water. There the larvae were supposed to grow and feed the salmon spawn also introduced into the loch, a bright dirk pointing into the barren Highlands of Scotland that lay between Gog and London.

Sometimes, if he half-closed his eyes and looked along the shining scales of the ruffled surfaces of the loch, Gog could see the glint and warp of water as a thrash of fish. Then the whole narrow crevice was a turmoil of salmon, twisting and leaping in Gog's blurred vision and mind's eye. And round the long pit awash with life, the children were pressing and wading and tearing with their teeth, filling their swollen black and yellow and white bellies with the red meat of the sea that was always giving and giving and giving to the need of men. And the faces of the multitudes of the children would fur into tears and Gog would blink to find the wind stinging his eyes and his sight would clear to see that the flashing sides of the salmon were only little chills and gusts puckering the loch in the sun, and the cries of the hosts of the hungry and tiny were the screams of Rosa and Josepha paddling on the rim. And Gog would know that nature was too stubborn to give her plenty easily.

> '*Goggie, Goggie, Goggie,*
> *Goggie is a doggie . . .*'

Rosa was shouting, shrieking with laughter. Josepha joined in the chant, bird-like shrill.

> '*Goggie, Goggie, Goggie,*
> *Goggie is a doggie . . .*'

Gog smiled and went on tipping the larvae into the loch. The little girls were often dumped on him in the summers and autumns when the sun seemed to linger in the north as if loth to abandon the bleak hills to the snow and ice massing in the Arctic above. Gog would put a child on each shoulder and stride off with them over the hills and the moors and the stony beaches, feeling their wet warm fingers clutching his skull in a helmet of loving. So armoured against his loneliness, Gog would laugh and tell them long tales of Odin and Wayland the Smith and the Gods of the North, of the snake that girdled the world nine times over to tie it together and the Thunderer trying to drink up the bottomless cup that was the sea, and of the old tree of life and death that held up the roof of the sky. And Rosa and Josepha understood not a word, but they liked the low sound of magic in his voice mumbling into the wind, and they beat on his skull with their small fists, singing their own incantation:

> '*Goggie, Goggie, Goggie,*
> *Goggie is a doggie . . .*'

After their high tea, Gog would play with them on the rush mats on the farmhouse floor, trimming the oil-lamps as he watched their endless and absorbing game with its many variations and one purpose. Rosa was always the hunter, Josepha the hunted, Rosa the striker, Josepha the struck, Rosa the thinker, Josepha the foil of thoughts. Rosa would lunge and Josepha would take the blow, usually without protest, occasionally howling for comfort. But even when she was crushed to the hearth of Gog's chest, she did not complain as other small girls did. She never said to excuse her tears, 'Rosa hit me.' She would say, 'Josa hurt.' No more.

Gog saw their roles already fixed in life, irreversible at the age of four. No schooling could change their natures, no cant about environment could alter the inexorable engineering of their first making. Rosa would grab at everything in her life, seize and plunder and run. Josepha would accept all she was given and suffer all she was made to suffer. She would smile and help and stay. The few minutes of birth that had made Josepha younger than her sister, so that she stood between Rosa and her mother's total love, had made Rosa jealous unto death of her twin. But now, the two small girls were hugging each other, sleepy and sticky and close, in an embrace so tight that they seemed a pink spider of arms and legs.

'Bed-time,' Gog said and rose and sorted them apart. Tucking one under each arm, he carried them up the stone stairs of the farmhouse to the infinite pleasures of the bath, where a rubber duck and the Queen Mary floated on the water, and Gog could soap and feel the plump flesh of Maire's flesh to his heart's ease, seeing in the fat cherub that splashed and hung about his huge hands, the presence of the woman he loved in her absence and beyond her future death.

1950

The man stood on the bombsite. His army greatcoat was pulled over his ears and neck until it met the back of his peaked cap, a war souvenir from the Afrika Korps – you had to shoot a German's head off before you could get his hat, but the Italians threw theirs away as they ran across Libya. The rusty bayonet lying along the man's forearm in his sleeve was also a war souvenir, blooded at Monte Cassino and then again in Munich – a woman that time, she shouldn't have screamed, he'd paid her the two cigarettes. His black boots were his old best boots, now muddy and gashed at one toe, and his six missing teeth were other combat scars, broken off by a Military Policeman's club in Salerno. The war had been all right, there were always opportunities, he had stuck it through, he was British, wasn't he? But it was that long year waiting to be demobbed while all his mates were on the fiddle, he had to go Absent Without Leave, why should he march in for bloody permission to quit in peace time? Five years a deserter now and still on the run, he was fighting his private war in the rubble left from the blitz. His country owed him a living and it had taught him only to be a soldier.

The seasons of those five years had changed the bombsites into ruined gardens. Wild flowers and weeds now spread over the holes and fallen bricks, greenery plaited floors in London, WC2. Willow-herb was dominant in the new Kews opened by death from the sky. It grew alongside dandelions, thistles, bindweed, ragwort, sorrel, and some rose-bushes, once tame and now wild in the wastelands of the seedy triangle of postwar London that covered the area between Aldgate and the Euston Road and the Elephant. The Germans had chiefly bombed along the river Thames, that led them into their target down its Quisling snail's trail facing towards Europe. On either bank now lay the spivs' world, the pubs furtive and dirty with the soft-hatted men in their drape shapes and crêpe soles whispering old cars and bent logbooks above their black-market gins, the caffs full of steam behind their boarded windows, glass and welcome to strangers long blown to hell with the air raids. In this wilderness of crookery, where the barrow boys could always slip you a pound of butter for thirty bob and fill your petrol tank for a fiver, no coupons or questions asked, Magog never went, except by mischance. His luck was out that day.

Of course, Maire had landed him in the mess. She always did. She had been told of a wide boy who had some Chinese mandarin silk which was a steal, literally. It was not the sort of errand to send a secretary to do. Magog had to keep up appearances, even though appearances wasted more of man's time than showing off his naked self. So Magog walked through WC2 in black overcoat and shiny black shoes, the stripes on his suit one-twentieth of the size of the stripes on the spivs' specials, the lines on the cloth so exquisitely narrow that they proved the discretion of the weaver and the wearer. Inconspicuous in Mayfair, a mark in Aldgate, Magog was crooked in by the deserter's bent arm as he passed a gap in the brick wall round the bombsite. Choking, he pulled at the strangling arm. Stumbling, he was thrust backwards. Jolted, he was brought up standing against a wall smelling of damp and piss. Scared, he looked at the bayonet at his throat and the fierce face of the scavenger holding the weapon that had once been a soldier's. Surprised, he found that he was in the gangster films he had imported from America.

'Let's have it,' the man said.

'When you put your penknife down,' Magog said. His nerve came back with the power of speech.

'Gimme.' The man's voice was hard, uncertain. His dialogue also came from the gangster films which he saw to give himself courage.

'Of course,' Magog said. 'When you've put your penknife down. You hang for murder here. It's not worth it.'

Grunting his despair, the man dropped the point of the bayonet and swung at Magog with his left fist. Magog grabbed his arm. He moved into the deserter, caught him in a hug, locking the man's elbows so that there was no chance of a stab in the back. Grotesque, joined, stomping in a war dance, Magog wrestled with the deserter. He put his left foot in, he put his left foot out, he put his left foot in and he shook it all about, he did the hokey-cokey and he turned around about, that's what it was all about. And the deserter put his left fist in, he put his left fist out, he put his left fist in and he shook it all about, he did the hokey-cokey and he turned around about, that's what it was all about. Then he managed to try a stab with the bayonet, but only pierced the cloth of Magog's coat, which caught the point of the steel in the ripped wool and twisted it out of the deserter's hand. The deserter began to sob. He struggled a little more, losing his breath as Magog squeezed him harder and harder. He was giving up. It was hard being James Cagney on a diet of bread and marge. Magog ate well.

Magog flung the man away so that he thudded into a broken wall. He picked up the bayonet and held it towards the deserter. The man, under threat, became cocky, defiant.

'It's murder for you too,' he said. 'You'll swing.'

'I doubt it,' Magog said. 'Manslaughter in self-defence. What did you want from me?'

'Tosheroons,' the man said. 'What else is there?'

'Going straight,' Magog said. 'You're a deserter?'

'What's that to you?'

'You're a deserter?'

'I heard you.'

'You're a deserter?'

'I didn't spend the war on my fat arse behind a desk.'

'You're a deserter?'

'So what?'

'You're a deserter?'

'Yeah,' the man said. 'Turn me in. It can't be worse than out here.'

'It's not your fault then?'

'I tried to stick you up, didn't I?'

'The war made you do it, surely. That's what you'll plead in court.'

'It's the fact,' the man said. 'But nobody'll listen.'

'Millions of people come back from the war and went back into civilian life without fuss. You didn't. There was something wrong with you, not the war.'

'Yeah,' the man said, failing to snarl like Bogart. 'There was something wrong. I'm *evil*.' He sneered. 'My mum always said I'd come to a bad end.'

'There are still twenty thousand deserters on the run,' Magog said. 'That's not many at the end of a world war. My god, we trained a whole population to murder their fellows. Why didn't more come back to do us in?' He smiled at the deserter. 'I would have thought there would have been armies of you.'

'You're a cool one,' the man said. 'No mistake.'

There was a thrash of feathers, a screech, a slow unflapping of wings. Both men looked towards the noise. One of the hawks that now hunted the bombsites was flying with slow beats, a mouse held in its claws.

'The war's still on,' Magog said. 'I can see that. Only you're out of date.' He waved the bayonet like a conductor's baton. 'Using *this*. Bayonets are over. You should fight with share issues, small print in contracts, loans, mortgages, the real weapons in men's lives. These rusty relics, all you get from them is blood poisoning.'

'You can talk,' the man said. 'You do talk. You'd talk a doll out of her knickers. I never learned to talk. Not many can talk.'

'Do you want a job?' Magog said. 'Is that what you really want?'

'I got to get a royal pardon first,' the man said. 'Some bloody hope.'

'It could be arranged,' Magog said.

'You have sausage and mash with the King, do you?'

'Every Wednesday,' Magog said evenly. 'I asked you, do you want a job? Bayonets are over.'

'Well . . .' The man looked down at his hands, blackish, cracked, hanging from the dirty sleeves of his khaki greatcoat. He was confused. Then he looked up, hatred in his face. 'It's a bloody con,' he said. 'You fucking conman, you're like that Donald Hume. You'll have me cut into bits in a baked beans box like poor old Stan Setty. Drop me chopped liver into the Channel from a Dakota.'

'If you'd rather live like a beast, do so. This is a free country. But who else is going to help you now?'

'I'll look after myself,' the man said. 'Till they get me.'

'They will,' Magog said. 'And Wormwood Scrubs won't be better than a job with me.'

'I don't have to take any balls in the Scrubs,' the man said. 'If a screw lays a finger on me, I'll have it off. But a job . . . I'd have to polish your apples with me arse. No bloody fear.'

'So the war did do for you? You'll never get out of it.'

'I went in at seventeen. Never knew nothing more. Too bloody late now. Had a mate was a commando in India. Fast MTBs across the Pacific killing Japs. Get stuck in, kill all the Japs, get the hell out. He must have done in twenty slit-eyes with Stens, cheese-cutters, the lot. When he was demobbed, they took him to a camp for six months to unlearn him. He unlearned, all right. First night out, he has a shindy with a bloke in a pub and chops his neck and does him in. His commando Captain got him off, 'cos it was '45, juries were sweet and all. So he went back to camp for more unlearning. It's '50 now. I ain't unlearned yet.'

'No, you haven't unlearned,' Magog said. 'And you won't.'

'I didn't ask to go to war,' the man said.

'You don't have to ask,' Magog said. 'War just came and you were sent. Want a job?'

'Piss off,' the man said. He turned and began running across the bombsite. His boots tore at the green weeds and flowers growing on the rubble. He stumbled over a jagged foundation, recovered, splashed through a puddle in a hole, bolted down a crack between two leaning walls, vanished.

Magog did not move. He watched the deserter run, then looked down at the rusty bayonet in his hand. He smiled. His first war souvenir. At last, he had been in combat. During the Blitz and the rocket bombing of London by the V-1s and the V-2s, he had been untouched in Whitehall and Regent's Park. Now, six years into peace, he had been ambushed, stabbed, victorious in Aldgate. Mistakes lingered on. That was the trouble about trying to do anything or change anything. So many mistakes lingered on from the past that they clogged the wheels of progress, hobbled society into a crawl. Mistakes lingered on too long. If they were well-dressed mistakes, they were called traditions and became virtues. But not mistakes in old greatcoats.

As Magog left the bombsite, he met a little lady who was examining a wild flower.

'Foxglove,' she said excitedly to him. 'There haven't been foxgloves in London for three hundred years. They ate the last of them to cure the Plague.'

'Really?' Magog said.

'Isn't it thrilling?' the lady said.

'Yes,' Magog said. 'But should you be alone on the bombsites? They're rather dangerous, you know.'

'Dangerous?' the lady said. 'Rubbish. I can look after myself. I've walked all across Africa. I once had to hit a lion with my brolly for bothering me. It cost me nine and six and I could never get that shade of green again. It was my favourite brolly.'

'I'm sorry,' Magog said. 'Things aren't what they used to be.'

'A foxglove,' the lady said. 'That's a miracle in London.'

'It is,' Magog said.

'It's for my Natural History of Bombsites,' the lady said. 'It should sell well. The war *and* flowers *and* ruins, it can't go wrong with the English public, don't you think?'

'There's a great opportunity in ruins,' Magog said – and left to find it.

'The moment we get rid of the controls,' Radzen said, 'the sky's the limit. Though we may build higher than that.'

Magog was sitting with Radzen in the tall rooms of the Ritz. They were eating pâté, pheasant, soufflé. The cost of each meal was regulated at five shillings by the government. The cost of the wine was not regulated. The Château Lynch Bages 1938, which they were drinking, cost six pounds a bottle. One way or another, the restaurant bill came out at what could be expected. There were people who had tried to eat a meal at the Ritz without buying any wine. The food took an age to arrive stone-cold in portions that would make a mouse laugh. These scroungers did not eat in the Ritz again. There were ways round regulations as long as there was a gentleman's agreement to ignore them. Only outsiders dared to break the holy unwrit of London conventions, and they remained outside.

'Food controls will be gone soon,' Magog said. 'The Labour Party has to fight another election and it's not too popular. People don't like being told what they can't have. They're not children any more.'

He ate the last of the soufflé. It clung sweetly to his palate like Maire's honeyed tongue. He sighed.

'Positively pre-war,' he said.

'But building controls,' Radzen said. 'They'll be with us for a time. Bricks, timber, window-frames, glass, there's a permit needed for them all, and even with a permit, you often can't get them. The local councils have priority. And rents are controlled at a minimal level. Yet there are all those lovely bombsites lying around, unused, undeveloped, dirt cheap. It's frustrating for a creative man.'

'It is also tempting,' Magog said. 'Great men, Radzen, make general frustration into their particular opportunity. They break the block. After all, you did put together your improbable Israel.'

Radzen smiled, his dark eyes briefly narrowing until lines ran all over the pits in his face above his beard. His good humour denied his ravaged cheeks.

'This will be easier,' he said. 'After making Israel, rebuilding

London is minibricks. By the way, Hadassah sends her love.'

'Hadassah?' Magog said. 'I haven't heard from her in years. How's life on the kibbutz?'

'She has a child called Absalom,' Radzen said. 'Her husband's very good with tractors. She says that's what Israel needs, strong hands, more hands good with machines and earth. Personally, I think it's admirable to marry for your beliefs – but I don't think the marriage will last.'

'Israel will last, though,' Magog said.

'Please God,' Radzen said. 'But not my daughter's marriage. You can't tune in a woman like a diesel engine. But . . . where were we? Building controls. When will they ever end?'

'In four or five years' time. But we must move now. Acquire the sites while they are still worthless, get the architects, prepare the schemes for the permissions under the Town and Country Planning Act.'

'How about the capital?' Radzen asked. 'We need millions.'

'I'll get that from the film industry,' Magog said. 'Bricks are much safer to back than celluloid fantasies.'

'I thought your job was to make films,' Radzen said.

'No. My job is to make money. If films won't make money, I'll have to find something that will, like skyscrapers. We must get moving, Radzen. The Tories will be back in power very soon. History won't let the Old Man go without a last gasp in Westminster.'

'Winston Churchill?' Radzen said. 'Him back?' He laughed. 'When he limps into the Prime Minister's seat again and he's rebuilt the bombed House of Commons exactly as it was, Big Ben will stop short never to go again. He's not only out of date, he halts time.'

'We need him back,' Magog said. 'Or we'll never be able to run this country again like we used to. There has to be a mystique of power, you know. You can't get that with the shoddy little men in big places now. You need a great old monster like Winston, ruthless and fat and old, hallowed and revered and grand, to persuade people to go about their own business and leave the business of governing in hands born to govern. Good God, the worst thing is to have a Prime Minister just like everybody else. It allows everybody else to believe that he could be Prime Minister. And then why should anyone obey anyone? And if nobody obeyed anybody, how would anything in this country work?'

'The answer is, nothing does work here,' Radzen said. 'Everything is run down, people are tired to death. They walk through their lives like golems, as if they had survived a sleepless ten years. You can't dragoon a population to fight for more than a decade. People are fed up with all this damn drabness and the war creeping on and on into the peace. Go to Israel, if you want a shot in the arm, a sense of hope.'

'I used to think,' Magog said, 'that countries got the leaders they deserved. But how do we deserve the Prime Minister? Some are born small, some achieve smallness and some have Clement Attlee thrust upon them.'

Radzen laughed again.

'He's campaigning to get back to power right now,' he said. 'One of the people. He may make it, you know. You're all so tired here, Magnus, you may be tired of glory.'

The Prime Minister sat in the front seat of the family car doing a crossword. He was early for his next speaking appointment and the crossword was difficult today. By his side in the driver's seat, his wife sat, doing her knitting. The windows were down to let in the country air and the birdsong. The Prime Minister had turned his election campaign into a sort of national outing.

'Time to move on,' the Prime Minister's wife said. 'Mustn't be late for the meeting. Finished the crossword?'

'Not today,' the Prime Minister said. 'Any ideas on "Trying situation for those who bag babies?" Eight letters, then five.'

'Not a clue,' the Prime Minister's wife said, putting down her knitting.

'How about "Christmas fairy found here in Essex?" in seven letters?'

'Can't help.' The Prime Minister's wife started the engine of the family saloon and took off the hand-brake.

'Or "City supporting nomads" in thirteen, or "To peel an onion with another vegetable makes weepy" in seven?'

The Prime Minister's wife put the car into gear and drove off slowly.

'I don't understand crosswords,' the Prime Minister's wife said. 'But they seem to have a strange power over great minds.'

The Prime Minister folded up the newspaper and put the crossword aside.

'It's easier to run the country,' he said. He looked out at the cows, the hedges, green fields, a shabby cottage with Tudor beams between its pink-wash walls, a postman passing by on a rusty bicycle. 'I've a good phrase for my next speech at our next stop. How about "I have seen a *puissant* nation"?'

The Prime Minister's wife was changing gears and didn't hear her husband too well.

'In how many letters?' she said.

The attempt at Churchillian rhetoric by the Prime Minister did not help him in the election. The Conservatives cried groundnuts, why waste twenty-three million pounds trying to grow groundnuts in East Africa? The Radio Doctor called planning another form of racketeering. The people grumbled at taxes and snoopers and queues and shortages. The Labour Government scraped into power again with an overall majority of six seats. Their time was not long to be.

Magog set about acquiring the cleared areas of London, Goering's gift to the speculators of capitalism. It was not difficult to persuade the bankers to switch their money to property schemes, now that the Tories were only a few aged Members of Parliament away from ruling. Magog found that his position as head of the Film Production Finance Guild was a great asset, as well as his control over Gog's fortune. Unctuous with fear at being asked by a good fellow like Magog to invest in a bad risk like the cinema, a banker found himself so relieved, when the loan mentioned over the brandy was for hard title deeds rather than screen daring-do, that he would give Magog anything he wanted, particularly when Magog would offer to deposit some of Gog's shares in the bank as a form of security.

So Magog began to acquire a ragged chessboard on the map of London – slum properties, ruins, demolished shops, run-down blocks of flats. Radzen also had funds sent from New York and Geneva. When Magog mocked him for not putting all his investments into Israel, Radzen replied that the money was better off in safety overseas, with the profits going to support the new nation. What Israel needed was hard currency, what England needed was new office blocks, what Magog and Radzen needed were fortunes. To unite these needs, their mutual property company was called Stratosphere Securities Limited. Neither of the two partners liked the word Limited at the end of their expensive expectations, but a limited company did hold back their personal liabilities to a mere hundred pounds. And something might go wrong.

Magog used other great persuaders as he plotted the graph of his wealth – Maire and the film girls. Maire was ripe and hanging, the slight droop of her breasts beneath her black dresses as full of offerings as Thanksgiving orchards, the innuendoes of her high voice as pinching-bright as the first chill morning of October. To rich men, with their power at summer and their bodies at late fall, Maire was irresistible, young enough to excite them, old enough to share some of their memories, rich enough to agree with their assumptions, dangerous enough to give them delicious fears of indiscretion, wise enough not to involve them in hysteria or embarrassment, cool enough not to exhaust them with the love-making that might blunt their business sense.

As for the actresses, they provided what many of the money-men wanted, a method of showing off in public without having to sweat it out on the couch in private. It was an agreeable arrangement for both parties. Fanny Bagle could dine at the Caprice or the Café Royal in the company of a man whose reputation of riches outstripped even his bank balance of millions of pounds. In such company, what producer would fail to think that he could find the finance for her next picture? And in such company, what rival tycoon would fail to think that his competitor was doing very nicely for himself? Naturally, if the actress really wanted the money and the rich man wanted her flesh, a bed might be reached by arrangement. But this was not usual. As in most film circles, the illusion of a public *amour* was more satisfactory than a secret romance. Everything was for show, not for sale. Keeping up the appearance of being kept was important for the ego, the gossip columns and the investors. When the actress so often said to the journalists, 'We are just good friends,' she meant it.

Occasionally, gatecrashers broke the rules out of ambition or desperation or some other form of bad manners. At the usual reception after the usual press screening of the usual British thriller, with a chase scene as exciting as a piggyback race, Magog was standing by Maire and a ratty man from *Variety*. Maire was dressed as a dandy, black-and-white check trousers, cutaway dark jacket, cravat and monocle and small cheroot. Her hair was brilliantined back against her skull as if she expected the imminent arrival of Dietrich and Garbo. But nobody approached the trio except for a young blonde with round and darting eyes and a mouth traced in a red pout three times the size of her lips.

'My name's Gloria Angel O'Connor,' she said. 'I can't decide which of you three gentlemen is the most beautiful.'

It was a bold attack. The two men beamed, whilst Maire sucked her cheroot.

'I am,' Maire said. 'And I am female. Glasses are free now, dear.'

'She is more beautiful,' Magog said. 'But I'm wiser.'

'Gloria Angel O'Connor,' the blonde said and stuck out her hand.

'Magnus Ponsonby,' Magog said, taking her hand. It was, after all, very hard to refuse a free offer.

At that moment, Fanny Bagle came across in her Arctic fox furs, to kiss Magog on the mouth. 'Darling,' she said, 'I must drift. Thank you for everything, for nothing, for something wonderful every time you introduce me to another of your fascinating moneybags.'

'It's their pleasure,' Magog said and watched her drift, after her last great smile towards *Variety*.

'Now you've had an actress's kiss,' Gloria Angel said, 'why not try a real one?' And kissed Magog quickly on the mouth.

Maire was not amused. She put her hands on Gloria Angel's shoulders and spun her round as expertly as a bouncer. She then bent until the tip of her cheroot burned the blonde's hair and the nape of her neck. Gloria Angel departed.

'Why don't you grow up and steal a baby?' Maire said, and turned to the man from *Variety*. 'Who is she?'

The man watched the blonde go out of the door, then he

looked at Magog rubbing the back of his hand across his mouth to remove the lipstick. 'Rub hard,' he said. 'I bet she's got the clap. She crashes every party. Climbs in from the gutter, or something.'

Gloria Angel's head reappeared round the door.

'Message for Magnus Ponsonby,' she called.

Magog moved towards the door, then outside into the corridor, hearing Maire's mocking laugh behind him. Gloria Angel blocked his path, her eyes wide and flickering.

'What message?' Magog said.

'The message is from me,' Gloria Angel said.

Magog laughed to be taken in by such an old trick. Maire would give him hell for it.

'I'm open to interpretation,' Gloria Angel said. 'I've got a baby and I'm looking for a flat. I'm open to interpretation.'

'Sorry,' Magog said. 'Full up.'

'You're in movies, aren't you? Give me a part. I've never acted, but I could.'

'I must go,' Magog said.

'Don't,' Gloria Angel said. 'I'm open to interpretation. And salvation.'

Magog went. Surprise attacks weren't funny for very long.

'But I really have a problem,' Gloria Angel called behind him. 'Help me. I've got a baby and nowhere to go.'

Magog went back to the reception. Other people's problems were the ultimate imposition. Once you listened to somebody's problem, you were stuck with it to the bitter end. Better to keep the barriers up, the retainers alerted, the notice on the door.

NO TRESPASSERS, HAWKERS OR CIRCULARS
PROBLEMS STRICTLY FORBIDDEN
GENTLEMEN WILL PLEASE LIFT THE SEAT

Why should the helpless demand help? By what right? They disturbed the peace of the comfortable, and disturbing the peace was a crime. So was loitering with intent to commit an act asking for charity. Or asking for involvement. Or asking for feeling. There was a right place for begging and a wrong one. Beggars should never intrude. They should announce themselves properly. A press reception was not even the time for a visitation from the Lord.

Yet Magog was not unkind. As he entered the reception room again, he saw a waiter with a tray of canapés. 'There's a lady in the passage,' he said. 'Offer her some, she may be hungry.' He watched the waiter go before rejoining the mocking Maire. 'I wasn't really taken in,' he said. 'I was trying to help. I've got her some food.'

'Don't tell me she was starving,' Maire said. 'People don't starve any more. What did she really want?'

'Somewhere to go.'

'Who doesn't? Isn't that what you want to do? Build places for people to go to?'

'That's right,' Magog said. 'Make more homes for better Britons.'

'What I love about you, Magog, is that you always have nicer reasons for making money than the Vatican. And it looks like you'll be lucky. There's going to be a boom, again. We've gone to war.'

'Really? Whereabouts this time? Acapulco?'

'Korea. I don't even know where it is, but it's no good for limericks. It doesn't rhyme with anything.

> *There was a young man of Korea*
> *Who had unspeakable diarrhoea*
> *He shat and he shat*
> *In his old tin hat . . .*

'Then what?'

'Korea is a pistol pointing at the heart of Japan,' Magog said. 'Or so I'm told by my friends who worry about strategic importance.'

'Why don't we let them fire it?' Maire said. 'Weren't we fighting Japan six years ago, trying to burn it down ourselves? What do we want to save it for now?'

'We defeated Japan,' Magog said, 'so it's joined us. Which makes Japan a jolly good thing.'

'The same people live there, don't they?' Maire said. 'Japs.'

Magog could not answer that. But then, he often could not answer Maire. Only men understood diplomacy and foreign affairs. Politics was a closed book to women like Maire, although in love, she also was open to interpretation without any hope of salvation.

They brought Gog the Stone on the last day of the year. He carried it out of the car alone, the monolith cradled in his arms against his chest, his heart spilling with joy and reverence, his breaths jerking in his throat with pain of labour. He would not put the Stone in his barn, where they said it would be safer. 'On my hearth,' Gog said. 'On my hearth. The Stone's no thief, to hide under the hay, now it's come back to Scotland in glory.'

When he had fed them bannocks and tea, and when they had gone away in their old black car, Gog sat on the Stone himself. King Gog on the Stone of Scone, Stone for the coronation of the old Kings of the Scots, Stone stolen by the English raiders and removed to squat under their own imperial throne like a pisspot, Stone holy and Stone regal and Stone blessed and Stone broken under the victors' gold seat in Westminster Abbey. Stone now sneaked back in dead of night from London across the Borders to Gog's northern farmhouse. Stone to found again the free Scotland springing up in the closemouths of the Glasgow Gorbals and the glens of Ross. Stone warm beneath Gog's bum that sat on centuries of pride until he was roaring with the clansmen charging down the braes at the redcoats, crying for Wallace, the Bruce, Mary, Mary, Queen of Scots, long gone to Fotheringay and the block, long gone, and Scotland taken along with her. But with the Stone come again to the North, a new beginning, from the highlands that held the Stone of Scone.

Hogmanay was howling in the evening wind, and Gog left the house to walk down to the village. The Stone would be safe, for nobody knew its shape any more, it had been that long robbed to London. As Gog walked by the dark sea that belched and rumbled to his left, he thought of his first washing up on the shores of the Firth of Forth those six years back, when he had fallen from the troopship in the suck, slobber, spew of the sea that had given him back to the land, not quite right in the head, like Karl Klock.

Karl was waiting outside the Thistle, propped against the wall on his stumps, the whisky songs raging about his ears that would never hear a thing, not since the day that the villagers had found him ten years before, lying legless and one-armed and deaf and mute on the stone beach, wrapped in his German overcoat where the submariners had left him after his accident, too ill to endure the long patrols in the cold fug of the U-boat beneath the North Sea, waiting to blow the enemy sailors on the dark Russian convoys to kingdom come and full fathom five. The Scots fisherfolk had taken Karl in and they had bound his legs and his arm and they had healed him. They had said nothing to the authorities, there was enough fish to eat. Since the time of the Vikings and before that time, the village had accepted what came from the sea. For the sea gave life and the sea gave death, the sea brought strangers and the sea took away friends.

Karl never said a word for he would not, and he never heard a word, for he could not. But each man in the poor village had his task, and no man could bear to be a man without a task to do. So Karl withdrew into the world of time, the slow countings of the submarines before launching their torpedoes, four three two one FIRE, the ordered rhythms before submerging and surfacing, the endless calibrations within the cold steel coffins lying in wait under the ocean. And as Karl now did not speak nor hear, he pointed to the time with his arms whenever anyone looked his way. And the time was always the right time, within a minute or two, for Karl was German and his watch had always mattered to him in some past and lost and punctual life.

So Karl became Karl Klock and the Scots children learned the game of asking him the time and he would point it out to them and to the fishermen and to their worried wives when the storms came and the boats were still out, he would show the time of day or night, with the stump of his left arm as an hour hand, his whole right arm at the full stretch of a minute hand. And the village had no need of a town clock, for there was Karl, always right to the quarter or so, Karl Klock, now sitting outside the Thistle on Hogmanay, when the dark stranger would be welcomed in at midnight, he the dark stranger, always welcomed in every year, carried about by the men and made bloated with drink as a man ten days drowned.

As Gog saw him, Karl pointed out the time with his short left arm, his long right arm.

'Aye,' Gog said, 'five minutes to seven. Thanks, Karl Klock. If I said, this is the rightest time there'd been in Scotland for many hundred years, now we had the Stone again, what would you say? That nothing was right in the human head, nothing at all, that nothing was right except time, which would do for us all anyway. So a Happy New Year to you, Karl Klock.'

And Karl Klock just smiled and shifted his right hand slightly to show four minutes to seven.

1951

One hundred years it had been since the Crystal Palace, iron and glass rising in cupolas over the trees, the sparrows shitting down on England's industrial might and Queen Victoria and the grand old Duke of Wellington, who sent up hawks after the damned defilers above, he knew how to clear a rabble out of trees or Waterloo woods. One hundred years since the Great Exhibition, when the godly prophets of disaster had warned of turning Bayswater into a giant Sodom, of pox and plague being spread by visiting Papist hordes, of fire and brimstone smashing the domes down onto the idolators beneath, only to see the revelation of the age of pride and assurance, *imperium in imperio*, steam-engines and crinolines, crankshafts and fossils, spindles and doilies, power looms and high hats, a full third of the people of England walking through the halls of glass and wonder, their vision stretching beyond the curved and skiey space that murmured with the power to girdle the globe with machines and good manners. One hundred years ago, and now the Festival of Britain.

It rained for two days out of three that January and February and March, and the site on the South Bank turned into a morass, and the new pleasure gardens in Battersea which were meant to rival the Georgian elegance of Vauxhall and Ranelagh looked like the shell-holes of Passchendaele where the Tommies had drowned in the mud. And Magog and Radzen cursed like all sensible people at the waste of public money and of scarce building materials for a mediocre memorial to muddle and muck. But May proved that once again the British could survive their own forebodings. At the first preview, visitors advanced into the Festival grounds as the workers retreated before them across the river, hammering a last few nails and details into their right place. The Skylon glowed in the spring light, airily astonished at being able to stand at all, a landmark as exclamation mark for the whole exhibition. Beyond, the Dome of Discovery, concrete scallop of grandeur, enclosing radar screens and cricket-bat makers and the cogs and the sinews of British industry and invention. Dominant, the Festival Hall for the lady harpists and the tuba players beloved of postcard jokes. Not to forget the Lion and Unicorn Pavilion, where whimsy reigned in the clutter of regality and spoofery that told of the country of Shakespeare and Edward Lear, greatness knowing its own absurdity even in its decline.

'Dog,' Rosa said, pointing to the huskies which lay about the Polar Theatre, tongues licking lollipops of air. Scott, Scott, why won't they let you lie in the Antarctic ice, forgotten as a gallant failure by all posterity? Why do the British only love their losers and regard their winners as cases of indecent exposure?

'Wolf,' Josepha said, as certain as only a five-year-old can be.

'Dog,' Rosa said.

'Wolf,' Josepha said.

The twins glared at each other. Rosa put her claws in Josepha's hair to pull it out.

'Husky,' Magog said.

Rosa was so surprised at this intervention that she let Josepha's hair go.

'What's husky?' she said.

'Half a dog and half a wolf,' Magog said. Not for nothing was he known as a master of diplomacy.

'Husky dog,' Rosa said.

'Husky wolf,' Josepha said.

The twins glared at each other again. Rosa's fist shot out and fastened on to her sister's ear. Josepha howled. Magog swept her into the air and on to his shoulder. Maire pulled Rosa back into the shelter of her thighs, two uprights of blinding white in swaggering trousers that met in a full M of delight at the crease of her crotch.

'Little savage,' Maire said. 'Just like your father, Rosa.' Maire winked at Magog. Little girls had to think that they only had one possible father. 'Gog always punches before he thinks, too.'

'Husky dog,' Rosa said.

'Husky wolf,' Josepha blubbed.

'Oh, let's go and get them some ice cream,' Magog said. The only way out of a fight was a bribe.

Queues were forming everywhere among the Festival crowds. The people hardly noticed they were queuing, they were so bemused by the bright colours and the towers and the music all about them, this true mirage on the South Bank among the shoddy ruins of London. One queue was waiting patiently at a locked door. There was nothing on the other side of the door. People were just used to queuing for not very much.

Maire was not used to queuing. Holding Rosa in her arms, she swept to the front of the line of people at the café, speaking loudly: 'Sick child, she must lie down!' The people parted as obediently as the Red Sea for Cecil B. De Mille, for they knew the voice of authority.

'I'm not sick,' Rosa cried out.

'A sick and naughty child,' Maire said firmly and deposited Rosa on an empty table, beating three old-age pensioners to it by a second or so. 'A very sick and very naughty child,' Maire said to the aged crones, who hobbled away, almost pleased to have been forced to do their good deed for the day.

Magog tagged along behind, Josepha on his shoulder, her hot little legs pressed to his chest and shoulder-blade, their soft warmth disturbing him slightly by their promise of the woman that must grow from the child.

'That was pretty bold of you, Maire,' he said, putting Josepha down into her chair.

'I am bold,' Maire said. 'With this population of sheep, there's no problem.'

'Husky dog,' Rosa said.

Before Josepha could answer, Magog popped a sweet in her mouth, kept in his pocket for such occasions. Her lips closed round the gift and she sucked, Rosa had had the last word as usual.

Magog could hardly recognize Hadassah when she suddenly materialized, holding her child thrust forwards on her hip, with her father hovering about her to ward off chairs and people, even though Hadassah was ploughing on so strongly that she seemed capable of taking her own furrow through a wall. She had grown fat, putting on some twenty pounds, hard-packed under her embroidered dress and filling out her scorched peasant face, a reversion to earthiness that Magog found both moral and distasteful. Just because she was making the desert bloom by her labour, there was no need for a Rachel to turn into a Leah. What was all right on a threshing-floor in Israel did not do in the Festival of Britain.

'Magog,' Hadassah said, 'it has been a long time.' She put the small boy into Magog's arms without bothering to ask. 'He's heavy, my Absalom.' She picked Josepha off her chair, sat down, and dropped the little girl onto her own lap. 'There's nowhere to sit. It's lucky you are here.' She looked across at Maire. 'I am so glad to meet you and your little girls. We haven't really ever talked.'

Maire smiled and decided on magnanimity, which was very good for her view of herself. This earth goddess was no threat, Magog would never lie again on such a mountain of brown meat. Besides, her own bursting on to the scene of Magog's locked embrace with Hadassah had been a famous triumph.

'It's so nice to see you again,' Maire said. 'You're much more appealing when you're sitting than when you're lying.'

Radzen was hanging about at the back of Magog's chair, apologetic and whispering.

'My Dossy's forgotten her manners. She doesn't even request now. She thinks all the world is a kibbutz, and children belong to everybody. I hope you don't mind.'

'Steal a chair and join us,' Magog said. Then he looked down at Absalom. The little boy looked back at him, with black steady eyes. He gave a small roar.

'Roar back,' Hadassah said. 'We took him to the zoo. He thinks you're a lion. He won't roar at women, only men.'

Magog roared. The little boy smiled. Magog roared again. The little boy laughed. Magog roared a third time. The little boy looked away. He had had enough of looking at Magog.

'Over for the Festival?' Maire was saying in her polite voice. Her questions were like reconnaissance patrols, probing for the weak spots in the enemy's defences.

'My father's never seen Absalom,' Hadassah said. 'So I brought him over. Father's too busy making money here. He should be out in Israel, but he says we need the money too, and I suppose we do.'

'I'm too old to be a ditch-digger,' Radzen said, pulling up a chair beside Magog. 'I had my fill of that in Treblinka. I swore I'd never dig a ditch again. The holes in the ground were mostly graves for Jews, anyway.'

'What's a Jew?' Rosa said.

'I am,' Hadassah said. 'It's another word for human.' She turned to her father. 'You won't even dig crops for Israel?'

'It's your turn now,' Radzen said. He smiled and shrugged towards Magog. 'I know how to leave the future to the young and bow out gracefully.'

'For the easy life,' Hadassah said.

'Easy lives can be quite hard,' Maire said. 'We have to endure being bored with nothing to do.'

'You've got enough rebuilding to get on with here,' Hadassah said. 'It looks a bigger mess than Israel.'

'We've got the Festival,' Magog said. 'The acme of comfortable mediocrity. It's a perfect case of the British middle classes patting themselves on the back without lifting their elbows.'

Unseen from within the café, a balloon painted in bright colours drifted off, holding two gentlemen in Edwardian clothes and a lady in bootees and a hobble skirt. The balloon was drifting to nowhere in particular and symbolized nothing of importance. As it floated higher and grew smaller, the people who watched it from the queues felt happier and sadder, filled with a nostalgia for a time that never had been. 'Yes,' they said to each other, 'I like that, it was like that.'

Within the café, Magog at last found a waitress who would
serve him.

'Ice cream for the children, miss. Tea and biscuits for the
rest.'

'It's off,' the waitress said.

'What's off?'

'Ice cream and biscuits.'

'Tea and orangeade, then.'

'It's off.'

'What?'

'Orangeade. And there's only powdered milk with the tea.'

'Well, we're off,' Magog said and rose. But at Josepha's howl,
he sat down again, defeated.

'Bring us what you have,' he said.

'That's better, ducks,' the waitress said. 'Tea, peas and chips,
just like everybody else.'

She went off among the chattering tables.

'Everybody looks so happy,' Radzen said. 'I just can't understand it.'

'Why not?' Magog said. 'We've got an atom bomb, which puts
us beside America and Russia, the tom tiddler of the Big Three.
We aren't going to join the rest of Europe because Europe is a
bad thing – look at the mess it's got us into just because of its
silly wars. We've still got a hunk of Empire, which is a lot more
than most people have. We're powerful and broke, suspicious
and full of pride. Good god, even the Labour Government's
come to its senses and is wasting our last pennies on guns for
some Asian war as irrelevant as the Crimea. So now it has to
ask people to pay for their false teeth and glasses on the free
Health Service. It has got its priorities just as wrong as the
nation has. This is the Festival of Complacency, my friend,
the jolly good show of what we think we are and soon won't
be.'

The children cried and did not eat their peas and chips. Magog
ran out of sweets to pacify them. Maire and Hadassah got on
well, for Hadassah secretly admired smart ladies in good clothes,
while Maire still dreamed of being a truly independent working
woman. Anyway, they were both mothers, and mothers always
had brats in common. As for Magog and Radzen, they ran down

what the government had really done very well, a Festival that persuaded the people that their ten years of drudgery had been worth it, that good times were just round the bombsite. For disparagement is a form of patriotism in England, a thwarted hope that things cannot be worse than they are now, so they must get better soon.

The great director, who had followed the failure of *Montrose Meets Mary Queen of Scots* with the fiasco of *Dracula in Springtime*, which fell between two stools flat on its sugared skull, was now preparing *Convoy Waltz*, a stirring drama that united the wartime thrills and chills of the daring sailors on their long trudge across the Atlantic with the gay dances of high society, bravely keeping its toes twinkling and frills flying through the ballrooms of Belgravia despite the Blitz. The film was going to combine the best of *In Which We Serve* with *Mrs Miniver*, or so the great director said at the party he was giving at his Hammersmith house. He knew he would get backing because he had lost so much money on his last two pictures that he had to be supported until he made a movie which would pay for all his disasters. To be a few million pounds in debt in the film industry was to be working all the time; to be a thousand pounds in debt was to be unemployed and dunned for one's gold teeth.

The great director was kneeling by his dining-table with a live maggot held between his finger and thumb. 'So that's what he eats,' a voice said. Then another finger and thumb, twenty times as small as the man's and attached to a wrist as thick as a pipe-cleaner, snatched the maggot and vanished under the top of the table.

'He took it,' the great director said with pride. 'He doesn't accept meal-worms from everybody.'

Magog was curious enough to bend down far enough to see the animal under the table. He saw a pale rat which had four long furry frogs' legs with ankles that grew into four hands. Three hands held the creature to the top of the table leg, while the fourth hand put the maggot into its mouth. Its face was dirty and pointed and seemed to hold nothing but a pair of enormous brown eyes, which were as expressionless and sad as the button-eyes of a teddy bear, sewn on to twin patches of inky fluff and staring forwards, luminous and unseeing under the shadow of the furniture.

'He's a slender loris,' the great director said. 'I feed him on meal-worms, raw meat, bananas, sponge-cake and brandy when he's under the weather.'

The great director reached under the table and brought out the slender loris hanging upside down by one hand from his forefinger. He put the creature on the silk shoulder of Fanny Bagle. She screamed.

'Careful,' the great director said. 'If you're beastly, he bites. Just like me.'

Fanny was hoping to waltz and trollop through the great director's next film, so she stayed still, shuddering, while the loris splayed out its legs and dragged its belly down the slope of her upper arm. Nobody could say that Fanny wasn't a trouper. She had once spent three hours in a swimsuit on an icefloe in Greenland, smiling her way through a short film for the tourist trade. There were still no tourists in Greenland.

Within ten minutes, the women of the party were competing to have the loris crawling over them. It was cute and it tickled human skin exquisitely. Only Hadassah, sitting between Magog and the Steel Lord, found the fuss over the monkey trivial.

'How can you bear to waste your time here?' Hadassah said. 'There must be better things to do.'

'My job is to waste my time here,' Magog said. 'The whole film industry runs by waste. Its luxury keeps thousands of drones alive. We're a sort of reverse sewage system. The activated sludge of our society, which is also called entertainment, is processed back by the film industry into real shit.'

'Then why take the job?' Hadassah asked. 'Money isn't worth that.'

'All jobs are the same now, my dear,' the Steel Lord said. 'From the point of view of the national economy, it doesn't matter whether we make our money by exporting machine tools or bad films. The money we get for them is still money. There is a curious Puritan subsoil in this island which presumes that money is somehow better if it's earned the hard way rather than by the soft touch. It's not true. Money is just money and has to be got.'

'All the same,' Hadassah said, 'the world needs machine tools more than bad films. I'm sorry, but what men need is the best thing to make and sell.'

'You'll never persuade us of that here,' the Steel Lord said. 'Power in England is not corrupt, as it is in other countries. It is amused. And the greater the joke, the greater the laughter in Whitehall. If we could make money selling London Bridge to the Americans to put in Arizona, we would.'

'We will,' Magog said. 'That's exactly what we will do.'

'I'm just as world-weary now as the rest of them,' the Steel Lord went on. 'I'd give up anything for a laugh. Look at the farce going on at this minute. The Labour Party in its death-throes is trying to nationalize my concern. Of course they will pay me out in full and I shall stay stinking rich, when the country can't afford it. The Tories, baying like a pack of hounds, promise to give the steel industry back to the rich when they win the next election. So I am doubly insured. But is steel the issue? Not at all. It could be mackintoshes or gumdrops. What the Tories want is office. And once they have got it, they'll smile and relax and say to me, "Old boy, have you heard this one?" And they'll tell me the latest good story, while the country gets on with running itself like it has always done. The trouble with power is, you cannot relax enough to laugh if you're in opposition. You have to rule to find everything the huge joke that it is.'

'I don't believe you,' Hadassah said. 'You've got the English disease, Lord Strezel. You pretend to be just after some fun, when actually you're the most ruthless nation in the world.'

The great director was now showing his guests round his private jungle, and Hadassah and the Steel Lord and Magog followed him. A hothouse had been built over a garden, and there the great director had created his Eden. Macaws chattered their ticker-tape to parrots in the steamy air. Humming-birds whirred like faulty neon. Green creepers bound bird-cage to bird-cage as streets. Order had been given to nature. A disinfectant even took away the smell of droppings on the breath of synthetic pines.

The great director pointed to the loris, now lying between Fanny Bagle's breasts in a position where ten million men would like to be. 'Well, who wants my loris?' the great director said.

'I'm giving him away. He's such a pet, but there's no room for him in *my* jungle.'

There were no takers, but the great director was determined. He rounded on Magog. 'You've got that huge house in Regent's Park with a greenhouse and garden. Just made for slender lorises. Take him, Magnus.'

So Magog did. He didn't really know why. But he had always found it difficult to refuse anything valuable going for free. And he was thinking again of Hadassah. The monkey needed warmth, Hadassah was going back to Israel, what better gift for her little Absalom than a loris? It would cost him nothing.

'What's he called?' Magog said, as he left to drive Hadassah home over Hammersmith Bridge, where the late cars were already padding with soft noise between twin iron peacocks' tails.

'Borgia,' the great director said. 'Nothing's too bad for him.'

The cold was. It was nippy outside and Hadassah refused to have the caged loris in Magog's car with her, so the chauffeur put the animal in the boot. It would be all right on the short journey to Central London.

On the way back, Magog found himself asking Hadassah to spend the night with him. It was not lust which spoke with his mouth, but curiosity to see whether he still had his old power over her. And when she said she would stay with him until morning, she only wanted to show that her overweight and her baby had not taken away her desirability. Neither of them could bear to admit the other was not fascinated, although both would have spent the night more comfortably alone.

The love-making was not a success. They did not want each other enough. Magog found Hadassah's plumpness rather repellent, and Hadassah found Magog's refinement pathetic after her mechanic husband's assaults in the kibbutz. Still, for old time's sake, they told each other that they had enjoyed it and vowed secretly never to do it together again. Yet it was worth while in a way, for the sake of the conversation that followed. At a certain age, chatting between the sheets with a cigarette is more fun than what comes before it.

'It's strange how everything is still there,' Magog said. 'Nothing changes really. It's just as good as ever between us.'

'Yes, that is strange,' Hadassah agreed. 'Do you really find me just the same?'

'Just the same,' Magog said, lying through his teeth and squeezing the excess of flesh on her upper arm.

'When a woman has a child, she doesn't think she will ever be attractive again. Then she finds she is, and she has a child as well. It is a great blessing.'

'It must be.'

So the two lovers who no longer loved each other were perfectly reassured that they were as potent as they had ever been. Ageing was denied and they lay back in warm satisfaction.

'Your brother Gog,' Hadassah said, 'what happened to him? He was so odd to be your brother.'

'As far as I can gather, he had some part in stealing the Stone of Scone. They're not prosecuting now that they've got it back in Westminster, but really Gog is intolerable with all his wild false Celtic nationalism.'

'How did the English get it back? I thought the clans would guard it with their lives.'

'Gog says the reason why the English always used to beat the Scots was that they could always bribe one clan to fight the next clan for them. The Scots are venal. I suppose we bought back their stupid coronation Stone in exchange for the welfare state.'

'The proud are the most corrupt in a way,' Hadassah said. 'They never believe they can be corrupt, so it's really quite easy to buy them. They don't suspect themselves. Perhaps you should buy the Stone now, Magog, to use as the foundation of your first skyscraper built with father. Think of all the publicity.'

'I'd rather the Stone sat under the throne,' Magog said. 'Concrete's much sounder, you know, and it costs less.'

The night turned cold. The loris was forgotten on the kitchen table. Magog and Hadassah slept. When they woke in the morning and went downstairs to get their coffee, they found the loris had turned its back on them. Its little buttocks were two mute curves of abandoned hope. Hadassah began to cluck and cry and tell Magog that he was a monster of cruelty. She filled the monkey's bowl with milk and left a piece of banana, some sponge-cake and even a thimbleful of cognac in the cage. But for an hour, the slender loris would not move. Then it turned about. It held its two hands in front of its circular eyes to ward off the light of the killing world.

Magog had to go to work, but Hadassah refused to desert the loris, even though it meant leaving Absalom with his nurse all day. The loris did little. Occasionally a tremor ran up and down its tiny ribs as though a bee were pinned within its chest. It would not eat. But in the evening, when Magog came home and Hadassah had to go away, it climbed up and down the twig within its cage, as though it were reviving. So Magog could easily press it on Hadassah for Absalom's sake. Every little boy needed his own pet.

Magog did not see Hadassah again before she went back to Israel. But he heard from her the following morning on the telephone. She was weeping.

'The monkey coughed all night,' she said. 'I did everything. It wasn't any good. He must have caught pneumonia on that kitchen table. He coughed up his lungs. He's dead now.'

'You shouldn't care so much for animals,' Magog said. 'That's just the English disease, part of our hypocrisy. We love our dogs and loathe our babies.'

'But he looked just like a little baby, dead, and all that blood.' Hadassah began to weep again. Magog could not make out another word from her, except he thought he heard her say, 'Murderer.'

All day, Magog remembered the loris. It was ridiculous. Why should the death of a monkey matter to him? He supposed that its death had proved his thoughtlessness, and so his vanity was hurt. He felt the need to apologize, so he put a call through to the great director. He feared the other man's reaction, but he did not expect the reply.

'Serve the little bastard right,' the great director said. 'Justice is done. You know why I gave him to you?'

'No.'

'There's one thing lorises eat that I didn't tell you about. They eat birds. Two nights ago, dear Borgia got out of his cage in the greenhouse. I'd just bought a very expensive Indian nightingale, which cost me sixty pounds in Harrods. Her singing was sheer Galli-Curci. I adored her. Then that little beast Borgia went after her in the dark, stretching his filthy paws through the bars of her cage, trying to grab her. My poor nightingale went mad with fright and beat her brains out on the bars and fell dead. Borgia ate her bit by bit through the wires. I'm delighted he's dead.'

Magog felt like laughing with relief. He had merely killed a killer. There wasn't really a Great Chain of Being, just a Great Chain of Doing In Others Until One Was Done For. Men were stupid in disguising their animal natures to themselves. At least in the film world, claws mattered more than consciences. To kill a loris had been a public service. His brief feeling for the monkey had been as sentimental and stupid as his fling with Hadassah. Whistling through his teeth like a corner-boy, Magog set to work to axe a film project or two before lunch.

The day Winston Churchill gave his one more heave and won the election, he sat selecting his Cabinet while Magog sat in his office, selecting his henchmen for his property dealings. Not for Magog the classic heavies of second feature films, the bruisers with the square jaws and the meaty fists ready for mashing or mauling at the flick of a razor. He preferred the young men green from two years of doing their National Service for King and country, or else adrift and shocked after being cast out of the cocoon of Oxford or Cambridge which had so long protected them from the viciousness of this world. These freshmen to London did not know that the big city was less evil than their fears of it. Thus they would make better villains than cockneys, because they thought that those who are no better than they should be were worse than they were.

Three young men passed the interviews. Sandy, who had been in the Hong Kong Police and had a taste for Peking duck, bare knees and flogging; James, who had studied history and rowing at Cambridge, and had found that both led to dulled senses and bruised arses; and Morrell, whose mind was so whimsical and rarefied that he despised everybody ordinary to the point of callousness. Magog rapidly explained to his little gang their jobs – the fixing of permits through lunches and gifts, the smoothing of officials by flattery and parties with film stars, the dealing with the black market in building materials knocked off from the sites, the shifting of baulky tenants from near-empty blocks by disconnecting their electricity and putting in criminal neighbours. For the over-riding considerations were to get permissions, clear the land and build, build, build. London needed more space for its business, which was business, not nicety.

So the young men fanned out, Sandy and James and Morrell, the Three Racketeers, dedicated to save all London from the machinations of Cardinal Planner and his minions. In their smart Edwardian suits, nipped at the ankle and hip, they looked like storks with crests of loose hair that flapped in the breeze of change. Plans were presented to the London County Council in blue harvests of paper. Some schemes were quickly approved after promises from Magog and Radzen to restore some ancient feature within their development; other schemes pended until next year, the year after, sometime, never. But there was enough to get along with, now that the Tories were easing the brakes on free enterprise, and the pirates were coming up out of their manholes, ready to sweep the loot off the streets.

Magog left his resignation as film boss to the last moment. Two jobs were certainly more profitable than one. But the redevelopment of the metropolis was heady stuff. Magog's brain was full of quantity surveys; his mind ran only on girders and concrete, not on the paint and canvas of film sets. He left his position with the declaration that his city needed him. He would convert the cinemas to better uses than the showing of films. True creativity lay in bricks and mortar.

As Magog watched his three young men grease the rusty cogs of London government, he sometimes wondered about his own role as corrupter. Was he really teaching the young the truth about financial life or was he creating new sharpsters, who would go on bringing the standards of British business down the snakes and ladders where they had been falling since the Depression and the Second World War? Soon the ethics of the City would be no better than those of Wall Street or the Bourse. Perhaps Britain had been more moral about business in her great days, just because she could afford to be. She could no longer afford to be. And perhaps Magog was merely practising a form of democracy. In the old days, only the artistocrats and the underworld had felt a divine right to fiddle and trick a living from society. Now their privileges and capers were spreading to the middle classes and the financial community, who could ape the dandy clothes and soft hair and easy morals of their betters and the worse. Only one step remained. Once the whole of England put on the dress and habits of the Edwardian gentleman and crook, who would be left to work for the goods and obey?

An appeal was sent to the office for the rebuilding of the Guildhall of the City of London, burned down in the Blitz. Magog had heard his half-brother tell of a night spent wandering through the incendiaries and blaze about St Paul's and ending in delirium in the Guildhall, as the statues of the giants of Old England, Gog and Magog, charred and fell. It was probably a vision, although Gog had produced a burned ball, which he said had rolled from the flaming wooden club of the giant of the people. The twin giant of power had perished utterly. Now the Guildhall was rising again, the honourable temple of money-changing and the survival of the sleek. Magog was asked for five hundred pounds and managed to spare five, earmarked for the new statue of the ancient giant which bore his nickname. Magog was not sentimental, but he had become used to being called Magog, and this was a cheap way of getting his likeness to last in the very ark of the covenant of Mammon.

1952–1955

For Magog, four years passed as one. He would later say of this period of his life, 'Nothing happened to me.' In fact, as much happened to him as happened in every other time of his existence. Yet the events of these years were not particularly memorable, and were not remembered. Magog lived through steady weeks and months and years of ordered business, of consolidation, getting richer faster than the rest of his countrymen, recovering from the effects of the war. As rationing ended and building materials became more available and permissions became easier to get from Tory councils and ministries, so Magog found the redevelopment of London a form of sophisticated child's play, of trading with greedy kids who had sticky fingers, of boasting about how strong his big daddy company was when its actual dealings were rather seedy, of putting up large ugly blocks where small pretty ruins stood. Occasionally, Magog and Radzen and Stratosphere Securities Limited could not proceed with one of their plans for changing London from a city of spires and houses and gaps and squares into a city of oblongs and offices and high density and higher rents; but on the whole, their progress was both solid and spectacular. Nothing they built failed to fatten the pocket and offend the eye. They even managed to reduce the great dome of St Paul's, which had reared over its blitzed surroundings, to the stature of a round-cherry sweet set in the box of chocolate blocks that was the new City of London.

There were a few unpleasantnesses. Magog did not want to know of such trifles. So the Three Racketeers, Sandy and James and Morrell, quickly learned how to spare Magog the ugly details. The King, after all, has no evil, although he may have bad ministers. Sandy, with his appetite for the whip and his police training, specialized in breaking the intention of the law legally and in labour relations. He studied the regulations of eviction and dismissal, of mortgage and compensation, of controlled rents and uncontrollable neighbours. He knew how to trick a tenant into defaulting on a payment or a worker into discharging himself. He knew how to threaten vaguely and act precisely. James, however, was the bluff figurehead, jovial and hail-fellow and one of the chaps; yet he knew how to drive a hard bargain at a bar, how to exploit heartiness heartlessly, and how to cozen the honour of old people and the self-respect of working people and the shame of young people.

By not seeming to be so, Morrell was the most effective rogue of the three. If a tenant would not budge from a building otherwise empty and ripe for redevelopment, Morrell would begin ornamenting the lead pipes with flame effects in the style of the Japanese sword-masters, thus happening to cut off the water. Or else he would declare that Hallowe'en was perpetual and decree gibbering pumpkin-masks and candles for the lodgers – no electricity, of course. He would announce that rats were a man's best friend and import them by the sackful. He would say that he was the Pied Piper of cockroaches, and then play the flute to make hordes of the insects suddenly materialize. As he hated racialism, he would quarter homeless Jamaican razor gangs next to immovable old ladies, who would then move. 'Our neighbours should be the unexpected,' he would say. And then he would add, 'Zoos should be daily,' and house a pack of hyenas next to the last hold-out of a family in a slum property awaiting refurbishing. All sorts of people seemed to prefer sleeping in the streets to putting up with Morrell's japes.

With the Three Racketeers clearing the ground and with Stratosphere Securites Ltd cluttering that ground by its clean cheap constructions, Magog could spare time for his home life. And he had one. For Maire and her twin girls came to live with him in his Nash terrace house in Regent's Park.

'It's not so much that Rosa and Josepha need a father,' Maire said. 'Nobody does. But as they are seven-year-olds, they are young women and they need a man about the house. As for me, I am tired of half of London thinking that passing through my door also means passing through my thighs, while the other half hates me because I never bother to invite them in or on. It is time, Magog, to off-load the envy we create. If we're together, at least the people we don't sleep with will believe that they are being turned down because of our togetherness, not their undesirability. And we will be loathed as two people, which means splitting the odium between us. And as both you and I have a horror of involvement or marriage, domesticity is fine. You can't marry your brother's rich wife. You are prohibited by God and the Income Tax. We were made to live together.'

Maire ran the household well with its weekly dinner-parties, where peers rubbed shoulders with actresses and skins later; where Portuguese couples overworked since they did not speak enough English to understand their slavery in their adopted country; and where nannies lived with the two little girls in the mews house at the bottom of the garden, since Maire refused to inflict the children on Magog, stating that such closeness was damn near incest. Magog did try to point out that her opinion made every family home into a sink of iniquity, as only the very rich could afford to live wholly apart from their children.

'Exactly,' Maire said. 'The bourgeois family is a hotbed of vice. They know each other's flaws down to the last pubic hair. Good god, how can a daughter *respect* her mother if she hears her flushing the loo?'

As the years passed, Magog found his habits changing. Used to being unable to sleep if he spent the whole night with a woman, now he had insomnia if Maire was not in his bed until morning. He discovered that bodies give more comfort than pleasure. By a form of unspoken agreement, Maire confined her peccadilloes to the afternoons and behaved just like a married woman, dressing three times a day, once when rising, once after her afternoon lover, and once after her evening bath. Her restlessness was leaving her and she plotted her major affairs to coincide with the summer holidays. Then Magog stayed working behind his desk and the twins went north to stay at Gog's farm, while Maire herself tried one of the few resorts she had not often seen and one of the many men or women who had not often seen her. As she said nothing to Magog about these affairs, he never felt betrayed and found his peace of mind in her silence. Maire was not coward enough to ease her conscience by admitting her crimes. Magog almost thought her a martyr to her own life; she did not lay off her sins by confessing them.

As for Rosa and Josepha, Magog found himself growing to love them. Rosa, dark and thin and nervous as a whippet, goading on the plump and determined Josepha to imitate her naughtiness and take all the blame. If there was a plate broken, a fit of tears, a fight or a quarrel, Rosa would always say that Josepha did it or started it, and Josepha would look sulky and say nothing. In a brilliant counter-manoeuvre, Magog decreed that, since both were inseparable twins, both would get punished equally for what either did. This just injustice destroyed Rosa's strategy for all of a week, until she began blaming every crime on the little boy next door, who was too young to talk, or on the Portuguese couple, who did not understand, or on the nannies, who could always be replaced. By a shrewd planting of a piece of Maire's jewellery in a drawer in the mews, Rosa did get her most awful nanny removed. But that was a rare triumph, because she was up against two masters of craftiness, Maire and Magog. Rosa could run rings round any visitor, but she had to deal with adult trickery in a hard school at home.

Familiarity bred content with Magog and content bred love. The little girls might scream in the garden, but their fuss was no worse than the honking of the Canada geese from the Park, and just as reassuring. For usual sounds tell a man that he is in the place which is his. A hush in the Nash terraces began to seem menacing to Magog, and a long silence scared him out of his senses. The paradox of family life was beginning to impose itself on Magog, when peace is only found in hearing fond noise, when solitude is peopled with horrors, when the company of the household seems the most private thing, and when listening to the little doings of the twins each evening appeared more important than the death of nations or kings.

Naturally, Magog did remember the death of the King, since he took Maire and the girls to watch the funeral from the garden of old Hamish Gorder's grace-and-favour residence on the walls of Windsor Castle. The aged ex-civil servant now had a seat in the House of Lords as Baron Tenworthy, and although he could hardly stand, he insisted on watching the full ritual in front of St George's Chapel, to bury the coffin of the monarch. Tears rolled continually down the old man's cheeks as he confused his mortality with the King's, but Magog could find precious little to cry about. There was a slight sense of the ridiculous about the whole occasion to a man who felt in his prime like Magog. Not enough redcoats were available to line the kerbs of the Castle, so young long-haired Etonians in baggy khaki stood looking down at their topsy-turvy rifles, resting on their arms reversed, while the brassoed magnificence of a few Horseguards was reserved for the last steps up to the Chapel. The massed wreaths made the emblems they bore seem out of place, an anchor in red flowers, a gun in green and yellow petals, a crown in lilies, and a wheel in multi-coloured blossoms. A white cat, blissfully unconcerned, strolled through the soldiers' ranks; it did not even have the decency to turn black. The boy soldiers saluted from time to time, not noticing that half the limousines had dropped their distinguished cargoes and held only their chauffeurs. And when the cannon finally fired and the bell began to toll and the Union Jack on the castle pole was lowered to half-mast and the brass band beyond the walls struck up the Dead March in Saul, no reverent procession came by, but six Rolls-Royces wheeled through the gateway of Henry VIII, with four veiled ladies sitting in each car, twenty-four Queens mourning at the Morte of their Arthur, but sailing in no black boat with dark swans to Avalon. But then the procession did finally come. Lifeguards *sans* nags and Pursuivants and Representatives of all the Foreign Forces there ever were and Marshals and Generals and Admirals and Pipers and Heralds and Knights at Arms and Black Rod and the Lord Steward and the Assistant Valet and then the guncarriage pulled by the sailors bearing its coffin and the coarse gaudy royal standard with a silvery tinsel crown on top and the doddering Yeomen of the Guard on either side and the royal families of Europe drooping behind from the last countries that didn't mind admitting to a useless royalty like France and Denmark and the Hellenes and Sweden and Iraq and Turkey and Norway and Liège and Luxemburg and the Netherlands and Denmark and even Vietnam, then all the way down through the High Commissioners and the Heads of Special Foreign Missions like the USSR (oh where have all the Czars gone?) to the Equerries and the Privy Purse and the Comptrollers, and then there was nothing but a bit of dung on the roadway and a boy-soldier fainting and being taken off in a stretcher and the old Hamish still blubbering and anyway, Magog could never afterwards really distinguish the funeral from the Coronation procession of the King's daughter next year, except that he was then sitting with Maire and the two girls outside Buckingham Palace, and everybody was riding in carriages under umbrellas except for the Queen of Tonga, and there were crowds of hundreds of thousands to watch exactly the same sort of peacocked fools troop by, even more of them and more soldiers, but as violent emblem succeeded garish flag, and prominence shuffled after dignitary, and even the gold coach looked just as tawdry and improbable as the royal coffin, Magog realized that Kings never did die because it was really just the baubles and the trappings and the troops and the gaudy manner of it all that the people wanted to see, the dressy illusion that the whole world would still meet under dyed feathers and bright banners to watch the crown put on the Princess's head, somehow all wasn't yet over with the Empire if such an international cast would still turn up to honour the royal première, there must be something still left as the whole show had been on the road for nine hundred years, with much the same trimmings too. And hadn't Everest been conquered that very morning, what a bit of inspired stage-management, it showed Britain could still be tops, oh yes she could!

Yet royal deaths and royal crownings did not affect Magog's life, for nobody cared very much for the New Elizabethan Age in property circles or at home. There had been a time when the death of a King had ruined his whole country and had delivered it to fire and sword, to civil war and hunger. Now even the passing from power of Sir Winston Churchill to Sir Anthony Eden made little difference. For the truth was that nobody was indispensable any more. The old Winston had been as necessary as any man could be in the Second World War, or he had made use of his opportunities to make himself seem so. Yet he had been discarded for a nonentity the moment that the war was won. The British no longer liked greatness thrust upon them. They were settling for lesser and cosier men to guide them, and the moving on of the Grand Old Man for a tailor's dummy whose only strength lay in his moustache was really rather a relief. Unlike a coronation, which was merely a parade of past might and magnificence, the luxury of keeping Churchill in office meant a beggared hanging on to navies and fighter-planes and bases that cost far more than occasional pomp and circumstance. The Queen might be a bit dear, but frankly, she was far cheaper and fancier than an H-Bomb, and not half so dangerous or dirty.

In the age of the totally disposable individual, Magog found the myth of indispensability his strongest weapon. There was nowhere a clerk so petty that he did not feel the nation depended on his pen or judgement. No man could function if he felt superfluous. All the piddling barriers and snobberies which minor English officials put up about themselves were really defences against the fear that they need not exist at all. So Magog only had to invite a borough surveyor to a drink and humbly ask his opinion about a million-pound scheme and then incorporate his least suggestion, for the surveyor to be convinced all his life that his ideas had altered the whole skyline of London.

Yet Magog often thought that he himself was not essential. Without him, he knew perfectly well that Radzen and the Three Racketeers would carry on their work of enriching the Company (and incidentally the country) while rehousing the office workers (and incidentally dehousing the city-dwellers). His personal sense of near superfluity gave him a curious liberty. He found that the only way to feel free was to know that it did not matter whether he was there or not. Naturally, Magog still did go to his office on most days, but he thought himself released from routine because he knew that things could continue if he died in an accident on his way to work. If that was so, what was suddenly quitting or resigning except a voluntary accident, a willed death of a usual way of life? Why wait for necessity to impose what choice could do just as well?

'Sometimes I don't understand you,' Maire said. 'I think I know my Magog, so obsessed with control and money that it affects all your life. Then I suddenly see you lounging on your hump-backed stripey sofa listening to Scarlatti and reading Homer for all the world like a man who could not care less about anything except exercising his leisure. Perhaps you no longer love power any more, you just enjoy its games.'

She was right, of course. The first article in Magog's credo was that Maire was always right. Detachment was creeping into Magog's wish to dominate and arrange. Now he often wanted to experience his new domesticity more than to carve up the metropolis. Riches would pile up their muck in their due course. One could jog along to a fortune without shitting in one's britches to gallop there.

A curious lull settled on Britain, five Indian summers of fond illusion that somehow everything could be fixed without losing too much. Luxury glittered again in the gold-painted Daimler of the Dockers, débutantes danced once more to the dated music of Tommy Kinsman, and the street gangs now dressed exactly like Edwardian gentlemen. The rise of the Teddy Boys seemed to prove that the lower classes were rightly back to apeing their betters. These narrow-trousered dandies who coshed and

robbed were as proud in their plumage as any aristocratic
Mohock who had terrorized Georgian London. The spiv with
his flash and anti-social ways was dead; the war of the classes
was apparently dying out as secretaries began to dress like
ladies and thugs like Guards Officers. The welfare state seemed
to have blunted the worst edges of poverty and inequality, and
the Tories were too wise to scrap it for the old class conflict
that might destroy their chosen strategy of levelling up rather
than breaking down. There were nasty brush wars in Kenya and
Malaya and Cyprus, troubles in Iran and Egypt, but really, even
Rome had never changed its empire so decently from control to
Commonwealth with so few dust-ups abroad and so much peace
at home. In this strange interlude of convalescence from a
great war and of national complacency, everything seemed
to be ticking over all right as long as nobody looked too far
ahead.

'It can't last,' Maire said. 'But all the same, it's very chic of
luck to let me play the wife and mother at a time when I feel
I'm slowing down. And it's very chic of whoever's responsible
up there to let you reach your first million pounds in peace and
quiet without too much fuss and bother. They always say the
first million's the hardest, but I do hope you're not one of those
men who never have a million enough.'

'No,' Magog said, 'I'm not greedy. Two million pounds will
be enough, just in case I lose one on the way home.'

Gog stood on Arthur's Seat and looked down on Jerusalem. Of
course, the false name of the city was Edinburgh, but as the
sinking sun set its bright scales on the dark leviathan of granite
that lay in its dry-dock walls between the north loch and the
south loch, then the Scots capital was restored as the golden
city of heaven. Gog could even pick out an exact correspondence
to the site of the Bible. There! Castle Rock was Mount Zion.
St Giles's Cathedral was the Temple, Princes' Street Gardens
the Valley of Jehoshaphat, Holyrood House high over the ruins
of the Palace of Lebanon by the Watergate which led to Joppa,
the same name for the port of Edinburgh and for the Jerusalem
of the Hebrews. West towards the low sun, the Dung Gate
leading to the Golgotha of Gogar's Mount, place of the skull and

the sacrifice. Ah Gog, Gog, you were at the ancient Jerusalem, and at the present Jerusalem, shall you not be there? And shall not the present Jerusalem be where you are?

City of bleak beauty, dark and ridged between water and water, city of northern light, city of shining westering, your shape the axis of the sun's rising to its falling, who can say that Jerusalem was not here or shall not be here again? Shall the place of the true Jerusalem matter, whether in Albion at London, or in Israel at the Dome of the Rock, or in Scotland at Edinburgh, when the city of heaven on earth may be built from any man's vision who shall walk himself through that city and touch its golden pillars and worship in its temple and lie down with its lambs and eat the olives upon its Mount? How shall a man live who does not seek his Jerusalem, how shall a man judge who does not know of his Jerusalem, how shall a man ask who does not expect his Jerusalem, how shall a man die who does not reach for his Jerusalem?

When the light went, Gog turned away from his Jerusalem to the Lothian Hills and stood still as a pillar of salt, looking towards the dark south leading to Sodom and Gomorrah, England.

1956

'Garden cities!' Magog said. 'Garden shitty! Enough of bloody greenery. I'm positively polluted with flowers.'

Asthma had bunged up his throat and eyes. In the sun, only his sinus was sweating. The pollen count was astronomical, while his breathing felt diabolical. In Regent's Park, his nose was worse than a hot honeycomb and he had to run for relief to Baker Street before he could begin to inhale. There, an acrid whiff of exhaust scratched his nostrils, soothed his sinus, cleared his head. A friendly diesel truck puffed out its black fumes as it idled at a red light. Magog sniffed and smiled. His lungs settled down, his chest tingled with vigour. What heavenly foul London air! He had better keep off the grass and far from the trees in summer. Only the streets were safe.

Yet this sudden asthma did not drive Magog to his retreat in the dirtiest part of the city. He had begun a clandestine affair with a woman he was ashamed of, and she knew it. Gloria Angel O'Connor, who had once announced herself at a film press show as open to interpretation, was interpreted. Magog never quite knew why he started the liaison or continued with it, except that he had just the right place for that sort of squalid affair. Perhaps the last sexual thrill was to live in contradictions. What was certain was that he had gone down to Limehouse one day with Sandy to look at a terrace of derelict houses on the river.

'In thirty years' time,' Sandy had said, 'the Thames will be dammed by a barrage and the river'll be a yacht marina and the docks will be duck ponds and all the smartiboots and posh tits will have cottages on the tenth floor in Wapping. We should have a foothold here, so we are first in the redevelopment area and the queue. A straight conversion job of a waterside slum into rich queers' studios will bridge the gap. They can watch the big ship brothels cruising in and then screw their favourite sailors and pretend they're artists – about buggery. And we can feel out the possibilities – of buttocks, of course. I've got contacts in that world.'

Magog had himself been seduced by the view from the derelict houses, which still had barge-builders operating from the cellars. The buildings were set on a wharf on an outer bend of the Thames, so that the eye was carried by the sweep of river towards Greenwich on the left and Tower Bridge on the right. Facing Magog across the Thames, two factory chimneys made a rifle's foresight to aim the view, while day-and-night sounds of machinery and wreaths of smoke flew with the gulls and the swans over the water from the working of ENTHOVEN and ESSO on Lavender Wharf. Around them, gutted ruins and a rubbish tip, where trucks emptied wastes down canvas chutes into barges to be towed away. On either side of the river, warehouses squatted and bulked below the arms and torsos of the iron cranes that were spiders in the blue fog of the morning or else were skeletal in the low slant of the evening sun. Below Magog, on the north foreshore, the long coffins of the Thames barges had slats over their maws and red-painted decks, the same size still as the galleons which had been made there in the first Queen Elizabeth's time, when Raleigh had sailed off to found Roanoke and the whole of North American history had been a dream of adventurers seeking Eldorado from the East End. Scrubby tugs also lay on the gravel bank, their hatches lime-green, navy-blue-funnelled, rust-arsed and ready for reconditioning to leave a cleaner wake. At the end of the buildings, the back of a pub called The Grapes (Charles Dickens drank here) and beyond, another great chimney of a power station smutting the air so that black rain fell on the twin giant cranes that walked away down-river into the last light, two red lamps shining at the edge of their platform. Magog called the warning lights Rosa and Josepha. To the west, the river crooked its vein into the heart of London, with a Wren church spire pushing up its white bill in the midst of a nest of the iron-boned cranes. On the rim of the City, Tower Bridge held up its two manacled wrists, while the street-lamps dressed themselves in single file to confine the water o'nights.

Such mystery and brutality of place, such stark demand of beauty, such harsh vision, made Magog decide to keep a hidden studio there for himself to flee from the Regency decencies of the Nash terraces round the Park. And when the long narrow studio was finished, with its white-painted pine walls leading out to a balcony that jutted over the tidal Limehouse Reach, so Magog could stand on his rope-caulked deck of beams and steer like Captain Ahab towards the two chimneys across the river when the storms hammered at the skylights and the barges banged against the watergate of the house trembling like *The Victory* at anchor before Trafalgar, then Magog knew why he was there, playing the sea-dog at the muddy ditch from where England had grown to Empire, black factories, coal-dark bricks, iron ships, the docks of London where any sailor could drop down on the foc's'le in a cone of yellow light from the deck lamps and begin like Conrad's Marlow to say: 'A funny thing happened to me on my way to Penang last voyage . . .'

There was also Gloria Angel O'Connor, ill-met in The Grapes and still open to interpretation. In her passion for Magog lay a desperation, a pitiful devotion and obedience to Magog's least

temper that made her lover feel a tenderness towards her that
he would have grudged a woman, but given to a neighbour's
child or cat. Bed was very good with her as long as Magog was
feeling lusty, although she worked away at his balls too much to
be supportable in times of fatigue. Sex did take it out of a man
even more than a game of squash. Gloria seemed to think that
her love-making would somehow kindle Magog's heart towards
her, when it wearied his fondness and disgusted his appetite.
At least, his indifference never allowed her to ask him to put up
with her child as well. It – a bump-browed snubbie called Jerome
Ignatius O'Connor – was kept in the country at her mother's
and she visited it at week-ends, when Magog was not available.

He was not available except for two evenings a week. Gloria
complained that she had nothing to do in the studio while he was
away. It was a rotten area, with the shops half-a-mile away and
little to buy in them. 'Crochet doilies,' Magog said. 'Sew. Spin.
Watch TV. Bake bread. Write letters to *Woman's Own*. Talk to
the milkman. Good god, there are a thousand fascinating things
for a girl to do.' But Gloria surrounded herself with scores of
magazines and sent off for travel brochures, dreaming of the
day when she would lure Magog off to permanent retirement
in the Canary Isles or Bermuda or some other palm-fringed
bide-a-wee nookery among natives.

'You never take me anywhere,' she used to say. 'That's
because you don't want to be seen with me.'

'You're here,' Magog used to say. 'That's better than having
nowhere to go. Shut up.'

Magog had never had a domineering relationship with a woman
before. He had supposed that the normal brutality of an Edwardian masher towards his mistress was no longer appropriate to
the nineteen-fifties. The arrogance of the British gentleman was
as out of date as the British fleet. But the very cheapness of
Gloria's thoughts and the vulgarity of her tongue drove him to
hit her a few times, although these easy victories were no fun.
For she blubbered and promised to be good, never to nag again,
except that her tearful apologies were even more wearisome
than her complaints.

'You're always free to go,' Magog said.

'Where to?' Gloria said.

'Back where I found you,' Magog said.

'You'll have to tell me where,' Gloria said. 'I belong to you now. You owe me something, you do.'

'We all belong to ourselves,' Magog said.

'I'm yours,' Gloria said. 'I didn't ever belong to me since I met you. You put me in here, didn't you?'

So when the quick nervous hard flesh of Gloria Angel O'Connor became not worth the price of her chatter and the boredom of her company, Magog had to do something about her which would cause no scandal and little expense. After all, she had insisted that she was his responsibility. Morrell had the answer. 'Kept women don't keep too well too long,' he said. 'You should catch her out. Common women are common to everybody, aren't they?' The jovial James was sent down to supervise the rebuilding of the other riverside studios and to seduce the lonely Gloria during his tea-breaks. She was always open to intepretation, so it was no problem for Magog to walk in unexpectedly and surprise Gloria flagrante delicto with his underling, who was lying fully dressed on top of her naked body on the nylon polar-bear rug in front of the antique French coke-oven, which held the drinks.

'I'm sorry, sir,' James said, immediately rising to his feet and saluting while dropping his left hand for decency's sake over his flies. 'I must be getting back to work. Will you please excuse me while I button up?' Then he disappeared about his business.

Although Magog had set up the whole débâcle, he found himself both furious and jealous, which was absurd. He would have been irrationally proud if Gloria had resisted temptation for his sake.

'You rotten bitch,' Magog said to her. 'Can't you save it till I come?'

'You never do come,' Gloria said, weeping. 'And I don't know how to do anything else. He wasn't much cop, anyway.' Then clutching towards Magog, 'Not like you, my love. Not like you.' Then hurled aside by a violent push. 'No, don't go, don't go, don't go. Save me.'

'Save yourself now,' Magog said. 'You had your one chance. Salvation doesn't knock twice. You go. A taxi will call for you tomorrow morning to take your things away. Bitch!'

When Gloria Angel O'Connor was gone in her broken flight, Magog found the studio curiously empty and sad, and hardly went there any more. It was as if he could salvage nothing for himself down in the docks, now that he had refused to save Gloria. Occasionally he thought of asking her back, but he had lost touch. So he would only go down to Limehouse once a month to watch the great cargo ships from the four corners of the world as they were towed into the wharves by the tugs. Sometimes he saw a couple of floating cranes move slowly past, hanging the low sun on the gibbets of their frame, the *London Hercules* and the *London Titan*. Once he saw a red-sailed Thames lugger making a bloody patch towards Greenwich, once a four-masted clipper training-ship, once even a painted galleon like the Ancient Mariner's boat mysteriously making towards the sea without noise or sails, by opening the air in front and closing it behind, presumably set on course for the new Eldorado of film sets in Spain. But most evenings, in the decay of trade and might and main, there were just some burping tugs pulling strings of barges loaded with bales of old paper, or a few lighters croaking their way across to France, or some navy cadets toiling at the oars in whalers on water too dirty even for a shrimp to survive in, or perhaps cold youths in racing-sculls which made a plaything of this foul river that had once floated counter-Armadas. For the little diesel freighters of rebuilt Rotterdam were now taking most of the trade of the continent away from the London docks, as Europe slowly began to unite and Britain stayed in her cold island, waiting for destiny to visit again and give her another opportunity or carry her away.

Yet only one monster came across the Thames from between the two chimneys that stood like a rifle's foresight. It bore down on the studio, its open jaws larger than a whale's, until Magog could almost believe that it would crunch up the river wall and gobble him down, a new Jonah, never to be vomited back to the safety of dry land. But the scoop-tug swung away downriver just before it bit into the moored barges on the foreshore, and Magog read its name which was his own, the name of one of the two guardian giants of the rebuilt Guildhall in the City:

MAGOG

PORT OF LONDON AUTHORITY

Magog could hardly believe his eyes, but he asked Morrell to look up the tug in *Lloyd's Register*, and it was so.

That November, Mulcree caught up with his old enemy. When the card bearing Mulcree's name was brought into the office, Magog thought he was in for a bad time. And Mulcree did not disappoint him.

'I'm in the Ministry of Housing now,' Mulcree said. 'Our business is to house people. We don't like your methods. Our investigators state that you have a thug called Morrell working for you.'

'A practical joker,' Magog said.

'It's a spiffing wheeze,' Mulcree said, 'to find yourself sleeping in a gutter. Our target for new houses is three hundred thousand a year. You're getting people out faster than we can build them homes.'

'People have to work somewhere too,' Magog said. 'Offices pay higher taxes as well as higher rents. A man has the right to work in comfortable surroundings, you know. And work is going to save this country's bacon, not lounging around at home.'

'So you intend to make living conditions so intolerable at home that people are driven to spend more time in the office?'

'It's a good strategy for the economy,' Magog said.

'I would always believe your disinterest, Ponsonby, if I didn't know what a fortune you made out of it.' Mulcree took a few typed pages from his pocket and put on his reading glasses. 'I have here a list of thirty-six violations by Morrell . . .'

'I never knew he was so lusty,' Magog murmured.

'Violations of the code of housing ethics. Now let me see . . . Item One: The said Morrell did declare that sundry properties in the Elephant and Castle were to be reclassified as Jungle National Park. Soon afterwards, one tenant found a crocodile in her bath-tub and another discovered some large spiders in her sewing-basket, later identified by the Public Health Authorities as tarantulas. Most of the tenants fled when a plague of tsetse-flies, never before identified in England, descended on their

Sunday roasts. When asked about this, the said Morrell replied, "Well, we cleared out South Africa, didn't we? Let's call this the Hottentot's Revenge."'

Magog smiled. Morrell was a minor genius, witty and paradoxical even about his villainies.

'Was it proven Morrell did this?' Magog asked.

'Nothing is ever proven against Morrell,' Mulcree said. 'But somehow he is always involved in driving the poorer classes out of their controlled-rent flats which are immediately redeveloped by your company. Look at this! Item Nine: The said Morrell did let the basement of 96 Lentilbody Buildings to a Mission for Bike Boys at a rent of a sponge of vinegar every Eastertide. As a result, the Buildings were surrounded by motorbicycles revving up night and day, as the Bike Boys visited the Mission where the clergyman, himself dressed up in a black leather jacket painted with a skull and crucifix, served free Coca-cola and gave sermons on Christ the Ton-Up Rider Steering His Norton To The Pearly Gates. The other occupants of the Buildings soon left, saying that they didn't hold with all this new-time religion, and also they were scared out of their wits. The Buildings were torn down shortly afterwards. When questioned, the said Morrell stated, "Is there a soul so speedy that we may not catch it on the wheel? Salvation is too serious a business to be left to God!"' Mulcree put down his indictment. 'It's shameful,' he said.

'As a practical joker,' Magog said, 'Morrell's got nothing on Sir Anthony Eden. The Grand Old Duke of York, if you remember, marched ten thousand men to the top of a hill, then marched them down again, and children have mocked him in their nurseries ever since. But what will the nippers say about Sir Anthony Eden? He had a hundred thousand men. He sailed them to the Suez Canal, then sailed them home again. What a jape! Making sure that the last stand of the British Empire should be on a banana skin. Ending Disraeli's gift to the Empress of India by the biggest fiasco since we surrendered at Singapore. We're the laughing-stock of the world! And you worry about Morrell.'

'I am sure that the Prime Minister had good reason for what he was doing,' Mulcree said. 'We are talking of Morrell, who also happens to be a liar.'

'No comment,' Magog said. 'I believe that the government

did assure the House of Commons that we were not in collusion with the Israelis. That is balderdash, and not even credible balderdash. What did Nye Bevan say, that Eden's gang of gentlemen are synthetic villains, who set off on a villainous course and can't even use the language of villainy. If we're going to bully the wogs, at least we should bully properly like Israel, not scuttle back home leaving a blocked canal and a ruined economy behind us. At least Morrell can be funny about what he's doing, and successful. If you have to be evil, don't fail and always make us laugh.'

Mulcree was shocked. His pale face flushed, while his eyes, magnified beneath his glasses, narrowed to normal size.

'You are unspeakably corrupt, Ponsonby,' he said. 'Words fail me.'

'Good,' Magog said. 'I enjoy hearing your silences.'

'You do realize that *death* is sometimes the result of Morrell's clearance schemes . . .'

'And Eden's . . .'

'Clearances which I may say have been more brutal than any since the Mulcrees were cleared off their Irish lands by Cromwell. I suppose you wish to buy your way into the aristocracy as Slum Lord Ponsonby, the scourge of the aged.'

'Progress has its price,' Magog said. 'I am prepared to pay it – for others, if necessary.'

'When you have old ladies put out on the street, don't you think it is a form of murder?'

'If we are to assign responsibility for killing old ladies, why doesn't the government accept some? How many millions does it kill by slow starvation on an inadequate old-age pension? After all, what is private crime compared with public crime?'

Mulcree rose, his rage a pallor on his cheek.

'You will hear more of this,' he said. 'I will see you and your henchman go to the Scrubs for ten years.'

'First catch your chickens,' Magog said. 'Can I lend you some salt to sprinkle on our tails?'

After Mulcree had gone, Magog sent for Morrell and gave him a mild reprimand about his methods and advised more caution and less whimsy in the future. Under threat of law, respectability was the best gloss.

'They will forgive you everything except your wit, Morrell. Villainy is pardonable if it is earnest like Eden's, and he will be ennobled for it. But, as Oscar Wilde found, the penalty for deviant wit is Reading Gaol.'

Every day Gog would walk from headland to headland along the tip of the lower jaw of the North Sea, looking towards Orkney and Shetland and Greenland that lay beyond the cold waves before the ice. Sometimes he would think of setting off in his small dinghy, which he had named the *Blake*, and trying to find that strait beloved of the Tudor adventurers, the North-West Passage to Tartary and sun and spices and silks of Serendip. And if the floes would close about him, and white bears would rise twelve foot over the solid water before falling to rend his frozen body that dared to enter their domain, why then, he would be seeking what all wanderers from Albion had sought before him, a way through the North Sea to a far haven of ease and mastery.

Yet as he looked down the cliffs to the biting sea that had marked the rocks with its teeth, Gog knew that Britain's way no longer lay on the surface of the waters. The rule of the air and of space was too costly, while the land was being taken back by those who lived upon it from the spoilers who had spread over the seas in their ships of wood and iron. The last empire, the third empire of Britain, could only be found in the maw of the ocean, with its sunken territories unmapped, unmined, untenanted, a drowned and weedy Atlantis of infinite food and riches, waiting for the first nation to lift up its treasures. On the shores of Albion had been bred a race of skimmers on the surface of the deep. Inland, a race of miners had hewed out the coal that burned in the fires of the ovens of the potteries and in the boilers of the factories and the steamships, the black base of imperial majesty. Now the miners should leave their dark earthy veins and put on rubber suits and sink to the depths by submarine or diving-bell, rather than by a cage. The riches of the future lay fathoms down, and only the explorers of that cold and pressing darkness would bring back the last Eldorado to their ebbing country and its peoples. For the British were pirates, the looters of the sea. Broadsides and nets would no longer bring bounty money from the ocean. Wealth had now to be found by crawling along the sea floor.

Yet as Gog stood on his headland, he could not find any good in his vision. What use for him to prophesy the future, to foresee what should be done for the good of Britain when nobody in power would listen to him? What should he do? Go with a petition to Westminster, write a letter to Sir Anthony Eden, or stand at Speakers' Corner in Hyde Park, crying the truth to anybody who would hear him, and knowing nothing would be done, nothing? Gog knew he might as well stand on his promontory, thinking nothing, as cast the runes of the future like a Celtic seer, and pierce through the nibbling and gobbling waves to the place where the last dominion of his country lay under the deep. Yet Albion was a white island that had risen out of the waters, and if she sank back into the lightless sea, perhaps it would be the death of Albion because of the terrible work to be done in the bowels of the deep, the chill toil to raise up the sunken spoils that might smut the white cliffs, smear the last few walls of liberty that still housed a man on his own in his right on common land. So Gog walked back to his farmhouse, melancholy in knowing what was to be done and would not be done, until it was too late. He knew why Cassandra had to be sad.

Back in his kitchen with the range roaring and the toddy hot in his hand, Gog's eyes fell on a battered brown book that he had used to prop up the wobbly leg of the kitchen table. If he had had anything else within reach to read, he would not have bothered to kneel and yank the book out from under the table. But as it was, he was interested to find in his hand a Victorian work called *The British Nation Identified With Lost Israel*. The book was dedicated to the (so-called) British people by their kinsman, Edward Hine. Below the dedication, there was an inscription in ink.

To Gog, who is the sign and forerunner of the end of the world and the coming again of the true Israel, I dedicate these hundred scriptural proofs of Britain's role in the world, as written through a previous incarnation of mine in 1877, Edward Hine.

signed
Wayland Merlin Blake Smith

The book must have been propping up the table-leg for a
dozen years, since Gog had moved to the north after the last
Pyrrhic victory of the British Empire at the end of the Second
World War. He could not remember how the book had ever got
into his hands. He could only remember that it had always
seemed to be under the kitchen table. He flicked idly through
its pages, reading the cock-a-hoop proofs from biblical texts
which made out that Britain fulfilled God's prophecies about
Israel by becoming the largest empire the world had ever seen.
The Jews were too weak to be the Chosen People, who simply
had to be British. To Victorian complacency and self-justification,
every deed of gunboat and bayonet and seven-pounder was yet
another proof of the island's divine right to rule the world by the
will of the Almighty.

Identification the Twentieth
ISRAEL MUST PUSH THE ABORIGINES OF HER COL-
ONIES TO THE CORNERS. We have seen that Israel must
possess Colonies; by the superior power of her people, by
the immense increase that God would give to her seed, she
would become so populous as every now and then to require
the extended use of these Colonies, and thus from time to
time the aborigines should gradually give way, and so be
pushed to the ends of corners of what was once their own
country. It is a prerogative solely belonging to Israel, a
covenant between God and them, that could not be violated.

THE IDENTITY, that this is the very thing that both the
British and the American people are doing, as all our Colonists
know. We have done it to the Tasmanians, the aborigines of
Australia, to the Maoris of New Zealand, the Caffres of the
Cape, indeed in every Colony where we place our foot; and
the Americans have done the same to the Indians, who are
pushed to their backwoods. How intensely valuable the Bible
becomes when we are able to trace the Word of God being
fulfilled! It is worthy to note, that this Scripture cannot refer
to the Jews, because they are not complying with it. So this
pushing Identity must be in operation now . . .

This pushing Identity was in operation now for the Jews, Gog thought. In 1877, naturally, Britain might have seemed the proper place for the fulfilment of the pushing prophecies of the Old Testament. But in 1956, with the Israelis now standing on the shores of the straits of the Red Sea, their South Passage to the Indian Ocean won, where was the Israel of Deuteronomy now, but back in the historical Holy Land of Moses and Isaiah and King David? At Suez, Suez, the glory had departed and the British had come finally home, leaving Israel to the Jews.

Identification the Thirtieth

ISRAEL CANNOT BE CONQUERED IN THEIR ISLES. The Lord said to Israel that 'All the people of the earth . . . shall be afraid of thee' (Deut. xxviii, 10). 'Happy thou, O Israel, . . . thine enemies shall be found liars unto thee, and thou shalt tread upon their high places' (Deut. xxxiii, 29). 'He increased His people Israel greatly, and made them stronger than their enemies' (Ps. cv, 24).

THE IDENTITY indicates the well-known fact, that the British nation has the most powerful army in the world: Israel's was to be the most powerful: ERGO, we must be Israel. Moreover, as God speaks of Israel as those who 'go down to the sea in ships, and do business in great waters' (Ps. cvii, 23). THE IDENTITY is further proven by the fact that 'Britannia rules the waves.' We are the only undefeated nation upon the earth. We never have been defeated since the Norman Conquest and the Normans were a tribe of Israel. The last of the Ten Tribes arriving in this country, it was necessary to receive them into our Constitution, otherwise Israel could never have become reunited and consolidated into a 'strong nation' in compliance with the will of God. THIS IDENTITY is peculiar to Israel, is solely her property, and is only found in the British, who have never been defeated.

No longer, no longer. When Russia rattles its rockets and the White House puts on its frown, the British gunboats scuttle home across the Mediterranean and the Prime Minister bursts into tears and has an illness for the good of the country and the whole national economy is ruined because the Suez Canal has been bravely blocked by the Egyptians and there's no thanks to be had for our pains, none at all, the Israelis were getting on much better without us, thank you very much. In fact, all Eden's intervention did was to stop the Jews from winning a bigger victory than they did. The British Empire lost what the Israelis won for themselves, and nothing would ever be the same again for a power that could no longer live on its dreams of enforcing what it did not have the strength to do.

Identification the Fifty-Third
ISRAEL CONQUERS AGAINST ALL ODDS.
It is the pecular prerogative of Israel to obtain decisive victories by the use of only a small force. One of the seals of God's favour upon them that they hold to this day is that 'Ye shall chase your enemies, and they shall fall before you by the sword; and five of you shall chase an hundred, and an hundred of you shall put ten thousand to flight; and your enemies shall fall before you by the sword' (Lev. xxvi, 7, 8).

THE IDENTITY. We are the only nation that can dare to face fearful odds. This seal of IDENTITY with Israel was verified in the Peninsular War, when the Duke of Wellington bravely withstood, by a small army, nearly the entire forces of the Continent. We withstood the people of China, computed by millions, with only a few boat-loads of men, and prevailed against them. We hold India, with her teeming millions, under the power of a few white men. We prevailed against Russia at the Crimea with but a very small force. We went into Abyssinia with but a handful of Englishmen, and put their millions to the right about without scarcely striking a blow. Thus again we produce a seal given only to Israel and which Israel must have with her this very day, proving that we must be Israel.

Yet what an ageing Goliath were we now, while David was risen again in the Gaza Strip and his stones were fighter-planes killing from the heavens and the giants of the Arab nations were fallen about him, and from his sling came death and destruction and the rout of the many by the few, of the great by the small. Israel was gone again to Jordan, Israel had come into its identity once more, the lost tribes wresting their land in Palestine from the grip of the sea-spread colossus of the world, sickening and sinking and letting go.

Identification the Seventy-seventh
ISRAEL TO BE A SEPARATED PEOPLE FROM THE GENTILES FOR EVER

Israel was not only to be high above the Gentiles, but, as a nation, a separate people from the Gentiles, and that for ever. 'I am the Lord your God, which separated you from other people' (Lev. xx, 24). 'Was not Esau Jacob's brother? saith the Lord; yet I loved Jacob and I hated Esau' (Mal. i, 2). Hence it becomes an utter impossibility for the seed of the Lost Ten Tribes to have become amalgamated with any Gentile people.

THE IDENTITY maintains that British people are a separated people – that neither Scotchmen, Englishmen, nor British can ever lose their IDENTITY – that it is not our custom to naturalize elsewhere. Hosts of foreigners do with us; but we, as a rule, never with them. There may be Esaus, but they are the exception, and generally regret it. Gentiles may merge with other Gentiles and lose trace of their nationality, but a foreigner can never merge into the British stock so as to become unknown as being of foreign extract.

This is surely an Anthropological IDENTITY WITH ISRAEL!

Gog closed the book of the Victorian British Israelite given to him by Wayland Merlin Blake Smith, the bagman he had met on his walk to London a dozen years before. Why was there always a terrible truth in the ravings and boastings of the past? Why did a lunatic prophecy often become fulfilled not quite as it intended? Why did the hazard or destiny of the book falling into Gog's hands make him see a vision of the British coming home at last, to set up their little walls in Bournemouth and Hastings and Cheltenham and Ongar against the coming of the very peoples who had taken them in, the slaves from the West Indies, the tribesmen from Africa, the millions of quick hands from India and Pakistan and Hong Kong? Why would they not see an identity in this reverse migration? By what right of isolation was

Albion sacrosanct from the invasion of other people when its own peoples had imposed themselves on the rest of the world? White isle, false whited sepulchre of an isle, that spewed out its hordes and took none back into its tomb, perfidious Whitehall that put the globe under the Queen's blanket and allowed not a fuzzy-wuzzy's hair to lie on Her pillow. Yet pride shall fall, separation shall end in joining, sundering shall come together, caste shall be class and class shall be race and race shall be species and species shall be spread over the whole earth and unto the far shores of the universe, Britain with end, Albion without end as the sanctuary of all men seeking the white holy place of the north beyond even Israel.

A man without a face slumps into Gog's mind. Putney Bowles, killed by Gog's hand in Egypt. I am the enemy you killed, my friend. And all for the British Nation identified with the True Israel in the occupied land by the Red Sea that would never, never wash Gog's guilt clean.

1957

Life in the African colonies began dying soon after Suez. The new Prime Minister, Harold Macmillan, was called in to revive the corpse, although he sensibly preferred to bury it. Like any undertaker, he had to reassure the family at home with visions of fortune and future ease, while actually pickling the body before it started to stink and could be carried away. The funeral procession of empire had to be done decently and discreetly – No wreaths nor forty-gun salutes by request. The Gold Coast was first given independence and took the new name of Ghana. The rest of the African possessions were assured that their freedom would come soon, even for Mau-Mau Kenya, if they would wait for the proper obsequies and not shoot the pall-bearers. By concentrating the eyes of the British people on the better life to come, Mac the Hearse hoped to drape a black shroud over Africa without his party or his country noticing that the white man's face was covered and gone. It was a shrewd strategy for a necessary grave. Britain could not afford an Algeria or an Angola of its own.

In the Nash terrace house, Maire announced her departure for Paris. Magog could not understand her reasons and Maire could not explain them too well, for all her articulateness. She said that she was irritated with domesticity and that even the show of monogamy was against nature. She no longer enjoyed the role of being hostess to the great nor of attending elegant deceptions from the Lord Mayor's Banquet to the opening of the season at the Royal Opera House. She was forty-five years old and the prospect of menopause made her want to cut loose with the last seasons of her beauty. She insisted that Rosa and Josepha were becoming hopelessly insular in England and needed another cultural influence to stop them from becoming lacrosse-playing neuters whose only word was 'soopah'. Perhaps Maire's dominant reason was the death of her mother Lulu, who had left her daughter a six-roomed apartment on the Quai Bourbon overlooking the Seine. Flats in Paris were unobtainable and requisitioned if left empty. Guilt about the memory of her mother, now too far gone even to forget to visit, and the gift of a place where she could live in freedom and nostalgia made Maire leave bag and baggage for her island in the Seine. Paris was worth the bore of a move.

There was nothing that Magog could do about it, except that the twins continued with their English education and visited their mother only in the holidays, which suited Maire admirably. 'I shan't miss you at all,' Magog threatened Maire, and did miss her. It was intolerable that a woman should get a man used to her, then flit off just when he had acquired a new set of habits based on having her around the house.

So Magog found himself nervous and lonely. He invited his friends round for dinners and drinking, then saw by the uneasy looks in their eyes that he was pressing them too hard to stay on after midnight. He went often to the theatre, but he didn't care for the new realism which had sprung up with *Look Back In Anger* nor for the mannered comedies set in Berkshire drawing-rooms where Magog would never have gone, even if invited. That he should have to pay for being bored by bad conversation in Shaftesbury Avenue added robbery to fatigue. He did not know what the theatre was coming to, and soon did not bother to go and find out.

Magog had never thought of himself as obsessive, certainly not sexually obsessive. He presumed he was like other men, more interested in money and work than in bed and women. It was almost indecent at his age to find his eyes slipping off the stock-market quotations to close their lids on a memory of Maire's full breasts flattened as she lay on her back or spreading like hot batter on his chest as she put her tickling head on his shoulder. And it was positively ridiculous to find himself suddenly bent double with desire while working through a quantity survey on a skyscraper, just because he imagined Maire's pubic architrave above her pillared thighs. Sex was all right in its place, but why the hell didn't it stay there?

Magog found other women useless as a cure for his obsession. They bored him with their flirting and he could hardly pluck up the interest to seduce them, let alone use the hackneyed words necessary to get them to lie down. Even if he did actually proposition them, his lack of enthusiasm made them refuse him. They soon learned that he would rather rant on about Maire's desertion of him and his love of her twin daughters, whom he always claimed as his own. So they spurned him, and in their spurning, he found new gall for his bitterness against all women and for his passion for one.

Against his better judgement, Magog did go and see Maire in Paris. He said that he came to talk over the future of Rosa and Josepha, also to discuss his administration of Gog's fortune in Maire's interests. But she knew better. He could not keep away.

'I never knew I had any hold over you,' she said to Magog. 'I always thought you were a cold fish. But you too, you too . . .'

'I just came over on our business and for old time's sake,' Magog said.

'Then you don't mind if I'm out all night?'

'Do as you wish,' Magog said coolly, a hook in his gut. He would have liked to shut up, but he had to add, 'Of course, I did fly over just to see you.'

'Yes, you did.' Maire stood by the window, looking out on the cascades of the plane-trees, their grey-water leaves falling down to where the fishermen stood on the quai, trying to catch the small gudgeon that swam canny and deep under the barges. 'You do come for old time's sake. That I do believe, because that's why I see you. All those years together. We couldn't forget that, could we?' She turned back towards Magog, the sleeves of her black dress with the high shoulders and low V-neck down between her breasts making her seem crow-bodied under her smooth full face. 'I know I'm a liar on principle. How else can a woman protect herself in a man's world? But I have to have at least one witness for what I've done, in case I forget or believe my own lies about the past. And you, Magog, are my only witness.'

'Glad to be of some use,' Magog said.

He had always told Maire that she was free to leave him whenever she pleased, but now she had left, he found that he was not free to leave her. He might feel dispensable from his property company, but he had been gulled into feeling indispensable to Maire and her daughters. So Magog persuaded himself that duty put him on the aeroplane to Paris every other week-end, until he arrived one Saturday afternoon to find Maire at the concierge's lodge of the Quai Bourbon with another woman, tall and gaunt and dressed in a Russian blouse, panta-loons, cloak and boots, with Maire oddly girlish in a white fur-trimmed coat and a plain black headband that bore a single pearl.

'You remember Anne-Marie, don't you?' Maire said. 'My doctor. She's just come across for the day to examine me.' She smiled at Anne-Marie so confidentially that she seemed to be in a conspiracy with her against all comers.

As Magog took the hand of Maire's doctor, he wanted to crush the cold fingers with the professional cropped nails. They had been touching Maire, feeling within her, palpitating her flesh, finding the liberty doctors take in the name of gynaecology.

'I hope there's nothing the matter,' Magog said stiffly.

'Nothing,' Maire said. 'Just a routine check-up.' She smiled again at Anne-Marie. 'I'm wicked, but I have to pretend I'm ill to persuade Anne-Marie to come over and see me.'

'It's my pleasure too,' Anne-Marie said, her voice too shrill for a woman of her size.

'I've never touched any other doctor since Anne-Marie helped me have my babies,' Maire said. 'In a way, I feel they are *hers* too.'

Magog's bowels clenched like a fist. His tongue clotted in his mouth.

'You're going . . . out,' he managed to say, swallowing. 'Perhaps . . . May I come too?'

'Women only tonight,' Maire said. 'I am sorry, Magog. Women only tonight.' And she left, hanging on to Anne-Marie's arm and chattering up towards the doctor's cheek, as they walked away under the waterfalls of the plane leaves.

So Magog went through Paris that evening, looking for a way to exaggerate his own pain into self-destruction since he could not destroy Maire. Masochists for money tormented him on the boulevards as he passed. In Pigalle, a bare-backed man, his skin scarred and pocked as an old tin kettle's, stuck hatpins through his nipples, whirled walking-sticks edged with razor-blades round his ears, ate broken glass and breathed out gouts of fire. 'Pay well,' his barker said. 'He needs a lot of money, messieurs, for his hospital bills every time he makes an error.' In Raspail, there was a frog-swallower, gulping down the little groping legs and bulbous bodies with a great indrawn belch, then with a hawk and a cough and a spit, the live frog was vomited up again to be put back into a bowl with six others. It was a very economical act. The frog-swallower did not digest his working capital.

Drinking through the Coupole and the Select and the Dôme, Magog planned what would hurt Maire the most. He would go to the Lorgnette, the local lesbian nightclub, and buy one of the girls away from the butches. He had never done that sort of thing before. It wasn't his style. But then he had never been so bitched before. And there was no need of style if one had enough money in Paris. Every man deserved his one night of Henry Miller.

The Lorgnette was much what it was meant to be, a bar down one side of the long room, tables down the other, a dance-floor in the middle, and halfway along the wall where Manet's naked

Olympia was painted wearing a lorgnette, a bandstand for the three old girls of fifty, wearing evening trousers and white bum-freezers with sequined lapels, as they thumped away on drum and piano and squeeze-box. At the tables, the coupled girls, the Bill billing and the Cul cooing, the dike wearing a navy-blue blazer with English regimental buttons and the doll in demure and dimity dress. Occasionally, a duet of girls in frocks, lookalike and narcissi, wondering under their fringes that their love could be such an image of themselves, glad to hug each other because it was more fun than hugging oneself, detached Siamese twins but Rosa–Josepha under the skin, joined at the loin as in Maire's poster because Sapphos know each other carnally and are inseparable in their secret knowledge of a sex unshared by any man outside.

Magog sat on the bar-stool and ordered a cognac, turning away from the breasts of the fat stripper as a Negress left her butch at a table and came to sit beside him.

Yes, a drink, monsieur is so kind to offer.

Champagne, of course champagne.

I want to be a singer, my name is Suzy from Martinique. Suzy like Suzy Parker, I could be a model too. My parents are very rich. I am here to study at the Conservatoire.

Lucky mulatress Suzy a white man gave you a straight nose somewhere in the Caribees, and your mummy left you her thick red lips, and you don't have rich parents as you say, but the richer sun of the West Indies bunged up your eyes to stop them being as large as brown pennies, and you put gold in your teeth for your old age, and you are tall and strong with muscles under the skin of your bare arms and shoulders, muscles as snap and whipper as the Sargasso eels that swim yearly across the Atlantic to breed off your island where they slither up the shores and into your bodies, eel-taut under bright-dark skin . . .

Monsieur, I'm strong, no sleep for two nights. I live for my singing.

I am having two dresses made, one hundred and fifty thousand francs each, all gold sequins, for when I start to sing.

Yes, another champagne, you are so kind, you help me pay for my dresses. You must want that I shall be a singer.

Now there is a broad-hipped crooner in a striped suit with a duck's arse of blonde hair, a female *voyou*, her hands feeling up and down the mike, caressing the cock she hasn't got . . .

Si tu veux un vrai copain . . .

Ogling the girls and the girl-men, slow roll of hip and leer of lip, take me, take me *copain*, take me for the man I'm not, voice harsh, fingers chopping the air, then slicing invisible women from the void . . .

C'est le plus beau cul . . . *cul* . . . *cul du monde* . . .

The girls are laughing and a merry butch with a roving eye winks at Suzy, who giggles and pinches my arm.

She is funny. A woman, like a man, you know.

Oh, too literal Suzy, as though Magog hadn't noticed, Magog with his power to see everything at the twinkling of an eye, why, he can see into the foul stew, the bad cess of a female bitch before she opens her mouth to tell him a lie.

'I'm a man dressed like a man, Suzy. You should throw me out.'

Suzy laughs and pinches my arm and an old woman selling violets comes over. Yes, I'll take your violets, violets for forget me never . . .

You are very kind, *chéri*. I saw your long face, sad yes, but a face that's what I said. *Donnes-moi un bise* . . . *Baiser* . . .

Oh, kiss, yes, then a dance, a tango anglais, but Magog doesn't dance, the champagne does, bubble, bubble, float, no trouble . . .

Merde, you don't have to *enjoy* it. He's not paying for that.

The merry butch bitches to Suzy, who defends her Magog, kind black girl, kind darkie, kind Africa when white treats you right . . .

He's kind. I do what I like. Over here, *chéri*. Champagne for the band. And the coatwoman. She is chic with me. The others are not chic. Because I am Suzy. I don't do it with everyone. No, I choose who I go with. I choose.

What did that planter say, the Jamaica Rum Fellow, no man's a man till he's split back oak and had a dose, had a dose, had a douse, more champagne, bitter bubbles, can't get them down . . .

Another bottle, *chéri*. You are sad. My friends will drink to you. Another bottle.

'I'd rather pay you, Suzy. Not the Lorgnette. Come back with me. I'll pay you well. Come back, little Sheba.'

I'm not for nothing, you know. Twenty thousand francs. Not for nothing.

That's for nothing. Africa's for nothing. It's a bargain. Don't bargain for a bargain.

'All right. But we go now.'

I'll tell the propriétaire. She has to know the price.

Oh yes, the propriétaire, white fat old lady, get your cut on everything, a cut on the drink, a cut on the cul, a cut on the customer, a cut on Africa, a cut on the unkindest cut of all. Suzy's off with a man, a man, a man, and the butches hiss me as I go out . . . Suzy won't come, she's just saying she'll get her coat, she and Maire and Anne-Marie wouldn't go to bed dead with a man, they take you to the limit, and all you get is a bise and a squeeze that's what . . . Then the click of heels and Suzy's there in her fake leopard-skin coat and the taxi's waiting . . .

'Quai Bourbon. Ile St-Louis.'

It's chic, your quarter.

My quarter? Maire's quarter. No quarter. Suzy's by the bed, Maire's bed, stripping down to her canary underwear, choc skin murkier . . .

Oh, chéri, let's do the money now, before . . . It's not chic to do it after. Not twenty, chéri, it's rich here. Make it thirty, chéri. Look at me . . . Look . . .

Then she takes off her yellow pants, it's as it should be, black coils of hair on rough brown skin. She gets the thirty thousand francs.

Now you chéri. Come.

Well, that's easier said than done with all that champagne. Why does she keep her bra on. Why?

You won't make me a baby? You're chic. You won't.

Of course, she was with women usually, she wouldn't be prepared.

'I'm chic. I'll make you nothing. Not even twins.'

Oh Rosa, oh Josepha, don't see me now, in the dark with a

black girl, pulling at those eels under her rough skin, her hair like a wire brush on my soft cock, it won't go up, no go down there, it's no good moaning in that silly way, Suzy, nobody's enjoying it, there's nothing to enjoy. The first time I've bought it, the first time I need revenge, and I'm flat as a flounder, limp as a cod. Blame her quick.

'Take your bra off, Suzy. I can't unless you do.'

Suzy doesn't want to, but I insist, so she does, saying . . .

Don't mind the operation. I haven't got a disease.

And she's right, her left breast isn't one, just like an Amazon, no breast to foul up the bowstring. She's a man over her heart, a girl-man from the Lorgnette. What can I do about that, when I'm breast-mad for Maire?

Don't worry, *chéri*. It's nothing. I just have to have another three hundred thousand for the left tit. It's for the singing. Then they can put plastic in the left tit too. I only had enough for the right one. They want it all cash in advance. They won't let you pay week by week. And if you're a singer, you have to have some breasts. White girls have breasts. We're born strong and pretty. But no breasts you see. Be chic, *chéri*. Give me some more *fric*. Then I can save up for my left breast. Give me some more. Then I can sing, *chéri*. I can sing in my dress of gold sequins, cut so low. Listen, *chéri*, I can sing, like an American.

> *Put another nickel in*
> *In the nickels odeon*
> *All I want is lovings you*
> *And musique, musique, musique . . .*

I sing good, very good. But how can I sing with only one breast? The white girls have breasts, black girls no, not from Martinique. Give me the *fric*, and I'll be good to you.

Suzy, I'll give you the money but you can't sing very well, and by the time you have your gowns of sequins and your plastic breasts, you had better put off the day of learning to sing, because you're not good at it. But if that is your dream, you must pursue it. We all have the right to foul up our dreams. And you can't go about with one breast flat and one plastic.

Oh Africa, what has happened to you, Africa, was it the trip across the Atlantic in those long shackles that made you slaves to the shiny vending-machines of the USA? But it's just as bad in Paris now, where the blacks come to forget racism, because the French only hate Algerians. What of that architect from Dahomey learning to build plastic huts for his people, so much more practical than mud and grass, very mobile, perfect for jungle, never rot. What is more dangerous, a colonist, or the car he leaves behind him? What costs more, a Portuguese bombing raid or a national airline? If you want what we want, you shall get less than we have, and that is not much . . .

When Magog told Maire what he had done, she laughed. She found it ridiculous, she said. At least, it was not invented, as usual.

'The worst thing about you, Magog,' she said, 'is that you're turning in on yourself more every year. You're beginning to love only what you think is your own, when it's not. Sometimes I think you're only fascinated by me because I'm your brother's wife. You have to add incest to injury.'

Although she denied that she was hurt in any way by Magog spending the night in her bed with a black girl from the Lorgnette, Maire would not let Magog come to Paris to see her again. The break was final, she said. His revenge had hurt her, although she could not say so. It had been a dirty trick.

1958

Magog's sexual obsession with Maire passed away. It was no good lusting over the lost. He had to work her out of his system, and he did that soon by overwork. Later, he found that the final bad trip to Paris was the only thing in the whole year that he remembered. Suzy would appear in his mind as he flew high in that curious limbo of jet-travel which made him exchange confessions with a stranger in the next seat, because there was little chance of ever seeing one another again. Magog talked too much only in these situations of forced intimacy on the interminable journeys and brandies of the flights over Asia to Australia or over the Arctic to Vancouver or to any city where Stratosphere Securities had an interest, a client, a banker, a plot of empire. On these odysseys of business, Magog would tell the story of the black girl and speculate ignorantly on the future of Africa. He often felt as blabbing and unnecessary as any other traveller. For the extent of the activity of men everywhere made Magog's own efforts seem local and puny to him, and the little was hardly worth the time.

One project, however, began to occupy his interest, for it was as radical in its way as the Victorian sack of London by hurling railways into the centre of the city. The need was to bring in a motorway from the West, so that the oil-lorries and week-end cottagers could get to their refineries and Celtic twilight and Camelot one hour quicker. The method was to carry the motorway into London on great concrete toadstools larger than the cromlechs of Stonehenge – four storeys high, the cars would sweep above the bewildered householders at the level of any gable or bedroom. Stratosphere Securities had won part of the tender for setting up the giant toadstools. The public authorities understood that Magog would be helpful in clearing the route, if necessary.

Owing to the ease of enforcing compulsory purchase orders by the councils, there was not much trouble from the citizens. Everything had been done to make it difficult to protest. Nothing was said about where the motorway was to go until the last moment; anxious householders were shifted from department to department until they were so lost in the labyrinths of town halls that they nearly starved to death; public inquiries were held in out-of-the-way places at outlandish hours, so that only the rich and unemployed could attend them; town planners consigned buildings of architectural merit to dust and oblivion without even bothering to visit them, in case they felt some pity; conservation societies wrote their letter to *The Times* and then sank back with nothing achieved except printing their warnings to prove their good sense. In fact, all that democracy could do to deny its own premises was done. The good of the whole was said to override the good of the part. Officials said so, who were not elected and who considered any consultation with people a waste of their time spent serving the public.

One old man called Evans objected. He lived in a Tudor manor, somehow preserved among the suburbs like a mole on a powdered cheek, a blemish that was called a beauty spot. The motorway rose on its toadstools through his Elizabethan garden. With pride, the minions from the departments told him that millions would now be able to see his ancient home as they drove by; but he was not mollified. He sat with a shotgun at his leaded windows and fired from time to time at workmen trying to dig up his gravel and low hedges. The police intervened and took away his gun; but the newspapers also intervened and gave him a more dangerous weapon, the publicity of the brave old codger fighting the state. He was tagged as the Motorway Methuselah. Magog went down to deal with the problem before it became a scandal.

Already the concrete Ts rose roof-high over the peaked tiles of the manor-house, as Magog walked from his Rolls to the dark front door, studded with nails. He banged on the wood a few times, then tried the iron latch. Bolted, of course. He walked around the house towards the gashed garden, muddied and pot-holed and growing only precast fungi higher than Jack's Bean-stalk for a more troublesome burden. The kitchen door was open. Magog walked inside past black timber, whitewashed brick, old frying-pans greasy on a coke range. As he stooped to enter through a low doorway into the drawing-room, he half-turned at a noise and a blow cracked him on the collar-bone. He staggered sideways to see an old man with wild yellow-white hair coming at him with a knobbed ash club. Magog easily caught the weapon and used it to force the old man into a dark oak chair.

'I'm not here to hurt you,' Magog said. 'Just to explain.'

'You creep in, don't you,' the old man said, ranting to himself in a whisper. 'They never tell you they're coming. Fight them here and, look you, they're round your back there. First it's one house in a field, then two, then a street, then a *development*. Then you're surrounded, bach, like Owen Glendower. Only what's odd is, you're still just as you were. Battles, they're easy. Once the enemy's all round you, they close in and finish you off. London's not like that, not at all. It closes all round you and *preserves* you, like a stone in plum jam. You can preserve a plum stone in green slime, and that doesn't make it a jar of jam. You've got to save the fields too, not one old bit just to say, it was like that here, and now it isn't . . .'

The old man was talking to himself. He was not struggling. He seemed almost glad to have another's ear to hear him out.

'Better something than nothing,' Magog said. 'I'll let you into a little secret.' A quick lie to show his concern. 'I have been here before many a time, looking in from the outside. You don't know it, but I've *fought* for this house. There was a question of a compulsory purchase order, but I put my foot down there.'

The old man began to speak again. He did not seem to be listening.

'That's what the Romans did, bach. Bloody great roads to split the tribes apart. Cut the people from the people to subjugate them. That's what bloody King Edward did in Wales. Roads and castles, castles and roads. It's just the same now as ever. Motorways and reservoirs to get our holy water to your foul Birmingham and Manchester. We'll blow them up, I tell you. Blow them up. Free Wales. There'll be an army.'

'Don't take it so personally,' Magog said. 'It happens to many people and they don't take it as personally as you.'

'There's an English Duke stopping you out in the Cotswolds, I hear. He says the motorway will divide his Hunt. If the fox runs across the road, the hounds and the horses will follow, look you. Then they'll be hunted, won't they? By the Minxes and the Jaguars. Or perhaps the Hunt will pull the cars down. That would be better.'

Really, the old Evans was very obtuse. One might have thought he was deaf. He did not appear to be listening to all that Magog said he was doing to save the house.

'Look, I am trying to help, you know. You can't obliterate the past, I said to the planners, just like that. So I had my engineers move the whole motorway, just to save your manor.'

'They say I won't hear anything when it's built. I'll get used to the noise, the peering into my windows. They say, we're wonderfully adaptable. We can get used to everything. But I ask you, is it worth getting used to everything? Being bloody slaves of the English. I'll blow it up, you know. I have friends in Free Wales. This is a military road to Cardiff. We know what it's for. It's to roll the tanks along next time we rise.'

Magog found himself getting angry at this wilful unreason.

'I might as well have been talking to myself,' he said.

'They said they'd give me compensation,' the old man said. 'And look you, I thought I might have it. Will you pay me in sticks of dynamite, I said? They weren't having that, oh no. They weren't having that.'

Magog fell back on his most effective weapon, cold irony. That usually brought the tribesmen to heel.

'Have you ever felt you were with somebody, and yet you were talking to yourself?' he asked. 'Two people in a room talking to themselves together? Some people call it conversation. I call it verbal masturbation.'

'It's a sin, you know.' The old man's voice was so full of denunciation that Magog felt like a small boy caught playing with himself. 'The clearing of the Celts off the land. The killing of old ways. It's a sin. I shall write to God about it. Dear God, I wish to complain, I do, I, Evans the Latin, the Chief of the Druids . . .'

At last, Magog knew who the old man was. Gog had once spoken of him, his old Welsh teacher in Holy Island off Anglesey, long since emigrated to London to stir up trouble there. Silly old fool, thinking himself a spy for the Celtic Revival in the city of the enemy. He was damn lucky that he was being left with a roof over his head to keep his delusions out of the rain.

'You don't have to stay here, you know,' Magog said. 'We could make it worth your while to move out. We could have this converted into a tea-shop, or something. There's quite a demand by the public for a genuine atmosphere to eat their buns in.'

'There's stuff, they tell me, just like plasticine. Explosive dough. You'll not buy this old house off me. It'll be sitting under your motorway like a time-bomb. Yes. As you drive by, packed in your tight little tin boxes, just you look down and think, That's a pretty old house, isn't that pretty . . . And it'll be full of bombs to blow you all up. You wait. You finish that thing up there, that bloody Roman road to take the guns and lorries to Wales, and I'll finish it for you. That I swear, by Glendower himself. Now get out. Get out.'

The old man rose, his stick in his hand, wavering, threatening. Magog also rose and moved towards the door.

'Don't wave that club about,' he said. 'You'll slip a disc.'

A sudden gleam of illumination sparked in the old man's fogged eyes as he looked up at his visitor's bony height.

'You're Magog,' he said. 'I know you.'

'You must be mistaken,' Magog said, and left.

The strange thing was that the old Evans did fulfil his threat. Seven days after the motorway opened, and the cars began to flick past in their tens of thousands, hundreds of thousands, strange eyes peeking into the leaded windows, voyeur after voyeur after voyeur, willy-nilly at seventy miles an hour past the historic flash-by, there was an explosion in the manor house. In a great huff of black smoke, tiles soared into the air like clay pigeons, while brick dust and splinters and dead woodworms peppered the underside of the track of the road. The manor was totally destroyed, but no damage was done to the motorway whatsoever. One car had a broken windscreen, but the insurance paid for that. A report from a motorist that an old man with yellow-white hair pushing a pram had been seen somewhere near Glastonbury Tor was discounted by the police. They did not think Evans worth pursuing. If any man was silly enough to blow up his own house he was better left on the road. God only knew what he would do in a police station.

The schoolgirls were drawn up in their ranks on the playing-fields of November. Their parents stood among them, rarely taller except for the few as large as Magog. It was a cold blowing day that fluttered the cloth poppies in the lapels of the brown coats of the girls and the dark coats of the men and women. In front of a solitary wooden cross stuck on the touchline of the hockey field and loaded with a wreath of more red poppies, Josepha stood. On a signal from the headmistress, she began her recitation into the wind.

> *'They shall grow not old, as we that are left grow old;*
> *Age shall not weary them, nor the years condemn.*
> *At the going down of the sun and in the morning*
> *We will remember them.'*

The words were hardly audible, although Josepha piped them out from her red round face. The sound tailed away into the Two Minutes' Silence of the memorial service for the dead of the Two World Wars. Magog glanced down at Rosa on his right hand, as she buried the tip of her cold nose inside her scarf and looked down at the muddy grass. She did not seem to be praying nor thinking of the millions of the dead who had fought for something or another that was quite irrelevant by now; she just seemed to be trying to survive as warmly as possible until she could get away.

Fifty yards to Magog's right, a Highland trumpeter in tartan and sporran and bearskin and bare knees sounded the Last Post. Each slow-drawn note was more clear and more cold than the wind. Magog felt that tears were appropriate and the wind helped, driving a drop or two out of his eyes to freeze on his cheek. But he did not remember the seas of mud in Flanders where men had drowned in liquid earth, nor the Japanese labour camps where the prisoners had crawled to death in shame and squitters, but only the moment of sad absurdity on a Veterans' Parade that he had seen in Birdcage Walk, when the strutting young soldiers were followed by old cripples driving their motorized chairs, and at the Eyes Right, one of the old men had turned his neck so stiffly into the salute that he had run into the kerb.

Still, it was cold all right, and that stopped the sneering short. However much a memorial service made the congregation suffer, the sacrifice of the dead would never matter enough to the living, who had won all by just breathing. Once Magog had visited a cemetery worthy of the Assyrians, the American Air Force graveyard outside Cambridge. He had been driving past on the Mildenhall Road, when he had seen squads of American soldiers and airmen wandering about under the shadow of an old windmill. Something about the glossy baldness of their helmets, the bright scarves about their necks, and their white spats had made him stop his car and get out to join in the celebration of the dead. He had thought it would be exceptional and it had been so, with the men drawn up facing a Colonel Chaplain among the thousands of equal marble crosses, every so often broken by a stony Star of David, all planted in a semi-circle facing the

American flag, which flew on a white pole below a golden
coconut. The dead had been buried standing to show respect.
It was a second burial for them since they had been scooped up
in plastic bags after the war from their shallow graves where
they had been shot down in Germany or France. Now they had
come back to the fields of England for the climax of the memorial
ceremony – a fly-past by an old RAF Anson, which dropped four
thousand sweet peas, one flower bomb each for those grounded
for ever in Cambridgeshire . . .

Afterwards, Magog had visited the cemetery chapel. On its
doors, copper reliefs of various types of tanks and guns. Inside,
the main wall bore an immense strategical air-map in many-
coloured marble to illustrate the British and American bombing
raids – lines of bright wire, straddled by model aeroplanes,
radiated from Cambridge, home of learning, to all the cities of
Europe. The map explained everything – Types of Target,
Military, Industrial, Transportation, nothing was omitted.
Even the German Air Force, when mentioned, had a special
Gothic type of its own. Above on the ceiling, God and his
angels in five-pointed Technicolor robes flew with the golden
mosaic bombers . . . Oh, a flight from Britain had meant
something then, those aerial legions on the thousand-bomber
raids, death from heaven more fiery than brimstone, destruction to Berlin, holocaust to Dresden, no kraut took our planes
lightly then, all raids led to Britain, and didn't the world know
it . . .

'We can go now, Mag,' Rosa said, pulling at Magog's arm.
'Have you froze or something? Can you get us to the tuck-shop
before they run out of fudge? It's super, the fudge.'

Josepha walked over to them. There seemed to be tears in
her eyes, more than were necessary from the cold.

'You were very good, my darling,' Magog said. 'You read very
well.'

'She's blubbing,' Rosa said. 'That's stupid. Nobody'd be seen
dead out here if it wasn't a school hol.'

1959

Magog was forty years old. He did not sleep well that night and he walked in the dawn. A red sun had risen in a slow bounce over the trees, calling Magog into the park. There the ducks and herons showed in the mirror of vapours that was the boating lake. As Magog walked towards the far whooping of the Zoo, he was enclosed in a bright ring of mist. Wherever he looked across the dewy grass, a white circle swathed him in an arena of haze. Yet overhead the sky was clear and a distant aeroplane made a shiny snail's trail across heaven. Then the sun upped and the mists were gone and it was everyday in the park, with the dogs walking their owners and tracksuits sweating out the early runners and the geese honking the bread from the hands of those who loved to feed living things and had no families.

Yet the day was no normal day for Magog. He telephoned his office and told them that he was not coming in. All appointments were to be cancelled. Magog was forty years old. He had heard that men had a menopause too, earlier than women, a time when they felt their lives were wasted and they needed a change. After twenty years spent in the pursuit of power and money, Magog had both. But what else? Money was worthless unless it bought things which gave pleasure, and Magog had more than enough money to buy his pleasures. And Magog's push for power seemed to have ended in a curious kind of powerlessness, a discovery that dominion was a form of inertia from a height.

Magog pondered over his coffee and scrambled eggs. If there was a conspiracy of power, it was a conspiracy of inefficiency. Responsibility lay in ruins like Camelot. If you had a friend in power who tried to help you, the subordinate he detailed to aid you would get the message wrong or turn against you, and then your masterful friend would have to back his subordinate to prove that he did not favour his friends.

It was a great mistake to try to fix anything in England. All the rulers hated pressures. They cringed from hard sell like a lancet, from soft sell like a hernia. The best policy was to praise your enemy to your friends. You would then be thought humble and a good chap and you would end by advancing yourself. Nobody since the war had understood the terms of power in England except Harold Macmillan, who never presented his virtues except in a tired and detached way. The use of power in London depended on understanding the fatigue of the powerful. They wanted to be amused, wined, dined, and never to speak of anything urgent. A casual remark or two over coffee could settle the matter, if the meal had shown you casual about the matter. The only error was to appear to care.

Magog had understood all these conventions in his rise, but now that he had risen, he found himself the victim of his own manners. If the end of all those intrigues and exquisite jokes and interminable dinners was merely to become as bored and flaccid as everybody else, surely a life spent chasing girls or binding the wounds of lepers with Albert Schweitzer might have been better spent. If power was only a cosy dream of action, an illusion of control, why had he bothered? There had been a time when he had wanted to do and do and do things while he was young. Or was all doing just another way of raising dust and ashes?

Magog the Great, Magog hero, Magog at Eton, Magog *in excelsis ego*. Magog eighteen.

Brutus Magog lay on the coir-matting, a tickle of dust in his nostrils, deep-breathing from his fall dead. Above him is Rupert's voice stressing, *'This was a man.'* He must have said it wrong. It should be, *THIS is MAN*. I MAGOG *am* A MAN. No longer Boy Magog. Magog the Youth in agony of pimples, but Magog the Man, *homo emergens*, slowly rising from his belly at the rumble of the smacking hands from the dark beyond the foot-lights. Man Magog, bowing to the homage, keeping a sad face to show feeling for the words he had not felt. Magog tragic, lion-heart while the fools clapped. Brutus Magog.

Then Friend Magog, walking with Rupert round Luxmore's Garden, in the utter delight of conscious mutual admiration.

Nostalgia put on for last summer and leaving; watching water-
snakes, playing Pooh-sticks down the stream as the war clouds
gathered over Europe; striking poses for the benefit of those
who passed them by and envied them in their seeming neglect.
For Magog is in sponge-bag trousers, purple his waistcoat with
silver buttons; he is white-tied and lounging, holes in his shoes.
Rupert the Beautiful, eighteenth-century flowered brocade between the edgings of his morning coat, listens. Magog, already
master of the ways of the world in his arrogant ignorance, lies.

Midnight, the folding bed down from the wall, Rupert's gold
curls a ram's head in the dark, the feel of his lizard hands
snatching at the release of their love, the muscles sliding away,
shuddering under Rupert's touch, then the running water and
basin gargling in the peace of it all, then Rupert lying beside
him, the warm crush of the thin bodies, yes, we will always see
each other *sub specie aeternitatis*, this is the good time, there
will be nothing better than to love oneself in another when first
a man.

Then there was scholar Magog, witty, erudite, effortlessly
successful. Scholar of Eton, Rosebery Scholar, Scholar of Trinity, Cambridge. Not to mention Magog the Athlete, strong,
scornful, Keeper of the Wall, Golf, Rugby and Strawberry Mess.
But were these titles anything to him? Hardly . . . For Magog
scorned success – he only identified himself with it. Unasked,
glory came to Magog. He took it upon his shoulders and framed
it in lists and photographs on the walls of his room. He displayed
his triumph so he could give an excuse for his public ridicule of
it. For Magog was a man apart from boys, Editor of the *Eton
College Chronicle*, winner of the Verse Prize, congratulated by
the Queen Herself for the ironic sincerity of his declamation.
Magog had achieved all his little world had to offer, so he could
afford isolation from all except Rupert. In the eyes of his school,
in the eyes of his society, Magog was total success.

Magog and Rupert in the graveyard by the old chapel. The
time is one in the morning. Moon splashes on the flat tombs
blacken the moss that lies across the stones. A yew tree,
traditional for weeping and long-bows since Agincourt, stands
sentry, crooked and warped with long duty. Magog's last night
before going, going, his kingdom gone, never to be found again,

the ease of ruling his little world of eleven hundred elegant youths, now over because of the silly passing of the days, cry halt time, enough of the hours, the outer world won't give a damn for his piddle of glory, *eheu fugaces Posthume anni*, what did the millions of London care for Horace or the starving billions of the Depression know of Homer? Tomorrow, Magog must leave his eleven hundred minions, never to come back, going home far from Rupert, with the Nazis already gibbering their menaces in Stukas over Spain, Magog never to be god again, never, never, never, never . . .

'Never,' Magog says, Lear in his voice.

'Never what?' Rupert says.

'Nevermore,' Magog says. 'Quoth the raven, nevermore.'

'We'll be seeing each other,' Rupert says. 'Evermore.'

'But what will we be when we do meet again? Nevermore like now. Do you think we'll always have open minds? I mean, look at them, our parents. All their *idées fixes*, conventions. Enemies of Promise. By god, Rupert, you'll be a shootin' man, or papa will know the reason why.'

'Bang, bang,' Rupert says, putting a forefinger to his temple and lying on a gravestone. 'I'll be dead at twenty-two. RIP. Here lies a City Man. Or a soldier, *Duce volente.*'

'Promise me you'll never die, you'll always have a mind that's open,' Magog bends and kisses Rupert, cold-skinned on the stone. 'Honestly, if I ever feel my mind's dead and I can't dream any more and I can't write or read Homer, I'll take a boat and sail out into the *poluphloisboio thalasses*, and I'll take a lead weight and tie it round my ankles and, hey presto, Magnus is sunk without a bubble.'

'Sure even unto death,' Rupert says languidly. 'How can anyone be as sure as you are?'

'Well, you and I, Rupert, we've won everything Eton has to offer. Why? Because we don't care. Because we're sure we're the best. They can't get somebody who's sure. Not me or you. As long as we're still *sure.*'

'*Hubris,*' Rupert says, 'but listening to you makes me believe. Nothing will stop you, Mag, nothing. I'll just follow on and admire. Any room for a Boswell, Johnson?'

So it is that last night, top of the world to you, Magog, on the ultimate Everest after your adopted family broke you in – we'll make a Ponsonby of you and did so – till prep school puffed you up again and Eton knocked you down at tiny thirteen, only to throw you up to the Chapel pinnacles five years forward, to look down at the first sick plunge of the train home with the years ahead a roller-coaster of diminishing heights and falls from the peak, lesser mountings and pitchings until the last slow bumps of near inertia at forty years and on, the slow rolling along of later days to the knowledge of a life not well spent, but spent in never, never, never getting again to the glory of eighteen, god at the brink, all possible, nothing tried, and Magog the pearl in the world his oyster that was to shut like a trap when Rupert would play the double agent for the Kremlin and be burned alive, and Magog watched him dying in the hospital for terminal cases in Oxford, just a log for bandages to wrap round, a plug for tubes of plasma, a hole for a mouth and a number to know him by. No hero's death now, not even a Hector's, body dragged round the walls of Troy at the chariot's wheels, at least seen by the wailing women in its blood and dust. But Rupert's just a bundle, a mute thing, stinking, shocking Magog *in piam memoriam* from the university into Ministry and Maire's arms, leaving risk and love in its mummy case round what was called Rupert. Nevermore, however hard the trying and high the vaulting, nevermore the ram's head easing in the dark, with every chance ripe to the finger-tip, and the absolute surety that all would yield to a touch and a classical tag.

> *Ask for past glory, it shall not come again.*
> *Ask for present forgetting, there is no oblivion.*
> *Ask for future hope, and the streets will cry old age.*
> *Quoth the raven, Nevermore . . .*

That afternoon, Magog decided that he had played the property game long enough, and for the rest of the year he prepared his going. He arranged for Radzen to buy him out for a million and a half pounds in share capital; in order to keep the prices of the shares high, Magog agreed never to cash in more than £200,000 worth in one year. The Three Racketeers were delighted at the prospect of Magog's departure. They could see themselves as troika under Radzen, ready to become a ruling trinity once Radzen himself bowed out. When Magog asked Sandy and James whether they felt they had *missed* anything by staying in property dealing, they roared with laughter and replied that they had only missed making more money by not going in earlier. Yet Morrell did say that he thought flying saucers were more interesting than building heliports; he was considering leaving the Inner City for Outer Space. Only Magog found his words more than whimsical – he also was bored and idle in the cage of every day.

'That's why your country's through,' Radzen said at one of their farewell lunches on expenses. 'You quit too soon. There was a time when you were called the bulldog breed. You'd hang on tight until the bitter end, and even when the bull was dead, they still couldn't part your teeth. Now you English give up the moment you're ahead, you relax, you take it easy. Go, then stop. Stop, then go. That's not an economy, it's an idiocy. Like a goat pissing, in jerks.'

'There are other things to do,' Magog said, scooping the brain out of his snipe. 'Look at your one-eyed General Dayan. He goes back to archaeology between wars. He likes digging up old ruins as well as making modern ones. I rather fancy going back into education myself. I could always build a university or two. There are projects for new ones, I hear.'

'That I respect,' Radzen said. 'Though you'd do better building shopping plazas and using the money to fund a university.'

'Your lot give too much to charity,' Magog said, 'to excuse the fact that you're too good at making money. We tend to do too many good works ourselves, because we've got too much time left over from earning a living. I really owe something to my mind. With the war, I went straight into the Ministry. No graduate studies, I miss them. Did I ever tell you about Rupert?'

'Your friend who died in the war?'

'Yes. I'd like to do something for the young men.'

'If you must,' Radzen said. 'And if they will let you do something for them. The young these days, on their Vespas and Lambrettas, buzzing over Europe like flies, non-committal and detached, guzzling all they can get for fear there will be another war again, there may be rationing, they'll lose it all just as they did when they were children and didn't have toys . . .' Radzen paused and smiled. 'I'm sorry,' he said. 'Old men run on, we lose our meaning. But at least we talk to each other. But will the young talk back to us? What have you got to offer them? Latin, Greek, culture?' Radzen laughed. 'I hope you can communicate, my friend.'

'I hope so,' Magog said and thought of Rupert, the gold curls bright above the white shirt and flannels, the grace of the bare arm moving in the fives courts, the easy laughter that met anything Magog said with a sneer or a turn of phrase. 'Youth's much the same as always, I suspect.'

'I hope so,' Radzen said. 'But even the Russians are complaining about their Nibos who don't believe in Marx and Lenin any more. I think we may be out of touch.'

Magog put his hand on Radzen's arm. 'My old friend,' he said, 'we'll have another brandy.'

Before Magog finally made up his mind to return to the pastures of the mind, he put his ear to the ground to find out what the plans of the government were in respect of the new colleges and universities. There were to be several new ones, all with opportunities, appointments, interests far outside scholarship. Did not the Pugwash group of scientists already cross international suspicions and barriers set up by the Cold War? The concrete towers of the new universities were to be no ivory ones; they would be lighthouses, even radar stations to detect the coming of a whole linked world.

Magog also took a trip to the West Country to clear his mind. It was sunny and coarse on the Downs with air so fresh that Magog sometimes felt himself laughing at the sheer joy of breathing. He knew that it was time to take a break from London life – if only his last walk had not brought him back to a new temptation of power and a fresh subject of study.

He had seen the monoliths and grassy banks from a low hill on the downs. When he reached the top of the tallest earthwork, he found himself looking at the standing stones, pitted and scarred and separate, that had been set up in broken arcs, shattered circles around the hamlet built on the crossroads across the grasslands. Sheep leaned against the stones, cows searched for tufts in their shadows. A pub with a thatched roof inveigled visitors into the great holy circle of time lost, ditched in by its dry moat and outer bank. Avebury.

Four thousand years ago, Magog might have known the meaning of Avebury. He would have still ruled, ordering the slaves captured in the Welsh wars and harnessed in their hundreds to each monolith, as they dragged the rock masses into place in still circumference, a minor heaven on earth from which to graph the eclipses of the sun and moon and stars. Magog would even then have been a priest marking down the set wanderings of the little lights in the sky, setting limits to the seasons and presuming that his special wisdom gave him the right to command the labour and the tribute and the deaths of tens of thousands of his fellow men. He would have known the meaning of the Gods, while staying within his own small skull that could calculate from the roundings of the stones the far circumference of the skies. From a pebble dropped into the pool of one mind, the ripples may spread out to the shores of the universe.

Yet the meaning of Avebury was now lost. The Druids were dead. The great stones were fallen. Many had been broken up to build farmhouses and walls to hold sheep. Silly meandering roads ran through the magic circles of old. A red oil lorry, articulated behind the driver's cabin like a lobster's claw, roared the horror of its passing into Magog's thoughts and belched its black fumes into the clear air. Something should be done about Avebury.

Magog began to dream a speculator's dream. If he had the Force, the power over England, he would clear the hamlet away, placing it a mile to the south, making the move worth while to the natives. He would re-route the roads so that their tarmac spoiled other meadows. He would grass over the spoiled centre of the great stones, build again the giant obelisk from which the priests had once watched the sun and commanded worship. He would have vast Sarsen rocks brought from the quarries in the Cotswolds to replace the ones that had been lost or broken. So a huge arena would grow, an encircled and sacred field, the scene for a yearly festival of pomp and circumstance to celebrate the long reign of Magog from time out of memory. And the carriages of mystery would roll on their golden wheels from

Whitehall down the Great West Road, they would stop briefly at Stonehenge to pay their respects to the lesser cromlechs and circles of other Druids, then on towards the setting sun between the standing pillars of stone to the gigantic ring of Avebury. There the people would be gathered round their rulers, the bearers of the mysteries of night, the orb and the mace and the chalice and the rod and the throne, all brought together for the ceremony of Avebury. Then the drums would beat, the trumpets sound and the people kneel, crying. 'Magog, majesty, Magog, mighty, Magog, mercy upon us . . .'

A sports car took the corner too fast. Its tyres squealed like a pig's death. Magog winced. His leg had gone to sleep. As he rubbed its pains, he sneered at his dream. He was getting as stupid as Gog. Perhaps there was something of his half-brother in him. To set Avebury to rights as the mystic English Nuremberg would cost a million pounds or so. And then who would come there to revere Magog? It would be another monumental folly to the mystique of power and to the good sense of mankind, who would stay away and leave Avebury to the cows. Better to take the old stones as the subject of a thesis, to date them exactly by the new nuclear and radio-carbon methods, to stake out an exciting bridge field between the long gone and soon to be.

Avebury and Nuclear Fission – or Who Split the Stones? It was an intriguing title. The only need was now to write the book as a passport to power in the university of Magog's choice.

1960

'They must leave at once,' the headmistress said. 'They aw expelled.' She seemed to haw without heeing like a bronchial donkey, as she sat on her chintz sofa, overweight, overwrought, beside herself with outrage. Maire sat on an armchair, perfectly in command and picking Persian cat's hairs off her black skirt.

'Do unto others . . .' Maire murmured. 'Why don't you expel yourself?'

'What do you mean?'

'This place is obviously too much for you, my good woman. If you let my baby daughters get you into such a state . . .'

'Dawghtaws?' the headmistress said. 'Monstaws of depravity. Liaws. Fawnicataws.'

'I do hope so,' Maire said. 'But really, I don't quite understand what all the fuss is about. Rosa can be a little trying, but Josepha is an angel.'

'Rosaw has cawrupted the whole Lowaw Fifth. And Josephaw is her aidaw and abettaw.'

'Loyal girl, Josepha,' Maire said. 'But are you sure that there was anything left to corrupt in the Lower Fifth? I have always found the girls absolutely unspeakable. By fifteen, the only thing I hadn't tried was a donkey.'

'You aw speaking of *riding*, I hope,' the headmistress said.

'I hope.'

'The Lowaw Fifth was a supaw form of little ladies until that rascal Rosaw got among them with her sistaw. And do you know now . . .' The headmistress panted and patted her shelving chest to calm her excitement. 'The *rubbaw frog*,' she said. 'Do you know about the rubbaw frog?'

'It sounds very stimulating,' Maire said.

'Rosaw came back to school one term with a rubbaw frog, the sort which inflate when you squeeze a rubbaw bulb. Then suddenly there was a craze for rubbaw frogs. All the girls were taking them to their bawths. But do you know what they *did* with the frogs?'

Maire began to laugh. 'I can imagine,' she said. 'It's worth a try at that age.'

'There aw ways and ways of coping with developing woman-hood,' the headmistress said. 'Inflatable rubbaw frogs aw not one of them.'

'I think it shows a bold experimental mind in Rosa,' Maire said. 'I'm quite proud of her.'

'Your pride, ma'am, does you little credit. And that was only the beginning of yaw dawghtaw's revolting conspiracy against school discipline. There was the affair of the bus conductaws!'

'Bus conductors? From Jamaica, Pakistan, or just the home-grown natives?'

'Only one, thank God, was colawed on the 97 bus. On the way to the swimming-bawths, yaw Rosaw persuaded all the girls to go to the top deck while Josephaw sat as a sentry on the stairs, only allowing the conductaw to pass. Then the girls *undressed* up there. They even took their knickaws off, I am told. Rosaw called it the Crazy Bus Strip Club, I believe, and made the conductaw the *talent judge*. One young man was up on the top deck for *twenty* minutes with the passengaws downstairs unable to pay for their tickets, which is a misdeme-anaw against the local Council. Not to mention the view from the uppaw windaws of Malmesbury Villaws. I have had *complaints* . . .' The headmistress could not credit the fact that anyone could have complained of her young ladies. Her voice dropped to a whisper. 'I am even told that the winnaw had relations with the conductaw.'

'Had relations?' Maire asked. 'On the top deck of the bus?'

'Lataw, in the hockey pavilion aftaw games. He was the *First Prize.*'

While Maire was laughing, she noticed on the walls of the headmistress's sitting-room the End of the Year school photo-graphs in their gilt frames. The plain faces of the adolescent girls smiled or gloomed towards the viewer, ranged in a graded pattern of heights and identical uniforms, blazers and skirts and white socks and striped ties and little boater hats, for all the world like a group of long-haired and dumpy boys in kilts. In the middle of these sexless and ordered squads, the headmistress sat with the teachers, smiling to present such a display of neatness and suppression of nature.

'I fail to see anything *amusing*, ma'am,' the headmistress said. 'I should point out that at fifteen a girl is still a Minaw. The Assizes deal with those who take advantage of Minaws.'

'But in this case, the Minors were taking advantage of the bus conductors. What then?'

'Expulsion,' the headmistress said. 'They can then be taken away from their parents by the Court as being in need of Caw and Protection.'

'If Rosa ever got had up,' Maire said, 'the Court would need all the care and protection it could get.'

'You are flippant, ma'am. You will remove yaw dawghtaws at once. I cannot allow this contamination to spread furthaw through the Fifth.'

Maire rose, picking the last of the long cat's hairs off her skirt, and she walked over to the window-seat to where the culprit pussy sat, white and otiose and totally absorbed in its own beauty sleep. Maire removed the cat onto the floor and sat in its place, which was pleasantly warmed, pretending not to see the headmistress scowl. She looked out of the window to where some of the girls were walking in the playground, slouching and giggling with their arms round each other, joined in the endless gossip and confidences of puberty and thereafter. They seemed perfectly able to cope with their silly prison costumes and their sentences to three terms a year of formal education. They were biding their time, waiting to break out into the world of men, stalker and quarry, hunter and prey, both.

'I fail to see why Josepha is guilty of more than loyalty to her sister,' Maire said. 'Her marks are very good, and all that.'

'I have not told you yet of the *Dawm Feast.*'

'What's so terrible about a dorm feast?'

'Nawmally we turn a blind eye like Lawd Nelson . . .'

'Lady Hamilton, surely.'

'Lawd Nelson,' the headmistress said firmly, 'to an innocent gathawring of the girls aftaw Lights Out if they want a bit of extraw tuck. But Rosaw, as always, awltered an institution into an awgy. Only last night, ma'am, unable to sleep and wanting to make sure that *my girls* were safely in the land of nod, I made my rounds . . .'

'*Your* girls?' Maire said. 'Is the real trouble that Rosa doesn't fancy you very much?'

The headmistress ignored Maire's remark completely, although a pink tinge in her cheek showed that Maire had pricked her.

'And *what* met my eyes? A positive *Black Mass.*'

'Really,' Maire said. 'That is advanced.'

'Rosaw had covawed her sistaw all ovaw with a mixtyaw of cocoa, honey and peanut-buttaw, a favourite of the girls which they call Awful-Awful. Josephaw was stretched out on the dawm table in the attitude of the *Crawss*. My girls were all licking the Awful-Awful off Josephaw, while Rosaw was reading some filth from *Salomé* by that awful Awscaw Wilde.'

'Serving up her sister to the lusts of the whole dormitory?' Maire said. 'That is a bit awful-awful. Was Josepha enjoyng it?'

'Ma'am, I did not pawse to verify yaw dawghtaw's *pleashaw*! I packed her awf to take a bawth, and I locked Rosaw in the Wataw Clawset. I sent for you at once. Take yaw dawghtaws awf of my hands!'

'Well, I suppose it's better for the poor dears to be fondled by their mother than by you,' Maire said. 'I'll take them. Home is the place, they say, which has to take you in when nobody else will.'

'There is Bawstal,' the headmistress said. 'You do realize yaw daughtaws have ruined their lives. They have not even secyawred their O-levels!'

'No O-levels,' Maire said. 'How can they possibly survive without O-levels?'

'Let alone A-levels.'

'Let alone A-levels,' Maire said.

'No academy will have them aftaw this awful awgy, no university, not even the Sawbonne. Poor Rosaw, poor Josephaw . . .'

Maire rose.

'Yet you are condemning the children to this stupid fate, headmistress. I suppose you don't feel at fault at all. You presumably think my dawghtaws were *caw*rupted by their *Mawmaw*.'

'Mawmaw?' the headmistress said. 'Maws Maws are cannibawls in Kenyaw.'

'Mawmaws are also carnivaws to teachaws.' Maire paused and considered what would hurt the headmistress most. 'You love your cat, I presume.'

'Butchey,' the headmistress said. 'I simply *adaw* Butchey.'

'That to your cat,' Maire said and kicked the Persian furball halfway across the room.

The cat miaowed, the headmistress surged up, jelloid with fury.

'Get out with yaw awffspring!'

'Pshaw,' Maire said, making slowly for the door.

'I will sign no refawrence faw Rosaw and Josephaw,' the headmistress whinnied. 'There only futyaws aw to be whaws!'

'Yaw futyaw,' Maire said, 'is to be a bloody *baw*.' And left to take Rosa and Josepha home, for there was no place like it.

Magog's thesis that most things could be bought made his thesis on Avebury most easy to buy. Knowing that professors were under-salaried and numerous and family men, and also knowing the laws of supply and demand, Magog offered a thousand pounds each to the specialists in the twelve fields that covered his ancient and modern approach to the mysteries of the great stones of Avebury. For his money, each specialist was asked to write an original monograph of fifty pages dealing with Avebury from the point of view of his discipline. Magog told his dozen disciples that he would be picking their brains on the subject, but, as Nietzsche had pointed out, a genius did have the right to steal from other men's brains. Moreover, Magog was behaving far better than the American professors, who used their graduate students as unpaid slaves to produce the material for the yearly book needed to keep their master's place at the top of the Ivy League. After all, a thousand pounds was at least ten times the going price for fifty pages of research. And money, like thought, had its value. The twelve specialists were to be ready to sacrifice their narrow ideas for the good of the glorious whole, which was to be put together by Magog himself. This was self-sacrificial and co-operative labour – and profitable as well.

Once the monographs were done, Magog hired the services of the Great Synthesizer, whose printed comments on every subject under the sun had broken the legs of countless coffee-tables. A tall, fat, bald poodle of a man, given to snobbery and leaping at the offerings of the great and lying at the feet of majesty, he would sell himself at the drop of a cheque or a titled name to anyone from the Queen Mother to the *Daily News*. Distrusted by his fellow professors as a dilettante, equally distrusted by the general public as too clever by three-quarters, the brilliance of his pen and the fear of being caught on the wrong side of a controversy with him had brought him a grudging respect and a decent income. For a high price, he was prepared to become a ghost writer without advancing his reputation or pushing his name. For a very high price . . .

'Five thousand pounds,' Magog said.

'Five thousand,' the Great Synthesizer agreed, 'and expenses. Got to keep myself in port, you know.' He laughed. 'It helps to keep the ketchup down.' Like the true climber in a society which increasingly pretended to be classless, he had learned how to make an advantage of his humble origins and how to own up to a couple of vulgar tastes with genuine pleasure. Dukes also were known to like bangers and mash.

'A limit of five hundred on expenses,' Magog said. 'Or else you might want a Tintoretto for your ceiling.'

'I thought that was *your* style,' the Great Synthesizer said. 'Being paid off in tax-free old masters, for looking after your brother's *estate*.'

'How do you know that?'

'I know, Maire,' the Great Synthesizer said.

'Who doesn't? Seven-fifty expenses. Overheads are normally charged at fifteen per cent. And just because it's literature doesn't mean to say that it's not business.'

'It'll be an expensive thesis,' Magog said.

'Status symbols cost a lot,' the Great Synthesizer said. 'Perhaps it'll found a new career for you. You must have motives behind your charity to us.'

'It had better be a good thesis.'

'The very best,' the Great Synthesizer said. 'I am a professional. Could I trouble you for a little more of that Cockburn? The only other Cockburn worth troubling about was an admiral who helped liberate Latin America – he also liked a good port in a storm.'

Magog gave a polite smile as the Great Synthesizer delivered his after-dinner jokes. He watched the other man posture, sneer, amuse – and he found him an arrant courtier and ultimate failure. For all his books on the Edwardian earls and the defunct Kings and Queens of England, for all his doggy tricks in flattering the great to let him get at their family papers and dinner tables, the Great Synthesizer would never be satisfied until he was the titled gentleman he could never become, even though he was a prince among professors and he could have been a grey eminence to governments. As it was, the students despised him as a lickspittle tyrant and his colleagues thought him a venal snob. If he had not been so devastatingly good at his trade and quick at the throats of his enemies, he could have been the best-hated don at his university. Instead, he was the best known.

'Five thousand pounds, then, half in advance and half on delivery. Seven-fifty expenses during the course of the work by attested bills . . .'

'Cash and guineas,' the Great Synthesizer said. 'Gold is the only currency between gentlemen – and it does confuse the taxman.'

'Seven-fifty guineas in cash expenses. Contract broken and money repayable in full if *any word* is ever leaked about the actual writing of the Avebury manuscript. I may say, my dear fellow, that I shall take the precaution of personally correcting a typescript in my own fair hand to prove authorship, as well as to give myself the pleasure of the final draft.'

'You're not doing much less than many footballers and Prime Ministers have done. The final draft *means* total authorship – when the cheques don't bounce.'

'Busy men have earned the right to make up their books with the help of other people,' Magog said.

'Also rich men,' the Great Synthesizer said.

'Also great men,' Magog said.

'Also great men, my dear Ponsonby. But you must realize, history no longer deals with great men. Only with economics.'

The speed of the Great Synthesizer at writing the Avebury manuscript was remarkable, his epigrams apt, his paradoxes impeccable, his conclusions judicious, his sense of balance worthy of Blondin on a tightrope over Niagara Falls. But all the same, Magog felt that something was lacking in the final product, a certain roughness, an unorthodox passion, a groping originality of concept that might suggest genius. As this was to be his only masterwork before he took up his duties as the head of a new college or Vice-Chancellor of a new university, Magog intended to settle for nothing that was not remarkable. The Avebury book was, after all, one which must seem to be the product of a lifetime's thought by a great brain. So Magog sent the typescript ahead to Gog in the Far North and followed it by train a week later to spend Christmas with his half-brother. Gog was a wild man, but there was no question that he had a warped power of perception. His mind was not as other men's were. His madness might, after all, make a contribution to Magog's rational intellect, based on the logic and style of his thirteen helpers. And ancient times were rather Gog's brew.

'I've read it,' Gog said. 'It's all right a far as it goes. But it doesn't go anywhere interesting. For instance, you state that all the evidence shows that Avebury pre-dated the Druids, so it wasn't a Druid temple at all.'

'Like most other people, I thought it was a Druid temple,' Magog said, 'until I did the research on it.' Really, the professors had dug up so much against the Druid theory of Avebury that it was untenable.

'Research?' Gog said. 'What the hell has research got to do with intuition and tradition? Radio-carbon dating is very fancy, but tradition is where the truth is. The Druids were at Avebury, everybody knows that. Druid originally meant "wise man". Its corrupt meaning is "false priest", and it only refers to the later Druids.'

'Not according to the evidence. When Julius Caesar invaded England, he found no Druids in the South. So they couldn't have built Avebury.'

'Perhaps, like most tourists, Julius Caesar missed a thing or two. He was looking for conquest, slaves, booty. Why the hell should he bother to mention the Druids, who had probably gone underground, as they usually do in time of neglect or trouble. Stick to tradition, Magog. The critics may laugh at you, but you'll be correct.'

'You can't rely on traditions about long ago. Or intuitions. By new archaeological methods . . .'

'What your Avebury book needs is a good theory, but you're too bloody sane to find one. Now if I told you the Druids were migratory Iberians from Africa, who brought along their Cult of the Dead with its human sacrifice and burial under huge blocks of stone, all the way to Britain across Spain, and then took the cult east to Egypt and built the pyramids, not to mention going across the Atlantic to Mexico . . .'

'Proof?'

'There are stone burial chambers of the same type in Africa

and the Orkneys. There are also huge monuments in stone, dolmens and cromlechs that stretch from Brittany to Peru to Easter Island. Perhaps the Iberians and the Druids with their foul theocracy drifted all over the world. Perhaps William Blake, our greatest prophet, was right that the first Holy Land was here in Albion, the first Israel, until the false Druids from Africa invaded with their crushing Aveburys and dead weight of religion and stone pillars of power that replaced the sacred oaks of nature worshipped by the original Celts, who made their white island a place of peace and joy and Jerusalem. Perhaps . . .'

'Perhaps,' Magog interrupted, 'I shall have to write a witty chapter on loony theories about Avebury. It might make the scholars laugh.'

'The truth always does make intellectuals laugh,' Gog said. 'But it's still the truth. Yet if you want to make your book seminal, you'll have to propose a new theory, you know. Even an unpopular theory. Why not this, which may well be the truth?'

'It's too romantic, too Celtic,' Magog said. 'And this isn't a romantic age. It's pragmatic. We must make things work, the few of us who know how to.'

'Yes, the people haven't much of a say-so now. And their last hero's dead. Nye Bevan. The last hope we had of a people's leader. Do you care?'

Magog nodded.

'Nye? We all cared for Nye. But he should have stayed down the Welsh mines. He used to go to Ebbw Vale in a Rolls-Royce, then change into an old Austin Seven to arrive as a mate among the miners. But he crashed the Rolls on the way once and the papers printed it and the miners got to know, after all.'

'People always do get to know,' Gog said. 'And their leaders always betray them.'

'Still, no more National Service,' Magog said. 'No more conscription. No more young men drafted to fight colonial wars. You must admit that's progress for the *people*.'

Gog poured out another tumbler of the clear malt spirits that passed for whisky in the Far North.

'Stopping an abuse isn't progress,' he said. 'We should never have had conscription at all. We lost the Empire in the last half of the nineteenth century, when we hadn't even finished founding it. Our industry began slipping eighty years ago, and machines now matter far more than red coats or blue jackets. Why did we hang on to the red on the globe for so long?'

'Perhaps we felt it was our duty to hand over to the black leaders of the Commonwealth countries in good order. After all, it has been the most decent retreat from Empire the world's ever seen. The Romans didn't do half as well. The British are really at their best at their Dunkirks.'

'Did you hear old Harold Macmillan saying a *wind* of *change* was sweeping through Africa?' Gog laughed and lowered half his tumbler of spirits in a gulp. 'It's just a little breeze at the rate we're clearing out. It's all so bloody slow, *giving* away independence to Ghana, to Nigeria . . . so bloody slow. As if it were up to us to *give* anybody their country back. We raped their independence. You can't give back what you took by rape. It's done, there's no forgiveness for it. You can just get the hell out of the scene of the crime as soon as possible.'

'We believe in leaving law and order behind us,' Magog said, 'things which work. Africa was chaos before we went in.'

'It'll be chaos again,' Gog said. 'The tribes all fighting against the artificial nations we've imposed on them. But it'll be *their* chaos. Every people's got a right to its own chaos, a birthright to make the biggest bloody mess it wants to make.'

'We did more good than harm to our Empire,' Magog said. 'No exploitation without more civilization.'

'It's coming home now, the Empire,' Gog said. 'Millions have been coming home to nothing from India, from Asia, from wherever we left a colony or culture or a bit of trade. What they did out on the far shores of Empire is forgotten. The government doesn't want to own up to them. They are the invisible men of our time. They feel they've wasted their lives for a lost cause and an ungrateful society. So they sit in their cold cottages and villas on short rations and marginal pensions, waiting to die off. They won't be needed again. Who cares about the old porter or nurse when the bailiffs are in?'

Gog's voice betrayed the tremble of the time when his blood was pounding away at the injustice of it all. Despite all his experience, he still thought society had something to do with equity.

'I would never have believed that I'd see you worked up about the fate of the imperialists,' Magog said. 'Is retirement turning you into a reactionary?'

'They're people too,' Gog said.

'Your son Arthur –' Magog said.

'Who?'

'You have forgotten you have an illegitimate son?'

'He was never mine. He has forgotten me. Have you heard of him?'

'Yes,' Magog said. 'You know he disappeared after he left Cambridge. He became rather revolutionary – some sort of protest against the Establishment and Suez, which was only an imperial swansong, not an act of aggression. Well, he's become a mole in Fleet Street. A minor official in a printers' union. Trying to become the youngest Father of a Chapel ever known.'

'He gets his interest in printing from me,' Gog said. 'I even worked as a printer in the General Strike.'

'Arthur would kill you for that,' Magog said. 'You were a government scab?'

'I believed then in getting the news to the people at all costs.'

'Arthur believes in getting the news to the people, but only the news he sees fit to print. Anyway, I thought you would be glad to hear of him.'

'I am,' Gog said. 'I am always glad to hear of people I used to know. I am very isolated here. I depend on the occasional visitor to tell me of what is going on in the world.'

Magog looked at his half-brother. It was time to settle an ancient war between them. No peace had been declared on that, only a silence.

'Talking of people you used to know, do you ever think of those who didn't survive the war? Rupert Fox? And Putney Bowles?'

'I am always thinking of Putney,' Gog said. 'I was in Egypt when he had that shooting accident. He tripped over his shotgun.'

'You were in Oxford when Rupert was burned in that explosion. It was dreadful that month he lingered on.'

'I was at Bletchley,' Gog said. 'And Rupert was a Russian agent.'

'Sometimes I feel you had him killed,' Magog said. 'Just

because you were jealous of his love of me. And Putney Bowles. I am sure you killed him personally.'

'He was my friend. How could I?'

'You killed him,' Magog said. 'I know.'

'You cannot know,' Gog said. 'You were not there.'

'You were. The inquest was fixed. I heard the truth about it from Max Mann.'

'He was the third member of that group spying for the Kremlin. You knew that.'

'They were not spying. We were Allies with Russia then.'

'Max was the third man, as well as hating me when he was my tutor at Cambridge. He would tell you I had killed Putney Bowles.'

'He did,' Magog said. 'You shot him in the back of the head when he was peeing against a tree. You did that to your friend. And don't you deny it. I am sure you had your orders, but they were the wrong orders. Do you know something? All truth is known in the end.'

'No truth is known,' Gog said. 'There is no truth in war. There is no treason. There is no friend. I suppose that is why I went a bit mad at the end of the war. And you having my girl twins by Maire.'

'You killed Putney Bowles,' Magog said. He rose to go. 'Thank you for your help on Avebury. I did not mean to rake up the past or accuse you, but every day I think of Rupert and his foul and unnecessary death.'

'That was not I,' Gog said. 'I had nothing to do with it.'

'But you killed Putney.'

Gog met Magog's stare, then looked away.

'I also remember Putney's death every day of my life. I was never the same after it. Good-bye, Magog.'

'I will tell Max Mann that you have confessed to me.'

'I did not.'

'I hate you for it,' Magog said. 'Good-bye, Gog.'

The table at the Ivy was cloistered beneath the windows of stained glass. Ranged in order of precedence and irreverence, a conclave of the Cognoscenti was assessing its port and armagnac as carefully as marking a First Class Honours Degree in the

Tripos or a pregnancy test. Magog had been a member of the Cambridge secret society for twenty-five years. He counted on its direct intelligence and indirect influence. The members were the brightest and the best over several generations; no major Cambridge philosopher or poet, mathematician or aesthete was not of their number. Exclusive and clandestine, they pursued the male bonding that was the cement of English society. Their obscure assocation was their intellectual aphrodisiac, inducing in their closet ways a sense of innate superiority. They would help Magog become a Vice Chancellor of a university or the Master of the College of his choice. He was one of them, and some of them were already Masters or Chancellors or Permanent Secretaries in the Civil Service. Where power was, there they were.

'Max,' Magog said to the stooped emaciate beside him, an ascetic who might have modelled for St Simeon Stylites despite grouse for dinner. 'I had to bring up your name.' He lifted his glass. '*In piam memoriam*. Rupert Fox. Putney Bowles.'

'Our two dear lost friends.' Maximilian Mann lifted his glass and drank. 'You talked of me to whom not in the Society?'

'My half-brother George. Gog.'

'Ah.' A trick of candlelight threw the flash of a bright blade onto Mann's eye. 'Did he confess?'

'He confirmed what you said, Max. He knows who killed Putney in Egypt, even if it was not directly him. As for Rupert, he knows you and he and Putney were in a Russian ring.'

'No longer. Any more than you are a friend of the neo-Nazis, though you may have been of the old ones. All that prewar enthusiasm for extreme solutions . . . But we did believe it.'

Magog smiled.

'When the solutions were as beautiful as Rupert and Putney. Oh god, Max, how I miss them.'

'And I.' Mann looked down the table to where two younger members of the Cognoscenti were balancing brandy-glass on brandy-glass, making an iridescent pyramid of small balloons. They were also lighting the gauze paper wrapped round hard Italian macaroons so that it floated away and ended in a puff of charcoal. 'Something is forever lost. Some grace, if that is not too strong a term.'

'Yes,' Magog said. 'A lost grace. Tell me, Max, after those two idiots Guy and Donald Maclean defected, you must have been investigated. How long did your clearance take?'

'It was quite civilized,' Max said. 'In fact, the case officer assigned to me – well, he is one of us, in a certain sort of a way. Need I elucidate?' He smiled at Magog. 'I know what you felt for Rupert – and he understood what I did too. And anyway, if once I had a passing interest in – shall we say – Kremlinology, my only passion now is for the rococo –'

'When Italian, male and under eighteen.'

'When eighteenth century and inanimate. My erstwhile passion is now necrophilia. I examine the dead closely – and mourn them.' Mann paused. 'I still believe your brother was Putney's murderer – and perhaps Rupert's. He was always violent and most misguided. He was with Graveling and that group at Bletchley Park decoding Enigma through those early computers. They were all demented over what they called security, which meant lying to our Allies in the hour of their desperate need.'

'There are people still looking for a third man, you know, who tipped Guy and Donald off. And a fourth and a fifth *ad infinitum* and *nauseam*. All for *soi-disant* treachery twenty years stale. Paranoia never stops. The file never closes on our generation, merely because we dared to be committed – that is the term now, isn't it?'

'Committed where?' Mann sighs. 'The Old Bailey, probably. Did you know Kim Philby? He'll be the next to go. He's blown already. That's why they've put him out to grass in Beirut. They hope those mad Arabs will do their dirty work for them.'

'And you?' Magog asked. 'Will they ever make you go public and beat your breast and bare your sins?'

'Neither my tits,' Maximilian Mann said, 'nor my testicles could possibly interest the English masses. As dear Morgan used to say about his policeman friend, one must love the working classes only one by one. But you, Magnus, have taken to scholarship like a duck to muck. Something on Avebury.'

'A small work,' Magog said with all the modesty that suggested profundity and long research. 'But all my own.'

'So all my friends tell me – your contributors. You wish to

leave the stews and fleshpots of the metropolis for the provincial groves of academe?'

'If the right offer comes along.'

'For you, Magnus, it somehow always does.'

A tinkle and a tintinnabulation at the end of the table signified the crashing of the brandy-glasses. Chuckles sounded the approval of the deed and the knell of the dinner. The Cognoscenti rose to go about their business in high places. Magog knew that they would do their work and aid one another without a word being said. It was a conspiracy of mutual understanding. He also knew that he should not record the meeting of Cognoscenti nor their existence, but in the manner of all the chroniclers in the Ivy, he did.

1961

Magog thought he should do a Grand Tour of the Great Antiquities before he settled down as an academic. He needed those personal memories, the gleanings and gossip about old sites which could only be picked up on the spot and at the dig. He had also heard that excavations at Jericho had revealed the most ancient human settlement yet known in the world, and he felt the need to take some credit for this discovery by others. There was also the problem of Rosa and Josepha and their lack of education. Magog hardly intended to act the paterfamilias; but Rosa was beautiful enough at sixteen, with her large restless eyes and agile body, to look good in his company, while plump Josepha was flattering with her seriousness and adoration of anyone who bothered with her questions. The girls were certainly presentable enough to be seen abroad.

There was Maire as well. Of course, Magog had parted from Maire finally for the last time. Of course, Maire was impossible and had caused him what passed for anguish at the time in Paris. But of course, in middle age, no parting was for ever. That was the stuff of youth, a total break with an intimate. In later years, to know somebody well was a blessing, because friends had already begun to die and too few days remained to spend the time in getting to know new people. The passing years obliterated quarrels, joined separations, healed wounds, and led to fresh voyages in old tubs. Maire and her twin daughters agreed to go with Magog to the Middle East.

Egypt showed itself to Magog in its dim world where beasts met gods and men. The great bronze cats in the Cairo Museum, green and thin, yet haunched like women. The Sphinx's face that sandstorms had changed from the goddess's mask to a negroid man's snub-nose above the couched lion's body – threat of Africa, advancing up the Arab Nile. The avenue of rams' heads at Karnak, each body holding a little human figure in eternal cat-and-mouse play between its feline paws. The strange painted motifs in the tombs in the Valley of the Kings, the Nile as a serpent carrying men on its curves, a cobra with eagle's wings and human feet, a scarab boat so made that the rower floated on a beetle. Then the golden lion's bed and bull's bed of Tutankhamun, more godlike than their divine burden long gone to rot. The musk of papyrus, the fetid warning approach of decay and dust in the nostrils, the lairs that were emperors' tombs made the past years pad like the ghosts of tigers through the museums and the pyramids, so that ancient Egypt seemed a sacred zoo where the Pharaohs had been the keepers and had fed their slaves into the jaws of the ravening holy beasts.

Nasser's dominion also had its animals and gods and men. Magog always visited zoos in cities to see what they showed of the nature of the citizens. Since the behaviour of beasts was constant, menageries were the measure of man. Where the animals were content, the men seemed kind and society in balance. Where the animals were ill-treated, men and the state were sick. In the Cairo zoo, so famous under the British occupation, tourists were now rare, and the keepers in their old khaki greatcoats from the Desert War waited to torment their charges for a few piastres. They would rattle and bang the bars of the cages, tweak a toothless lion by the lip, scream at a leopard, cuff a coati mundi. They knew how to put on a jolly good show.

Ignoring these tiny Roman circuses mounted by each keeper in a rage against his own poverty, Magog and Maire and the twins walked under the date palms and eucalyptus, between the flowering bushes and the rushes and the cacti into the gothic grotto of Sulemein Pasha with its black-glass mirrors and crazy passages, where the Pasha once hunted his houris before he broke them in a rest-house under the lazy spike of Cheops' Pyramid. Everywhere, a prevailing smell of shit, the acrid shit that came from hide or fur, not the faint aroma of human merde that made the whole delta whiff of blood pudding. House cats kept the zoo clean, stealthily wandering into every cage, ignoring the greater animals in their sacred scavengings. Anything the cats left was carried off by the high hawks and kites, which would even swoop to grab a fish in mid-air from a sea-lion. There were no dogs except in cages, the St Bernard as remarkable as the rhinoceros, the cocker spaniel mooching as sadly in his hutch as any baboon.

As Magog walked with his women past the cages and the empty tea-gardens called casinos and the duck-headed pleasure boats rusting in the ornamental pond, he thought of the British taking their Jockey Clubs and zoos all over the globe. Perhaps the British Empire had been acquired in a mania for natural history. When the Revolutions came and men were said to matter more than pets, then the animals decayed along with the imperialists. The Egyptian government had closed the Society for the Prevention of Cruelty to Animals at Luxor. Donkeys, bullocks, camels, horses still carried the loads, turned the waterwheels, stamped the seed, along with the beasts of burden called women. Men knelt to Allah and lazed, the snail's eggs sent by Osiris eating their veins away, prey to the parasites as they had always been prey to the Cat, the Ram, the Lion, the Snake, the Nile, the Pharaoh, the Gods, themselves.

In the small mammal house, the jolly good show could not be avoided. The fat keeper there was stimulated into an orgy of baiting by the entrance of four British tourists. He banged on the mesh of the cage of the desert foxes and made one of them run in crazy circles round the small box, up the narrow diamonds of the wire, quick over the low ceiling, down the far wall, back across to the wire in a prisoned panic. The fennecs and the agoutis merely shivered at the clap of the keeper's hand; they would not perform. But the lynx snarled, and the jewelled and blobbed Margay Cat fought back, hissing and striking at the keeper's palm, clawing at the mesh.

'Ho, ho,' the keeper yelled in a squire's laugh, proud of his act, putting his face close to the wire. The cat spat at his plump cheek.

'Don't torture them for us,' Josepha said, holding on tight to Magog's hand like a scared child. Both Maire and Rosa were smiling, uncaring, mildly interested.

The keeper grinned with brown teeth, clearly not understanding English. He slammed the flat of his hand against the wire again. It was to be a virtuoso act, for the Margay Cat spat again.

'No,' Josepha said. 'Stop it.'

The keeper gave a greater grin and once more smacked his hand at the cat's face through the mesh. Magog saw the pain in Josepha's look and decided to intervene in the most effective way, not the most aggressive. He took a banknote out of his pocket and pointed it at the next cage, where a grey fox was cowering. At the sight of the money, the keeper moved sideways and thumped his hand obligingly on the fox's hutch. The animal shuddered.

'No,' Josepha screamed. 'Stop him!'

As the keeper laughed and banged again, Magog put the banknote into his hand. The keeper bobbed, smiled and spread out his palms in gratitude.

'Effendi,' he said. 'Thank you a thousand thanks. Thank you a million thanks.' His accent was good. He knew English all right, and the English.

Magog shepherded his women from the stench of fur and caged fear into the bright gardens under the banyan trees and the poinsettias. Josepha was crying.

'There's no need to blub,' Rosa said. 'You can't do anything about it.'

'You bribed him,' Josepha accused Magog. 'You *paid* him . . . He'll do it again . . .'

'What did you expect me to do?' Magog asked. 'Give him a good right to the chin and land up in jail? We're not the masters

here now, you know. Our last gunboat got sunk in that Suez
mess four years ago. These aren't the good old days.'

'That wog only does it to annoy because he knows it teases,'
Maire said. 'The moment he sees an animal-loving Britisher,
biff, bang, bam! He tortures the beasts till we pay him off. He's
really torturing us for going biff, bang, bam to him when we
ruled here. Don't cry, Josepha dear . . . Probably he doesn't
get any wages. He has to earn his keep off the animal show.'

'It's icky,' Josepha sniffed.

'Very icky,' Maire said, 'but that's the way it is. We all
blackmail each other through our weaknesses. Look what
women do to their lovers . . .' She smiled across at Magog,
who still found her appealing, although she was straddling fifty
years on her long tapered legs. 'Those foxes are treated quite
well compared with some gentlemen I have known.'

'Who do *you* torture?' Rosa asked.

'Never you mind,' Maire said.

'Magog,' Rosa said and smiled sidelong at her mother.

'Magnus is just a friend and your uncle,' Maire said. 'As though
I'd have anything to do with your father's brother.'

'Oh,' Rosa said as if it were an old story. 'I've always thought
Magog might be our real father.'

There was a pause. A crow croaked in the distance. Josepha
forgot her tears and looked at her twin, hot-eyed.

'Where did you get such a frightful notion from?' Maire asked.

'Gog told us,' Rosa said, looking steadily at her sister.

'He . . .' Josepha said, then shut up at her twin's stare.

'He couldn't have been such an idiot,' Maire said.

'Gog's absolutely super,' Rosa said. 'He'll tell you absolutely
everything.'

Magog was curiously pleased that things were now in the
open. The two girls were really very passable. They promised
him the guarantee of young company in his old age.

Maire looked hard at Rosa, who looked back at her mother.

'You're tricking me, Rosa,' she said. 'Gog never told you a
thing.'

'He said Magog might be our father,' Rosa said. 'After all,
why is Magog here now? Poss, he's our uncle, but he's hardly
known as a *sacrificial lamb* to his dear ones.'

There was a short silence, while Maire decided to admit something rather than be told she was a liar.

'Gog shouldn't have told you two,' she said. 'He's normally so discreet. I'll have to talk to him seriously.'

Josepha could not hold her tongue any longer.

'Gog never did tell us that,' she said. 'Rosa tricked you, Mummy. I didn't want to know. Why did you tell?'

It was too much to bear. She, Maire, tricked by a sixteen-year-old! And then reproached for being honest!

'*What!*' A rare redness bit at Maire's cheek as she swung on Rosa. 'You *dare* be smart with me?'

'I'm learning from you,' Rosa said. 'I thought it was super for a girl to learn from her own *mummy.*'

Magog could not stop laughing. It was too funny. Maire, who had outwitted the whole human race, now sprung by her own baby daughter. It was like the wily zoo-keeper, knowing how to squeeze piastres out of the fading sentimentality of the British Empire.

'For that, my girl,' Maire said, 'I'll take you off the Pill.'

Now it was Magog's turn for outrage.

'The Pill? Do you mean to say, Maire, you've put the *child* on the Pill?'

'She needs to be,' Maire said. 'With *her* nature.'

'Quinine,' Rosa said. 'A quinine pill. One has to be super careful, if poss.'

Maire's anger suddenly turned to laughter as she saw Rosa now outfacing Magog. She was back in her own youth. Sweet sixteen.

'You meant a contraceptive pill, Rosa,' Magog said. 'I know for fact Maire takes the Pill. She's always trying the latest fad from America.'

'You do know, do you?' Rosa said innocently. 'How? First-hand experience?'

Maire's laughter shrilled higher than the parrots and monkeys in the distance.

'Oh, Magog,' she said, 'do I have a daughter!'

Magog looked at Josepha, whose face was burning with tears and shame.

'Two daughters,' he said. 'We have two daughters.' He put

out his arm towards Josepha, but she moved away, almost roughly.

'Gog's our father,' Josepha said. 'I don't believe you.'

'Don't,' Magog said. 'Gog may well be your father.'

'Don't you know?'

'Maire's your mother,' Magog said. 'Be sure of that.' He turned on Rosa. 'I won't have you on the Pill. You're too young.'

'What Mummy says goes,' Rosa said. 'She is *definitely* my mummy.' She gave a sidelong grin towards Maire, then turned again to Magog. 'They're trying to make a male pill. You should take it. Then me and Josie mightn't be here. One has to be super careful, if poss.'

As the four of them left the zoo, Josepha staying angrily apart from Magog, Rosa and Maire with their arms round each other in gales of conspiratorial giggles, two hundred Cairo schoolgirls met them. The schoolgirls were plump and brown, unveiled and educated at last, wearing the little uniforms of the Revolution in their training as schoolmistresses for the Sudan and the Yemen and other benighted areas. They looked just like little ladies from the twins' old school, but they found the sight of Maire in her check suit and the tall sisters in their flared red skirts and Magog in his bottle-green outfit as comic as a treeful of orang-outangs. They burst into a chant, taunting and mocking at these four white Western grotesques.

> '*Hull – low, Hull – low*
> *Hull – low, Hull – low . . .*'

Their teacher, screaming, could not hush them. They were berserk with glee, as if the visit to the zoo had already begun with the jolliest of shows.

Jerusalem was not golden, nor with milk and honey blest. But the war did not seem to have poxed it overmuch. It was still a Crusader's stone city with little streets meandering upstep and downhill under arches and projecting window-seats, the shops of the artisans spilling out their sheepskin rugs with the black cross designs, the prayer meetings hailing Allah Allah to the squatting Bedouin, and men as donkeys carrying swollen loads through the hugger-mugger of alleys that led to the myriad holy places of the sects and lost the visitor seeking Calvary. The Via Dolorosa was a sorrowful way, a crucifixion by car horns suddenly blaring after the walking streets of the Old City. There was a bus station under Golgotha, and the Garden of the Tomb drew tears from black whiffs of exhaust. Had Magog and his women been Christians, they might have become apostates to gain the surpassing peace of the Great Dome of the Rock, which had miraculously survived Israeli mortars, or so the bazaar said. Sitting under its octagonal walls and curved heaven of tiles, Magog was almost seduced by such propaganda for the Almighty and the faith of man. Upon this rock, Abraham had nearly sacrificed Isaac, Solomon and David had built their temples, the Ark of the Covenant had been placed, and Mahomet had landed from his steed Burak which had skipped from Mecca to there and back again in one night. Upon this rock, too many churches were built.

Magog did not go on the journey to Bethlehem, for where was the archaeology in a manger? He took Maire and the twins to Jericho to look at the hole in the ground which claimed to prove that civilization had begun nine thousand years ago in the usual umbilicus of the Middle East. The evidence was mere trash, shards of pottery, scraping tools, horn knives, pounding stones – primitive, yet enough to dominate all living things. Was this the source of all the Western world, a hole in the ground and a few armfuls of tat? Later, invited by some rich Palestinian refugees to sip mint tea in their orange groves under the Mount of Temptation, Magog thought that perhaps he had fallen rather head-over-heels into excavation as a subject of study. Still, looking at meaningless holes in the ground had always been one of the great pleasures of mankind. Perhaps archaeology would soon qualify with the movies as popular entertainment. By each picture palace, a huge pit. On the big screen, *Samson and Delilah*. In the hole, human moles delving into why the hell the rubbish below had produced the rubbish above . . .

'We will go back,' their host the sheikh was saying, pointing towards the River Jordan. 'We will drive the Jews into the sea where they came from.'

Maire picked an orange from the tree above her. It was irresistible. 'You've got lovely citrus groves here,' she said. 'Why go back?'

'We work,' the sheikh said. 'We have made this desert bear fruit. But in our lands back there, we had olives, figs, a sea wind. We will go back. We will never flee again.'

'Won't you ever accept Israel?' Magog said. 'Is there no solution short of eternal war?'

'None,' the sheikh said, 'until we win. I have six hundred men. None of them will forget their land. Not their sons. Not their sons' sons. Your crimes drove the Jews from over the sea into our land. They drove us out. We are suffering from your crimes against the Jews. You should help us, not Israel. Do you know my doctor? He is a Lord and lives in Harley Street . . .'

Help there was of a sort from the United Nations, doles of flour and corrugated iron to the million poor refugees living in their dirty camps along the way to Petra. Hatred, too, in the voices of the screaming announcers invoking the jehad daily for the destruction of Israel from the car radio of the big American limousine that swept Magog and his party along the desert roads past the camels and the Bedouin in their composed definitions against the dawn as perfect as postage stamps. Vision also, as Magog rode his horse with the mounted Maire and Rosa and Josepha through the entrance called the Sig into the lost city, the crack in the red rock fifty feet high, with the first pillars of pink sandstone beckoning beyond the slit in the cliff, the lintels and the corbels of the Nabatean Treasury cut out of the flesh of the rosy scarps, the wonder of the hewn temples and theatres and palaces melting with sun and time back into the hazard of natural shape of scarlet and vermilion stone with odd veins of azure, the body of the city lying on her back open to the spoiling of the dust devils on the wind, all this secret intricacy spread out beyond the slit of the Sig . . .

Magog looked back at the women behind him as they straddled their horses that were led by their Arab guides, and then he remembered the birth of the twins at the end of the war – abysses coming from the abyss, the continuity of the fault within flesh, the rose-red daughters that came bloody into the world from the black crack of Maire's being. Shameless and hot, Rosa pulled up her horse and used her guide's locked hands as a step to help her down to the sand.

'Isn't it all super?' she said and picked between her legs at the crease in her tight corduroy trousers, wriggling her buttocks and ignoring the Arabs watching fascinated and repelled. 'I won't be able to sit down for a week. Those bloody saddles. I haven't hurt so much since I was hurdling and I missed and it got me halfway.'

After Petra, the other lost cities of the desert. Jerash with its huge horseshoe of a forum where Pegasus must have left his print and where the soaring pillars were still waiting for Artemis to come down again to roof them with a cloud. Palmyra's oasis of palms, booby-trapped for acre on acre around with pediment and pilaster breaking the desert, mourning stumps of stone for Zenobia, sometime conquerer of the Romans. Then the Krak des Chevaliers, the original genius of the Crusader castles with its infinite capacity for taking defensive pains, a hill saddle made into a peak of blocks, impregnable and futile and lasting. And finally from Syria over the mountains to Lebanon and the evil of Baalbek, with the fields of marijuana scenting the air with blue flowers and acrid leaves round the ornate temple ruins, wrinkled and golden and fallen in their ancient venery.

At the hotel, Magog walked into Hadassah, gaunt now, her bold eyes ringed with kohl, her face browned with powder rather than sun, her hair short and permed, her dress from Paris and her shoes from Rome, elegant and Western, her peasant self gone to ground.

'Hadassah,' Magog said. '*You* here? I hardly recognize you.'

'I don't believe we've met before.' Hadassah turned and went away.

Of course, she was a Jew in Arab Lebanon. She had worked for the Haganah in Britain before the founding of Israel. She must be on a mission for her country. Magog felt the thrill of secret knowledge and conspiracy. He followed her to the stairs of the hotel.

'The temple of Bacchus,' he said softly as he passed her. 'Be there at three.' Then he climbed the stairs and did not look back.

Hadassah was not at the temple at three o'clock. The omnipresent guide was, nagging as a blister until he was bribed to leave Magog alone. Unfortunately, Magog could not bribe him easily, because he had forgotten his daily rule, always to have some small change in his pocket. Sighing, he had to buy his peace with a banknote worth a pound. Expecting little, he had to wait for his change. He knew that getting the right amount of money back would be like flaying the guide's fingers, then breaking the bones of the hand one by one as the Bedouins did when they caught a thief – if the guide at Baalbek was like all the other guides of the Levant. He was.

The action of his hand searching in his pouch grew slower and slower as he gave filthy notes and small coins to Magog. He began to shake his head, looking into Magog's eye to judge the exact moment when Magog had had enough. A pleading expression crept into his face, then a worried one, then a righteous one. When he was still three coins short of the demanded total, he stopped feeling in his pouch altogether. He had paid all, sir, OK, sir? Magog insisted on more cash, because Hadassah had not come and he still had time to waste. Another coin appeared. Magog's voice scolded and threatened. Another small coin was surrendered by a wincing, palsied hand. At this point, Magog did give up. He would never get his full change, even if he spent the whole afternoon visiting the police station with the guide. He shrugged his defeat and was rewarded with a great grin and a bow. He had lost half-an-hour and his peace of mind to save ninepence. 'It's a matter of principle,' he told himself and was not convinced.

Hadassah came at four to find Magog bored in the Temple of Bacchus, but alone. She did not apologize. She seemed angry that he had forced the meeting upon her.

'As you guessed, I'm on a mission,' she said. 'Why did you make me risk this meeting? Oh, you'll be all right, my old goy. But I could get a firing squad, just for being a Jew.'

'This is Lebanon,' Magog said. 'They're civilized here.'

'Only the most cultured people massacre the Jews,' Hadassah said. 'Forgive us for thinking that Buchenwald was just another great German musician.'

Magog smiled. Age had made Hadassah waspish.

'I know you won't tell me your mission,' he said. 'But tell me your cover.'

'It's simple,' Hadassah said. 'I'm buying hashish, beautiful dreams. The place is loaded with it. I'm the front woman for a big European combine, which has just decided to hook the next generation on hashish rather than alcohol or tobacco. The profits are bigger as it's illegal; it will appeal to an adolescent sense of rebellion against their parents' pleasures; and you don't have to pay for it in dollars.'

'It sounds a very profitable idea,' Magog said.

'Good cover stories must be good ideas,' Hadassah said. 'They've grown hashish at Baalbek ever since it was Heliopolis and they used to have all those orgies to Aphrodite and Venus. Baalbek's also a staging-post for a gang of Palestinian refugees who play at being guerrillas and are trying to get guns from China – along the old Marco Polo silk route, I suppose. They're mad, but we have to worry about it.'

'What'll you do to them?' Magog said and remembered the killing of Putney Bowles in Egypt.

'There's only one ruthless power in the Middle East,' Hadassah said, 'and that's Britain. Talk to the Arabs of the black Canberras with the engines always running in Aden, ready to rocket to hell a man or a village if the word's bad. Talk to the Iranians about which Old Man had their Prime Minister assassinated in the Second World War . . .'

'We've always understood the Arabs,' Magog said. 'What they want is gold, force, intelligence and respect in that order. We pay them only in sovereigns, we kill without question on the best information, and our whole air force will fly past for the birthday of any minor sheikh. Not to mention that we have the most desirable things on God's earth – dogs which *point* at hidden game. And if you add the fact that the desert's another kind of sea, and the camel is the ship of the desert, why wonder the Arabian Gulf is British?'

'If you're so good at being ruthless to the Arabs just for the sake of your oil,' Hadassah said, 'why grudge us our toughness when we're fighting for our land?'

'Because I don't want Israel to become a little British Empire,' Magog said. 'It's better than that. It's Zion, the Light of the World, or should be.'

'We want survival,' Hadassah said. 'We have to fight and scheme for that.'

She looked round the ruined temple of the wine-god with its fluted and dewlapped pillars on their heavy plinths, its massy charms whorishly asprawl to the fingering clouds of the sky.

'Up there,' she said, pointing to the top of a pillar, 'they've just found a woman's torso, ravaged and headless and forgotten. Things still go on here, evil things. Places stay what they were.'

'Oscar Wilde's swallows used to fly to Baalbek to nest in winter,' Magog said. 'They liked it here.'

'Baalbek is evil.' Hadassah shivered in the sun. 'The place of abomination and desolation, cursed by the Old Testament. Not like Israel.'

'Israel was cursed too, when it turned to false gods in the Bible,' Magog said. 'Gog told me that Britain was the first Holy Land before we sinned. You were only the second. Don't lose that sacred privilege to Africa. Will it be the third hope of the world?'

Hadassah smiled.

'We'll see what we can build,' she said. 'If we survive. Who's that?'

In the yellow leer of the temple entrance, Rosa stood. She looked like a boy, pausing in flight, excited to catch Magog in a rendezvous with a woman. The sun that softened the stone into fat shapes of dropsy now lighted a glint of conspiracy in Rosa's eyes, now defined her young body into hard lines worth the chase. Magog hungered for her suddenly, longed to catch her, wished she had not found him with Hadassah, was ashamed to see that Hadassah had surprised the need for Rosa in his look.

'See you later,' Magog called to Rosa. She smiled as if she shared something only with him, then went.

'Rosa? Maire's daughter?' Hadassah asked. 'Are they with you?'

'Yes.'

'I must go then. Maire will know me.'

'Yes.'

'That Rosa will cause you trouble. She is too like Maire. Wicked and bored. Baalbek suits her. Any love goes at Baalbek.'

'Don't be silly,' Magog said. 'I can't think of Rosa in that way.'

'I came here by the Dog River,' Hadassah said. 'That's where they killed Adonis. The river's blue naturally, but every spring it turns blood-red for Adonis, just as the oleanders come out with their pink flowers.'

'Why mention that?'

'Because I thought of the Dog River, seeing Rosa and you. You'll have trouble with her, right here in Lebanon. I feel it. If not this trip, later.'

'Never. She's sixteen and perhaps my daughter and I won't ever come back here. Don't give me all that Jewish prophecy!'

'We always say we'll never come back, things won't happen, then they do,' Hadassah said. 'We all do what we must do and in the places that make us do it.'

'Must we meet again?' Magog asked ironically.

'Once more, I think,' Hadassah said and smiled. 'When Israel is Zion at last, we will meet. I will arrange it and you must not refuse to come. I shall make you confess in public that you are a damn cynic and unbeliever. For we will have our Jerusalem . . .'

The party in the Piccadilly bookshop for the launching of Magog's masterwork on Avebury, now subtitled *The Riddle of the Stones*, was a diplomatic triumph. Magog had done his research on the literary editors and the reviewers, and he had found that the critics were not in a conspiracy against the creators, as long as they recognized the writer's reputation and could hunt in a pack. No reviewer liked to find himself out in the cold, praising a book which everybody else damned, especially if there might be factual mistakes in the work which would show up the critic's negligence or ignorance. Busy reviewers had to be careful about the company they read – or failed to read if they were dashing off their piece in a hurry. Equally, no literary editor wanted to give space to a book which his rivals ignored, for fear that he might seem to lack discrimination or to favour friends. The world of reviewers could not be bought, but it was prone to influence by a general susurrus for months beforehand that a coming book was good, good, good.

Magog had arranged a whispering campaign through his twelve disciples and the Great Synthesizer, who had demanded another two hundred and fifty guineas to cover his literary lunches. When Magog received advanced proofs of the reviews for his book, he thought the money had been well spent. Like the professional that he was, the Great Synthesizer had suggested the right adjectives in the right ears from the *Sunday Times* to the *New Statesman* – 'remarkable', 'penetrating', 'cogent', 'major work of scholarship', 'elegant', and one 'seminal' from the *Spectator*. Magog was glad to find that he had played safe and had discarded Gog's wild notions. Such adjectives from such quarters showed his fundamental learning. Magog had to begin with an established reputation. Only learners could afford to run risks.

Magog acted with becoming humility at the gathering on the panelled first floor of the best book emporium in London. He disclaimed his evident achievement. 'Written in the intervals of public service . . .' he murmured. 'A minor first fruit . . . The need for the interpenetration between the business and the academic worlds . . . A little work, but my poor best . . . I never talk of my future plans, it might only embarrass myself and you . . .' He bent his scythe of a nose deferentially to the level of the bald crown of the most lethal critic of them all, he mumbled answers to the complacent roaring of the king of the beasts whose ground was the most-read page in town. 'So much to learn from the reviewers who don't like me . . . Beneath every civil servant's bowler there's a Baudelaire trying to break out . . . I dabbled in property only to learn more about building at first hand, through the modern to the ancient . . .'

The weary marchers stood in their tens of thousands or sat at Nelson's feet as he perched blind and high above them on his column, a roost for the pigeons of Trafalgar Square who did not care a fart for his victory. Swollen feet, hot bodies, cold faces filled the paved acre. The statues of the lions were swarming with spectators, the barriers set up by the enclosing policemen were bending under the weight of the mass of protestors. Three days, three nights, most of the crowd had marched from Aldermaston, where the nuclear research station was. Some women had wheeled babies in prams all the way, others had carried them on their backs like papooses. The marchers had slept badly, they were hungry, their hope was high. 'Ban the Bomb,' they chanted, 'Ban the Bomb!' Or else 'Macmillan No, Macmillan No, Macmillan No No No No No!' Now they were listening to the old beaked eagle of a philosopher with his white crest of hair, who had somehow risen from the grave and the last century to speak for the rational progress of humanity against the dirty deaths of burst megatons seeping invisible through the air.

Gog was pressed into the pack of the crowd, squashed against Josepha, his head blurry, hearing nothing, feeling only the warmth of the plump girl against his arm and left side. Ah, daughter, who summoned him from the peace of the north to her turmoils, cry, Gog, Gog, they are spraying the seasons with pesticides, the rays of the sun are radiation, the dew is leukaemia, Cancer is in orbit over Moscow, Scorpio spins over Washington, between the crab and the spider we shall be sucked and stung and webbed into extinction, we must march now on a crusade for the cradle and the bed, a crusade for the garden and the children, a crusade for the fruits of Eden and the joy of Jerusalem. We must march, Gog, in our thousands and our tens of thousands, until the people are all marching, million on million against the rulers, saying, We have life, all we have is our lives, ban the Bomb, ban the Bomb, ban the Bomb . . . And the rulers do not listen, for they fear to hear the people.

'What was that you said?' Magog could not make out the murmurings of the gossip columnist beside him, who was suggesting something so slyly that he seemed to want the words to be part of the discreet hubbub of the whole party.

'*Adopted* by the Ponsonbys,' the gossip columnist said. 'That's what they say.'

'The Ponsonbys have always been a father and mother to me,' Magog said shortly, but not rudely. The gossip column was read by ten million readers. It would help the book.

'In the file we have on you in the morgue, there's a clipping about you as a civil servant. You were mentioned in a Tribunal. Bribery, wasn't it?'

'I was innocent, therefore acquitted, except in the stale memory of newspapers.'

'Your property dealings . . . everybody's fascinated by

property. You become a millionaire in a *very* short time, in spite
of our tax structure . . .'

'I had good luck.'

'Your brother, George Griffin I believe, is a landed gentleman.
I don't understand your *adoption* if your actual parents were so
well off . . .'

Magog felt anger.

'Old families don't talk of their affairs. We leave that to
guttersnipes.'

The gossip columnist smiled. He was an old hand at fielding
bouncers thrown at his sleek head.

'That's all the people want to read about, bless them,' he said.
'Lords and Hons and rich men like you.'

The paving slabs were hard on the bum, Gog felt himself
petrifying, chipped by the chiselling wind into his own statue,
squatting at the entrance to Downing Street, his arms locked
over his knees, alongside the odd hundred who were holding
the last thin red line against the bully boys in blue, waiting in
their three ranks with the twelve mounted coppers on their
brown horses beyond, cossacks ready for the charge that
wouldn't come at such passive resistance. Now the sirens of
the evening and the Black Marias parking nearby and the
police squads picking up the limp squatters by the armpits and
hoisting them into the vans with the barred windows to spend
the night in the cells and to be on a charge in the morning.
And god knew where were the rights that Pym and Hampden
had fought for, the rights of assembly and free speech, the
duty of saying No to the tyranny of Whitehall, No, No, No,
No, No, I am a Briton, I will not, I refuse. Now the coppers
were taking Josepha away, she sagging in their dark grip,
what had the anarchists sung on the long march from Aldermaston, the old Wobbly songs and the songs of Spain and the
chant to tease – 'All fuzz are bastards . . .'

So Gog rose and smote the bluebottles on face and chest,
hip and thigh. He brought one down, he brought two, he
grappled with a third. They dropped Josepha and came in a
wave on Gog. And he swung and thrust and hulked and bent
and bowed and fell under their blows battering him down, but

the last sight he saw was the weeping face of Josepha, white and wailing above the blue legs and black boots trampling, a voice from the sky, 'Gog, it's for peace, it's for peace . . . '

The final guest had gone as Magog turned to find his publisher still there.

'I never told you,' the publisher said. 'The advance subscription is six thousand. It's unprecedented for a serious archaeological work.'

'I know how to operate,' Magog said. 'Authors should know a bit about business. Then they wouldn't let you exploit them so much, would they?'

The publisher laughed. Magog would have his little joke.

'A message,' the bookshop manager said behind Magog. 'Your brother and your niece, Mr Ponsonby. They're at the police station. Something about a *demonstration*.'

The word seemed obscene in the empty room lined with oak and books on solid shelves, with only the three respectable men looking at each other and a few waiters in tails already putting away the last of the champagne glasses and the silver trays for snacks.

'Relations,' Magog said. 'If I were to define the word trouble, I would say – relations . . . and not even intimate ones.'

The bookshop manager and the publisher laughed. They both thought Magog should perform well on television when promoting his book.

'Still,' Magog added, 'one is born into a family and a country. One just has to put up with it, I suppose.'

1962

'Your new appointment's a sort of dictatorship, I presume,' Sir George Germain said. 'I can't imagine you settling for anything less than control, Magnus.'

'Officially, the dons can vote on various things,' Magog said. 'But I doubt if I will let things get to that sorry pass.'

Magog sat with his old chief in the Athenaeum. The leather armchairs were dented with wear, the cigars were mature, the port venerable, the waiters exhumed. Sir George was now at the top of the Civil Service, the Prime Minister's most trusted adviser, always at the ear of the Patronage Secretary. He had put in a word for Magog, who had been made the Master of the second new college at Cambridge founded since the war – the College of Charles the Martyr, the result of a stupendous and surprise bequest from a Scots shipbuilder who still thought that krauts shouldn't sit on the British throne and wanted to provide for a new breed of students for the Stuarts. Naturally, nobody cared about the delusions of the dead benefactor as long as his money was good, and it was. Magog was grateful to Germain for getting him the plum post; but then, as Machiavelli had pointed out, a man's opportunities were only half his luck. The other half was his skill, and Magog's skill lay in knowing how to use the right people.

'Are you going in for co-education?' Sir George asked. 'That's the way to drag Cambridge mewling and puking into this century.'

'Boys and girls together at Charles the Martyr?' Magog said. 'What do you want me to do? Run a college or a crêche?'

'Co-education's in the wind, you know. If you don't opt for it, Magnus, somebody else will. Churchill College might as your rival in the novelty stakes. And as for King's, you can never trust it not to leap on the bleak future without sacrificing a single luxury from the fat past. Also, there's nothing like a bit of fanny to disguise the local fairies. I'm sorry, incidentally, I couldn't arrange a Vice-Chancellorship for you. But really, there were only those rather experimental northern universities beyond the Potteries, and a fellow simply can't exist more than sixty miles from London.'

'I couldn't have expected a Vice-Chancellorship,' Magog said, 'with only one work of scholarship to my credit.'

'And a very good work too,' Sir George said. 'Without disrespect, I never knew you had it in you.'

'Hidden talents,' Magog said, then laughed. 'Sometimes I feel there are dozens of academics marching to the beat of my brain.'

'Still, what has writing books got to do with running colleges? Your appointment was absolutely just. There was your Civil Service experience, your knowledge of building and your wealthy contacts. Administration, architecture and fund-raising are the three qualities that the Master of a new college needs. Charles the Martyr is very lucky to have you.'

'Too kind, George.'

'I presume you're not going in for any of that silly stuff about student representation on the College Council, are you?'

'No need if I throw the girls to the young men. Who has time for politics when he's got a free fuck in the same corridor? And anyway, George, I must confess that I am personally concerned about the lack of places for girls at Cambridge. I actually have two daughters . . .'

'Really? You always kept rather mum about them.'

'One doesn't mention brats until they are fit to come down to dinner,' Magog said. 'Of course, I wouldn't actually have Rosa and Josepha at Charles the Martyr, it might smack of favouritism. But I am sure I can trade with Newnham or Girton. Four of their girls whom they can't quite fit in for two of mine.'

'Horse-dealing at a university? Shame on you, Magnus. All undergraduates are chosen strictly on merit now, without pulling any strings. You've spent too long manipulating property schemes. The air's pure in Cambridge.'

'Not when the wind blows off the Fens,' Magog said. 'I bet you a Cambridge college is worse than any corporation. Good god, it isn't even answerable to its shareholders. And whoever heard of a student *strike*?'

'Is that why you're going up there?' Sir George asked. 'To find total control and respect?'

Magog studied the acute oldish man sitting opposite him. He was grey-haired, his face chalky with only a faint wine-flush in either cheek, his weary eyes ringed with small cysts, even his knighthood a mere sneer at such fatigue endured in the name of duty. Magog wanted to do better for himself in the end.

'I'd like to pull out for a while, to think, to get back my own self-respect before I earned anybody else's. And . . .' Magog fell silent. He closed his eyes, trying to conjure up again the vision of Rupert's helmet of short curls, his grace in the fives court, his languor in the Eton graveyard that last night when Magog was in love and in supremacy of self. He saw nothing, however, behind his lids but red fire burning out Rupert's image, so he opened his eyes to the sight of his friend Germain, who had survived into premature age. There was something to dying young.

'Absolute mastery over a little world . . .' Sir George Germain said. 'Wasn't there that fellow Tom in *The Great Gatsby* who reached such an acute limited excellence at twenty-one that everything afterwards was an anti-climax? To be King Frog in a respectable puddle at only forty – I'd rather like that for myself.'

'You can't get absolute control over a whole nation,' Magog said. 'Even Napoleon failed. You can only get it in a group where you know everybody's face and they know you. That's real power. You have to limit your range.'

'I hope you get it,' Sir George said. 'Power's a slippery fish. I've seen it wriggle out of too many men's fingers.'

'I'll gaff it,' Magog said and finished his port.

The meeting between Merry, Maire, Magog and the Ponsonbys could no longer be postponed. Rosa and Josepha had precipitated the crisis. Suddenly, anybody who could possibly be connected to them wanted to own up to them. Two desirable young women, who might have male children to carry on family names as well as interesting adults with the sexual problems of adolescence, could hardly go begging for kinship or for guardians in this world. A family council was summoned to settle their fate and their holidays. Gog was not invited. There had to be a rational solution.

'There must be a way of establishing their . . . um . . . paternity,' the Honourable Digby Ponsonby said. He stood in front of the open fire at Cormonderley, his hands pushing his trouser pockets forwards to make the seat of his pants tight across the buttocks. As with many old men, his rear seemed to have slid across to his belly, so that he had a paunch and an inconsiderable bum, the opposite from old women, whose fore tended to slide aft. Digby fancied the fire. It made his arse warm and eased his piles.

'Blood tests are rather unsatisfactory,' Magog said. 'Especially when the two fathers are half-brothers. Anyway, one could hardly go to court and tell the story there. Not even Solomon could judge this misbegotten matter.'

'I should think *not*,' said Amy Ponsonby, Lady Burke-Gotha-Stubbs, Baroness in her own right and damn anyone who forgot it, she was the fourth of a quartet of wealthy sisters who had danced away the twenties, frittered away the thirties, hoarded away the forties, soused away the fifties, and were now looking for a way to malinger through the sixties. She had been called handsome, a fine figure of a woman, when she was young and rich; now that she was sixty-one and still rich, she was told that she was imposing and wore well. Her aged nanny of eighty-eight still called her 'Child', but this was the only licence she permitted.

'There must be a . . . um . . . resemblance,' Digby said.

'Well, Josepha's well built like Gog, but has a studious temperament like me,' Magog said. 'And Rosa's thin and well-made like me, but has an adventurous streak like Maire or perhaps Gog. It's hard to know where the blame lies for them.'

'They're both *mine*,' Maire said. 'And I'm part of the family. I really can't see the problem.'

'You could have been more careful,' Amy said.

'Who couldn't?' Maire said.

'The problem is . . . um . . . inheritance.' The Honourable Digby Ponsonby looked round the high Palladian room, the two noble horse-paintings, the ancestral portraits of clodhoppers in red coats and plain ladies with breasts like turnips above ruched jewelled gowns, and he considered the view of the deep park through the french windows. 'Childless as we are in a manner of speaking . . . um . . . Not forgetting you, my dear Magnus . . . um . . . The very last of the Ponsonbys, all good things come to an end . . . um . . . We would not like to see five hundred years of effort all go in death duties . . . um . . . There's the estate to think of.'

'A trust for the grandchildren, or better, the great-grandchildren.' Amy turned to Maire. 'You're a woman of the world, evidently. Couldn't you get one of your daughters to buck up a bit and breed?'

'They'll breed in their own bad time,' Maire said. 'I can't be expected to be a madam for my own daughters.'

'They're old enough to Come Out next year,' Amy said. 'During the course of the Season, I am sure we can arrange suitable matches. By Ascot, I remember turning down a score of young men, but then I was very eligible . . .'

'You are still eligible,' Digby said, 'for an . . . um . . . old age pension. That is the problem, you see. Amy and I are not in the first flush of youth.' From behind him came the delicious odour of roasting chestnuts or toasting marshmallows. Or were his trousers beginning to burn?

'You'll live for ever,' Magog said, hoping this was not true. Statistics were on his side.

'That wicked law on death duties does mean we have to live for five years beyond the time we have given everything away . . . um . . . One might call it a life duty . . . um . . . One has a duty to live that little bit longer to pass on the goodies, what?'

Magog could see that he was meant to laugh. He laughed. Then he made a quick suggestion.

'If you passed it on to me now,' he said, 'I could pass it on in due time to my male grandchildren.'

'You're wealthy yourself,' Digby said. 'Your . . . um . . . mother, Amy, and I . . .'

'Mother be damned,' Merry said. She had been swilling gin all lunchtime and had relapsed into a coma on the sofa, a fat red lady suffering from corsets and heartburn. But the mention of motherhood had revived her. 'Magog hasn't got two bloody mothers. Even if those poor bloody twinkins have two dads.'

'I use the word mother . . . um . . . as a shorthand for foster-mother . . . um . . . I am sure, dear Mrs Griffin, you will take the remark in the spirit it was intended, what?'

'Give her another tot,' Amy said. Magog took the decanter of gin across and filled his mother's glass.

'Neat, dear,' Merry said. 'I do like everything neat.' And she gulped her drink down and fell back in a sprawl on the sofa.

Smoke was now rising from Digby's rear. The stink of scorching smelt more like worsted than bread. Digby seemed unaware. His sore bum was being grilled into the peace of ashes.

'As I was saying,' Digby said to Magog, 'you have made your own piles and you must sit upon them . . . um . . . it, I mean . . . Suppose you pipped off before us by some mischance, terrible road accidents these days, and it doesn't help telling the Lord Lieutenant about it . . . um . . . What we need is a Ponsonby family trust for the twins' male children . . .'

'And the girls do need to be pretty nippy about putting something in the oven,' Amy said. 'Digby's getting rather gamey and I can feel my old bones.'

Magog had always admired the way that people from ancient families seemed indifferent about death. Perhaps a sense of the continuity of their name made the grave seem merely a stepping-stone on the family way.

'What about giving it all to the girls direct?' Maire asked.

'Don't be a twit,' Amy said. 'They'd spend it all on froufrous. A trust for their male heirs, who must take the name Ponsonby-Burke-Gotha-Stubbs.'

'Four barrels are better than one in a name,' Digby said, 'as long as Ponsonby comes last.'

'What's changing the brand name from Griffin worth to the girls?' Maire asked.

Magog looked horrified at Maire. As usual, she had crossed the barriers of good taste. One never mentioned the size of an inheritance until the meeting in the lawyer's office after the funeral, and then one could only hint blue murder at the foul wrongs of the will.

'Is this quite the time and place, Maire?' Digby asked.

'How much? They're *my* daughters.'

'Tell her,' Amy said. 'She always did have a heart of gold. It clinks all the way to the bank.'

Maire laughed.

'I never knew you were so witty, Amy. I always thought you were just plain nasty. How much?'

'I don't guarantee . . . um . . . nine figures,' Digby said. 'But a comfortable eight.'

'Ten *million*?' Maire asked, and even Magog was surprised. He felt his heart jump slightly. Once love had made him palpitate. Now his tremors only warned of cardiac trouble or future fortunes.

'I don't quite say that much, but with shares doing tolerably decently, and our investments in South Africa really rather sound . . . um . . . stout chappies out there, know how to manage their labour problems . . . um . . . but don't let's talk about money, it makes me feel rather like a Jewboy . . . um . . . and I don't think even my worst enemy could call me that . . .'

As Maire said, 'Anti-Semites are the very worst,' she saw that Digby was on fire. Wreathed in smoke like a pantomime Lucifer with flames licking from his lower regions, he suddenly leapt forwards as Maire rose. The fire this time.

'My arse!' he chanted. 'My thundering arse! My balls are burning!'

Maire caught him in her arms and rolled with him across the Feraghan carpet, smothering the smouldering trousers on the galli-henna design and the red lotus-herati border. Both Digby and Maire knew their carpets, because Digby was always having his rugs appraised for insurance, while Maire was always calculating a man's income by what he trod upon.

'You're out,' Maire said and rose from her embrace with the fiery Digby. She picked up a petit-point cloth off an occasional table and wrapped it round Digby's singed rump like a kilt.

'I'll get the vaseline,' Amy said. 'When in doubt, get the vaseline. Digby, you are a chump.'

She rose and left as Merry woke up, screaming.

'Call the Fire Brigade.'

'It's only Digby getting parboiled,' Magog soothed his mother.

'Thank god it's not serious,' Merry said. 'As long as it's not my baby.' She clung on to Magog's arm and began to weep. 'My baby, I never meant to give you away.'

Magog was embarrassed. He tried to loosen his mother's grip, but she hung on to him.

'That's all in the past, Merry,' he said. 'I'm a middle-aged man. What's done is done. I don't hold it against you.'

'I shouldn't have,' Merry blubbered. 'I shouldn't have done it at all. But you couldn't keep an illegit then. Not like now, when you can flaunt your little errors.'

Digby lay on his stomach on the ground and looked upwards. He seemed strangely happy.

'I've burned them off,' he said. 'My piles. Singed them off.'

'There's was a Yorkshire squire who once cured the hiccups by setting his bed on fire,' Magog said. 'He got scorched, but it did the trick.'

'I couldn't sit down anyway,' Digby said. 'And it's more . . . um . . . dignified to say you've set your arse alight than to say you've got piles.'

Merry started sobbing again, pure gin trickling down her swollen cheeks.

'You don't know what it is to be a mother,' she wept. 'Every time I see you, Magog, I don't see you six feet tall, a bloody great ox. I just see a little tiny baby . . . and I gave you away . . .'

It was Maire's day to be a Samaritan. Sometimes she surprised herself by her good behaviour, though her help could be dangerous. She never allowed people to forget it.

'I know,' Maire said. She sat beside Merry on the sofa and let her weep. 'Men can't know. That great lump coming out of you and then growing bigger and bigger and somehow you always think of that small dependent thing clinging on to you for dear life. Men don't know. I do.'

She held the sobbing Merry, while Magog helped Digby to his feet.

'There's only one thing wrong with your plans, Digby,' he said. 'We haven't told the girls. I don't think Rosa will care for Coming Out, and Josepha's at the French Lycée in Kensington. She wants to study and be useful, or something.'

'Girls will do as they're told to,' Digby said. 'I say, Magnus, I bet you never thought your old *father* would go down in the annals of medicine as a . . . um . . . pioneer. Ponsonby's Instant Pile Cure. Anybody can do it in his own home by his own hearth. Ponsonby's heroic experiment. Could you get a snifter of brandy, old chap, for a . . . um . . . guinea-pig needing revival?'

Dearest Rosa–Josepha, Gog wrote, I'm sorry you won't be coming up to be with me this Christmas. I'm glad you're potty over French, Josepha, you'll make your mother very happy, and if you have to take time off to find yourself, Rosa, everybody does that some time or another, though I'm not sure that the jazz cellars and riverboat shuffles and cappuccino bars are where you will find your soul. Still, I did know a sailor in the war who had his first religious experience when a gull dropped a perfect cross of white birdshit on the guardroom windowsill at Malta. The spirit moves in mysterious ways, his wonders to perform . . .

It's just as well in a way that you're not coming up, though I shall miss you both sorely. Karl Klock died with his arms pointing to thirteen minutes past midnight, which gives the local witches something to worry about, as nothing much has happened here since Macbeth. And the fish farm is progressing well. I am sure it is the only future of these highlands. I have been rereading the *Compleat Angler* lately, and I am trying to follow old Isaac Walton's advice from Ecclesiastes – STUDY TO BE QUIET. I recommend strongly that advice, although I am always fighting against the enemies of my salmon and salmon fry; the lobsters are armoured enough to look after themselves. Dear Isaac praised the Otter-Catcher, but I may not catch him – he is too delightful a beast for that. So I must just go along with Isaac and say, 'the poor fish have enemies enough besides unnatural fishermen; as, namely, the Otters, the Cormorant, the Bittern, the Osprey, the Seagull, the Hern, the King-fisher, the Gorora, the Puet, the Swan, Goose, Duck, and the Craber, which some call the Water-rat: against all which any honest man may make a just quarrel, but I will not; I will leave them to be quarrelled with and killed by others, for I am not of a cruel nature. I love to kill nothing but fish' – and frankly, I even hate to do that, but others must eat, and I suppose I have to.

Still, enough of that. As they say, come and live in the country, nothing ever happens round here. What do you think of the Chinese invading India, then going home again? They're really fine fellows. I hope that when we get out of the Empire finally, the Chinese will come in to take our place. Their trouble is that they like home so much that they can't be bothered to boss people abroad. I've always felt that somehow the Chinese had wisdom, and if the Celts weren't the original wise people, the Chinese were. Anyway, it's hard to believe

in the remnants of our ancient wisdom when that old poseur
Macmillan goes on being Prime Minister without end, amen,
and nothing happens at all except the rich get richer, and the
poor don't notice they never had it so indifferent. There must
be a bit more to Britain than a weary Harry reading Latin
verse to send himself to sleep while the whole island sinks in
a coma of inertia back into the North Sea. I'm afraid we are
handing on to you not much of a heritage, I know you'll do
better for Albion than we did, Magog and I and our lot, we've
made such a sad mess of it when we had such an opportunity
after the end of the war. But what won't flower in this green
and ancient land from your brains, from your loins, Josepha
my lovely, Rosa of England . . .

all my love
Gog

1963

'Have you heard about what fun and games the three Cardinals
had?' Maire asked.

'I have heard about the nine High Court Judges having an orgy
in the Middle Temple,' Magog said. 'I have heard about the
naked member of the Cabinet serving as a maid at dinner and
wearing only three white feathers and the motto, *Ich Dien – Me
Flagellate*. I have heard of the Royal Duke caught between two
tarts like caviar between rye crisps. And I have heard of a War
Minister lying publicly in the Commons about not lying privately
outside it. But I haven't yet heard about what fun and games
the three Cardinals had.'

'Nun,' Maire said.

She laughed, and Magog did not.

In the storm of the great scandal that was blowing down the
Macmillan government, nobody stood so high that he might not

topple from his crow's nest. Something was rotten at the top, and everyone knew it. Naturally, there were always weaknesses of the flesh, although hardly of the spirit, in the cabins of the great. Yet the hold which the government had over the people depended on keeping everything battened down. The gossip about the scandal in the Cabinet had breezed about the clubs for months before it had reached the press and the vocal members of Her Majesty's Opposition, but now that the gale was rising, the whole anchor of power was dragging. The Conservatives were usually chosen to command because they seemed to have some sort of divine right. Apparently, a High Tory was better than you and me. But with rumours flying as loose as gulls and as far as the Hebrides, the Ark Royal of England seemed no more than an ancient bum boat where aged panders were trying to sell stink-fish to the sailors while they waited for the latest virgin, guaranteed farm-fresh from Suez.

'I would think there was a conspiracy against this nation,' Magog said, 'if only I didn't know that we could ruin ourselves without any help from abroad. Of course, God did send us a terrible freeze-up in the winter and de Gaulle did prevent us from joining the Common Market, but we can certainly survive the spite of the Almighty. What we can't do is to live under a government caught exhibiting itself in a urinal in Fleet Street. Pissoirs are only for mass use. Gentlemen do not patronize public lavatories. If they have natural functions, they deal with them in private.'

'Don't be so pompous, Magog. Everybody's got a right to a mistress. Look at you and me.'

'I'm not married,' Magog said.

'I am, to Gog. And I'm still your mistress.'

'If I were in a responsible position, I would not allow any indiscretion.'

'Are you going to give me up, when you start being Master of that silly new Cambridge college?'

'Nobody gives you up, Maire. That would need surgery. But I won't let you visit me at Charles the Martyr. People would talk.'

'People always do. That's what they have tongues for. But how are you going to stop me from coming? Suppose I'm visiting my daughters? Or are you going to have no curtains on the Master's Lodge, just to show what a Holy Goldfish you are in your beautiful bowl?'

'If one's trying to set an example,' Magog said, 'one might as well set it. The rot's spread awfully far and awfully high. The young must be able to look up to somebody.'

'You?'

'Why not?'

Maire began to laugh.

'Oh, Magog, do look in a mirror one day. Can't you see what others see? A rich, domineering, paunchy fellow, so much in love with his own art of manipulation that he's forgotten hands can do more than pull strings. They can play flutes, touch up women, pick noses, thumb a lift. The young men don't want to learn how to play the power game for twenty years only to find, when they've won, they're too old to enjoy the victory.'

'We'll see,' Magog said. 'The young have to look up to something or they fall over their own feet. And even if I can't inspire them, I can guide them. And keep an eye on Rosa and Josepha.'

'Josepha will get to Cambridge all right,' Maire said. 'She's top of her group in the Lycée. But Rosa . . . she never goes to school. You'll have to break a few arms to get her into Cambridge, and then you won't keep her there, even if you steal her clothes – she never seems to wear any. She's talking of Art School now, which means she won't learn a damn thing except to do what she wants, only more so.'

'I'm worried about Rosa,' Magog said. 'She won't let me do anything for her. Perhaps it's a phase, the natural rebellion of seventeen.'

'You can't do anything for a girl who won't let you help and can always find a man to live off,' Maire said. 'I can't get through to her mind these days. You know, Magog, sometimes I feel Rosa's sick . . .'

Sweetass I thought of you in Piccadilly and it was nearly fatal.

Listen, I'm walking along Piccadilly carrying this super bag with a new striped dress to witch you when you came back

from Africa, but passing Fortnum and Mason I am suddenly
diz. Fainting for you that's normal daily only to be expected,
but not this – this way I bleed for you, in warm sticky rushes
from all the joins of my body and my stomach all tight as I
long for you. Bleeding bleeding I must find a chemist a friend
a locker before I am a bloody mess a spectacle in Piccadilly.
I begin to hobble full of shame somebody may notice and I
hold my clothes to me so I kind of jive at every step my legs
close. All that way from you Sweetass knifes me inside soon
the blood will show below the hem of my dress are the backs
of my knees oozing too? What shall I do where shall I hide
can I make it to the loo in the Underground and wait till it
passes – if – and then maybe wash away the stains the wounds
have a heart in one piece again. Blood also from my armpits
like soft glue oh Sweetass how much worse is your curse than
Eve's. Thighs together to hold this from the crowd I cannot
make it down those steps. Look *A Taste of Honey* at the
Criterion Theatre there's dark below let me in I'm a goner
Rosa poor Rosa. But the bitter ones at the box office have no
mercy as I lean at their window whimpering May I go please
miss may I? Oh no, you'd never find it down there in the dark
and we get enough of your sort anyway. My sort? Like this?
Haemorrhaging in their foyer? I move scaredy-cat from the
window of their cage. I can no more go out into Piccadilly
Circus traffic roaring gas Eros, so I lean weakly against the
dark wood between the mirrors and sobs come in rhythm
with the blood. Sweetass Brown, bang that thing, break it.
Here comes a bright-glassed woman plasticked against the
rain to buy tickets for the show tonight and I will still be here
empty of blood then with the others she will slush through
the gore while I lie in my mess and they in their wooden safe
will make tea and say No miss you can't not your sort.
Sweetass Sweetass Brown. Jerks of sickness of loss of never
see you again. Are you all right dear? You don't look too good.
I am not too good and they won't help me I am suffering from
a miscarriage I think. Oh you poor duck, sit down I'll get . . .
I can't sit I can't but just make them, let me telephone who
to? to Kenya? Sweetass what shall I do help me I'm bleeding
in the foyer of the Criterion Theatre Piccadilly he said he'd taken

the baby out I'd be all right in a couple of days this is a week
later why do men have to lie why do men have to lie why did
I forget the Pill did I want it? I'm bleeding for you Sweetass
Brown I want you to come back to me no troubles just the
same as ever can it ever be just the same as ever? At
the box office they drink their tea crammed together with the
money the telephone the seating plans and it must be stuffy
in there pretty soon they won't be able to come out for the
blood they have let spill drip filter smoothly along the nylon
my legs. Look, love, I'll call an ambulance from the chemists
they're difficult here. No no I don't need an ambulance I
need . . . But she has seen the blood (it's real then, this
draining for you, Sweetass). Now it's much too late there is
blood running hot from my eyes salt my face is shivering my
hands move over my tummy trying to find each other to hold
on to don't look in the mirrors and see me miz so miz it is bad
I know because people coming in to buy tickets back out
mustn't get involved. Ha you manky money-changers I am
bad for your takings today. I cannot cannot hold my body
together the blood is moving from me taking over from me.
She's back in her apricot rims super lady – It's coming soon
coming soon. When Sweetass when? We wait she wants to
stroke my hands but they move too fast for her to catch. It's
all this traffic dear but any minute now I expect. I'll hold your
bag and umbrella mustn't forget them must we? (Sweetass,
my skin used to keep me from the weather the world but not
now since you touched me you leave me bleeding somehow
new skin won't grow won't grow at all now you have touched
me all over. Sweetass I have no scalp not even) Here they
are you'll be OK soon. Never never you don't understand
(this is a miscarriage of love spooned out it can't grow now
the boy if it's not even afterbirth just after-mess mine own
abortioner nowhere for the boy to hold on and feed gently
within lying on your flank Sweetass come back come back I
want him again if you want him Sweetass) No no she can't
walk to the ambulance can't you see she's lost a lot. The
muscles move in my face, they won't stay still, too tired to
keep them down. The men carry me in a little chair to the
ambulance past that murdering box office quickly quickly or I

will die of exposure to the curious of Piccadilly. Those are lovely black windows I wish I had some to wear. My friend with the apricot rims and prawn curls explains about the box office all is good in her world. Oh yes, they get a lot of trouble with the drug addicts going to the all-night chemists probably thought you were one. But anyone can tell you're not, you're a young lady who likes a bit of fancy dress. (Thank you, but you're the only lady even though a Pommy and too short and too fat you are a true lady they haven't forgot how to help a stranger out there. I am no lady I am Sweetass's tart he does as he does with me I am drilled through by his beautiful prick pounded under his brown chest oh damn you Sweetass). It must be the movement dear makes you so sick. No I retch for fear I'll die among the green tiles and green ceilings while you look for drum beats man in Africa where it came from way back in Africa.

Sweetass they have transfused me tranquillized me dripped into me another's blood not mine not yours now I am resting. How long will strange blood protect me I have none of my own left I must rest rest for months here under the green ceiling no green jungle like over you where you are Sweetass in Africa.

Sweetass how long the longing they say I may die next time I've always got to be ready for something to go wrong with me.

Sweetass Brown.

Rosa did not make medical history, but it was a rare case all the same. She lay in the London Clinic for five-and-a-half months at Magog's expense while she was pregnant. The doctors told Magog that she would have had twins, perhaps they ran in the family. Magog nodded. The doctors said that her abortioner had only removed one of the two fertilized eggs, he had not delved deeper to find if there were more. Rosa could save one baby if she rested in bed until the actual birth. And she did so, although at times she wept at her swelling belly and brown nipples and distorted body, only to weep even louder at the thought of losing one child when she could have had two.

The Ponsonbys were secretly delighted, although publicly shocked. Of course, it would have been better if Rosa had got herself fertilized on the croquet lawns at Hurlingham or in a coach at Ascot or below decks on a yacht at Cowes. But her Coming Out had been notable only for her disappearances and her début had been only through back doors marked Exit, so the Ponsonbys had hardly expected her to pair off with the elegant noddlepates who dummied about the young ladies, sniffing for riches. Even if Rosa would not admit who the father was, one could presume on her natural good taste in biological selection when it was a matter of keeping the family going. And the absence of a father made the taking over of the baby by the Ponsonbys seem an act of Christian charity and mercy rather than a lawyer's plot to keep the estate from the government and preserve the family name. Visiting Bath Abbey, Amy, Lady Burke-Gotha-Stubbs, had been shaken by seeing a relief of a broken Corinthian pillar with the inscription:

Robert Walsh, d. 1788
By the death of this Gentleman an ancient and respectable
family in Ireland became extinct

Now, in the London Clinic, Amy had to pat Rosa's huge belly through the blankets in order to reassure herself.

'I must say, Rosa, you have been splendidly nippy about it,' Amy said, surrounded by the roses and chrysanthemums that hallowed the bed like a border in Harrogate. As she spoke, she popped Rosa's grapes one by one into her mouth. 'Couldn't wait to be a mum, could you? – plop – Get a bun in the oven, that's the ticket – plop – Can't look after the nipper yourself, not a chance – plop – He's got to have a nanny in the country like everybody does – plop – What do you say to a spin down to Monte to put the roses back in your cheeks? – plop – We'll get the nappies changed and all that bore while you whoop it up down on the Riviera – plop – Blasted nuisance being a young mum these days – plop – No fun sticking a thermometer in the milkies, I can tell you – plop – You don't want to go in for any of that breast-feeding lahdidah, I'm sure – plop – A girl needs her tits later on and suckling does turn them into sponge-bags – plop – Got to think of the future, you know, lots of carryings on to come, I shouldn't wonder – plop – Digby's going to make you an allowance, the generous old sod – plop – Two thou a year if you stay away till after the christening – plop – You don't want to be bothered with all that C of E argy-bargy, do you? – plop – Of course, you don't, lace and parsons, that's what grannies are for – plop – As there isn't a dad on the birth certificate and the poor little nipper has to have a name – plop – He might as well have a string of good names, can't do him any harm in later life – plop – We'll call him Simon for Digby's side, simple Simon if you ask me – plop – And Drogheda for my side, that's where the Irish land came from after Cromwell cleared out the bogmen – plop – Simon Drogheda Burke-Gotha-Stubbs-Ponsonby, that'll get him on in the world – plop – If you're agreeable, Digby says he'll run to an Aston Martin for you – plop – That's *your* christening present, baby can't drive – plop, plop, plop.' Amy put the last three grapes into her mouth, squelched them, swallowed them, sucked her fingers, and looked down at the ravaged stem. 'There's not so many grapes on a bunch these days, it's the fault of the government.'

'Three thousand a year,' Rosa said, 'after tax. And a Ferrari.'

'I'll have to talk to Digby about *that*, my girl.' Amy was shocked. 'You *dare* to bargain, when you're an *unmarried mother.*'

'I'll keep the child,' Rosa said, 'and call him Sugarcock.'

'What cock?'

'Sugarcock Griffin. That's all.'

Amy knew when she was beaten, but she did not like the experience.

'Three thou, then, and a Ferrari. If you drive too fast, perhaps we won't have to pay much of your allowance.'

'After taxes,' Rosa said, then wondered. 'What if he's a girl?'

'One thou and an MG,' Amy said. 'And no bargaining over a girl. Take it or leave it.' Then she reassured herself. 'But he'll be a boy. Twin sisters always have boys.'

'I hope so for my bank manager's sake,' Rosa said, then smiled sidelong and wicked. 'Does it matter how he *looks*?'

'Not at all. A boy is a boy,' Amy said. 'They all look the same when they're boys.'

Actually, Sweetass Brown was a dinky sort of caramel custard cream. He wasn't coming back from Africa, he was tuning in to those basic drums, he'd go straight on to New York, not a whisper from him, he would never know. Of course he had lovely bedspring red hair, but he cooked it in lye till he had a flat conk, the colour needn't show too much, baby Simon would always look like he was just back from a cradle-snatch to Capri. Golden tan for the silver-spoon kiddo.

'His dad had a very healthy complexion,' Rosa said. 'I think Simon may take after his super dad.'

Simon Drogheda Burke-Gotha-Stubbs-Ponsonby did not take after his super dad. He came into the world pale and freckled, with only the soft dark mouth and the red curled hair to hint at any connection with Sweetass Brown. In less time than was decent, he was taken from Rosa down to Cormonderley where a nurse and a nanny watched over him, washed under him, weighed his ounces, dandled his tantrums, waked him with diddums, fondled his sleeping, fed him, changed him, clucked to him, chuckled and chucked his chinnikins. As soon as Rosa could move, she was driven to the South of France to get her figure back and her breasts into shape so that she could attract more lusty fathers. As the milk dribbled from her nipples, she found herself crying at the waste of it, but the slackness of her stomach and the blue veins on her swollen breasts gave her such a disgust and yearning for her lost beauty that she began to think of her baby as the cause of her ugliness, which he was. And as the milk dried up in pain and her bosom shrank firm and the blubber melted in the sun from her hips and the muscles tightened their ropes across her stomach and the beach boys began to whistle and eye her in her swimsuit, she almost forgot Simon, as if he were a growth that an operation had removed for her own good. The Ponsonbys, too, were careful to write nothing about the baby's progress to his mother.

Magog's child was progressing in mud and tribulation, brick and manipulation at the rear of the Backs in Cambridge. By the squat tower of the University Library, the first temporary huts of the builders had spawned two legs of Magog's vision of the spider College of Charles the Martyr. Influenced by the Dome of the Rock at Jerusalem set high over its surrounding Crusader alleys, Magog had given the architect instructions to draw up the plans of a college that spread its eight legs of dons' and undergraduates' rooms over its two acres of ground, enclosing triangles of greenery between the long buildings instead of the usual Cambridge quads surrounded by hollow squares of rooms. The legs would join up at the base of the flattened dome, which would hold the dining-hall, library, reading-room, common rooms, buttery and a meditation room for those of various religions who missed a college chapel or just wanted a bit of peace and quiet. On top of the great dome would be the Master's Lodge, a circular eye projecting above the tarantula of Charles the Martyr.

Domes were not fashionable any more, the architects said. What's good enough for St Paul's is good enough for me, Magog said. Domes are too expensive, the architects said. Magog smiled and went to the City and raised another two million pounds in four lunches, five dinners, and two hours spent between three offices, having drinks. The price he paid for his money was not great – the admission to the College of half-a-dozen moronic sons or nephews, the naming of the library and each of the eight spider's legs for some wealthy unworthy or bitter spouse, and the making of the meditation room into an Anglican chapel with an attached parson, who happened to be the white sheep of a blackly successful family. This last concession had to be rather clandestine, for the original Scots benefactor had stipulated in his will that there was to be no chapel for the Church of England as there was in every other Cambridge college. King Charles the Martyr was a Stuart and a Scot, so to hell with the Church of England, even if King Charles was its official head, though pretty much of a Papist for all that. Religious intolerance had made King Charles into a martyr with his head officially off. The important thing was Students for the Stuarts, be they Jew or atheist or Christadelphian. So the benefactor willed. Yet Magog would let no dead man's error thwart him. He wanted his spider's eye, his dome and his eight long brick legs, and he would get them.

When the parson of the new College, the Reverend Simpkin-Smith, came to be interviewed by the Master, Magog gave him few illusions about his holy role.

'No dog-collars,' he said. 'No clerical black. We have the problem of a will that stipulates that you should not exist. Like your God, therefore, you may be present, but you must be invisible. You may not convert the young men and women, but you may encourage them to go and pray to your version of the Almighty in the meditation room, which will be called a chapel by a mason's slip of the chisel on the stonework over the door. The Anglican altar will be on a tea-trolley and will be removable. At the flick of a switch the hanging crucifix will fold up into the ceiling in three parts, yet somehow one. The religious tapestries on the wall will be mounted on roller blinds. Within moments, your Anglican chapel can be converted into a barren kirk fit for the Wee Frees. Render to Caesar that which is Caesar's . . . I have always believed that the Holy Spirit should obey the letter of the local law.'

'It sounds rather hypocritical,' the parson said.

'The fact that you are here at all is rather hypocritical,' Magog said. 'If you want to fish for souls, you have to tart up your hook with feathered flies and tinsel. In sum, my dear reverend, you are permitted here, but you are not encouraged.'

The parson nodded and left, but he did not acquiesce. Magog thought the holy fool would make trouble in the name of Christ once the dons had begun to arrive and claim their minor share of the major decisions. But until they did come, Magog's lay spider could push out its legs and raise its bulbous head from the dream made concrete of the Master's mind.

Josepha came down to Cambridge to visit Magog at the end of the year. She was still plump, but there was a harvest in her ungathered, a store of pears under her skin that made Magog's mouth pucker at the thought of the sweet juice flowing at one bite of breast or thigh. Damn this lust in him for his own likely daughters! It was idiotic, unfit for Magog. Rosa was a slut, evidently, but Josepha had a mind, an innocence, a goodness that showed in her clear eyes and easy grin. She needed education, that was all.

Magog took her on a tour of the women's colleges and she

opted for Newnham. There was no trouble about getting her accepted. She impressed everybody in her personal interviews, she was evidently intelligent and studious, the entrance examinations would be a mere formality. Magog was delighted, for once, not to have to use his influence, and Josepha was proud to succeed on her own merits. She chose to read Moral Sciences.

One thing about Josepha foxed Magog. For all her placidity, her acceptance of her sister's domination, her willingness to follow the reasonable lines drawn by others, she had a streak of stubbornness that showed in politics. Her left breast usually sported at least five tin nipples, badges for the Campaign for Nuclear Disarmament, the Congress of Racial Equality, the War on Want, Oxfam, the Committee of One Hundred, and other buttons for good causes current among the radical young. She believed wholly and fanatically in the ultimate virtue and victory of each and every crusade for a better world; she would not listen to the base facts of experience and history that each and every good cause must compromise or fail. In mid-sentence, she would slip from the sweet reason and obedience of the good daughter into the jargon of radical reform. Her only illogical tears were for the death of President John F. Kennedy. But then, who could be sensible about such active beauty and grace of power cut down by a crazed gunman in Texas?

'You've got a monument here all right,' Josepha told Magog. 'Now there's been a nuclear test ban, your smashing spider may be here for ever. What a crappy ziggurat! And Kennedy's already got his memorial in London – the new bile-green Hilton on Hyde Park, with all those fascist businessmen with their discredit cards fouling up the view. But what will remind people about *you* and JFK is the wrong sort of things you left behind you. Not your good stuff, your little acts of love, but your conspicuous waste, Charles the Martyr and the space race. You're spending enough on *one* college to build a whole university. You could house four thousand students for the luxury money you're spending on four hundred privileged bourgeois goons. What's *really* important, educating more people now, or leaving behind a Magog memorial? I don't want to get at you, Magog, you're kind to me, I'm sure you want the best for those you love. But there's always yourself, yourself, yourself big and shiny in the way of you loving people. You've got to love them through a great big daddy longlegs of you. They have to *know* you're loving them.'

'But I love you, Josepha, and I love my college.'

'I know. But when will you become big enough to make yourself so little you won't even have to show what you do for us all?'

'Even Gandhi in his loincloth,' Magog said, 'had special aeroplanes, nannygoats for his holy milk, girls to warm his old flesh. His monument was a million spinning wheels when power looms were really better for India. Don't expect too much of me, Josepha dear. I'm only human. That's the trouble. Even Masters are only human.'

1964

Gog stood by the great hole in the belly of Glasgow. He could not say that the guts had been ripped out of the city. The city had never had any guts, just ulcers, hernias, wens. Round the hole, the dark granite of the old offices tagged away into the closemouths of the slums, with the sluttish mothers and the chib-men and the far-from-bonnie hairies hanging out on the street corners. But the great hole was not for housing. No, it was for motorways, concrete leggy tapeworms crisscrossing high and low firth and forth to make foul intestines for the city centre, evacuating the lorries and limousines to the south and the airport from the maw of the great void called Glasgow. Once sheep ate men, now cars ate men, but men could eat sheep. Cars were a harder diet and their breath was bad.

Yet as Gog turned towards the north-west, he was lost in a glory of evening. There was a gold scar flung across the hills towards Loch Lomond. Out of the brightness two black thunderheads threw up their dark feathery turbans into the pale sky.

Soot seemed to be dusting the air, the stone walls were blotters to the late light, so that the spires of the churches were dark dirks at God's shiny throat, the heavy blocks of terrace houses were warts on the cheeks of heaven, the galleries of cranes along Clydeside were chains to the arms of the last of the sun. Yet all this counterpoise of dark and light, of grind and grace, of Satan and Jerusalem, made Gog's heart strain its walls and put a blur in his eyes for grief of toiling earth and hint of millennium.

'Ya sully aul' bastart,' the chib-man said behind Gog. 'Whaur's yer wullit? Mibbe ye'll no want a face like a pun' o' mince.'

Gog turned. Behind him, a squat heavy man with crossed slashes on his right cheek, in his eyes glims of madness or whisky. His right hand held his open chib, steel streak of slash and run. A hard case from the Gorbals, a nutter.

'Gie us some cash or Ah'll cut ye fae earhole tae arsehole.'

Gog transferred his parcel from his left hand to his right hand and took out his wallet. It held a few pounds. He gave it to the hard case.

'Reight, Santy Claus. Noo gie us the wee parcel.'

'It's only got a dead fish in it,' Gog said. 'A poisoned fish. It's no good except to throw at politicians.'

'Doan't ye gie me tha'.' The chib-man snatched the parcel with his free hand. 'Naebuddy but a nutter would hump a stinkin' fish tae Glesca. We've the Macfisheries alreidy.' He looked to right and left. People were coming. He closed the chib. 'An' doan't be stoappin' tae talk tae ony polis, or Ah'll cut off yer heid an' hit ye in the face wi' it.' And so he ran off, hunching and scuffling as a broken-wing tern.

Gog looked after him, smiling. Magog had told him once of being robbed by a deserter on a bomb-site; but this Gorbals hard case was no deserter; chance had deserted him. All that risk for a few quid and rotten fish. For the parcel did only contain a small poisoned salmon. Gog's shrimp larvae for his fish hatchery in his dammed loch had once come from San Francisco Bay. But the pollution had grown so bad there that the larvae had all died. So now the larvae were hatched in Vancouver Sound and flown to Scotland. Gog had fed them to his spawn in his loch, only to see the smelts begin to die. He had sent the dead fish and the

larvae to Glasgow for analysis and had flown down to discuss
the results, carrying another corpse wrapped in brown paper.
The chemists said the smelts were sick to death with mercury
and traces of arsenic, carried by their food. Nobody had yet
noticed in Vancouver that the larvae were being bred near the
outflow from a chemical plant. The millions of embryos, innocent
Crippens, had spread the taint of mercury to the young salmon
half a world away . . .

Gog faced once more to the north-west. Now the pitchy
shapes of kirk and slum and crane had nearly joined the gloamed
dusk except where a scrap of final sun capped the hills in a red
cockade. Chill now, time for a wee drop in the pub, a dram to
keep the warm in, a fug of sweat and plain talk of work and
wages and Celtic and Rangers, a barmaid that had long lost hers,
a folk found again for Gog in the hot dens where people herded
against neglect and the night.

The chapel issue did come to the vote at the College of Charles
the Martyr. It was not mismanagement on Magog's part, but
misjudgement of the character of the philosophy don. Magog
had selected Angus McInnes, because he had seen someone
who was fat, spectacled, drunken, yet very quick and apparently
selfish to the point of disinterest in the affairs of others. The
philosopher had seemed wrapped up in Wittgenstein and whisky
rather than College politics. 'For god's sake,' he had said at
the interview, 'don't make me a moral tutor to the young –
their righteousness puts *me* to shame.' So Magog had given
him a Fellowship, presuming that he was manipulatory. Now
Angus McInnes was the wily leader of one wing of Magog's
opposition, who wanted no chapel, while the Reverend Simpkin-
Smith led the other wing for God, King Charles and the Church
of England.

'Angus,' Magog said, 'I'm sure that we can settle this matter
out of school. We cannot be so nineteenth-century as to quarrel
over what brand of religion gets taught here. It is quite irrelevant
to the era of electronics.'

'Aye. But what about the will? Our founder and benefactor
does say there's to be a meditation room and no parson. And if
you meditate upon that, it does seem to be incontrovertible.

Yes, another drop, Master. They say the whisky fuddles a man, but I always find it a wonderful sharpener.'

'Removable religious symbols, Angus. A parson in a sports coat. Who cares about such little nonsenses in the space age? And think of the educational value in all that extra City money for the college, just to have an occasional chapel and a clown to perform in it.'

'It's attractive, vurry attractive. But what about the first cause, the *primum mobile*? Without the money from the will, there would have been no College at all, not at all. So we should always be remembering the founder and respecting the first cause – especially when it has to do with God. Suppose He takes it out on our founder's soul? And he, poor body, a fellow Scot too.'

'Wills should be accepted gratefully and applied gently,' Magog said. 'The dead ought to help us, not chain us. It is rather incongruous, Angus, to find you talking of our founder's soul, when you would say the soul was not even a meaningful statement.'

'Aye, it's not meaningful to me, the soul or this chapel. But they were meaningful to our founder and they are meaningful to the poor old parson. And who can say any man's version of God is not meaningful to *him*? The problem is, there are dons who really believe with our founder in the meditation room. And there are dons who side with the parson. We'd like it settled one way or t'other, a chapel or none. To those who care, Master, you seem to be taking money from both sides and settling for neither . . . a kind of false pretences.'

Magog looked at the fat philosopher swilling his whisky. Where was his weakness? Every man had a weakness. The problem was finding it. Once found, there would be no other problems.

'It must be odd for you, Angus, to have *holy* bedfellows.'

'Where I come from, we don't ask what a man is in a fight. As long as he's fighting, that's enough.'

'And who exactly is in the fight?' Magog asked, wishing to pick off the list of his likely enemies.

'Gadby, for one.'

'Gadby?' Magog laughed. 'He's no interest outside the Classics. He doesn't know anything's happened since the fall of Rome.'

'Aye, but he thinks Christianity made Rome fall. He's against the chapel. And I'm with Davie Hume and him on that.'

'We could do without Dr Gadby, you know.'

'Could we now?' Angus said. 'You asked him to come here in the first place, Master. Are those more false pretences, would you say?'

Magog did not like the way things were going. He decided to end the issue through his authority and his reassurance. What did a person want to know, really, except that everything was in good hands and that most people thought so? Nothing comforts a man more than siding with a winning majority.

'I assure you, Angus, that I have made the most careful private soundings among the twenty Fellows who are already here, the real founders of the college even more than my humble self or our rich benefactor. These pilgrims to a new concept definitely tell me that opinion favours a removable Anglican chapel . . .'

'Is that so, Master? Then why not put it to a vote?'

'The press might get hold of it. And nothing is worse for a new institution than to appear to start in dissension.'

'The press might get hold of it if there *isn't* a vote,' Angus said.

Magog stared at Angus McInnes. The man looked away, his spectacles bouncing light into Magog's eyes. Magog had read that, in nature, an animal which dropped its eyes was not insecure. It was merely checking that it was on its own territory. Angus's territory? This was Magog's own ground.

'Is that a threat, Angus? Would you be so indiscreet as to publicize our differences?'

'A journalist protects his sources, a politician his leaks, and a philosopher only tries to tell the truth.'

'Very sibylline, your answer. I don't suppose you'd even mind if it were quoted against you.'

'Not a bit.' Again Angus moved his head, flicking light from his lenses into Magog's eyes. 'Could you let me know, Master, how you managed in your soundings among the Fellows to miss out Gadby and me, so we only heard of the chapel matter indirectly?'

'I assumed your opposition,' Magog said.

'That's bad philosophy, assuming anything. What were the exact numbers, for and against?'

'I am not a mathematician, Angus. I leave that to professionals and clerks.'

'Do you now? Well, Master, *I* checked with the Fellows before coming to see you. I'd say you might be short of a majority for your compromise, for taking money from God and the Devil at the same time.'

'I have news for you, Angus,' Magog said. 'The Civil War is over. We don't fight about Protestants and Catholics, Kings and Puritans, Divine Right and Reason any more. We don't persecute the Jews. Religions simply don't matter because most of us don't go to church. Do you?'

'That's not the point, Master. We'd just like our say, that's all. The Fellows here would like their say.'

'On a *chapel*? Why not on a *kennel*?'

'Even if it were on a lavatory, we'd like our say. Aye, that we would.'

Magog found McInnes both stubborn and irritating, particularly his clinging to a slight Scots accent to prove he really cared about the rights of democracy. If one was part of the élite, one should have the courage of joining it, diction and all.

'You must excuse me, Angus, I have an important meeting . . .'

Magog yawned, then put on his look of weary amusement.

'How very important we always are,' he said, 'to ourselves.'

'Aye,' Angus said, 'we are that. I've got a petition with me, Master, signed by over half the Fellows asking for a meeting over the chapel. You will not resist, will you now?'

'So you've taken it that far?' Magog rose and walked to the end of his oval living-room on the south side of the spider's eye that looked over the spreading College of Charles the Martyr, still only four-legged as yet, but with turf and plants already browning in the days of October. When he was against the window, he turned back towards Angus, so that his body would be black and looming against the panes of light, half-blinding his enemy. 'So you want *my* place, McInnes, then?'

'No, Master, I do not.'

'Yes, you do. You're forming an opposition. But remember,

tenure here for Fellows is only for four years. It is renewable
. . . or not.'

'By decision of the college committee, Master. Normally, it
is renewed, unless there is cause . . .'

'Is not opposition to me cause for me to oppose you?' Magog
said. 'Do remember, my dear McInnes, I write the agendas of
College committees. I call the meetings. I notify people. I control
most of the funds. I think I shall get the vote I want. A wise
civil servant, Sir George Germain, once said to me, Give me
the agenda and I will get the necessary result.'

'You're like Wee Jock Elliott,' Angus said. 'Who dares to
meddle wi' you? But I'm like John Buchan, you know. A poor
Scot has to make his way in this world, especially against the
English Civil Service.' He rose. 'I don't like staring into
the light,' he said. 'I'm a night owl.' He put a piece of paper
on his chair. 'There's the petition of the Fellows, Master,
a humble petition and advice, asking for a meeting on the
chapel. You could ignore it and have another Civil War,
but look what happened to King Charles of blessed memory for
doing just that. You'll keep your head and hold the meeting, I
think.'

'The Vice-Master's an old man,' Magog said unexpectedly.

'Aye,' Angus said. 'That old Miniver should never have been
appointed. Friend of the family, isn't he now? Did you want to
get him a free pension?'

'He'll give us the benefit of his long experience to set up the
College,' Magog said. 'But he'll retire in a couple of years. Well,
Angus?'

'*Vice*-Master,' Angus said coolly. 'I'll leave that to Miniver.
He's lickspittle enough for the job.'

'You want it all, don't you?' Magog said. 'But you must
remember, the Master of this College is a royal appointment.
It's done at Cabinet level.'

'There's a new government,' Angus McInnes said. 'Haven't
you noticed? Harold Wilson. I used to know him at Oxford.
Clever chap, always knew who could help him and who couldn't.
He taught me how to count heads.'

'Well, you'll have to make me resign first, and that won't
happen,' Magog said. Damn this gutter-fighter from nowhere,

damn the shifts in power and patronage, damn the need to get to know a lot of new fixers in the lobbies of Westminster and Whitehall. This was his College. He had earned it.

'I don't want you to resign, Master. The Fellows just want you to deal with us, not do it all yourself.'

'I'll outlast you, McInnes. Be sure of that.'

'That you may,' McInnes said. 'But not if you try to take all the decisions yourself. You'll overwork, die young. It's because we want to keep you with us longer, dear Master, that we want to share responsibility with you. We all love our College, don't we?'

I know I shouldn't have come over, Sweetass, but then a girl's gotta do what she's gotta do I pay my own way the Atlantic's only a plane hop nobody's lived who hasn't seen the Big Apple like New York yeah. OK what if I did come to see you I'm not asking you for anything in fact I'm giving you bread if you don't want me around just chuck me out there's plenty more back on the old plantation where you came from Sweetass Brown don't think you soul brothers are so special. Whitey's got a prick on him too how come you're chocolate anyway Sweetass on your mother's side or your father's? I didn't mean that Sweetass I do love you but hell what's all this Black Muslim bullshit you go in for? No I won't scrub your floor lick your ass lie down and kiss your big toe be your seventh whore – some Wives of the Prophet ha! I didn't choose to get born grey any more than you chose black I give my bread to Elijah and the Cause I don't have to take your crap I don't have to ball your whole group chicks have their rights too, even grey chicks, yeah we're super. Soopah soopah what's so funny about me saying soopah, it's English that's what you speak only it gets lost in your fat lips didn't learn to speak so good did you country boy? Oh Sweetass I don't mean it I don't mean it just let me stay I'll give give I'll go to Miami Beach and get me a tan just as sweet as yours, but hell Sweetass what's all this exclusion crap, black is beautiful, well white is beautiful, Rosa's beautiful in England, this isn't my country this isn't my fault why take it out on me? Sure we brought you over to our colonies took you from Africa

raped your mommas, why sure we did but it still isn't my fault
my money's not off your backs it's Magog's it's for bearing
your bastard Sweetass son, that's who. You don't care do
you, screw all the grey chicks cut a hole in the french letters
get your own fucking back your brown bastards will inherit
the earth but they won't love YOU any better for it than they
loved US not one thing or the other you nigger bastard you.
Oh that's better Sweetass that's better yes again my Africk
Prince Prick that that that soopah. And those drums they turn
me on make me wild no horseshit grey chicks can dig be cool
no abalone none. Grey chicks got soul, soopah soul, what
about Miles Davis, he says only white boys can play drums,
Miles isn't an Uncle Tom, why the hell should you think
Sweetass you can play Bach and Bartok while Whitey ain't
allow to play dem blues? Music's for everybody soul's for
everybody you don't have a monopoly on suffering even if we
did hand out shit for centuries to your people, you didn't bleed
in Piccadilly damn near to death, fact is Sweetass you've
never bled at all at all, maybe your mommy did and your
poppy did they swung dat hammer and wore dem chains, but
sure as Harlem ain't Alabamy, you were always on an easy
jive play that thing MAN not like Malcolm X there's a hero
cat red kid from the mainline to nowhere got to the top, you
never had to sweat for it much Sweetass and you didn't have
to sweat for me just beat that drum and I came running.
Seems you're taking this whole city, you and the Afro scene,
taking it all, subways and streets full of trash and cans and
white guilt, climbing up the garbage and old horrors and coke
bottles to the tippy top of the Empire State. What about your
black kiddies. Gen. Geo. Washington Mr Thos. Jefferson,
isn't them the founding FATHERS? Black is beautiful black is
easy if black man plays or black man sings or black man says
hot words burn baby burn fire on fire bomb on bomb blow
down Moses, oh screw the grey chicks fuck 'em put 'em down
they'll be back for more and more and more but we goin' back
to Africa back to Africk. I'll put you down, Rosa pussy, do
your trick for Sweetass and his black is beautiful pals then
Rosa go home Rosa go home to England you ain't wanted
here you ain't wanted nowhere till we is acomin' to fuck you

over from America Africa Arabia China power is black power is beautiful power to the people as long as they black people some people are more equal than other people oppressed people are more equal than white people pay Rosa pay Rosa pay Rosa you pay for all that shit on Africa pay Rosa pay Rosa pay Rosa go home and fuck yourself Sweetass done gone back to black back to beautiful back to Africk ain't no time for white folks no more.

I'm going home Sweetass Brown.

Although the question of the chapel came to the vote, Magog got his way with the twenty Fellows without much difficulty. For he wrote the agenda. It initially proposed only two possible ways of voting; for or against the meditation room pure and simple; alternatively, for or against the permanent Anglican chapel. This method of voting, copied from de Gaulle's tactic of never asking for a referendum unless the only choice lay between him and chaos, split the opposition neatly in two, with the seven rationalists and the six Anglicans voting on opposite sides and cancelling each other out. This allowed Magog's own minority, the seven compromisers led by the old Vice-Master Miniver, to vote with the Anglicans against a meditation room and with the rationalists against a permanent chapel. Although the Anglicans and the rationalists combined could have easily defeated the seven supporters of Magog's own policy for a removable Church of England, he never presented his solution until both the meditation room and the permanent House of God had been easily voted down.

Then Magog brought forward his own wish as the only possible compromise, giving something to the meditative and something to the religious. What reasonable man could refuse this half-a-loaf? Magog also hinted that, if the vote did not go his way, he might feel obliged to resign, because obviously he would not be able to hold the College together. And think what a bad effect the going of the first Master would have on the future of a new College, not even built! Despite his wishes, the millions he had raised to found the College might well disappear if he were to leave. Magog won his vote by seventeen to nothing with Angus

McInnes, the Reverend Simpkin-Smith and Professor Gadby abstaining. It was a skilled victory.

Only Gadby resigned his Fellowship on a matter of principle; he had an income, of course. Angus McInnes and the parson stayed on. McInnes was still waiting for his hour of palace revolution to strike, while the poor reverend was trying to turn the new undergraduates to God and against the Master. Magog was amused. Even if he chose to leave for greener fields or loftier domes, he would arrange his own succession. He would see that McInnes had not a chance. There was a principle in protecting oneself, never to forgo revenge. It discouraged the enemy so.

One thing Magog forgot in his victory, the idealism of the young. He could deal with the world, but not with his own family – in that way, he was like other men. So when Miniver came through the door on his twin sticks, swaying and hobbling like a small ruin announcing a huge disaster, Magog was caught out.

'Your niece and twenty other *hooligans*,' Miniver complained in his reedy rasp, 'have occupied the occasional chapel. A non-violent sit-in, they say. Did I hear one of them talk of Martin Luther?'

'Martin Luther King, I should think,' Magog said.

'We are no rotten Papacy to call forth Protestants,' Miniver said. 'We sell no indulgences. We need strength. Shall I send for the proctors or the police to clear them out?'

'Neither,' Magog said. 'I will talk them out.'

'They'll shout you down,' Miniver said. 'Empty barrels make the most noise. A hundred words won't fill a bushel. What do you get from asses but hee-haws? Even his fart to a fool smells sweet.'

'A stitch in time, Miniver. You, with your wise old country sayings . . . But what the students want now is dialectic, not dialects.'

Miniver stooped, bent and tiny, venomous to the end.

'If they'll listen to you, Master. Yet if ifs and buts were apples and nuts, wouldn't I just fill my guts?'

The protestors sat round the bare meditation room in their frayed jeans and their heavy sweaters, their short blue donkey-jackets and their peaked caps. One youth picked at a guitar, another sang *Lord Randal, my son.*

> '. . . *I fear you are poisoned, my handsome young man.*
> *Oh yes, I am poisoned, mother, make my bed soon,*
> *For I'm sick to the heart I fain would lie down* . . .'

Josepha was wearing a denim skirt and a sheepskin coat; she sat cross-legged, her knees covered delicately. Alone, she did not look up and hush as Magog came in. For she was already silent, contemplating.

'Having a nice meditation?' Magog said pleasantly.

'You won't get us out,' a voice said.

For a moment in that warp of time that trips each man into the pit of the past more each year that he lives, Magog thought he saw Rupert again in blaze of red-gold curls, at elegant lounge on the ground, in quiet arrogance of speech. Then he blinked into sense to see only a ginger youth in gym shoes and corduroys lying on the floor among his grubby and sneering mates. Had Cambridge come to this? Where were the flutes of yesteryear? The church clock at Grantchester had no longer stopped at ten to three, but ticked on the fuse of the bomb.

'What do you want?' Magog said. 'Or don't you really know?'

Immediately a howl, hubbub, tumult. Magog raised one arm imperiously and waited until the voices fell.

'I will speak to your leader,' he said. He looked down at Josepha, now looking up at him. 'You, I presume. It's in the blood.'

'I was chosen by the committee,' Josepha said.

'Come up to my lodge,' Magog said. 'We'll discuss it there.'

'Up to the spider's eye? No, we'll speak right here. We're for open conferences. We're not afraid who'll hear.'

There was nothing soft in Josepha's tone now. A harsh wind had come with autumn, a stridency calling for the quick settlement of wrongs, real or imaginary. Bitter harvest for such ripe crop.

'I'm listening,' Magog said.

'I should begin by stating,' Josepha said, 'that our demands are not open to negotiation. We are not *asking* for what is right, we are presenting minimum terms for settlement by you. This College of Charles the Martyr is costing in excess of two million pounds to build, I believe.'

'That is hardly your affair, Josepha,' Magog said.

'There has been a diversion of the reactionary meditation room for use as a fascist Anglican chapel, I am informed.'

McInnes again, probably. But really, to fight Magog out of the mouths of babes and sucklings.

'Your information is suspect, Josepha.'

'We have occupied this room for the People until such time as the College elects to carry out one of the following things . . .' Here Josepha looked at a paper which she pulled out of her pocket. 'Restore the use of the room to education and turn over to SNCC or CORE the money for its conversion into an Anglican chapel. Or convert this room into a crêche for the babies of mothers who wish to return to their studies, uninterrupted by male chauvinist demands and house-slavery. Unless one of these two uses is forthwith made of this area, we, the Freedom Action Group of the Cambridge People's Socialist Party, will remain here indefinitely.'

There was a murmur of support and a hand-clap. Magog smiled.

'You'll get awfully tired of sitting in the dark,' he said. 'We'll cut off heat and electricity.'

'We've got sleeping bags,' Josepha said. 'And rations. We'll sit it out till the SS comes.'

'In the real war against the real Nazis,' Magog said, 'people really lived like moles in dark shelters. The bombs were real too. We didn't play at fighting Fascism. We really were.'

'People are being bombed right now,' Josepha said, 'in Vietnam.'

'That's not our war,' Magog said. 'Nor is the fight for racial equality in America our fight. Nor are we Fascists.'

'After the Smethwick election,' the ginger youth said, 'the race war's started over here. If you want a nigger as a neighbour, vote Labour.' He spat on the floor. 'We're all in this thing together.'

'One world, to be sure,' Magog said. 'I think I am still a human being, whatever you may think.'

'So are we,' Josepha said, 'whatever *you* may think. So we also demand equal representation on the College Council, diversion of half the College Building Fund to set up educational facilities for the deprived children of the town, an ending to the artificial distinction between students and workers . . .'

'Why not just ask me to hand over to you?' Magog said. 'Why not just ask me to leave? All power to teenagers.'

'The door's behind you,' the ginger youth said. 'Piss off, *Master.*'

Magog pissed off, wondering what had happened to the traditional respect among undergraduates for authority. He called on the College Porters, paid each of them ten pounds in cash, and had the squatters removed from the meditation room without any fuss. The students were not yet ready to fight; non-violence was still their creed. Magog also took the appropriate steps to see that all news of the affray was suppressed from the local and the student newspapers, under threat of libel suits or being sent down.

When one of the under-porters asked to see him on a personal matter, Magog granted the man an audience. Cherry was his name, his eyes sly and nervous above his humble smile.

'Begging your pardon, sir, seeing as how you're busy . . . It must be a fair strain, running this big place and all. I wouldn't be in your place . . . I've trouble in the family . . .'

'What can I do about that, Cherry?'

'Twenty pound would be a matter of life and death, sir.' The phrase gave Cherry satisfaction by its importance. 'A matter of life and death.'

'The welfare state deals with life and death now, Cherry. We just deal with food and drink.'

'Begging your pardon, sir, you don't know as how it's hard to make ends meet for the likes of us. You with all your money and giving your girls the best of everything . . .'

So Cherry knew. Did everybody know his connection with Josepha?

'You think there's a reason I should give you twenty pounds?' Magog asked.

'The kindness of your heart, bless you sir. I always say in the porters' lodge, it's something to be thankful for, a kind Master . . .'

'I hope you still say it when I tell you to manage on your wages like the others,' Magog said.

'I was hearing the talk of the students,' Cherry said, 'as did them wild things in the Chapel. Saying as how your Miss Josepha had put them up to it. Of course I paid no heed, seeing as how they weren't the sort of young gentlemen we used to have here . . . But I haven't seen any mention of it, not nowhere.'

'I believe you came to tell me about your family, not mine,' Magog said. 'Don't be so damned impertinent.'

'Begging your pardon, sir, I never did mean . . . oh no, sir, not Cherry, sir . . . It was just when I picked up that Miss Josepha to carry her out, she was the only one as put up a bit of a fight. It took me and Terry to get her out and I sprained my coccyx, that's what the doctor says. I've got a weak coccyx, that's what I have. She didn't half lay about her, and what a lovely young lady she is too . . .'

'You dared touch her?' Magog was angry.

'On your orders, sir, I had to physically restrain her, though my coccyx wasn't half playing up. *Physically restrain her* . . .'

There seemed to be a glitter in Cherry's eyes. Magog found himself shaking. He felt tremors run from his stomach to his arms, fury belch incoherent from his throat. He was on Cherry before he could think, his hands slapping the under-porter's face and shoulders. 'Out . . . You dare . . . My flesh . . . *Mine!*' And as Cherry ran for the door, his arms hiding his head, Magog heard that the shouting was in his own voice. *'Mine!'*

Cherry was dismissed. It cost Magog five hundred pounds to hush up his assault, and he was not at peace until he knew that the under-porter had left Cambridge to join the police force in Nuneaton. Cherry did not seem to have talked to anyone; his gratuity had closed his mouth. When he was safely gone, Magog summoned Josepha, but she would not come to see him until Maire arranged a meeting for all three of them at the Blue Boar Hotel on one of her rare visits to her daughter.

'I really don't know,' Maire scolded Josepha, 'which one of

you two girls is the more terrible. Rosa speaks like a Manhattan sewer rat, while you spew some ghastly Trotskyite jargon which might come from a discarded pamphlet of the thirties when things were really serious.'

'Things are really serious now,' Josepha said.

'Things are always really serious for the young,' Magog said. 'The trouble is that only the old know how to deal with serious things seriously.'

'Revisionist hyena,' Josepha said amiably, then passed her plate to Maire. 'May I have some more pud, Mummy?'

'There had never been a student strike or sit-in before you came up,' Magog said unhappily. 'Did you invent the idea or is it another ghastly transatlantic infection?'

'That, and Gog saying it would just be like another Peasants' Revolt. Only he said we weren't to listen to our Lords and *Masters* this time, or we'd have our heads chopped off as usual.' Josepha took back her heaped plate of white pudding and dug her spoon into it. 'Brainwashed imperialist lackey,' she said to Magog, then popped her heaped spoon into her mouth.

'You've got a sweet tooth, Josepha,' Maire said. 'You just get a sweet tongue for Magog, too. He's old enough to be your father.'

Josepha went pink. The allusion to Magog's possible paternity still hurt her, despite her tough surface. She swallowed and put down the spoon, her pudding unfinished.

'I should watch my weight,' she said. 'And my words.' She turned towards Magog and hissed, 'Dupe of the cult of personality.'

'Why don't you just say old rich powermen don't understand young ducky girls, darling? Why do you have to use all those long boring curses nobody understands outside a purge in Omsk?' Maire yawned. 'I know people say we don't communicate with the young any more, but that's because you talk the old political junk which our great-*grandfathers* did.'

'Bourgeois capitalist lackey,' Josepha said to Maire, then blushed. 'I don't really mean that, Mummy.'

'Gog's fault, is it?' Magog said sadly. 'Passing on all his wild notions to you now. The people's revolt and all that. When will it ever end?'

'When you give up,' Josepha said blandly. Magog wanted to hit her, but he knew his fist would become a stroking hand before it reached her.

'Give up what?' Magog said. 'I have nothing. No love, no respect, no wife, no daughters, no sons, no ties with my brother or my mother, nothing at all. I have some money and less power, both of which I lose more of every year along with my hair and my health. I have no glory, no thanks, and thus no mercy on those who wish to take away the very little I have. Why the hell don't you let me die away in peace?'

'Deviationist paper tiger,' Josepha said. 'Elitist class enemy.'

'This is my country too,' Magog said.

1965

Gog stood in the queue that was one and a half miles long. Its tail began at County Hall and the people slowly moved west in front of the doomed five brick cakes of St Thomas's Hospital with the river on their right, doing no Lambeth Walk as far as the bridge over the Thames, but a shuffle of grief over the water, turning back to the east with the river still on their right hand as they wound round towards the brown sugar pinnacles of Westminster and its Hall, where the Grand Old Man lay in state. The people did not question why they were there, after all, it would be enough to say in the years to come, I was alive in Churchill's time, I heard him say on the wireless, We shall fight them on the beaches even if that fight never came, blood toil sweat and tears and we had a lot of that let me tell you what with the blitz and the V-2s and the coupons, I was alive in Churchill's time and it was his time, you know, the last of the great men he was, we shall not see his like again, and for that reason I am standing here in this great worm of sorrow that is passing through the Hall where he lies. He saved us once, he did. He said we saved ourselves and that's true, but it was really him after Dunkirk. We're here to pay our respects. He'd like that. He was a gentleman, you see.

Frost and bitter wind, snow to sleet to January rain, and the queue still inched on with the almost lost patience of the war. Feet frozen, hands cold deeper than the knuckles, heart the only errant warmth under huddle of overcoat, nose a nubbin of ice, the people still waited in line, moved on, waited, moved, waited, moved, waited with Gog among them. They had come from the corners of the island, they had come from over the Channel and the seas, they had come to say to themselves, I was there, he spoke to me once, I heard him plain, I never spoke to him, but he knew I was there fighting with him, he knew, so now I am here to meet him, I must. Almost fainting in the chill, Gog found himself half held upright by the fat cleaning-woman behind, incense of sweat and Guinness, and the hatted schoolgirls in front, as they urged him as far as the Hall of Westminster where the carpets at last soothed the drag of the feet and the six jerky candle-flames made a hundred bright leaves and berries of mistletoe on the grove of bronzes above and the four Horseguardsmen of the apocalypse bowed their shining plumed helmets to consider their sabre-hilts and the points of their steel digging between their black high boots and beyond them on its raised steps the red and the white and the blue flag, garish and grooved over the Old Man's coffin under the gold crucifix that should not have been there to bless this preserver of his people and destroyer of his enemies. Better he should lie under the shadow of a Spitfire, a Hurricane, a Repulse, a Revenge, a Blenheim bomber than under this cross of gold that never hurled back the stormtroopers, Old Guard or Armada at any Trafalgar, Malplaquet, El Alamein, we kill more than we get killed, we last longer than you last, we lose only to win in the end, this island has not fallen since the Normans and it will not fall again, we shall strike back across the seas and we shall bring in our hands the Götterdämmerung that you have seen many times before and before that. I am a Churchill and there were Churchills before me and before the Duke of Marlborough, and if the Hitlers go back in history only to primitive insignificance, why, that is where they will go back again while I shall in honour and memory and family, Sir Winston Churchill, with the people and their children plodding by in their queues of mourning, yea, even unto Gog, the enemy of my greatness yet the friend of my fight for Britain, for Albion, for the glory that has departed with me and the people who are staying on . . .

Magog stood in St Paul's Cathedral, angry at his bad seat in the back. It was really no good the Earl Marshal telling him that he was lucky to get in at all, what with the company, mostly foreigners no better than Dr Erhard, Mr Ben-Gurion, Aristotle Onassis, Earl Warren, The Grand Duke of Luxemburg, Marshal Korniev, General de Gaulle, Paul Reynaud, Mr Kishi, Mr Krag and old uncle Moise Tshombe and all. The Queen was there and the royal family and Lord Avon and Lord Attlee and the old soldiers like Alexander and Slim, but these were the figures of the past while he, Magog, was the understanding and the force of the future. What did Sir Winston want to do, lie embedded in his coffin drawn on a gun-carriage by an escort of blue-jackets with steps solemn mournful and slow all the way from Westminster to the City cathedral saved from the incendiary bombs by his order and God's mercy? Or did Sir Winston want to live on by the actions of the new Magogs of England, who had learned by the Old Man's ruthless tricks and matchless rhetoric how to snatch victory out of defeat, only to be thrown from power by the traitor public bent on defeating the victorious peace? At any rate, Magog's vanity was hurt at being present unnoticed at the great burial service under the dome of St Paul's, where the chanted echoes were trapped for the eardrum of God, who hearest all.

> '. . . There's no discouragement
> Shall make him once relent
> His first avowed intent
> To be a pilgrim . . .'

As Bunyan's hymn said, the Old Man did have courage, the British usually had courage, they muddled ahead in what they thought they had to do, but why did they have to wait until their backs were against the sea before they would fight? Why wait that long to forget their grumbling and distrust of those who were set to rule over them? Why did they have to be in the last ditch to accept greatness? Old Sir Winston had been twenty years in the wilderness before the trumpets of defeat had called him back to his grudging country's service. And he would have stayed out in the cold until his forgotten burial in his village church, short of the disaster that gave him an old man's opportunity.

> *'. . . Glory, glory, halleluiah*
> *Glory, glory, halleluiah*
> *Glory, glory, halleluiah*
> *For his soul goes marching on . . .'*

Too cheery, really, the Battle Hymn of the Republic for the ceremony in St Paul's. Odd that the Old Man had been half American, perhaps that was why de Gaulle would persist in calling us Anglo-Saxons and keeping us out of the Common Market and Europe. Old Generals do have such a personal view of things. Yet, as always, there was something in that ancient French prophet's ravings. English was displacing French as the common language of the world, the shared culture. Galling for Paris to see itself lose the Nine Hundred Years War against England that had begun so well for France at the Battle of Hastings. One might call it a Two Thousand Years War since Julius Caesar first brought Latin speech across the Channel. Empires fade, languages remain, for in the long run, words survive better than power or glory. Sir Winston was right to polish his phrases, de Gaulle right to fear the Anglo-Saxon tongue, Magog right to give up politics and business for the life of the mind and the pen. In the beginning was the word – and in the end, too.

> *'God save our gracious Queen*
> *Long live our noble Queen*
> *God save the Queen*
> *Send Her victorious*
> *Happy and glorious . . .'*

No, send Her a good press-agent, poet-laureate, speech-writer, Shakespeare Minor, if She wanted to live after death. What had She said on the BBC to match Tilbury? That She had the heart of a King and a King of England too? There was a greater She before Her. There was a greater Magog before him . . .

The cranes all dipped their necks and the shrill pipes blew as the launch called *Havengore* took the body downriver from the Tower with the swans and the black-hulled policeboats all about as far as the Festival Hall Pier where Gog stood waiting with the last thin line of the faithful and the unforgetting and the watching to see the Old Man taken off the water (O First Sea Lord where are your fleets, sunk sunk by the shipyards and by the estimates not by the enemy) taken from the Thames to the slow train home from Waterloo to lie at last in his grave at St Martin's at Bladon down the fields from Blenheim, the names of the battles no more than the marks on stations and houses now and the old warrior six feet deep under the turf and cypress tree, never to rise again like Arthur from his magicked cave at his country's final hour, for Britain shall never have the time to call again in that brief flash of the cloud and the rays and the megatons and the fourth final burning of London to the bedrock of Albion, waiting to green again in peace over the bones of the last of the warrior chiefs, no need for the likes of you, Winston Churchill, not any more now . . .

It was the year of the plastic horn at Pamplona.

One hundred thousand of these tiny trumpets had been made from tinted grease and had been brought into town to keep the Basques happy. They did keep the Basques happy, day and night and night and day. Perhaps a thousand of the Basques had also brought huge drums and brass horns of their own, and they processed in a hundred bands through the town streets in an interminable celebration. If there was any pause for holy hush, the other ninety and nine thousand peeped with their plastic horns. As the placard in the town square said proudly in English:

DAMN FINE FIESTA
HEMINGWAY

Rosa had to admit, it was a damn fine fiesta, Hemingway. Playing the role of Lady Brett, she started off in the Ritz Bar, picked up a French youth in the Select, drove him in her Ferrari to the Spanish border before bedding him, then found out his name the next day in the Café Kutz at Pamplona. Jean-Roger Garde, handsome in that skully dark way that starved Parisian intellectuals can be, when they believe that burning ideals can only show in the hollows of their cheeks. He disapproved of her all the way through yet he had to have her, quivering like a puppy dog on her flanks. It wasn't bad for a week or two, Rosa supposed, but he was too broody to last.

Rosa would have avoided Pamplona at all costs, knowing what a student mecca it had become with the young men running in front of the bulls in the name of Ernest and Manolete, and the myths far too vulgar and Yank to have much to do with the festival of San Martin. But Josepha had written that she would be there and Rosa hadn't seen her all that year what with Cannes and Rio and that flip to Bali with Socrates Demetrios and hell, a sister was a sis and Josepha was a twin sis, it was closer than being blood brothers really. So Rosa watched the square in the morning from the Café Kutz with the Spaniards eyeing her Ferrari even more than her legs, and the American boys massed at the opposite café where the drinks were a peseta cheaper and they didn't have to meet the locals because they'd taken the whole place over as it was.

Josepha showed up that evening in the company of three tall English youths from Cambridge, one with ginger hair and one who looked like a melancholy bloodhound and one with nothing going for him except the hope that he might grow into something in a decade or two. They had nowhere to stay except for a room for the four of them on the main street above a bar where even a stone-deaf saint would not have found a moment's peace. So Rosa offered to share her bed with her sister, Jean-Roger wasn't all that hot, he was getting too keen on her, these young lolitos

thought one night gave them rights on a girl when she was just
being friendly.

'See you, Jean-Roger,' Rosa said. 'You can sack down with
the Three Mosquitos from the Cam. I'm going off with Josie.'

And she did go off with Josepha to the swank hotel room
thoughtfully booked for her by Socrates, such a wise man too,
always knew how to order the best in advance even though he
had to run a tanker fleet in his spare time, two front-row *sombra*
seats every day for the bull-fight too, Socrates didn't expect her
to go alone even when he couldn't show up. For a Greek he
really wasn't jealous.

The sisters talked most of the night and would you believe it,
Josepha was still a virgin and didn't seem to *mind* about it, she
was as Victorian as Karl Marx, she wouldn't even accept a silver
lamé jersey that was too big for Rosa but fitted Josepha to a T,
even lifted her breasts up, larger than Rosa's, but rather saggy
because Josepha would hunch up her shoulders as if she expected
a forward posture would somehow urge on the revolution. As
for the jargon, well, Rosa just wouldn't waste her time on that,
there was so much to tell her twin and Josepha really liked
listening best, she was the best listener a sister ever had, Rosa
had so much to tell, the world was so full of bargains and places
to go and men were so awful, and how was Simon by the way?
Josepha said Rosa's little boy was doing very well, he walked
and he talked, very quick and bright and just like her except for
his red curls. 'That's his father,' Rosa said and remembered
Sweetass Brown for the first time in months.

Jean-Roger was a bit of a bore, he would not leave them
alone, but he was useful for the dancing at nights and keeping
other boys away, really, those American kids were a crashing
bore, they never seemed to know when they weren't wanted,
they seemed to presume that the world owed them a free drink
a free fuck a free flop and the time of day, why the hell did they
have to wander all round Europe without a cent getting in the
hair of people who lived there and had a bit of money to get
around with? Still, the Yanks had one nice gag, persuading the
Basques that a machine for lighter fluid really served white wine,
but even that palled after the tenth victim had been sick on the
floor, and they would drink the local rotgut called Chinchon

which seemed to be distilled grappa, it took the top off your head and the lining from your tum, Jean-Roger even fell on his head off the car watching the fireworks and didn't seem to feel it at all, which wasn't because he was that thick, just because no sleep and all that booze and getting up at six to run in front of the bulls between the barricades in the streets or just not going to bed at all was a total anaesthesia which made you feel like life was a doze a drowse a laze all day. But the damn matadors wouldn't risk themselves, it was the beginning of the season, they weren't going to lean over the horns for a clean kill, not them, no they'd rather stab at the neck-bone with that nasty spare sword with a bar on the end of it, all messy too, nobody was getting awarded two ears and a tail let alone one ear, and Josepha just couldn't stand the butchery, she said it was like Lidice Sharpeville Amritsar the Western Front, just typical of the Fascist mass opium of the people set-up under Franco, symbolic blood and death. She wouldn't go to more bull-fights and so Rosa asked Jean-Roger to come, but he wouldn't go either, he had begun to talk seriously all the time to Josepha, words like Sorel *syndicalisme* Comte Saint-Simon *commune activisme* Bakunin and all the old jazz, he really was a drag but he did keep Josepha happy, she had really never had a man or how could she put up with all that chat? So Rosa went with a bull-breeder called Aragon just like the province and maybe he gave his name to Arrogance, he was that proud, and he wore cool grey suits like another skin except over his heeled boots and he fought bulls from horses with little lances and his eyes really burned, would you believe it, and Rosa asked Josepha if she would mind moving out, could she find a bed for a couple of nights, and Josepha did without a word. Aragon wasn't all that much, he was all flash and no timber, and when he began bossing her around, the great macho Latin lover, did he get his. But Josepha didn't seem to be hanging around anywhere, until Rosa heard that she could be found at a swimming-hole with Jean-Roger and a lunger–writer who'd also had polio and was trying to get fit. So Rosa drove down to the water-hole and there were the three of them getting the lunger to swim, and afterwards they all sat round and Rosa said, 'What are you doing, Josie, I'm bored, I'm going to blow, care to come?' And Josepha said she was going back to Paris with Jean-Roger, she'd started sleeping in his bed, they were *sérieux*, they'd spend the summer together till term started at Cambridge again. And Rosa said, 'He slept with me first, I won't have him sleeping with you baby, you little bitch.' And Josepha said, 'I know all about that, it won't happen again, he didn't really want to, did you, Jean-Roger?' And Jean-Roger said no. And Rosa began screaming and said, 'I don't care, you slut, you cow, you can have him, he's a lousy fuck anyway, you're welcome.' And she went off, driving the lunger back to town to show she was good too, but he had big ears, he was going to write all about it, the bastard. And after that Rosa went straight on to Madrid and ditched the car in a garage and flew off to Socrates in Chios. And all the time in the plane she thought that she really loved Jean-Roger and her pie-eyed baby sister had stolen him behind her back because she trusted the little so-and-so and she'd kill Josepha, she really would, oh those goody-goodies are vile, those holy ones are really rotten down inside, never trust anyone not even your own twin, I'll kill you Josepha or kill myself, either would do, we can't *both* live in this world. And then in Chios she told Socrates that her baby sister was still a virgin, wasn't that sweet, and they'd had a fine time in Pamplona.

While the students all went on their summer vagabondage – for all were bound to wander or lose face – Magog did not let the new space at Charles the Martyr go to waste. He invited experts from everywhere, from East and West and North and South and many uncommitted directions, to confer about the need to help the poor, the undeveloped and the plain backward nations. Since the high table at Charles the Martyr already had an international reputation – even the second chef had studied at Claridge's – and since Magog wanted his College to stand well among the conference jet set, he offered lavish expenses, retainers, accommodations and contracts to the great thinkers of the world. Like any aristocracy, they were only happy when they were being seen by each other in the right places and the same places, and they were only fulfilled in a cosy lecture-hall where the guests shared common assumptions, that experts were heard, that wise words led to good deeds, and that conferences really mattered. After all, it was not as if they were giving away the taxpayers' money in rich countries. They were merely recommending that it should be given away. This eased their consciences and spread their countries' budgets.

The conference recommended that the developed nations should devote at least two per cent of their Gross National Product to the welfare of the poorer nations, instead of the one per cent now doled out in tied shopping deals or disguised arms sales. It was a good idea, a practical idea, even a noble idea, and it fell far short of being a religious idea that the rich should share equally with the rest. Yet it was an impossible idea, because no government would listen to it. And so the conference broke up, putting on a few ounces and putting away a few expenses, prouder than ever of its expert help in saving the human race from itself. Even Magog, who personally drew up the conference report to send to the United Nations, the various world governments and anybody else he wished to impress, thought that the result wasn't much cop for the fifty thousand pounds he had laid out for the carnival of the best minds on earth.

After helping others, Magog's duty lay in helping himself and his family. Feeling that art prices could not continue to break probability and approach inspiration, he liquidated his entire collection at Sotheby's and Christie's. His twenty years of handouts to himself for helping to run Gog's estate realized over two million pounds. His cash then went into municipal bonds, property and gold. He expected the fever of speculation to burst its blisters within a couple of years, and he wanted to be out of harm's way early.

Magog was also a trustee of the Burke-Ponsonby Fund, set up as a charity for the sole relief of the infant Simon. Caring for the future of his grandson or grand-nephew, Magog apologized to high heaven and decided to go to South Africa. He knew enough, however, not to talk of his trip. In university circles, South Africa was a dirty phrase, tainted by apartheid, Boers and bad sherry. The fact that Britain had so many investments there was forgotten in the condemnation of those liberals who found it easy to love black people because they did not live among them. Our virtuous wrath, Magog consoled himself, is reserved for other people's problems, not our own. Did we not already have our ghettos of blacks and Paks, our controlled immigration, a police force that seemed to think a dark skin was an admission of crime? South African solutions were already creeping over here. Perhaps Magog's mission to Johannesburg was really more to find out the facts for the future than to feather his own nest – for the Fund did pay him a retainer of twenty thousand a year. Duty, honour, patriotism, realism and the need to keep informed took Magog to South Africa. Or so he told himself.

Actually, Magog hardly left Johannesburg. And he was quickly reassured about the stability of the two million pounds which the Fund had placed in the city. There was no question that the economy was booming, and so was the security system. In the white areas, the blacks were so well behaved that they might have been detachable shadows for their masters, dark genies that came out to serve when the magic lamp was rubbed and then went back to their hidden places when they were not wanted. There were a few who said that things were not quite as cosy as they seemed, but that was only talk. There were always red guerrillas in the hills – wasn't that what hills were for? Magog prided himself on being able to sniff the wind in any place, and as he put his sharp nose to the air, he smelt wealth and torpor and fear and control. It was a good climate for investment. Magog switched the Fund predominantly to gold and diamonds, the silly dross of the earth that people trusted when money went mad. Slump or no slump, Simon would inherit some of the hard stuff.

For one occasion, Magog was to treasure his trip to Johannesburg, when he had forgotten nearly everything else about the city of greed. He had heard that the old-time Army Angel was going to sing there, but he could not admit to the strange nostalgia which made him go to hear her. In public to his banking friends, Magog said that her performance would be the giggle of the year, the Army Angel coming all that way to wring the cockles of the veterans' hearts with her repertoire of war numbers, her Ivor Novello lilts and runs and trills. Second only to Vera Lynn herself, the Army Angel was sure to make strong men weep. In fact, Magog got to her performance early, for fear of missing anything. To hear Vera Lynn, he would have moved mountains; to hear the Army Angel, he was prepared to wait a bit in the foyer.

The audience in the theatre was not as other theatre audiences are. The people had begun arriving in the city the previous day in their old cars, blue-suited, short-haired, red and fat as bully beef, wearing their lapel buttons with MOTH on them, *Memorable Order of Tin Hats*. Their wives were at their sides in best flowered frocks and white gloves and white bags and white shoes as if they were going to be presented to the Queen Mother Herself. Half an hour before the performance opened, the theatre was filled by slow-moving men and women, pushing together as inexorably as a herd on a trek towards water in the dry veldt. There was no laughter in the house, just the occasional mutters of pleasure as old soldier met old soldier, the mass needing to slake its thirst for the time when all was simple in the North African desert, no worries far from home, death not very likely, life a matter of mucking along with one's mates, and a single voice singing tunes that seemed gay and smart to those who had been sent away for the first time from farm and small town into the World War.

The warm-up comedian was a barrack-room boy and he knew his bit. The old jokes came round, what the sergeant said to the prisoner and what the corporal said to the call-girl, and the blue puns got the steady laughs, play on words like holes and rings and browns and tits, allusions to French etceteras and Dutch caps and British walking-out fingers. Magog laughed with the rest, it was so easy, so natural, so male, a memory he had hardly had of bars and long evenings to waste with nothing better to do than ease the belly with beers and merriment.

Then the Army Angel appeared in a spotlight from heaven, and all stood up for her coming, and when they sat, she began to sing, plump, short, dark in her period white dress, a fading nightingale from Berkeley Square. Magog wanted to mock the pathetic stretch of the notes, the quaver of feeling at the pulpy lyrics, but there was a yearning in her, a sadness that made him silent until she stopped and the roar of the men froze his sneer and sent her voice skimming and soaring along its next high number in a gale force of love. No songbird this, to beat its

brains on the bars of its cage as the loris's hands ripped it apart
and ate it, meat and blood and throat, but a nightingale high in
the heaven of the lost past, where the circles of men sat in the
dark tents round their wirelesses and heard the far sweet sound
and felt each that the song was for him alone among the mates
he really loved.

The Army Angel left and the comedian returned, smut-voiced
and awful. He smirked and said:

'I'll tell you something you all want to know.' A pause for
effect. 'The donkey on Darling Street is dead.'

The silence at the end of this remark seemed to pull crimson
up every veteran's neck until a howl of laughter and shame
clapped at the theatre's roof and shuddered down the walls,
and the wives plucked at their men's shoulders wanting an
explanation, and the men would say nothing, choking with delight, and Magog understood at last what it was that still held
the Commonwealth together in a kind of a way, not the sterling
area and the regalia and the old boys' network, but the shared
dirty memories of the pubs and the changing-rooms. Magog
knew that the donkey on Darling Street was Apuleius come
again, no golden ass but a donkey with a prick as long as a black
mamba that served some cavernous fat tart in the whore's alley
in Cairo called Darling Street, where the soldiers came to jeer
more than to risk the pox, and the sad gyppo orgies were the
myths of all the armies chasing Rommel from Alamein to Rome.
The donkey on Darling Street was more famous than the Old
Man in Downing Street, and both were dead now, the myths
were moribund, Ichabod, Ichabod, Ichabod, thy glory is departed, old soldiers do slowly die, wars are forgot, empires
erode, voices still. The British had served their turn. The
donkey on Darling Street was dead.

1966

The attack, when it came, was unexpected. Angus McInnes was a neat fighter and he found Magog's weak spot before the Master found his. Josepha was reading Moral Sciences and the philosopher first lectured to her, then put her in his seminars, then gave her private supervisions. He said that he was devoting his time to her as he had never met such a brilliant pupil – it must surely run in the family. Josepha might well get a First and few girls could manage that in Philosophy. In fact, he was preparing his ground against Magog, finding a spy in the Master's Lodge and a thorn in the Master's heart. For he knew that, while Magog loved Josepha, she thought of him as a False Father, a Mammon and a Moloch ready to devour his own children through his greed and power and machinations. And Josepha was at the age of reaction from her family, rejection of her mother, rebellion from riches, and absolute assurance that she knew all the answers – which exposed her wholly to the latest radical frenzy. Violence was the new thing and McInnes spoke to her about violence.

'Violence,' he said to her, 'is neither good nor bad. It has no morals. It is an act of aggression, and we are all born with aggression in our natures. The question is then, violence for what? And violence from what? The guerrilla like Mao or Fidel or Che uses violence as an instrument of social policy. He wishes to replace a bad society by a better one, as you and your friends wish to do. There is no morality in the killing during the fighting. If the guerrillas become the government, their murders on the way become acts of revolutionary virtue and are taught in the schools. If the guerrillas are beaten by the government, their murders become acts of adventurist futility even to their own side. Success hallows a revolution, failure makes it folly. Violence in itself is abstract, as is non-violence. Their purpose and result determine their morality. Who is more guilty, the man who kills a tyrant and delivers his country, or the man who surrenders his whole people into slavery to save a life? Aye, Josepha, violence is all right, if you know what it's for and what it's against.'

'Magog,' Josepha said and went and blew up the Anglican chapel of Charles the Martyr.

Such a scandal had not rocked the Senior Universities since Percy Bysshe Shelley had been sent down for blasphemy. A petrol-bomb placed in a chapel dedicated to the Almighty and right beneath the Master's Lodge! Had Magog not smelled the smoke, he might have seen the whole central dome of his College flaming to heaven as he slid to safety down the curved concrete to the ground, or, even worse for his dignity, as he was evacuated by the Fire Brigade in his pyjamas. At any rate, Magog's sharp nose smelt the smoke in time to save the dome, and he also sniffed out arson as the cause of the blaze rather than a fault in the wiring. The defect lay in envy, not electricity.

'Whenever you come to see me, McInnes,' Magog said to the philosopher, 'I expect the apocalypse. My brother always used to tell me that Gog and Magog were the signs and forerunners of the end of the world. But you must be the actual herald of doom.'

'I try to do my wee worst,' Angus said. 'I really should compliment you on your malt, Master. You must loot all Scotland for it.'

'And you must loot the Master's Lodge to drink it back. If I put a match to your breath, McInnes, doubtless you'd burn like a bomb yourself. You're a Molotov cocktail on two legs. I'm surprised the police don't make you sleep in an Armoury till you're defused.' McInnes laughed almost complacently. He seemed very sure of himself. 'I suppose you've come to give me more bad news about the outrage,' Magog went on. 'What else can I expect from *you*?'

'Replacement,' McInnes said. 'Perhaps you'd care to cast an eye on this.'

The photocopies of the drawings which the philosopher gave to Magog were very detailed. They showed with a clarity worthy of Descartes the method of making a petrol-bomb. The notes scribbled in the margins came from two different pens. Magog recognized one of the scripts as Josepha's.

'An interesting experiment in design,' Magog said. 'What is it? A Roman Candle for Guy Fawkes' Day?'

'Come on now, Master. You know it's for making a petrol-bomb. And you know the writing on it. Josepha's.'

Magog pointed to the other script.

'I've never seen that writing before,' he said.

'It's her boy-friend's. Jean-Roger Garde, now at Nanterre. Do you know him?'

'I have heard of him. I thought he was all logic and no application to anything useful.'

'He applies his logic all right. I'd say the chapel made a fine proof of the theory of the petrol-bomb.'

'Just because Josepha has been sketching incendiaries as a form of love-play, I really can't see any connection between that and the *accident* here.'

'Take a look at this.'

Another photocopy was put into Magog's hand. Again, Josepha's handwriting. Again, irrefutable evidence. As a revolutionary, Josepha appeared only to want to be a martyr. The draft proclamation began:

STUDENTS OF CAMBRIDGE!
WORKERS OF CAMBRIDGE!

The fire that has burned the new College will burn the old ones. The bomb in OUR hand is also the bomb in YOUR hand. Unite to ignite the centres of fascist reaction that are brainwashing the young and the workers into consumerism . . .

The message was dreary and predictable, a plain incitement to riot, worth a prison sentence without even the bombing. It was signed CAMBRIDGE LIBERATION FRONT. Magog had heard of some printed leaflets from the same organization which had appeared in the Common Rooms and had been treated as a joke. Here was the original pen behind the propaganda, the first cause of the mischief. Magog felt a moment of cowardice, then of anger. How could Josepha have been such a fool? Even the words were hackneyed, and Magog could not pardon dull prose.

'Where are the originals of these photocopies?' Magog said.

'Safe enough,' McInnes said.

'How did they get into your hands?'

'That is my affair.'

'I gather you have become Josepha's part-time tutor. Or should I say *inciter*?'

'The philosophy I have taught your *niece* . . .' Here McInnes gave Magog such a hard stare through his owlish glasses that Magog knew Josepha had piled idiocy on folly and had talked of her family skeletons to her tutor, his enemy '. . . is neutral in terms of commitment. I never encourage a course of action. I merely clarify intentions and purposes. My job is not to build up belief or action, but to examine them. That is what I am doing now, Master. Examining an action, the bombing of Charles the Martyr by your *niece*.'

'You will give the evidence to the police?'

'Surely that is what you wish, Master. You cannot leave a pyromaniac running around putting Cambridge to the flame.'

'No, I cannot.' Magog looked out of the windows of the Lodge. Beneath him, the eight legs of the spider College were finished, the undergraduates were already living in its joints and cells. All was in order, in place, at peace, except for the small hammering sound beneath the floor of the Lodge where the workmen were repairing the chapel. Josepha might be Gog's child, after all, if she behaved like that. And yet, she did have her excuse. All her revolt was explicable as a violent reaction from the trauma that he, Magog, might be her father . . .

'Well then, Master, shall I go and call for the CID . . .?'

'No,' Magog said. 'Tell me your terms.'

'Terms?' McInnes took off his glasses and began to wipe them. It was a calculated effect, which simulated thinking. Yet the philosopher's terms had surely been defined before he ever came into the room. Only when the answer is known before the question is asked can there be any stability in this world.

'Terms,' Magog said. 'Don't try to tell me you haven't got your terms.'

'I would never have thought, Master, that you'd try to obstruct the course of justice.'

'I don't want your irony,' Magog said. 'Just your terms.'

'Of course, there's a higher law, as the great Aquinas said. There's human justice and there's natural justice, and natural justice can be better than the mere judgements of the courts. I'd say it was naturally just for a poor man who had given up his life to education to end his days profiting a wee bit from the spending of his life. More just, at least, than a rich man who had spent his life making money, only to end by profiting from education without much of a contribution to it.'

'You do want my place, then?'

'Miniver to go this autumn, I won't oppose his pension. You to have a hernia, duodenal, prostate operation – choose your own surgery – in the course of the next year. Then you retire for the sake of your health, nominating the new Vice-Master to succeed you.'

'You?'

'Aye,' McInnes said. 'I!'

'It won't wash with the Prime Minister. This is a plum job. He's got more important people to give a plum to than even you, McInnes.'

'I'm advising the government of the moment,' McInnes said. 'An honorarium of five thousand a year to evaluate certain aspects of our defence policy. It's so secret I don't dare mention it even to myself. But you'd better know that I have my contacts where they matter . . .'

'The students wouldn't like that,' Magog said. 'How would your radical views look to them, if they knew?'

'I can't tell them of my government work. I'm bound by the Official Secrets Act, as you are. But I do tell them what I tell the Committee, weapons are neutral, just as violence is. I evaluate defence systems as a philosopher, because the Prime Minister knows my judgement is completely un-biased. It's not for me to say what a weapon is *for*, but to find out whether it works and how much it costs. Incidentally, I've let it be known at Downing Street that your health isn't too good.'

'Very prophetic of you,' Magog said. 'Not to say premature.'

'The Prime Minister says he won't forget me. He hasn't forgotten you either. Apparently, he was President of the Board of Trade, trying to preserve the British Film Industry, while you were scrapping it.'

'I was also saving it, but by a different method,' Magog said. 'By not making films. And look, the film industry is saved now. It still exists – and still makes no films.'

'Well,' McInnes said, 'you'll accept my terms then?'

'Decent of you to offer me a year's grace,' Magog said. 'Could I have Josepha's follies in my hand, please?'

'Just the copies till I'm Master here,' the philosopher said. 'I presume on nothing in my trade, not even good faith.'

'Josepha is costing me pretty dear, wouldn't you say?' Magog said. 'That is, if I really am such a hard-hearted villain as she makes out.'

'Aye, you do love your family,' McInnes said. 'Too much, by all accounts. That porter you sacked told me you lost control when you heard the poor fellow had touched your daughter, even though you'd ordered him to throw her out. Well, I said to myself when I heard the tale, there's his weak spot, there it is. Every Rasputin has to have his Achilles' heel, to mix a wee metaphor or two. *Fatherly* love. Farther than that, I'd say . . .'

Magog hated. He had not felt hate since Maire had put him on the rack. Its violence in his gut made him double up. He could hardly steady his voice, though he managed.

'My private feelings for my family are none of your concern,' he said. 'You will find, McInnes, *if* you ever reach the high positions you are unfit to occupy, that nothing makes a man fall faster in England than trying to use people's private lives against them. That is considered intolerable here and you are intolerable. A bloody shit.'

'What's this?' McInnes said. 'The *Master* talking like you or me?'

'Turn Josepha over to the police,' Magog said, 'and I'll break you for it.'

'Don't bluff me, Master. I'll do it all right. You know that. She'll be put away.'

'Do it. And get out.'

McInnes rose and walked over to the door. He paused, his hand on the knob, waiting for Magog to call him back, but Magog did not call. He half-opened the door and paused again. Still

Magog did not call. So McInnes had to turn back himself, closing the door behind him. His face showed a kind of smile.

'Wha's the good?' he asked. 'There's no need to break your heart, man. There's no need. I'm a reasonable man too, and you love your children like a good father should. Why not just quit, enjoy your millions, bring up your girls and leave education to people who have made it their whole lives? It's enough, Master.'

'I won't be blackmailed,' Magog said.

'Then I'll not blackmail you, I'll just say, I'm the best man for the job of Vice-Master, and I'll take over as Master when you're ready to enjoy the leisure you have so richly deserved . . . in a year or two.'

'You'll always hold Josepha's case against me.'

McInnes walked over to Magog's desk, picked up the photocopies of the evidence against Josepha, and began to tear them up.

'There,' he said kindly as to a child.

'Don't baby me,' Magog said. 'You won't destroy the originals.'

'Yes I will, Master. In my own good time.'

'You really think I'll go?'

'I don't know what keeps you here at all. Your *ivory tower*? Your prestige? You can get more of that in London. We're *provincial*, a backwater . . .'

'That's the first thing I can agree on,' Magog said. 'Nothing keeps me here.' He rose and walked over to the window to look down at his monstrous masterwork. The concrete sprawl seeemed suddenly rather grandiose and tasteless. 'The College is completed, my creation done. And I've always been much more interested in setting things up rather than running them down. Furthermore . . .'

He looked back towards McInnes, who stared at him almost humbly, as if waiting to hear an important truth that would bind the Master to quit, condemned out of his own mouth.

'Furthermore,' Magog repeated in disgust, 'I came to Cambridge to find a quieter place, more sympathetic people. But you lot intrigue more with less result than any City Corporation. You *do* educate the young, but only to act as badly as yourselves. McInnes, you can have Cambridge with my contempt.'

'Thank you.' McInnes was grateful. 'I will.'

'But I will not leave under duress,' Magog warned.

'Leave under choirs of angels,' McInnes said. 'We are not worthy of men of your spirit. But you are leaving?'

'That is for me to say, McInnes.' Magog pointed the door to his enemy. 'All the same, don't go to the police.'

When McInnes left, Magog sent for Josepha. She was defiant, but she did come to see him. He showed her the torn photocopies, told her of the philosopher's betrayal and use of her, then said he had decided to quit the College of Charles the Martyr to stop her going to prison. If she felt self-sacrificial, the scandal would make him resign anyway, while she would get several years in gaol at the very least. Even a Labour Government, or especially a Labour Government, did not encourage radical solutions. The Home Secretary and the Cambridge judges would not be amused. If Josepha wanted to be a heroic victim, this was not the country to do it in. Her martyrdom would be both forgotten and useless. It would change her society in no way. Britain was an island unto itself, much too pleased with itself, suffering change ungladly.

'You do yourself no good going to prison, Josepha. You do me a favour in giving me a reason to leave this mess of pottage on the Fens.'

Josepha began by insisting on going immediately to the police to give herself up. Then she wept, then she said she was sorry. The bomb had even scared her, and when she had set it off, she had found herself wanting to run upstairs and warn Magog that his life was in danger. But her comrades had pulled her away. She felt too soft to be a revolutionary, too compassionate. She did not mind destroying things, but she could not destroy people. And she had not really thought of the consequences, the several years in prison.

'Prison would be destroying a person,' Magog said. 'Yourself.'

Josepha nodded. Prison seemed too long and brutal a consequence for such a brief and inept act.

In the end, Magog fixed a deal with Josepha. She would leave Cambridge at the end of her second year with her degree half-done. She would spend her final year in Paris, studying philosophy at the Sorbonne, and presumably living with Jean-Roger. She would marry him, Josepha said, only they didn't believe in marriage. The Cambridge Liberation Front would be disbanded now that it had been penetrated; it would commit no more acts of violence.

'Of course, you could set fire to your pickled nark, McInnes,' Magog said. 'He'd burn like a distillery, and I would have no objections whatsoever. In fact, it would be an act of passionate patriotism.'

But Josepha decided to spare even the philosopher. What could you expect from a bourgeois revisionist except betrayal?

'Not mercy,' Magog said. 'For mercy, you will have to look to your own flesh and blood.'

So Josepha wept and kissed Magog and said she was sorry that she had ruined his career. And Magog said that resigning the Mastership was perhaps best for him. He did not flourish in academic life. He would have left sooner or later. Saying this was a lie to comfort Josepha; but all the same, Magog did feel that the loss of his whole College was tolerable, now that Josepha had begun to feel for him again. God knows, getting money was easy enough, but getting the love of people, especially those who were very close to a man, was hard. And at forty-seven years old, Magog was more worried about the few who still touched him than the state of the nation or his investments.

To bring the walls of Troy tumbling down, the Greeks must have gone into their wooden horse on a ladder through its arsehole. But Rosa walked into the plastic woman at Stockholm through her slit, between the great spread legs decorated in bright rings and circles. She followed the crowd entering the giantess who sprawled on her back inviting her clients to try her black inside under the dome of her belly and the twin canopies of her breasts, headless though, what thought can a plastic body have when people are walking up her, to watch a Garbo film where her heart should be and poke their heads through a trapdoor in her navel? The giantess of Stockholm was eighty-two feet long and twenty feet high and thirty feet broad and was billed as the biggest and best woman in the world, notwithstanding other versions by Phidias and Michelangelo. The Troy she was meant to destroy was the walled city of hypocrisy, puritanism, reality, commonsense, decency and the canons of art. But the visitors to her dark belly came out exactly the same as they went in. The Troy of bourgeois values still stood in Stockholm despite the immense woman installed in the Moderna Museum. The trouble was, as Rosa saw, the giantess was too shoddy. You can't seduce a man, let alone a whole civilization, if you're an old bag.

As Rosa walked out of the slit of the plastic woman, she did not feel reborn. No embryo memory reminded her of the bloody convulsions and contractions of her birth with Josepha from her mother Maire. And yet, looking at the swelling tattooed legs on either side of her, she did think of bearing Simon. So, on a whim, she flew back to London and then drove down to Cormonderley to see him, unannounced. The giantess of Stockholm had had the wrong effect. She had driven Rosa back to the duty of motherhood.

The Ponsonbys were not glad to see Rosa, but they could not keep her from Simon. She walked with her son in the park outside the Renaissance house. She called herself just Rosa – Mummy would have confused him and Auntie would have been a lie. He ran in circles round her through the leaves like a dog chasing off from his fixed centre of love and security, only to return to a whistle or a call of his name. Rosa found his immediate doting on her peculiar; but there was no doubt that he kissed her without question and took her for granted in his little world, as if she had brought him up all her life. Amy Ponsonby found this most unfair.

Rosa did feel a twinge of regret, even a yearning for her child. Yet it was impossible, impossible. She was still young, she had to keep free, the Ponsonbys were bringing up Simon admirably, look how happy he was in the country, all children should have stable homes, he seemed to love her without the bore of bringing him up, there would always be a time later for her and Simon when she was less restless and had been through her freedom kick and had reached the point which the nice French poet told her she would reach, when she did not need liberty so much as only to be chained by what she loved. But Rosa loved herself now more than Simon, so she waited until he was put to bed, then she drove away, saying she would come back soon, which she did not.

*   *   *

When Morrell came into the Lodge with a metal stake in his hand, Magog felt his molars with horror. Surely he had not yet grown fangs, even if people did think he drank the blood of the young for breakfast.

'I am not a vampire, Morrell,' he said, to settle the matter. 'How do you do?'

'This stake is not for your heart, Magog,' Morrell said.

'Magog? My name's Ponsonby.'

'You're Magog. I've been talking to your brother and he identified you at last to me.' Indeed, Morrell was not recognizable as the dandy young property dealer, so expert at kicking out poor tenants for the benefit of profits. He now wore a many-coloured Joseph coat with a strange talisman round his neck, wavy lines on a silver disc. His hair was looser, his crown balder, his eyes both bright and restless. Gog did seem able to persuade people to indulge in their wilder natures.

'Magog, then, if you insist,' the Master said. 'What took you to my brother?'

'He lives on one of the nerves of the earth. His farm is near a radial point. He helped me to drive in a stake there on top of a scree.'

'Morrell, you seem a little *different*. Has something changed you in the last seven years?'

'The truth,' Morrell said. 'I have seen the whole lost earth, and it is mine to discover it again.'

'When we last met, you were joking about flying saucers and outer space. Now it is the whole earth. I'm glad you've got your feet on the ground now.'

'They must have had the flying saucers in Atlantis, Magog, when they mapped the earth out, when they drew all its lines, its nodes, its nerves. Then Atlantis was destroyed and we inherited only its wreckage. Few of the lines of the earth remain. Yet the Atlanteans must have flown high to map out the Nazca lines in the deserts of Peru, the Great Wall of China, and our own radial hub that spokes out from Stonehenge and Avebury, the moon and the sun of Albion. I read your book, incidentally, on the Riddle of the Stones. Rational trash. How could you do it, when you have a great genius like Gog as your brother?'

'How could you do it, when you made your money by evicting

the helpless?' Magog asked. 'You always were a whimsical fellow to the point of carelessness. How did you lose your way in faery land?'

'The same as you,' Morrell said. 'By a vision. This lump of property, this horrible dome of your College, who told you to build it *here*? On the leyline from Gogmagog to Castle Mound?'

'The money was given. The land was available. Cambridge needed a new College. I built it here.'

'Why a dome, then?'

'Well, when I saw the Dome of the Rock in Jerusalem . . .'

'*Jerusalem!*' Morrell's eyes glimmed like will o' the wisps. 'You did say Jerusalem?' With a cry of delight, he lifted his spike and jammed it into the oriental carpet that flew over the chapel roof below. Magog pretended not to notice such an aggressive action. Danger, if ignored, might go away.

'Yes, Jerusalem,' Magog said. 'Jerusalem, Jordan, not the New Jerusalem, Albion, courtesy of William Blake, idiot and poet and deranger of my brother's mind.'

'You call the river here the Cam? What was it called in the time of Atlantis? Perhaps the Jordan River. You built this dome for the sake of Jerusalem, didn't you?'

'It's just coincidence. The Dome of the Rock happened to strike me *en passant* . . .'

'Is it just a coincidence that your dome of Charles of Martyr is exactly on a radial point between the Stonehenge line and the line of the Great Pyramid and the Great Wall of China? *You* did not build the College of Charles the Martyr. It was built *through* you.'

'Precisely, but by my decision.'

Morrell laughed and began to bang the spike into the floor with a club-hammer which he produced from his glorious-patched coat.

'*Your* decision? Well, Magog, each man to his own folly . . .' Bang . . . 'A huge *dome* over one of the nerve centres of the planet, and Magog calls it *his own* decision? . . .' Bang . . . 'Do you know Lethbridge himself discovered the great figure of the Sungod Himself . . .' Bang . . . 'Lying across the Gogmagog Hills just a few miles from here? . . .' Bang . . . 'And do you

know where his axis points? . . .' Bang . . . 'To the centre of
the Dome of Charles the Martyr . . .' Crash.

The spike was well and truly driven home. At last Magog felt
his anger overcome his fear of this dandy turned Tom O'Bedlam.

'Would you mind,' he said, 'taking your spike out of my
exquisite Tekke-Turkoman?'

Morrell gave the spike one last thump, then swung on the
Master, his hammer in his hand.

'I have cured it,' he exulted. 'This College will now begin to
get well. It will be convalescent by next summer. Of course,
you'll have to go.'

'I am going,' Magog said. 'Was that a guess or information?'

'Going by your *own will*?' Morrell asked sarcastically.

'Not actually. By an unfortunate chain of circumstances.'

Morrell shouted with laughter.

'That's good,' he said. 'That's very good. Well, by a fortunate
chain of circumstances, I am here to cure the ills of this College
and all Cambridgeshire, by driving in this magic spike exactly
where it is, in the centre of the head of Charles the Martyr.
Have you heard of acupuncture?'

'The Chinese system of *faith*-healing,' Magog said. 'Doubtless, the needles are more painful than the aches, so the patient
has to say he's cured, or he gets tortured again. I'm not very
good at *magic*, you know.'

'Nobody is any more,' Morrell said. He took Magog's remark
without irony. 'The Chinese also applied acupuncture to the
body of the earth as well as to the human body. Wherever the
nerves of the planet ran, you will find the ruins of an old temple,
a pile of stones, a dragon's path, and a metal rod or statue. How
do you cure a polluted stream in China? By driving in copper
poles. What have we done to the body of the earth? Poisoned
it by its metals, chemicals, pesticides. But I have begun its
cures. I have gone back to trace out the old nerves of the earth
which the Atlanteans once marked out before they were destroyed, the diagram of the globe now hardly seen and often
destroyed by Roman roads, towns, farms, fields. But from the
air, you can still see some of the lines. And whenever I find an
old nodal knot, a crossing of the ancient lines of wisdom and the
sun, I drive in my needle to cure the currents, the palsied nerves

of the earth, the frayed ends of our lost and lovely world.'

Messianic, Morrel stretched out his hands. The weight of his club-hammer made his right hand sag, so he put the hammer in his pocket.

'I suppose it's as good a way to waste one's time as any other,' Magog said diplomatically. 'You must have got along well with Gog. He'd understand just what you're about.'

'Gog is a saint, a misunderstood prophet. He gave me money. He worked at the local forge with me to make my stakes. Iron, copper, a trace of silver, the contents according to the golden mean. On the head of each needle, the Celtic rune of the motion of the universe which I wear about my neck. Once I drive it in, it never fails. The broken currents of the earth begin to connect again. The old wisdom returns.'

'Am I supposed to leave that spike in the middle of my carpet?' Magog asked. 'I mean, what shall I say it is? A freeform statue? A scratch-post for my tame tiger? Or a toothpick with notions?'

'You will call it what it is. Morrell's Magic Marker, SOS, Save Our Society.'

Magog had had enough. He pressed the button of the intercom to the Porters' Lodge and spoke into it.

'I have a guest whom I would like shown out,' he said.

'I'm going,' Morrell said. 'I have done what I had to do. Cambridge is saved at last.'

'If anyone else tries to save me or my College by burning the chapel down or driving a pin into my carpet, I shall only say, I don't understand saviours. I don't understand revolutionaries. I don't understand you new freaks of the earth. None of you will listen to reason, and I haven't got anything else to offer you except force, and you won't take that. All I understand is that you want to change me, and it's too damn late.' Then he thought of McInnes and of his own going soon. And he smiled at Morrell. 'All the same,' he added, 'you're better than the envious and the intriguing and the mean. I do understand them very well, and they will listen to reason. But they want to see the back of me by now, and it's mutual. So perhaps I'll see you to the College gate after all, just to remind myself of the way out. This is a very nasty place to be sure, and I hope your pin pricks it.'

1967

Magog sat above the bowl marked *The Clanzer* and thought of
Montaigne. Even a king, Montaigne had written, sits on his own
bum. Now even a Magog was sitting on the hidden throne at
the Opera House, on the dark oak polished by the bare secret
skins of the Blood Royal and a few lesser bottoms. Magog
relieved himself more satisfactorily than Ladysmith, then sighed
with content. At last, he had rubbed cheeks with the great. He
rose and wiped and buttoned his trousers to his braces, then
walked through to the anteroom where the large angular basin
with the silver taps waited for his ritual cleansing. The bowl of
the basin was marked *The Reginus*. It was the perfect mixture
of the sacred and the profane. Magog rinsed his hands, dried
them on the towel and went out of the washroom into the private
supper-room behind the Royal Box. He closed the door behind
him and watched the privy chamber disppear into the Regency
panelling of the wall. The hidden throne might never have
existed, the most arcane and powerful pleasure-seat of them
all.

Round the table sat the other members of the Royal Commission for the Fine Arts with their dowagers. Also Maire, who
could still set, thank God, an ambush of possible danger at any
stuffy occasion. The guests were variously dressed in tails and
tiaras, white ties and décolletage, medals and jewels. Except
for Maire, who wore black satin pyjamas of a mysterious and
flowing cut with a white choker that seemed pinned to her throat
by an enormous baroque pearl in the shape of a mermaid. Magog
smiled at her distinction. There was no confusing her with the
rest of womankind.

'Chocolate cake,' Magog said. 'If there's one thing I can resist,
it's chocky cake.' And there it lay on the plates, chocky cake
between the Second and Third Acts of *Der Rosenkavalier*, not

inappropriate, as long as nobody had to eat it. Why the royal family of England had a craving for a chicken and ham salad and chocky cake, Magog had never discovered. It was as if the House of Windsor had never left the nursery. But however it was, the users of the Royal Box at the Opera House got the same fare, chicken and ham salad and chocky cake, just like at Garden Parties in Buckingham Palace. It had been a long time since there had been a gourmet on the British throne, who could have put *The Clanzer* to good use.

As Magog washed down his cake with some reasonable claret, he tried not to listen to the chatter that passed for musical appreciation among the Royal Commission for the Fine Arts and their ladies.

'. . . She growls like a pussycat in her pianissimo . . . Really, one shouldn't sit above Joan when she's playing an ingenue, her wrinkles look like the wreck of the *Hesperus* . . . I only come to opera to see women dressed up as boys, except it does stretch the plot so . . .'

Magog had been put on the Board of Governors of the Royal Opera for his wealth as much as for his connections. Subsidies were expected from time to time. Magog, however, was tone-deaf and found the long arias of caterwauling and large areas of posturing a torture to the eardrums and a travesty to the eye. But it was the thing to sit in the Royal Box on non-Royal nights under the great insignia, *Dieu et mon droit*, and so Magog sat there. Particularly as he had no better place to sit. The government had kindly kicked him upstairs to head the new Royal Commission for the Fine Arts, when he had said he was willing to resign from the College of Charles the Martyr. All governments in England played the rules of the patronage game – that a man who has not offended may only be dismissed by being promoted. This prestige had allowed Magog to announce his resignation as if he had been called up to save the nation's culture. And now he was being cosseted into understanding why the Royal Opera bagged the lion and the unicorn's share of the state money given to the Arts, even though it only appealed to a minor audience. Magog did know the brief of his Commission in advance. He was to find the state of the Arts in good shape, needing only the least of adjustments. And he must not attack the holy of holies, the Royal Opera, for he was now within its portals.

It was time for the Third Act. Magog rose and shepherded the Commissioners and their ladies and Maire into the Royal Box for the final term of trial by audio-visual archaeology. At least, he could set his chair behind Maire's and block out most of the stage by her exquisite black hair that was cut into the glossy helmet of her initial and his, M. There was admiration to be had in her agelessness and triumphant denial of time, however painful the sound was from the stage, however vulgar the surroundings of gilt and red velvet.

'Going to the opera,' Maire whispered, 'is no worse than going to the dentist's. You never expect to survive, but then it's never as bad as you expect.'

'At least you get gas at the dentist's,' Magog whispered back. 'Where's the bloody anaesthesia here?'

Josepha never knew whether her arrival in La Paz at the same time as Che Guevara was by accident or intention. Of course, she did not meet Che or even know that he had come there, but later, when the news was out and she found that the beginning of Che's sortie to Bolivia had been in the same month as hers, she always wondered at Jean-Roger's itinerary. As she understood it, their trip had been entirely for archaeology's sake, to see every old stone below the Rio Grande. Yet they had arrived in Bolivia at the same time as Che, and nothing would ever be the same for her because of that.

It was a fine trip. The money had been easy to get, the Ponsonby's chipping in five thousand dollars without a murmur, although Jean-Roger said they would probably have doubled the sum if Josepha had traded in her dutch cap. The two lovers hired a car in the sad industrial shanty-city of Monterey under its black saddle-mountain, then set off to the ruins in the West and Centre and South of Mexico, the Temple of the 365 Niches at El Tajìn, the pyramids of Teotihuacan with the mile-long Avenue of the Dead, the lost monolith of Malinalco with its eagle and jaguar stone seats, the eroding skull altars of Calixtlahuaca, the helmeted La Venta blockheads by the malarial Laguna de las Illusiones, the step-pyramids in the jungles at Palenque where the camouflaged moths crackled as they flew, the peaked temples shadowing the sacrificial chacmools at Uxmal and Chitchen-Itza near a sweat-holy cave in the limestone leading to the mysteries of heaven and earth and the final still clear pool of infinite death where blind shrimps swam, then down by little aeroplane to the first sight the Spaniards had of the cities of the New World, the degenerate stucco of sea-girt Tulum with its topsy-turvy God falling from heaven headfirst into the destruction of Mayan times.

Yet for all the beauty and wonder of the old ruins which Jean-Roger photographed and checked off against his guidebook to see if they matched, Josepha remembered only the Mayan Indians with their fierce noses and terrible stillness, waiting without expectation by the road that was their way of life, their long stares as they stood with their machetes in their hands until the white people went, the brown women in their white huipils embroidered with flowers at hem and neck or washing bare in the jungle pools, unearthly clean after the mud floors of their shacks where the yellow dogs and cats and guinea-pigs and gobble-gobble turkeys all mixed together in indifferent harmony. Why did they wait and watch? Surely the black Christs crucified in agony, the Indian saints that flew on the sugarcake walls of the marzipan shrines and churches such as Tonantzintla, the tinsel Virgins standing on the silver cup of the moon, the bleeding effigies of thorned hearts as vile as the smoking sacrifices of the Aztecs, surely these false hallowings of slave suffering imposed by the conquistadors could not still inhibit the Indians from hacking the rich tourists to bloody bits? What did they care that Jean-Roger called them oppressed comrades, hermanos, when he could not even get as near to them as a friar or an Inquisitor, he brought no guns, the Revolution had been and gone too often in Mexico, yet nothing had changed for the Mayans in their jungles, little hope to be had on this earth, only memories of might and past glory to sustain, waiting for a last Quetzalcoatl to come flying over the sea, no Holy Ghost in his white-feathered redemption, but as real as a Mig or a Mystère, a winged snake as deadly as the white-wafted galleons of Spain, this time to bring salvation without subjection. But God takes his time in coming.

'The Indians,' Josepha said to Jean-Roger, 'we'll never get through to them. We'll never get through. The whole coast from Veracruz to Villahermosa now stinks of sulphur. The sea's a film of oil. The Mayans don't want that. We inflict it on them, calling it riches, revolution, progress, and they don't see any of that. They pull back to their jungles, their last refuge, their lost dream. Jean-Roger, leave them alone.'

Damned as a bourgeois sentimentalist in her turn, Josepha was flown on to the jungles of the interior, the hidden city of Tikal in the Guatemalan Peten, where the high-hat temples swaggered over the forest roof, and death by jaguar was still more likely than death by alligator or green fer de lance or guerrilla, and where only twenty thousand people now survived on the land that had fed a million Mayans, twenty thousand stalking each other through the trunk-dark labyrinth in the name of poverty and humanity and liberty, but however much they killed each other, who would go back to Peten now, when he could live in a barrio and watch the football match come Saturday, far from the mosquito-pricking swamps without hope of draining, where the creepers and growths covered the clearings in a season, making mock of the burn-and-slash of men. The guerrillas now fought from the houses of the third Guatemala City – the first two destroyed by flood and mud, fire and quake. Even the red rebels had left the Peten to the jaguar gods of the Mayans, forever crouching in their trees as they wait for the winged deliverer who does not come.

On to Peru and the strip of coastal desert and the road fringed with crosses – bury them where they crash – past the great mud fortress of Paramonga to the mazes of Chan-Chan and the copulating skeletons of the Moche pots up up Andes-high to the massy blocks of Cuzco and Ollontaytambo making Cyclopean Greece look like crazy paving in the perfect dovetailing of monumental stone, where every boulder is sacred in shape and curl, and the sunrise comes over Macchu-Picchu through the fogged peaks to spit itself on the point of the heart-shaped sacrifice rock, and then the railway rolls for a day across the brown grass of the altiplano and past the llamas and the vicuñas and the Indian women in their ponchos and brown bowlers and the bare-foot men chewing cocaine against their tuberculosis and the despair of slow starvation and it all, then across Lake Titicaca by night in an old Victorian steamboat, brought up piece by piece on the backs of porters, its engine rooms all brass and shining copper, its smoke-stack black and belching, marble the bar and cast-iron the swivel chairs, hail to thee, W. Denny, Engineer of Dumbarton, who built to last! Then on by the little train to Tiahuanaco, the matrix of all the Andean temples, battered square Stonehenge of monoliths, set in barren plain, gap-toothed to rim of mountain, then back to train dropping down to La Paz, a tin-roofed city of mud walls with the men shitting in the open sewers and even the buzzards gone away in disgust, leaving the dead dogs to lie in the streets.

Of course, the papers said Che was already there, dressed as a priest on a bicycle, and of course, Jean-Roger and Josepha did not believe the papers, but Che was truly coming as a balding businessman off the aeroplane, and a farm was being prepared by the Peredo brothers down on the Nancahuazu River, and the slow harsh struggle of the guerrilla for survival in the jungle and on the scarps was in its beginning, doomed to its bloody ending cut in two parts thrashing like a severed snake, and Josepha was never to be the same again, she would never know if Jean-Roger had not been using her as a decoy to prepare Che's coming, she would never know if he was not sent in advance as a minor Régis Debray, she would never believe that chance had brought her to Bolivia in that month, she was always guilty that she had been there and known nothing and had done nothing to help the only hope of the Americas since Bolívar with his plan to call the continent into one struggle against poverty and disease, one great crusade against the jaguar gods and the stone masses of the temples of the dead for a future where each would help all and frontiers would separate no more. But Josepha did not know that Che was in Bolivia until that Easter back in Paris, and Jean-Roger said that he had not known a thing too, they had only gone to the Americas to look at old stones, there had been no other purpose, but Josepha never quite believed him and she never quite forgave him for not trusting her with the revolution, so she decided to have a child by him to still her doubts and because they seemed to be slicing apart like Che's guerrilla on the Nancahuazu, but as soon as she got pregnant, she knew it wouldn't work, it was too late, why was it always too late?

The old man stood in front of the supermarket, skivvying. Once a year he walked from Wales to stand outside the United Dairies off Portman Square, screaming curses against the government for raping the land from the people, grabbing the clean air, the pure water, the health, the happiness, the time of day and night. His old cap was a lid on the last of his hair, his eyes were blurry with passion and rheum, his pram was piled with his rags and stores and set like a rostrum in front of him, his three mongrel hounds were tied with ropes to the sides of the pram, as he shouted to the deafness of God in the high heavens and embarrassed the tidy passers-by who did not want to listen.

'They have stolen your ground . . . We must boil all our food now . . . Why? . . . We have to have hankies over our mouths . . . Gags against the poisons . . . No more govern-ments . . . Fucking fools . . . We must go back to candles, bach . . . We don't need all this stuff now . . . We've done enough work for four hundred years . . . Stop . . . Just fucking stop . . .'

His voice fell away as the street cleared about him, the housewives hurrying off at such language. He was right naturally. The whole world was wrong. It was a rubbish-tip of unwanted factory goods. But nobody wanted to hear. So he lit up a butt-end to cancer his lungs a little more and undid a plastic bag in his pram to give his hounds some discarded synthetic biscuit. And he waited to catch his breath. There was more skivvying to do. A Sinn Feiner had taught him about skivvying. Once a year for hundreds of years, old Irish families would curse the stealers of the land at their gates, inviting attack and the continuing of the blood feud. It was an old Celtic custom, lost this side of the Irish Sea. But Evans was reviving it, Evans the Latin, the last of the Druids, the only voice of reason left in the land, and he half-dead with not a boy to follow him. Still, he must stand and skivvy for the whole people of Albion, somebody would stop and listen, hear the words, carry on when he was gone. He finished his butt-end and cleared this throat and began to curse again to the passing cars and the empty street.

As Rosa drove to Marble Arch, she turned to Aristides sitting beside her, Socrates' nephew and one of the twenty-seven Greeks studying Maritime Law at London University. There were only twenty-eight in the whole class, and the last one was a Chinaman.

'Isn't this a quaint country?' she said.

'With lovely girls,' Aristides said, and Rosa thought that good looks ran in his family as she smiled, then heard through the car window as they revved away the distant voice of Evans the Latin cursing at nothing.

'They'll steal the planet from under your feet, then what will you walk on, bach? . . . Fucking fools . . .'

The tarmac beneath the Viscount's wheels hurried backwards, shuddered, tilted, as the aeroplane climbed over the suburbs round Heathrow. The wheels folded back into the wings just as the ground was lost in wreaths of low cloud, and Magog called on the stewardess for a double whisky. He was flying to Venice to spend early October there with Maire, for nostalgia's sake, for the sake of seeing once more the most beautiful city in Europe before it sank beneath its salt marshes or before its canals were filled with concrete, also for the sake of the Fine Arts Commission which had turned Magog's appreciation of beauty into service of the state. Not that the Commission ever did anything except pass a few afternoons a year in elegant regret for the erosion of the English national heritage through Sotheby's and speculative builders, but it did enable Magog to feel in the right frame of mind for North Italy. The noble homes of England, after all, sometimes seemed no more than portholes onto Venice, what with all the Canalettos and Guardis on the walls. To go to the very source was to confirm the good taste of the British aristocracy, which had always patronized the old pirate city power of the Mediterranean, as soon as that sea had become a lake as safe as Windermere.

The dulling warmth of the whisky and the jogging thrum of the engines bumped Magog's mind into the intermittence of his memories – the bloody birth of the twins, Hadassah's thigh-lock on him at Maire's entrance, Josepha's bombing of the chapel of Charles the Martyr, the deserter's attack at the bombsite, the

death of his beloved Rupert during the war, the loris eating the
nightingale in the greenhouse jungle . . . Scenes of the past
jinked high in no pattern of time . . . Consequence leapt up
before cause as in the shooting of a film which was more faithful
to place or person than to sequence or reason, only to make
final sense in the editing, in the cutting room, by post mortem
of mind or pen that tried to connect and analyse the haphazard
happenings in the material of the years gone by. What remained
in Magog's thought from each year but two or three highlighted
scenes, made abnormal through unnecessary drama or made
paradisiac through perception and season – mere gobbets of
sense or nonsense that somehow formed a whole human character out of their impression on one flesh that hung together round
its bones till death did them part. Magog could hardly distinguish
between what had happened to him and to others. The stories
told by those close to him became his own, he had been Hadassah
at the fall of Jerusalem, Rosa in faint at Piccadilly and in rage at
Pamplona. A few sentences spilled late at night grew in his
dreams until he stood in another's skin, remembering now in
drone of aeroplane what had not happened to him, in that elastic
warp of time that expands the minutes of a journey into years
of living and wandering in lives which are not always one's own.

Room 29 in the Grand Hotel was arguably the grandest room in
the world. A cube of thirty feet at every edge; the walls of dark
green silk; the glass in the gilt mirrors glacier-old, grey and
nobbled and opaque with reflections broken into swarthy drops;
the ceiling of close-set beams, each one decorated with an undulat-
ing golden plume that seemed to move in the night like a sea-swell
of light; a centre chandelier cascading down three yards of globes
and bubbles and baubles towards the ancient oriental carpets on
the marble floor; two oils, one of a Venetian sea-battle and the
other of a red Cardinal, looking disapprovingly across at the
square cloth-of-gold spread on the vast bed; scrolled gilt furniture, all curlicue and cluster round the silk upholstery and marble
table surfaces, with arched legs thrusting out like the prows of
galleys; then the tall windows out on to the stone balconies,
with the dome of Santa Maria della Salute on the far side of the
Grand Canal, rearing its curved skull on its octagonal neck in
gratitude for God's mercy and deliverance from the plague,

while behind the dome, the October sun set in a furry orange beyond the grey waters, already smoking with damp and sounding with the soft noise of engines and oars and horns. In this room, they said, Napoleon had slept after his conquest of the city, and Mussolini had met Hitler in conference, and Pope John had spent the night, and now Maire and Magog.

'Darling,' Maire said, 'I feel so swollen with pride and joy to be in such a place, I'd almost get pregnant again just to keep the memory of it.'

Magog was too much of a gentleman to suggest that Maire might be past fulfilling her wish, and, as it happened, her remark skipped a generation and came to rest in Josepha in Paris. The letter announcing the glad news did not arrive until their last morning in Venice, after Magog had held their farewell dinner in the grand room by the light of a five-branched candelabra with liveried waiters to serve the Orvieto Secco, giant shrimps, sole in wine, zabaglione. The little candle flames shone thrice, on the wave-rippling window-panes, in themselves, and in the ghosts of themselves shown by the glacier mirrors, which also held the twin ghosts of Maire and Magog, simulacra of their living bodies sitting under a huge squid that was the dead chandelier reaching down its tentacles towards the old lovers. Afterwards, the black gondola took them through the silent dark alleys of the backwaters under the dull humps of the bridges, its only beacon one plastic rose. In that hour's journey at night, Venice too seemed the ghost of its past, the negative of its faded empire and lost might, and Magog felt himself the captain of the death-ship of another great seaborn empire now slipping through the last ditches of its Eastern glory.

'If we died now,' Magog said, feeling the wet chill, 'it would be good, for nothing will ever be so good again.'

The morning brought Josepha's letter and nothing was ever so good again.

Dearest Maire, dear Magog,

It's funny and appropiate, I suppose, to write to you at the Grand Hotel, Venice, when Che Guevara's just been murdered and his body's being exhibited like a freak show and nothing will ever be the same. They have finally killed the hope of America, the voice of the Third World, the only excuse for the human race to go on existing and not lie down and die and hand it all over to the rats or the dolphins. I know you'll think this is extreme, but how else can I feel when they have done to death the finest man of us all? There was a time when England would have leapt to arms at a wave of Garibaldi's red shirt. We did help to liberate South America, after all. And what do we do now that this new Garibaldi is gutted and put out on a slab? Just wipe our napkins over our mealy mouths and say he was a bit rash and his prose was overrated.

At any rate, by the time you get this, you'll find that I'm in Cuba. I'm flying there via Prague and I will post this at the airport. Jean-Roger and I have split up. He is a futile theorist, an armchair revolutionary, a bourgeois Maoist who won't ever soil his white collar. I am going to have this child, but first I am going to work in Cuba to help bring in the ten million tons of sugarcane which Fidel has promised to the Revolution. And when the child is born, I will give it to the Revolution to carry on the struggle for the liberation of the Third World, another Che, another Tania. By the works of our hands, we will wipe the stain off the hands of those white gorillas who killed Che. Not to do anything now is almost as vile as murdering Che. We are all murderers or accomplices in his murder unless we help the Revolution with our lives.

Patria o muerte venceremos
Josepha

'How do you get to Cuba?' Maire asked.

'With a visa,' Magog said. 'You may have to wait until Josepha asks you to come out, if she's in with the Cuban government.'

'The Ponsonbys won't like that at all. A child, yes, but a child given to the *Revolution*, not to the *estate!*'

'That's Josepha's extreme reaction against her sister and us,' Magog said. 'She always was excessive. Just like Gog is. She'll spend her whole life bloody well reacting from somebody or something until her final fanaticism shoves her over the abyss.'

'She was such a good child,' Maire said, and real tears formed in her eyes. 'You never believe they'll grow up, and when they do, you always think they'll be just the same, and they aren't.'

1968

When Hadassah summoned Magog to spend the Passover with her in Salzburg, Magog went. She had prophesied and he had promised in Baalbek that they would meet once more and now their meeting had been arranged. Salzburg seemed a perverse place to hold a Passover feast, since the city lay in the heart of the pro-Nazi part of Upper Austria. Perhaps this choice was deliberate, a form of peaceful provocation, the triumphant return of the Jews from Israel to the stony places of their persecution. So Magog flew to Munich to appease his pact with the past, then took a car over the border to Salzburg, ignoring the signs that pointed off left to Hitler's eyrie in Berchtesgaden, where shattered bunkers still kept a trickle of tourists passing by.

The city was full of horror and kitsch, nibelung castles and cream cakes, ornamental graveyards and waltzing cafés, slush-stained streets and dirndl-skirted milkmaids in beer cellars. Magog had once seen a Peruvian triple pot, where a jolly skeleton sat between two naked plump women and felt them up with his finger-bones, while they laughed and worked away at his pelvis where a last organ was meat in their hands. This image of lascivious mortality, of sexy decay always came into Magog's mind every time that he went into Germany or Austria, and now he saw it again. The loudness and merriment of the Salzburg café merely accentuated the spectre of death-in-life, until Magog felt that he would have to scream or go straight back home. But like a guardian angel, Hadassah appeared to save him.

She was superb now. Age had fleshed her and fined her down. The bones of her cheeks carried her brown face as exultantly as the wings carry a hawk. Her body was full and proud, her walk arrogant. She looked round the café with her fine eyes and the lids fell over them in disdain. She might have been a conqueror wondering why the defeated natives were allowed to eat in the same room as herself. Magog could not keep back the compliments.

'You are a miracle, Hadassah,' he said. 'I have never seen anyone rout age more. Good God! Boadicea in ecstasy of revenge after burning Roman London wouldn't be a patch on you. You might have mastered the universe and all its secrets, from the elixir of life to total power over mankind. What has happened?'

'We have Jerusalem,' Hadassah said. 'I told you we would. That is why I brought you here.'

The reason the Passover feast was being held in Salzburg was not provocation, but business. The Steel Lord, who valued irony only a little less than Jehovah, was setting up a chemical plant nearby; its profits were to be donated to the Hebrew University. He had invited his friends to the feast, the Hagadah, and they had come to honour him and the Jewish people, Hadassah and Dr Radzen and also Magog because his name had been put on the list by his old lover and his old partner. No one had forgotten Magog's arms for Israel in its time of need. So he sat at the gathering in the dining-room of the largest hotel in Salzburg, part of a great circle of visitors and businessmen and grandmothers and children, mostly from Israel, but with a leavening of goyim. For the nineteen hundred years of losing and lamentation were past. The Jews had taken back Jerusalem by act of war. The crusaders of Israel now held the Holy City, and they wanted witnesses of their victory.

As Magog ate the Matsoh bread and shank of lamb and egg, and bitter herbs dipped in salt and washed down with wine, all brought in by angry waiters with shaven skulls, he listened to the Hebrew and the English words, spoken or sung by the sixty guests.

'Blessed art thou, O Lord, our God! King of the universe, who makest a distinction between sacred and profane; between light and darkness; between Israel and other nations, and between the seventh day and the six days of labour . . .'

Each had been given his or her part down to the smallest child, who joined in the nursery games at the end. But as he heard or read the text of the Hagadah, Magog found that the words no longer matched the facts. History had overtaken the ceremony. Listen to the Steel Lord as he held the unleavened bread and spoke:

'Behold! this is the bread of affliction, which our ancestors ate in the land of Egypt; let all those who are hungry enter and eat thereof; and all who require, come and celebrate the Passover. At present we celebrate it here, may we celebrate it next year in the land of Israel. This year we are here in exile, but next year we hope to be free men in the land of Israel . . .'

Exile? Voluntary exhile now, paid exile. Next year to be free men in Israel? Free men already fought for Israel and now the Egyptians ate the bread of affliction. The wailing was by the enemies of Israel; the wandering was for the refugees fleeing from greater Israel; the Sinai Desert and the Red Sea had swallowed up the beaten hosts of Egypt.

'Now,' the Steel Lord said, 'the question of the Wicked Son at the Passover.'

And Magog read:

'What mean YOU by this service? By using the word YOU I intend to exclude myself: and thus withdrawing from all the duties belonging to every member of the community, I reject the faith of the Jews.'

'And now,' the Steel Lord said, 'the answer to the Wicked Son.'

And Hadassah spoke, her voice like a warning bell.

'This is done because of that which the Lord did for ME, when I went forth from Egypt, For ME, but not for you; for had you been there, you would not have been redeemed.'

So superb Hadassah, so strong in the sting of her rebuke that Magog felt ashamed, idiotically ashamed, for the words put into his lips. He opened his mouth to protest in earnest, forgetting he was playing a part, but already the Wise Son was asking, 'What is this?' and already the reply was being given by the Steel Lord, 'With a strong hand did the Lord bring us out of Egypt, from the house of bondage . . .' So Magog settled back to drink his wine at the due time and watch the guests flushed with conquest after their centuries of regret, their millennia of oppression, their faith eternal in scripture and in God's promise to the Jews that was now writ on the Rock of the Holy City itself. Listen to the prayers of Radzen exultant:

'O Lord, our God! Have mercy upon us, on thy people Israel, and on thy city Jerusalem, and on Mount Zion, the residence of thy glory, and the great and holy Temple, which is called by thy name. Our Father! Feed us, nourish us, sustain us, provide for us, grant us abundance, and relieve us speedily from all our anxieties, and let us not, O Lord, our God, stand in need of the gifts of mankind, nor of their loans; for their gifts are small, and their reproach is great; but let our dependence be only on thine hand, which is full, ample, rich and open; so that we may not be put to shame in this world, nor be confounded in the world to come. Restore also speedily in our days, the Kingdom of the House of David, thine anointed, to its ancient state . . .'

'What is the ancient state of the Kingdom of David?' Magog asked, when Hadassah had taken him to bed at the end of the feast, and in her mastery and exuberance, had transported him back twenty years to their first loving, when the explosions of the flesh had blown up the mind into a no-man's land of uneasy peace. In this truce after grapples, Magog voiced his doubts.

'Now you have Jerusalem and the West Bank and the Golan Heights and Sinai, where will you ever end? Were there not Jews once on Babylon, in Egypt, in Damascus? If Jerusalem had only been enough – but now you want Zion, and Zion stretches over the whole world!'

'We have enough now,' Hadassah said. 'We have Jerusalem and we can defend our frontiers.'

'The British, who have been another wandering race and have often confused themselves with the Old Testament and the Israelites, should have had enough when they reached the Isle of Wight. But it didn't stop them grabbing a whole Empire that girdled the globe, in the name of Christ and the King. They didn't know when to stop. There was always another strategic route to protect. Once India was had, Africa had to be had to protect the route to India. And then we had to have Egypt to protect the Suez Canal. Now you have one bank of the Suez Canal, won't you want the other, in the name of Dayan and Zion?'

'No,' Hadassah said, 'never. We want peace. Peace and Jerusalem.'

'You want Zion,' Magog said. 'That is the worm in your Promised Land.'

'Jerusalem is all,' Hadassah said. 'Believe me. Just Jerusalem and peace. No doubt about it.'

'We have lost,' Magog said, 'you have won. Our empire has gone back to London, yours begins at Jerusalem.'

'Israel stops at Jerusalem.' Hadassah was getting angry now. 'That is the end of our state, God's city on earth. No more. No more, I tell you, or I shall take up arms against Israel. We stop at Jerusalem.'

So she closed Magog's mouth and fears with her own.

A mutual fund called Nogoco was begging Magog's millions in Geneva, so he decided to drive back from Austria across the Alps. As always, when he drove in the sun through beautiful and empty country, Magog considered the scenery as an opportunity for investment – cheap land and labour, the snowy peaks exploitable for the skis to come. Yet he felt too old to deface a whole mountain chain in the manner of the Aga Khan dealing with the coastline of Upper Sardinia; one had to be young for such a commitment to mutilation for the sake of money. Even if Magog could hardly enjoy a view without thinking of how to exploit it, yet he did see a vision of peace in highland Austria and did decide to leave it undisturbed. Once over the frontier into Switzerland with the belching smog of Zürich puffing its poisoned breath onto the slopes above, Magog felt there might be a case for underdevelopment and natural wilderness. This heresy persisted in his mind all the way to Geneva, where Chairman Max of the mutual fund was waiting for him in his château by the lake.

'Lord Byron woulda stayed here,' Chairman Max said, 'if he hadn't hired that other dump over the way. Yeah, it's distinct, a real conversation piece. Fourteen turrets and every one of them has to be nailed down in a puffa wind. Still, the broads go for it. And as the Nogoco Fund is goin' through the roof, we don't need no tiles, do we? Give us a million, friend, or make it two, and you got double next year.'

Magog was amused enough to look into the workings of the Nogoco Fund. Its operations were so simple that they were almost feeble-minded and thus seemed sophisticated. But then, as Magog knew, making money was such a boringly easy affair that only fools could bear to do it all the time. For every ten dollars that the Nogoco Fund took from the good plain people trying to insure their families, one dollar stayed in the salesman's hands and two in the Fund's numbered Swiss accounts for its expertise and brokerage, while seven dollars actually went into buying land and property, the title deeds of which were deposited in the Winterhalterzimmer Bank, Liechtenstein, which happened providentially to be owned by Nogoco. As the mutual fund was mutual only to those within its common conspiracy and was so far off so many shores that it might well have been a yellow submarine, stock market regulations and national taxes were as harmless as the drops of the dew. Nogoco also had ample funds to buy prestige names to squat on its boards in various countries, usually politicians who had served their countries once and now wished to provide for their imminent retirement by writing solid advertisements for the insubstantial.

'Who actually recommended me to you?' Magog asked as a matter of curiosity.

'One of your leading noblemen,' Chairman Max said reverentially. 'His family dates back to the Anglo-Saxon Conquest, he says. Can you believe it? It makes him a sort a national monument, Class One.'

'Who?' Magog asked.

'Lord Morrie of Bethnal Green,' Chairman Max said and never knew why Magog laughed himself into a fit of coughing, remembering the old rogue who had finagled his way up through riches and Merry to his ambition at last.

What Magog particularly admired about the Nogoco Fund was its habit of employing optimistic accountants, who doubled the value of the Fund's properties each year or sold them off at high prices to members of the Fund's board who never had to pay, but whose promissory notes were treated as more secure than gold sovereigns. Like the South Sea Bubble, the Nogoco Fund had only one purpose – to expand. If it stopped or had to redeem its shares for cash, it must go pop.

'Yeah,' Chairman Max said, when Magog pointed out that the Fund was really bare-faced robbery which could only go undetected if the boom went on forever. 'That's it, friend. I'm not ashamed to say the boom's gonna last forever like God or the great American people. You join the Fund, you gotta get richer. We're like the universe, we're expanding in a Big Bang. Jesus, sometimes I feel kinda holy just workin' for profit. There's a serenity in it all. Tell me, friend, have you ever seen somethin' more pure than a profit forecast?'

Magog shook his head, which might have meant nearly anything.

'That sweet curve on that graph,' Chairman Max intoned, 'just climbin', climbin', climbin' like up Jacob's Ladder to heaven. I tell you, this is just the beginnin', friend, it's gonna boom forever. The Fund's in land, isn't it? Grade A disposable liquid land – highly redeemable, aren't we all? If the bust does happen, and you can't trust those Chinamen not to rock the boat, though Moscow understands, you get me? As I was saying, if there's a Chink in the works, why, you'll get out in time along with us. We'll give you the dope in advance. You'll get out.'

'I've already got out,' Magog said, and did, to Paris.

He had read of the street-fighting and the troubles in France that May, and he took the precaution of buying full cans of petrol at the Swiss frontier to take with him through to the Channel; but as he drove past the manufacturing towns on his way to the capital, he saw sights that he had only imagined – red flags flying over factories with their gates welded together and with lines of silent workmen in their blue denims looking out through the bars, ready for any attack – the leaders of the country, pleading on television like whipped boys to the masses, they would never be so naughty again, no sir, please sir – the slack surprise in the faces of the officials now that they said, Do that, and the people just laughed and said without malice, Do it yourself – the fact that authority could just disappear overnight, and the people wake up to the knowledge that all government is merely a confidence-trick, and when, pfft! the confidence goes, why, there's no government, no need for government, for the sun still shines on the same streets and fields, the farmers and the townsmen go about their business, there may be trouble tomorrow and the need for new directors and commanders who will consult with everybody, but today, nobody needs nor wants orders, each man and woman knows what has to be done – Get the Old General out – Make Paris listen to the voices of the country – Neglect us no more, for we can do for ourselves. And the Old General watched and heard. And as Magog drove into the City up the Autoroute du Sud, already the armed policemen were searching the cars, and the lorries filled with troops were waiting down the sideroads, and somewhere, like a storm on the horizon, the rolling of the tracks of the tanks.

Yet in Paris itself, the theatre was in the streets and the streets in the theatre. Magog drove to the Odéon with its black and red flags flying high, the graffito painted on the stone *ex*-THEATRE DE FRANCE, the banner blazoning overhead *Odéon est ouvert*, and inside, the day-and-night free debate that had run longer than any political discussion since the French Revolution, with the students and the workers filling the elegant seats, and the orators haranguing from the boxes and the stalls, and anyone with a tongue delivering his or her plans for tomorrow's France, *le pouvoir au peuple, merde aux gaullistes, nous sommes vous, nous sommes tous*, and yet Magog lounging back on his plush, amused at the sincerity and the faith and the hope in the voices which believed they were also winning their Jerusalem in the ancient beautiful sink on the Seine, the Sodom and Gomorrah of *le tout Paris* that now had put on its red pants again and was shouting *ça ira* from the gutters, but Magog could already see the police agent in his new student clothes snapping the faces of the speakers with his Minox, evidence for the retribution that would surely come, the fire and the brimstone raining from the Palais de Justice, the truncheons splitting the skulls, the interrogations, the solitary cells, the slow despair of losing, of having lost, the post mortems in the back room, the *analyse, toujours l'analyse,* the waiting out of the interminable years, hidden and skulking and plotting until the next chance came again, this time we must win, the people will win – and they won't.

Outside now, Magog walked through the streets to the Sorbonne, the roads curiously empty and expectant, the citizens staying in their rooms, watching through the cracks in the lace curtains or from the upper windows, already withdrawing from the students at the sight of the burned-out cars, the broken glass, the trees cut down to make barricades, the destruction of the normal for battle against the riot police. Of course, when the barricades had first gone up with the students digging up the cobblestones to lob at the flics, why, even the flint of the concierges' hearts had suddenly struck sparks, the whole of Paris had skipped back to the lessons of the lycée, the great days of the fall of the Bastille, the mobs in the streets, the *aristos à la lanterne*, the people drunk with power, then again in 1830, 1848, 1870 and the Commune, 1944 and the Liberation, the songs of revolution first on the children's lips after the nursery rhymes, the tumbrils clattering to the guillotine, the heads of the great rolling into the baskets, the women knitting the tricolour while they watched the blood spurt, so let's chuck a flowerpot onto the policemen's helmets, bravo to the young folk fighting for the people, help them, France is rotten now. Then the young began burning up property, and everybody had his pension, her *dot*, his auto, her *meubles*, take away property? But everybody has property. Property is not robbery. It is robbery to take property. After all, somebody has to see thieves don't break in, murderers, Algerians, perhaps we do have to have a government, even the flics aren't all bad, the Old General up there, remember the war, the free French, the *maquis*, de Gaulle, Gaul, France, *gloire*, Napoleon, the Fourteenth of July with the big parade from the Arc de Triomphe, French tanks, French aeroplanes, our glorious history, remember, remember, for the revolution will take it all away. And so Paris was changing sides, giving up its brief plunge into the hot blood of playground memories, and the streets were empty and foreboding as Magog walked towards the Sorbonne and the centre of the revolt. Paris was waiting for the General to come back, and he was coming.

'Magog,' a voice said in the corridors of the university, now sprawling with students in sleeping-bags or huddling over the free-food counters and trestle tables stacked with leaflets. Magog hadn't been so shoved and hustled since in the Souk at Damascus. Now he was stopped by a young sheikh, head turbaned in bandages, left arm in a sling, wounded in the fight.

'Jean-Roger,' Magog said. 'Josepha wrote to me that you'd never go to the wars.' He spoke in French. Maire had taught him the lingo.

'The war came to me,' Jean-Roger said. 'What brings you to Paris?'

'Curiosity,' Magog said. 'An interest in seeing whether anarchy works, after a lifetime spent failing to use power except in the pursuit of futility. And I may confess, I am also disgusted with a vile sort of capitalism which breeds in the marshes of Geneva. There mosquitoes called mutual funds sicken me almost enough to want a cure.'

Jean-Roger smiled again.

'Josepha did always tell me that your only saving grace was a certain honesty. She said you were too worn-out to conceal even your power-mania from yourself.'

'Just too worn-out,' Magog said, 'to bother at all.'

He felt a violent blow in his back that smashed him against the wall. Swaggering by, a black-jacketed crop-headed gorilla, swinging an iron chain in his hand.

'*Fiche le camp, crapouillot,*' the gorilla said and went on.

'*Ah, les Congolais,*' Jean-Roger said and shrugged.

'This may be a free university,' Magog said, rubbing his bruises, 'but it's too much of a free-for-all for me.'

'We can't fight the SS police without the *Congolais*. They don't like de Gaulle either. He betrayed them too. They learnt how to smash the flics in Saigon, Algeria, the Congo. With them we can beat the SS.'

'Don't they beat you?' Magog asked. 'Don't I hear they rape your girls just as much as the riot police do?'

'Ah well,' Jean-Roger said, 'there are always unfortunate acts in the course of a revolution. That does not make the revolution less necessary.'

'Josepha always said you were an arm-chair philosopher,' Magog said. 'Rape's lousy under any name. I do know one thing. Lie down with the Devil and you get fucked by the Devil too. And something else. I also know you've lost. So does Paris.'

'How do you know that?' Jean-Roger said.

'The tanks and the troops are coming in. You can't fight them.'

'We're negotiating for the big trucks to come in. We'll use them to smash the SS and the tanks.'

'The unions have joined the Gaullists, even the Communist union leaders. Neither lot of old men on the right or the left are going to let their followers rebel against their authority. The union won't let you have the trucks. You've already been sold down the Seine. Look, I'll give you a lift out of Paris, Jean-Roger. Go to Cuba for me. See Josepha has her child all right, she needs you out there. She doesn't want me to go out. She'll see you, now you've fought in Paris.'

'I'm staying,' Jean-Roger said. 'My place is here. France needs me.'

'You sound just like the General,' Magog said. 'Does France really need you? Look, I've sat on too many committees. I've dealt with bureaucrats and officials all my life. Now you've lost the unions and the army's coming in, you're done for. Go to Cuba, I'll pay for it. Save your child, prepare him for the future revolution.'

'I must prepare myself for that,' Jean-Roger said. 'Now you go. I have work to do. Give my love to Josepha. Tell her that I also have fought. We must lose, Magog, by your terms. But because they are only your terms, we may win. We do not accept your terms, so we may still win. You can only do what you are when we let you be, and when we don't, your terms don't exist. Goodbye, Magog.'

On his drive to Calais where British Rail was still running ferries away from the ferment, Magog picked up five students hitch-hiking on their way home. He asked them why they were leaving Paris when they had gone there to help in the revolution. And they said that they had fought on the barricades too much, they had slept on floors too much, they had starved too much, and now that de Gaulle and the army were returning, they were too scared and they were going home. And Magog knew that the revolt of the children in the cities of the world that summer was doomed, for they could not endure. There were no quick victories to be had. Old men did not go out that easily. Yet because the children had to lose did not mean that they should not have tried. The only thing which ever moved the inertia of the ancient was a determined assault, hardly beaten back.

I didn't ask Magog to come over, but now he's come, at least he's somebody I know. I've never felt so liberated as in Cuba with everybody loving me and trusting me and working together for the Revolution. It's like a hot soak every day all day, nothing to think about except how to survive without sweating to death and how to get in those ten million tons of zafra and help Fidel. Everyone believes in him, we all believe in him, we stand in that big square when he is speaking to all of us, and he is so tall, so bearded, so personal, and he has all those statistics showing that the Revolution is winning, and if he makes mistakes, he doesn't cover them up, but he admits to them which is more than any other *jefé* would. Now my belly's grown too big and my back hurts and I have to lie down in the mornings with my legs apart to ease myself, and I think of the child coming and putting it in that high-rise Circolo Infantil with the fifty little ones on each floor all reaching up their hands for anyone to pick them up and hold them, and I wonder, Can I give him up, can I? Then I think of Fidel the father of us all. I and the flesh of my flesh are given to the Revolution, I know THIS! Yet they say opposite things of Fidel . . . First they say Batista cut Fidel's balls off in the Moncada Barracks like he did with the other prisoners, and that's why Fidel never married, and that's why he has this obsession with breeding bulls like the great Rosafé Signet who had 70,000 children before he died and even when he was fallen on his side in his dying, he gave a last spasm into the false cow's vagina so that there would be another hundred sons and daughters to carry him on with those coloured pills that they use for artificial insemination. Second, they say Fidel has every girl who goes and interviews him, particularly those busy Yankee girls, all fire and vinegar, and perhaps when I've had my child for Cuba and I go and see Fidel, I'll find out . . . I mustn't think like this, I mustn't, it's just gossip, it's unworthy, but the baby's kicking and I've got a belly that's splitting open in all this heat. At least, it's not so bad in Conrad Hilton's gift to the Revolution, the Havana Libre, when I'm ten floors up like a fatted sow, the guest of the government, ten floors above the queues, the colas for everything from a new book to icecream. It's just like in Britain in the Second World War, Magog tells me, what with the people being worked to death to do their office jobs and farm the land, and everybody tired out and getting slower

and more inefficient because of their effort. But there IS a
Third World War on, I tell Magog. Cuba is fighting the USA
in the Americas. It is helping the liberation struggle all over
the world just like Britain was fighting Fascism alone in 1940
all over the world, and just like Britain, the people are giving
up their present for their children's future. I may rest in the
Havana Libre, but I do take the *wawa* Leyland buses to see
the doctors for my weekly check-up just like everybody else,
and it's a long journey what with waiting for an hour or more
at the stop, then there's the standing and the jolting. It'll be
a strong baby if it doesn't come too soon. And he's yours,
Fidel, he's yours. ARM HIM!

I've even learned how to strip down and assemble a
machine-gun in the dentist's flat down the way where the
Black Panthers are. They come into Havana on the hi-jacked
planes from America and they come with their guns and
they're always on guard in their flat. They seem to be
expecting attack from the CIA or even the Cubans. Some of
them are bitter about how they were treated when they got
here. There's one called Sweetass who says he gave Rosa
her child. Magog knows this now and he swears he won't tell
the family, but you can see he's hurt deep down in his pig
racist heart – NIGGER blood in the Ponsonbys, he'll stay
mum for sure! Well, the cops bust Sweetass for pushing in
New York, really for Black Power, he says, and he jumped
jail at nine in the morning, hi-jacked a plane at twelve to Cuba
and was back in a work-camp in Cuba by six in the evening.
Jail to jail in one day! I say he has to remember that the CIA
is sending in black agents as hi-jackers, and the Cubans are
quite right in taking months to screen everybody out. Didn't
we put all the German Jews inside camps for the duration of
the war in case the Nazis were sending spies over to Britain
among the refugees, and the Jews didn't complain. They knew
it was for their general good and we were fighting for them.
Can't the Panthers see that Fidel is fighting for them too?
It's a slave racist society here, Sweetass says, worse than
Babylon because it pretends not to be racist. Down in the
South a black man really knows if a white man's his friend,
but in Havana, he doesn't know. Sure, there are some black

Uncle Toms from Santiago close to Fidel, but why isn't Fidel
INVADING America with the Panthers? Where's the guerrilla
war way down in the cotton patches of Alabama, with the
Appalachians the new Sierra Maestra? Don't be a fool, I say,
how the hell can Fidel allow his whole island to be blown to
bits just to support a wildcat invasion by a few black men,
doomed to disaster, a reverse Bay of Pigs that would just be
a bloody Bay of Panthers down by Biloxi? Fidel's got a
responsibility to the whole Cuban people. Yeah, Sweetass
says, he's got a responsibility to the Cuban white people and
to the Cuban polished niggers. Yeah! Bobby, who's the genius
who bosses the Panthers out here, says that it's really a clash
of life-styles between the Panthers and the Cubans, because
the Cubans don't understand the wisecrack. The government
spies take everything so damn literally. If Bobby gets some
grass and the spy asks where he scored, he says, 'Fidel gave
it to me,' and the spy puts in a report, 'Says he got marijuana
from Fidel.' Or if Bobby says about the black mammy cook
the spy gave him, 'If I gotta have a cook, make her white,
beautiful and sweet sixteen,' the spy writes down, 'Wants a
white young slave.' The only conflict, Bobby says, is a sense
of humour, but that can lead to more trouble than the war of
the poor and the rich, the black and the white, the young and
the old.

Bobby won't have anything to do with Magog and says he's
a pig, which he is, only a pig you've known all your life is a
person too, and Bobby agrees with that. Bobby goes out of
his way to shock Magog and call him a mother-fucker and
generally shove a pistol down his teeth. I must say, Magog
takes it pretty well. Sometimes I think Magog only wants to
die, he's so indifferent to threats, he's so out of touch with
what's really going on in the world. Magog says that the fact
that the Black Panthers are all ex-cons makes them so
thin-skinned that every failure or frustration for them is
interpreted as racism. They feel that history's treated the
blacks so badly that every demand a black man makes must
be accepted to tip the scale back. Because we made them
slaves, they now feel that they have the right to make us
slaves to get their own back. Magog says they see through

their dark glasses too darkly. They make racism the only explanation for every action, when there are many other reasons. They spread the cult of race war, when there is too much race war already, and it will mess up the world for the next few decades without any more propaganda. Magog says, why don't the Panthers just fight their just fight for black pride and power and dignity, and drop their unjust yelling for partition and hate and black apartheid? The Cubans also agree with Magog in saying that the Panthers are too American, too individualistic, not enough discipline, bandits playing at guerrillas who won't make it. But I tell Magog that he's a prejudiced reactionary imperialist, and he's got a good reason like all ofays to hide his bias against radicals and black men. He'll never forgive Sweetass for being Rosa's lover. He really just wants what every white father wants, to keep his daughters out of black hands. Magog goes silent then, and says nothing.

Magog spends all his time nagging at me and saying he must take me out of here. He says I may not ALWAYS want to work for the Revolution. And if my child is born here, he will be a Cuban citizen, and then the government will always have a hold over me, the perfect blackmail. Unless I work for Cuba, I may never be able to see my child again. I tell Magog that the Revolution despises tricks like that, I trust Fidel and the Cubans trust me. They will never use my child as a hostage to keep me on their side. Anyway, I won't ever change my mind. I want my child to be brought up as a new Che, a new Lumumba, even if he turns against his own mother because she has betrayed the Revolution. Magog says I am sick, women have strange fantasies in their last months, he knows best how governments work. Even if the government's good and Fidel's good, spies and secret services are the same the world over. Secret policemen will use ANY method to get a useful agent to work for them. They won't tell Fidel about it, and he won't be able to control them. No government has real power over its secret agents, its dirty workers. Josepha, please come home and have the child on a British birth certificate. Then, if you wish, you can bring him back here, and we will always be able to get him out of Cuba again as a British citizen. But I don't trust you, Magog, you'll take my child away from me like you took Rosa's. I have given my child to the Revolution, which will grow and grow in power and strength until it covers the whole world, I know it, I know it.

I try to educate Magog by taking him to see what the Revolution has done for Cuba, but he only agrees to see two things, the mental hospital and the old cigar factory. The ancient Casa de Dementes had iron bars and chains and used to be a freak show for the bored Batista rich just like Bedlam in London two hundred years ago, but now there are modern buildings and all the inmates are drugged into a kind of peace and they can do what they CAN do, calisthenics or raising chickens or singing in tuneless choirs or playing football or drawing pictures that gradually break up into little bits as their minds go. The doctor says the chief illness in Cuba is schizophrenia. Magog asks, Is that because there's such a huge gap between heaven and earth, between promise and performance, between dreaming of the good life and having to put up with this, between Jerusalem and Havana? The doctor doesn't understand, but I do and I am angry and I say, Do you realize what has already been done in this island? Unique in Latin America, all Cuban children are properly fed and go to school and read and write and wear shoes. This IS heaven on earth to what it was before the Revolution. Havana is already halfway to Jerusalem. And when we bring in those ten million tons of zafra, Havana will be Jerusalem. Just a little more effort, a little more. I worked in the cane till my hands bled, Magog, and only when my belly made me faint three times in an hour did they stop me from going to the fields. Believe, Magog, you must believe. WE all do.

In the cigar factory, where the women sit at their desks handrolling the Henry Clays and the Punches and the Perfectos for the rich imperialists overseas, they don't listen any more to the Hebrew tales of Moses and Jesus and the Promised Land as they work, but the reader in each room reads of Che and Mao and Fidel and Lenin. And the women workers are inspired to more productivity, since every cigar rolled means more foreign exchange to buy the machines

Cuba needs for the harvest. But Magog only jokes and says he thought his cigars were rolled on the bare thighs of beautiful Cubanas, and it is rather a let-down to see that old grandmothers actually roll the leaf with withered hands on slabs of wood. The factory manager tells him that England is the last export market that still won't take any machine-rolled cigars. England is so plutocratic that all cigars must be made by hand. That sounds about right, Magog says, but he makes the manager laugh by saying that Cuba will soon bring America to its knees. America must soon sue for peace and end the blockade, because now the Rockefellers and the Fords can't buy their Perfectos, they'll burn down the White House to get a good smoke after dinner.

The Cubans all seem to like Magog. He is just what they expect an English gentleman to be, a sort of dummy, a caricature of a capitalist, the actual walking talking effigy of everything they stand against. They even have a sneaking respect for him. They still believe the myth that every Englishman's word is his bond – probably because they have been dealing lately with the Russians. They certainly would do business with Magog. He says that this proves his point that power is much the same in every country. Power is always against the people. But I say, No, no, power IS the people here, you can see it, you can feel it. And he says to me, Forgive me, Josepha, I am getting old, I am half-blind and half-deaf, and all I can see is rationing, queues, fatigue, drabness, and the hope that you will find in everyone is spoken in a language which I do not understand.

There is something funny going on round the Havana Libre. I came down one evening to the lobby and found blood on the floor and the glass broken and they said there had been an accident, an incident. There is always trouble from the CIA and the gusano terror groups. They also tell me I shouldn't be seeing the Black Panthers now, they will be moved on soon, they are not wanted, their morals are not good. There is a lot of talk of infiltration. Spies are setting the sugar-cane on fire. There are many agents about. I should be careful. But how can I be careful when I have given myself to the Revolution, when there is only one Revolution, when anyone who fights for the Revolution is a friend, when anyone who is against the Revolution is an enemy, when there can be no enemies within the Revolution, for we all fight for the Revolution in our different ways TOGETHER! Until the baby comes in two weeks' time, I will see anybody I choose, it is not breaking revolutionary discipline.

The news in GRANMA stays good. The students and the workers are just about to win in many of the countries of the world. But Magog tells me the opposite. He says that we have lost in Paris. We would, with a wet like Jean-Roger fighting for us! Magog says that it has been like 1848 in Europe with risings in most of the great capitals. None of them has succeeded and now we are in for the years of repression, of oppression. As I can't do anything else except lie on my bed, I'm working on a poem for *Ramparts* or the *Black Dwarf*. It's to CHE, of course!

> *Now you are dead and nine months are gone*
> *The young are being bloody born*
> *You would not fight without a gun*
> *Their hands were bare, they fought too soon*
>
> *Now you are dead and nine months are gone*
> *The millions have stood and fought and run*
> *Paris and Prague saw them shot down*
> *Chicago cops were Al Capone*
>
> *Now you are dead and nine months are gone*
> *East has met West, the deal is done*
> *Left boot, right boot, both are one,*
> *The jackboot's stomping every town*
>
> *Now you are dead and nine months are gone*
> *The powers that were are on the throne*
> *Little is changed, old men hold on*
> *Reaction rules Jerusalem*
>
> *Now you are dead and nine months are gone*
> *Next year will be still bloodier born*
> *In hush or howl, the young go on*
> *To ambush the ageing garrison*

> *Now you are dead and nine months are gone*
> *Your name is to each of us our own*
> *While we live for you, shall your death die?*
> *While we die for you, shall your life lie?*

Of course, this is only a first draft, like everything it needs work on it . . .

Magog never saw the gunman who killed Josepha. He was waiting in the hotel lobby and, as she walked towards him balancing her belly, he heard the small noises and saw the little red hole open in her throat and the red cockade of blood spray up behind her neck. He caught her belly as she fell forwards, then lowered her to the ground and tried to stop the blood pumping out of her with the palm of his hand. Then he was crying and saying, 'Josepha, why you, and why not me, I have nothing left, why *you*?' And the militia girls came around and they took her away to the hospital and there the doctors struggled to save her, but she was dead within the hour. They did save the child by ripping it out of its mother's womb, another girl, another little girl.

Magog was given every apology for the death of his niece. She was doubtless a heroine of the Revolution. There would be a cane-cutting Brigade named Josepha La Trabajadora. Her name would stand over the door of a score of schools in the Oriente. But that did not bring back Josepha. Who was her murderer? Ah, *compañero*, the CIA naturally. Yet there were no arrests. So Magog would never know if Josepha died from an accident, a silly militia girl dropping her gun, or from an agent shooting at the wrong person, or from a paranoiac who thought Josepha knew too much, or as the result of a false spy's report, or because of this or because of that. But Josepha was dead and the Cubans were so ashamed that such a thing could happen in their country that, after a few weeks, they let Magog take the baby girl home to England.

When Magog arrived with the child, the Ponsonbys offered a few hundred thousand pounds for her, but Maire would not give her up, insisting on keeping her for Josepha's sake. So the little girl was not called *Tania La Guerrillera*, but Mary for Maire and Griffin for Gog. People had to go on, didn't they?

1969

Magog was fifty years old. He had read that the reaching of each new decade in a man's life was the birthday of terrible doubt and fear. Magog's answer was to buy a new address-book and to transfer on to plain paper the names and places of his family, friends and acquaintances. He was scared by how many of these had died like Rupert and Josepha or had disappeared from his life, leaving no sign to follow them by. He had meant to drop the names of those whom he hardly ever saw; but he found that his fiftieth year had made him into a hoarder of the last man who had given him the gift of his address.

Were these two hundred names or thereabouts the residue of half a life of meeting people and organizing the affairs of countries? And worse than that, were these eleven names the only ones that Magog could call the names of friends? There had been so many at Cambridge, where every undergraduate had been a kind of comrade, even if never met. Now, with age setting its grey cap on his head, Magog wrote down again the names of some open enemies such as McInnes. At least, they were *his* enemies. They would recognize him for who he was before they slammed the front door shut in his face. Worse than enemies were strangers, who might look straight through him, not seeing him at all.

Fearing the loss of his friends, Magog arranged to meet them all for lunch or dinner. And when he had met them all, and each had covertly examined in the other the effects of growing older, and each had flattered himself that age told less in him than in his friend, then Magog remembered the hard definition of the Irishman at the bar of the French Pub in Dean Street. 'A friend is someone who will take you in when you've murdered the Pope. The rest is just say so.'

Seeing his eleven friends and agreeing how friendly they all were, Magog knew himself to be a solitary. None of them would take him in, if he committed a crime. They were all too righteous about their own integrity. They had forgotten how to be tribal. Magog had no friends. Like the British Commonwealth that had once been an Empire, it creaked along because the rulers of each independent country knew one another, talked much the same language, and were frightened of being exposed to contact with strangers. There was no comradeship in it. Better to be an old boy than to be alone.

In fear of ageing on his own, in regret for a life passed in pursuit of power that had slipped through his fingers as insidious as sand, Magog felt a restlessness rise within him. He wanted obsession, some fierce commitment to an intolerable situation that would at least fill him with the pain of needing to live.

I never saw such a slow spring coming, he wrote to Josepha dead in Havana. *The buds stay in their crusts on the branches. Damn barnacles, they won't open! Leaves, flowers, grass linger in a winter's daze. The ducks in Regent's Park just slouch and huddle, their beaks under their wings. None of that frenzy of mass rape that the spare drakes go in for when the sperm is rising in the sun. Altogether, that grey interminable hanging on that the English call living in London and anybody else would call surviving in limbo . . .*

So, with the first soft drug of an April day, Magog found himself yearning. That is the most dangerous time. When an ache without a cause fills the heart, then beware. For all yearning finds its object. As in the fairy stories, if the yearning is there, the object it first sees can be ugly or lame or brass, but the yearning is all at once converted into love of that object. Beware of the rootless desire. For once it has settled on a thing, there is passion. And the passion, however truly felt, may dote on the false or the worthless or the casual or the impossible. Pray to weather the spring.

Magog's yearning fixed itself on the long legs and wandering eyes of Rosa. A man may want his daughter and resist the want – if he is not so poor that he has to share a bed with her. But Magog did not know whether Rosa was his daughter or not. At first, he did not notice anything in his feeling for her that could not be put down to a sense of responsibility or some acceptable emotion. Then he began to telephone her almost daily rather than once a week. He always had a pretext for doing so, but these excuses were so trivial that they often were no better than asking after her health because he had heard cholera was spreading from Turkey. But at least they allowed him to feel outraged when she was out or did not return his call.

In the middle of reading *The Listener*, Magog would suddenly be furious that the careless or callous Rosa had not bothered to reply to his concern for her. 'She has something better to do,' he would say to himself ironically, when the plain truth was that she did have something better to do. Magog would even hear himself talking viciously at dinner parties about the heartlessness of the younger generation, although the subject had hardly been mentioned. He could not stop himself being a bore about the way youth seemed to want to waste its opportunities, when all it needed was a little wise direction from its elders. But these remarks were never said to Rosa. She would have laughed at them and him.

When Rosa came through the door, the scene he had rehearsed for her was never played out as plotted. He would resolve to be magisterial, understanding, tender, until she dissolved into tears and he could forgive her from a full heart. In fact, he always burst out with the resentment which had been building up since she last forgot him. But the mutiny on her mouth and the misery in her eyes at once changed his petulance into an apology and a gracious downgrading of her offences, which hardly existed anyway and had never been noticed by her at all. Magog would then hurry on to the telling of all the funny stories he had heard since their last meeting, and when he had raised a laugh, he would dig into his pocket to give her the latest beads discovered in the Deepest Africas or Furthest Asias of the Antique Markets, or else he would promise her a dress for the spring or boots for the autumn. These simple bribes always made Rosa friendly again, except in her brief moments of worry about the starving Biafran babies or the homeless of London. Even then, her friendliness would return if he listened with polite compassion to her rehash of the latest problem of the world that happened to be in the news and needed no research to suffer deeply. But Rosa usually took the gifts that Magog offered, although she always explained that she only accepted things from him because they were given from love, not for a purpose. And after she had praised his generosity, Magog was silent about the conditions and concessions he had meant to demand as his price.

'Of course,' he would say, 'there are no strings.'

So Magog became weak. For his weakness brought the greatest gift from Rosa – her confidence in him, because she knew she could control him. Her grey eyes would stop their restless search about his ears for an excuse or a defence, and they would fix themselves on his eyes with a luminous stare, while she said, 'I tell you things, Magog, that I simply never tell other people.' And Magog's heart would swell with the certainty that, whatever she did, he remained the first love in her life, the firm base which was necessary for all her flits. He was the hub of her freewheeling.

Yet Rosa's confidences that Magog wanted to hear so desperately also hurt him. All the time he was listening, he had to smile and smile with a brave face. For if he showed his pain, the confidences would stop. So he had to hear, with needles in his heart and his grin fixed, her gossip about the pop scene and the drug scene, the Roundhouse and the Marquee, and the constantly changing string of men's names, Ron, Bill, Hugo, Vergil, Pierre, Antonio, Larsen, Poopoo, Red. Rosa's careful lack of precision about what she actually did with these men would confirm Magog's worst suspicions about her, especially as she talked of sex as coolly as all her generation did, even though she might be as cautious as most girls were in their choice of lovers. She chatted in the cruel jargon of her time, that excluded the old and hinted at a Garden of Allah and Eden that was nearer than Kew, but only for the young. *Age and Experience Keep Off The Grass. No Professionals Need Apply.* In this age of arrogant adolescence, which knew everything first time round, Don Juan himself would have had few takers.

When Rosa felt she had put Magog deeply in her debt through her confessions, carefully edited to spare the susceptibilities of a dodderer of fifty, then she would make her demands. He would grant her almost anything, even when the demand was against his best interest. She would say she was off to Marrakesh for a while, could she have a cheque, she had run through her allowance from the Ponsonbys, she didn't know how. And he would give her the money, certain that she would be cut off from him for weeks, perhaps months, without taking the trouble to send him a postcard. But at least he would have the relief of knowing that she was not in London to plague him by her presence, more off than on. He could stand her absence, he adored seeing her, he only found intolerable the fact that she could come and go in his life without warning. He could not even ask for the smallest explanation without being told he was the Grand Inquisitor. And Rosa would never explain, since she thought that a reason for doing anything made it not worth doing, and a fixed date was the death of spontaneity. Anyway, as her unpredictability was her power over Magog, she remained unpredictable. Yet to some men like Sweetass Brown, Magog knew, she could be a slave – for a time. But it never lasted. She would always come back to Magog, if he could last that long.

This was the pattern of Magog's relationship with Rosa, while he was still deluded that he felt for her as for a spoilt daughter. He had been so rarely good or generous in his life that he clung to this righteous view of himself as the man who had risen above doubts of paternity to play the role of the selfless father. He considered that most men could not have acted as well in the circumstances. So the truth of his desire for Rosa did not show itself to Magog until she fell ill in Beirut. When most men think they are better than other men, they want to hide the worst from themselves.

Rosa's hotel was called the Phoenicia Casino and stood on stilts overlooking the bay on the edge of the Old Port. Magog approached it on a carpet of severed chicken's claws, discarded from the nearby market. He thought of Pushkin's witches' houses that ran about on fowls' feet, and he supposed that the wily Lebanese had netted them and lopped them off so that the houses had come to roost in Beirut and could be let at a profit. The Phoenicia Casino itself was no smart gambling den, just a tea-barn where small businessmen could play dominoes and smoke their nargilehs in peace. The great ground-floor room, where Magog waited to be taken up to see Rosa, was a ramshackle collection of yellow wooden arches overhanging marble tables. Its hush was only disturbed by the clicks of the dominoes and by the sucking of the sad waves or of the players' mouths at the tits of the hubble-bubbles, that sprouted up their red hydra necks to each pair of lips. Inside the glass bowls of the nargilehs, a small turd of best Baalbek hashish was stuck on a pointed reed. As Magog watched, a waiter changed each ember on the top of the turds for a live coal, while the players ignored him and concentrated on their game, occasionally blowing out through their teats so that the water bubbled in the glass bowls as the coal burned down the brown cake of easy dreams.

The Manager who took Magog up to see Rosa was not pleased to see him. He was fat and wore a red fez. Late nights had sooted the lids of his sunken eyes. His skin seemed to have been smoked and cured by the fumes of the nargilehs at infinities of playing on the marble tables. He spoke in French to Magog, as one man of the world to another. *'J'ai dit à elle, pas nécessaire, pas nécessaire du tout, de vous faire venir ici d'Angleterre. Ne vous dérangez pas votre Magog, j'ai dit à elle. Mais elle ne veut pas m'écouter. Elles sont comme ça, les jeunes filles d'aujourd'hui. Pas de respect, pas de respect.'* But all the time the Manager grumbled about the bad manners of youth, Magog thought he was really grumbling that Magog had arrived in the nick of time to stop him doing a deal over Rosa, five thousand sovereigns or louis d'or for a new white slave for some oil-rich sheikh. Yet perhaps this was another romantic illusion and Rosa had asked Magog to fly to Beirut to prove her mastery, not because she needed rescue. All the same, Magog wanted to enjoy his role as her saviour as long as he could. So he replied in English, the language of gunboats in the Middle East, not of diplomacy.

'If my daughter is not all right,' he said sternly, 'I think you will find that I know the authorities.'

A vague threat always worked best. It was bound to touch on the fear that every man had of some power higher than himself.

Rosa was ill, no doubt of it. When Magog kissed her in her feverish sleep, his lips puckered at the dry heat of her skin. She woke almost at once with a cry of fear, then smiled radiantly to see who it was.

'Oh Magog,' she smiled, 'I'm so glad to see you. Get me some water, iced water.'

So Magog fed her ice-cubes until she fell asleep again with him holding her hand. And he asked for another bed to be moved into her room so he could keep watch over her. The Manager smiled and was not surprised. It would still cost Magog the price of two rooms. The police would not like a father sleeping in the same room as his daughter, even if one was called Ponsonby and the other Griffin. Beirut was a respectable city.

At this assertion, Magog laughed. 'Cost does not matter,' he said. 'If you don't steal it one way, you'll steal it another.'

So Rosa was a child again and Magog looked after her, feeding her lemon drinks and penicillin and chicken jelly and the jam that makes Levantine breakfasts into foretastes of heaven. He helped her to the lavatory and stood at the door until she was finished, in case she fainted and he had to go in to pick her off the floor. He sponged her face and shoulders and arms in the bed. She even let him give her baths, lying back in weakness while Magog's curious eyes and soapy fingers lounged along her thin ribs and hip-bones, her little breasts that floated like water-lilies on the surface of the bath above her brown skin, the sunken weed of her belly hair. Then Magog would help her to stand, and he would wrap her in a rough towel and dry her too thoroughly, feeling with his hands the fold between her buttocks, the wrinkle between her thighs, cupping her pelvis on his palm as he pretended to rub her warm for her own good. Although he bent himself like a hinge in the middle to ease the thrust of his cock against his trousers, hiding his desire, once she slipped and fell with her belly against his, her bright child's eyes glazing into a woman's appraisal, then she held the towel around her and walked away to her bed without a word.

One morning, when the rain was gone and the sun was out and Magog slept late for once, exhausted after his long vigils, his dreams heavy with Hadassah's tale of the Dog River turning red with the blood of Adonis, he woke to find Rosa standing beside him in her cotton shift, embroidered with pink flowers, like the oleanders by the Dog River in the spring. In her eyes, the glint of conspiracy he had once seen in the temple of Baalbek.

'My turn to bath you,' she said simply. 'I feel better. We'll have a bath together.'

'What?' Magog said, thinking he dreamed.

'Isn't that what you want?' Rosa said. 'I'll start it.'

When Magog heard the water running into the iron tub next door, he felt his lust rise and he did not dare to leave his bed. But Rosa called him. 'Aren't you coming?' And he had to go to join her, a towel wrapped about his waist.

'There,' she said, 'I'm even sitting at the tap end. Like what more can a chick do for a man?'

So Magog dropped his towel and quickly sat in the water at the round end of the bath. And Rosa looked at him and said nothing and wetted the bar of soap in the water between her legs and put his feet on her shoulders and began to rub each of them in turn, the toes, the soles, the ankles, the calves, the knees, the thighs. Then she put his legs back in the water to soak, and she began soaping his arms, the fingers, the wrists, the fore-arms, the elbows, the biceps. Then she soaped his shoulders and his chest. Then she squashed back in the bath to allow him to duck his chest below the water to rub off the soap with his hands. Then she asked him to stand. And fearing greatly, he stood. Then she soaped his buttocks and the space between them, then his thickening belly, then the hair below it.

'The rest you'd better do yourself,' she said.

'I want you,' he said.

'Not yet.'

Twice Rosa tortured him in the bath, learning his body, before she would let him make love to her. And then, as he kissed her after their bath, she pushed him gently until he was kneeling by the bed and kissing her belly and the hair between her legs. Her fingers felt his scalp and ears, as her thighs began to move against his cheeks. As he knelt, he began to pray to himself, 'Clever tongue, find her, make her happy, make her come. For in her coming, she will have me too, for a while, for long enough for me to come, amen.' And his tongue heard him and searched and pried and found and worked on and on, and she sighed and moved and said, 'Magog, Magog, Magog,' and she used his hair to pull his face up to her kiss and he laid his body on hers and she felt the back of his legs with the soles of her feet and he was as one great pin piercing through a moth fluttering on its death-mount and she locked her legs behind his waist and he groaned and he clawed at her buttocks and she said very kindly, 'Magog, yes, yes.' And he could see that she had that secret smile of a woman who feels the ultimate power of giving pleasure to a man. And Magog felt a peace beyond understanding and knew that it was the beginning of all hell on earth.

The torment began almost at once.

'I may be your daughter,' Rosa said. She looked away moodily and put down her coffee cup.

'It doesn't matter. In Ancient Egypt, brother and sister, father and daughter married. It strengthened the line of the Pharaohs.'

'Sure. And where are the Pharaohs now?'

'Still around. In pyramids, mummies . . .'

'Talking of that, you fucked my mummy for years,' Rosa said. And she suddenly began to cry and pushed Magog away when he turned to comfort her.

So the torture was worked out in Beirut in the next two weeks of her convalesence. Only once did Magog get to lie with Rosa again, after she had made him sleep in another bedroom in the hotel. And then he bribed her with a gold-and-pearl collar and took her to the new Casino de Liban on the horn of the great bay to the north of Beirut. From there at night, the shoddy city that wheeled and dealt between east and west, between ancient and modern, between Muslim and Christian, between feyadeen and Israeli, at last achieved a small beauty of lights at the end of the silver curve of surf and the arc of black sea. Rosa won fifty pounds and more at baccarat under the crystal pillars, and she was flushed with luck and greed. She and Magog were picked up by two Arab businessmen and taken to a *boîte de nuit*, where a German girl stripped on the back of a white stallion. The rapt audience, with its desert traditions that prized horses above blonde women, was silent as the girl – naked except for her riding boots – rubbed her white breasts and body along the haunches of the horse and pulled its mane as a tassel between her legs, until even the stallion grew restless and it pawed the wooden floor with one hoof and its huge cock began to point out of its black sheath of skin. But the girl knew how to quell desire in beasts and men as well as how to arouse it. So she hit the

stallion over the nose with her whip and turned to the audience
and clicked the heels of her boots together. Everyone was
staring at the little trimmed blonde triangle above her thighs as
she put up her hand in a Hitler salute and said in bad French,
'*Messieurs, messieurs, il faut regarder haut comme ça.*' And there
was a huge laugh and she walked behind her stallion and leapt
onto its back over its tail as if it were a vaulting-horse and she
rode off-stage. The applause and whistling were tremendous.
Any man or woman in the audience would have given her an
oil-well for one night with her. As it was, Rosa smoked some
hashish and let Magog make love to her till dawn, and her only
cruelty was to make him swear that she was ten times better
in bed than Maire.

But conscience always lived in them like a knife. And Rosa
knew how to exploit her conscience as well as how to kick at
its pricks or to be ashamed. If Magog demanded anything of her
from sex to a little thanks for all he was doing or paying for her,
she would talk of how he had done the worst thing of all to her,
she had always thought of him as a father, now look at the pair
of them. And she burst into tears and made him feel that he had
ruined both of their lives just for a fuck or two. Then, when she
was feeling high and stepping, she would glory in the situation,
boasting of how none of her girl-friends had managed to steal
their mother's lover, let alone somebody who might be their
father. Incest was the ultimate boast – at least, the idea of incest
in the past. For if Magog tried to use this Byronic gloating to
get Rosa into bed, her conscience would immediately savage
him through violent accusations that she would have anybody
except him, he disgusted her, he only wanted a younger version
of her mother, if she hadn't been so ill she would never have
touched him, she would kill herself or kill him if he ever laid a
finger on her again. So her conscience made her angry, tearful,
bold, bitchy and destructive. The moods never lasted, for no
mood ever lasted with her. But they ruined a love affair that
never had a chance, and they kept Magog in a permanent rash
of guilt and an irritation of passion.

They went home after a scene with the fat Manager that came
back to Magog in the many white nights he was to know. When
he paid the hotel bill, the Manager opened a drawer below the

desk and took out a junky bracelet, heavy with little elephants and rabbits and crosses. This horror was slipped onto Rosa's wrist with a caress of her arm. *'Un souvenir de moi, Rosa,'* the Manager said. Magog expected Rosa to take the bracelet off and throw it in the fat man's face. She hated familiarity from ageing men even more than she loathed charm jewellery. But she took it and smiled and thanked the fat man with dark-lidded eyes, then she left with the angry Magog.

'Sure I slept with him,' she said in the taxi to the airport. 'What do you expect? Stuck in Beirut without bread. I'd have been all right if I hadn't gotten too ill to move on. And sure, he might have been aiming to sell me to some sheikh. But what makes you think a lay is so important? I didn't even think of it till you brought it up. Look, it doesn't mean a thing if you think it doesn't mean a thing. It's only thinking that makes fucking mean so much. Forget it.'

And so they came home from Beirut. They had meant to split apart immediately. But Rosa had let her flat go and it was hard to find another and Magog had the flat in his basement free. There were separate entrances. She would be wholly independent. She could come and go when she pleased. The contract was liberty.

'You really mean that?' Rosa asked. 'I'll test you, you know. You're never to say you're keeping me. Besides, there's no harm in a father helping his daughter, is there?'

When Rosa accepted to live in Magog's shadow but by her lights, both he and she felt that each had won a victory and each had suffered a defeat. So Magog began to move towards some wisdom, when he knew that victory and defeat might be the same thing. There had once been a great Emperor in India called Asoka, who had ruled India between the time that the arrogant Alexander and the arrogant British had both tried to rule India and had failed. Asoka had kept up an army of a million men and had gone out to punish rebels in Kalinga. He left behind a stone pillar of victory, which still stands. It records that the great Emperor Asoka deported one hundred and fifty thousand Kalingans and killed one hundred thousand and allowed many more than that to die of starvation or disease. But then the pillar of victory becomes a pillar of moral defeat. It records how the

Emperor grew ashamed of what he had done and was converted to the ways of Buddha and enforced the law of peace, even giving up his favourite dish of roast peacock because life was sacred. There is no other triumphant arch nor stone like it in the world. Magog also found only ashes in his conquest of Rosa.

So the basement of the Nash terrace house was set up as Rosa's flat and she padlocked the internal door that connected with the ground floor on the top of the stairs and she used only her private entrance. She was wholly free and Magog had to telephone her to fix an appointment, which she often did not keep. On the nights when he could not sleep for despair and rage, he would walk down the wide stone steps that fronted his house and look down through the iron railings towards her semi-circular bedroom window in the basement. Sometimes shadows of men crossed the lighted blinds behind the bars, set there against burglars. Occasionally there were sounds of flutes and gongs. Then Magog would catch himself spying on her and caution himself as he went back into his house. 'I will not say a word to her. I will not ask. I said she would be free. She is. I have surrendered.'

At last, by living in a state of surrender for two months of summer, Magog learned what it is to lose a war. He understood how a good German – that mythical creature of the Second World War and certainty of the Common Market – could look round the ruins and devastation of Cologne, Hamburg, Berlin, Dresden with the wild pigs eating the corpses of children and the stone melted into glass by the fierceness of the fire-bombs, and that good German could raise his hands to heaven and say, 'Lord, once we surrendered to our sin. We thought we could dominate the world. Now we surrender to our retribution as wholly as we surrendered to Hitler. This is the condition of a new Germany. We accept.'

So Magog, after a lifetime in the pursuit of power, surrendered wholly to Rosa. The months of pain gave way to periods of few feelings, lulls that were as exquisite as the ecstasies of the young Magog, for the pain was no longer there. And though the pain came back with sudden lusts unsatisfied, or on occasional nights with her always followed by her long absences, or after her continual extortions, yet the lulls in feeling grew to an almost constant serenity. For days on end, Magog could feel a humble pride in himself at his acceptance of every wrong that Rosa could do to him. This was a full expiation of his incest. Above all, this was the denial of his life of ambition and intrigue. Power had corrupted him, and perhaps corrupted him absolutely, but in that absolute corruption lay the birth of a strange purity. Magog was bored with the endless chores of manipulation. He wanted to grow old in peace. It was merely unfortunate that the lusts of the body lasted longer than the mind wished them to last. Or perhaps these idiotic appetites that would not die provided the humiliations that led a man stumbling towards wisdom.

Sometimes an old dog, he wrote to Josepha, *lies like a puppy with its paws in the air, inciting any man to put his foot on its stomach. It does not care whether it is scratched, pressed or crushed. The puppy rolls over because it knows no better and has not learned yet to fear the world. The old dog rolls over because it has yielded to the world for better or for worse. The French are always accusing us of lying on our Anglo-Saxon backs and letting the Yanks treat us like old dogs. Perhaps we do. Perhaps we are tired of being the meanest old hound on the block, and we just want to live out our age now in peace and a patch of stagnant prosperity. We are learning to lose gladly.*

Magog's surrender made his relations with Rosa easier. She might take him for granted, but she began to love him a little again. Her sudden generosities, when she would give him her company or her body or a plant for his garden, made him abjectly grateful. Now he understood about the happy slave, the Uncle Tom. There was a certain voluptuousness in subjection. Magog suspected that inside every iron man there was a seraglio lying in wait for its sultan.

In search of a way to bind Rosa to the house, Magog began negotiating with the Ponsonbys to allow the adopted Simon to come and stay from time to time with his mother. The Ponsonbys resisted fiercely. The child was only six, it would unsettle him, he must put his school work and his cricket team before his mother. Magog insisted, almost threatened, but the ultimate menace lay with the Ponsonbys, the withdrawal of the huge fortune settled on Simon, if they could find a lawyer smart enough to break the trust. Frankly also, Magog had to admit that Rosa was in no way maternal. Perhaps she would grow a motherly nature with time, if he could survive that long.

As Magog and Rosa had no common language except for gossip about her childhood and the family, they went to the cinema to find one. Magog could hardly remember the time when he had been the czar of the British film industry, and he had found the medium was just a dreary hokum for the masses. Now he was like any small boy, ready to be amused, only his childhood lay forty years back. The only star who seemed as good as in the old days was Belmondo with his broken boney mug and his spread lips; but Rosa said Belmondo turned her off. Still, films were a form of dialogue, for the images on the screen spoke to Rosa while Magog could be mercifully silent and feel her thigh or hand. It was marvellous to have her company and not to need to distract her.

Afterwards, Magog would find that Rosa could never analyse a film. She would say that it grooved or didn't groove, that it was out of sight or a dog. She would repeat whole scenes almost word for word, mimicking and laughing. But the metaphysics of cinema that interested Magog, the difference between reality and illusion, between the image and the thing itself, were dragsville to Rosa. Except when he read her the item in *The Times* about the Phantoms.

JORDAN: Hundreds of rioting Arabs wrecked a cinema in Amman. They tore down the screen during the showing of the John Wayne film, The Green Berets, *after American fighters had been shown in action in Vietnam. Apparently referring to the recent sale of 50 jet fighters to Israel, the rioters shouted: 'Phantoms! Phantoms!'*

Magog put down the newspaper, expecting to catch Rosa's usual expression when he read her anything out of *The Times*, a look of mixed boredom and indifference. But this time, the story set off some chain reaction in her mind. She began to tell a story; her answers were rarely direct.

'I was at the National Film Theatre,' Rosa said. 'You know, under Waterloo Bridge. Rudy Valentino was on in *The Four Horsemen of the Apocalypse*. The film was draggy, like twenty hours long. And Rudy never met his Cousin, who was a real baddie. It was the First World War, Rudy on the French side,

Cousin with the Huns. But first we had to sit out the whole bit, draggy Gay Paree, Rudy getting the chicks in a clinch but never getting them in the sack, then off he goes to the Western Front, flares, shells, hell's bells, one big yawn. Then wow, Rudy goes out on patrol. And you know he's going to *meet* someone! That old man at the NFT who's been playing his piano ever since the silents were silent, is really banging the bass. Then pow, up goes a Very Light, and pow pow, Rudy's on the edge of a hole in the ground looking into Cousin's evil grinning bare teeth. And Cousin's got a gun and a knife.'

'And how did Rudy get out of it?' Magog asked.

'I never sussed,' Rosa said. 'Just then, I mean, just when the whole show was right at it, the film caught fire. Of course, the movie was in black and white, being so early, like before cameras were invented. Then suddenly there was all this orange and yellow with black curly edges. Like a Light Show. Real fire on the Western Front. Then the screen goes blank and the lights go on and there's smoke pouring out of the projection room and chicks begin screaming in the seats. And there's smoke everywhere and we wait outside under Waterloo Bridge and it's just like Waterloo, till those groovy red engines come and they roll out the hoses and hose it down and there's even more smoke when the water gets on the fire. Like the Blitz was, I suppose.'

'It wasn't like that,' Magog said. 'There weren't enough engines to put the fires out. Gog saw the Guildhall burn down the night the Jerries set on fire the whole of the City. But you're too young even to imagine it.'

'Don't pull that age-gap stuff,' Rosa said. 'This was worse. I mean, I thought all the old movies might be burned up, they're on nitrate, it goes up like a light. And that would be the Apocalypse, I mean, the end of the world. I couldn't drag myself out any more in the mornings. What's there to live for, anyway, except hash and rock and old movies?'

'What happened to the old man who played the piano?' Magog asked. 'Or did you trample him down in the rush to preserve flaming youth?'

'They helped him out. Like he was wounded before, half-gassed or something. They really used chemicals to put you down in that First World War. But the old man's back, you know, still grooving for the silents. Like he's got something to live for. We dig him and we all give him a shout at the end. He's like the last survivor.'

Magog looked across at Rosa's shining face, alive with her memory of excitement. She was there in the body and he loved her. No image, the flesh itself, the passion itself. Only he knew that her love for him was his illusion that she sometimes shared from kindness. But not for much longer. The movie was nearly over.

Phantoms for Israel.

Eros.

That late summer, when it was all over with Rosa and she had disappeared, Magog went out to look for her in the shadow of the boy-god of love. Standing at Piccadilly Circus, Magog surveyed the stone chop of the famous traffic island with its tip lying towards Swan & Edgar's and its tail towards Leicester Square. A circus used to mean a place people went round to go about their business. But people were not going round Piccadilly Circus any more, even if the traffic was. They were sitting having their own circus in the middle of the stone chop, dressed in their granny dresses and caftans and torn jeans and Afghan jackets and shawls and love-beads and frayed buckskins and tatty boots, the uniform of the survival experts of the urban frontier. But Piccadilly was not meant to be a sanctuary for refugees from the world set-up. London never has much to do with street carnivals – they would only disturb the pigeons.

'Are you the fuzz?' a young Mohican asked, his skull shaved bald except for a central ridge of hair. His simplicity was winning, as though he expected Magog to flash a badge and say, 'Why, yes, how did you guess?' But Magog only nodded miserably and said, 'I'm just looking for somebody,' which sent the Mohican running away. As he fled, Magog noticed that he had an ugly unhealed scar on his skull. He must have trepanned himself to let off the pressure of his paranoia.

The wind blew the water from the jets of the fountain under the statue of Eros on high. The little silver god shot his stringless bow at the passing traffic and scored no hits. The street people sat to leeward, where the steps were dry that led up to the fountain; like old sailors, they knew which way the wind was blowing. The traffic roared and stopped and started in intermittent complaint on the other side of the grey barriers, while above them, the Edwardian buildings hung on until the next rebuilding scheme for the Circus which was never rebuilt. Foppish façades stood by, old dandies left out of this new happening where they were not invited. Four stone nymphs huddled under their conch shells over the All-Night Chemists, where the registered addicts were waiting for their legal fixes, while the learners were blowing out their grass smoke in hopeless competition against the exhausts of the buses besieging them.

Magog stayed in the Circus, looking for Rosa, remembering her bloody collapse there in her pregnancy, but she was not carried up to the street before the bad bright neon signs began to taunt the close of day – *Coca-Cola, Where Eagles Dare, Cinzano, Oliver, Guinness-Time, I A Woman, Wrigley's Spearmint Chewing Gum, Laughter In The Dark, Lilywhite's, Easy Rider*. Something for everyone. The shortest way out of Soho was once a bottle of gin. Now it was a shop or a ticket to the movies.

Night came. The police began to patrol the Circus. Time to move on. The street people picked up their sleeping-bags, blowing with the paper down Piccadilly towards Green Park. Magog moved with them, drifting with the drift from the Circus against the tide of suburban people, coming in for an evening in the West End. Somewhere at the end of the street, perhaps Rosa.

At the end of the street, a siege. Several hundred squatters had occupied a large building in Piccadilly. Now they were surrounded by a turmoil of tourists and television men, policemen and photographers. The babble of publicity outside was louder than any anarchy inside. As Magog fled away into the peace of Green Park, he saw, high as an eagle, a bearded man in coloured patched trousers putting the last strokes to a great graffito on one side of the occupied building – WE ARE THE WRITING ON YOUR WALL.

The Park was an encampment. Deck-chairs had been set up in little wigwams or porches to bushes. The branches of the trees made natural roofs to those bundled in their sleeping-bags below. Indignant, the blazing square eyes of the millionaire flats in St James's Place stared out at the migrants in the Royal Park. The lights in the Ritz blinked fiercely on and off at the mess of free sleepers on its own back lawn that happened, by an error, to be a public area. And the policemen stayed outside on their beats in Piccadilly, thankful to sweep the problem of the street people from the gutters on to the flowerbeds until dawn.

Magog wandered among the shapes on the grass, peering down at the faces that could hardly be seen. Some slept with their foreheads buried in the crooks of their elbows, sure to be smothered by midnight. Shadows patched the cheeks of those who lay on their backs, blankets and hair obscured the profiles of those who rested on their sides. Magog could never make out a whole face, just the features of the tired young, soft and slack in their weariness. The sleepers moved and sometimes shrieked, then muttered into a doze again. There were enemies in their night. The Park would not hush.

Under a dark clump, laughter and action. Two boys, a girl between them. They moved beneath an old shaggy robe, their bare legs making a six-footed beast rolling on the ground. The head of the girl broke free from the top of the robe and looked up at Magog looking down at her. She was not Rosa.

'Why don't you go and blow a key-hole?' the girl said.

Magog turned and began to stride away, head held low, towards the lamp-posts and the streets. A duck quacked from the dark.

What was it Barbellion wrote as he lay dying?

Cupid and Death once met at an Inn and exchanged arrows, since when young men have died and old men have doted.

Eros in London.

Gog rarely read a newspaper. It so happened that he was wrapping up his lobsters for market when a paragraph of newsprint caught his eye. A rock north of the Orkneys, inhabited only by gulls and too small to claim in more human times, was now the object of a territorial battle between England, Holland, Denmark and Norway. Ever since treasures of minerals and oils had been discovered on the sea-bed, every maritime nation wanted to annex each pimple which showed above the breakers in order to claim twelve sea miles of sunken land about its perimeter. Gog was reminded of the fable of Hengist and Horsa, who were granted by the English King all the land that a hide could cover. They cut the hide into strips and made a circumference big enough to contain a castle. And thus the invading Danes got a foothold in England.

Perhaps the strange still November sea drove Gog finally mad. Perhaps it was the fine chill day that made the waves break up into a million million particles of radiant energy, like the unseen atoms and electricities that worked Gog's body. Perhaps he remembered his loved Josepha and had to join her. Or perhaps, like some American Indian chieftain, Gog knew his proper time of dying before the valves of his heart clotted with blood or seized up with fat, before his blood cells were gobbled in the claws of cancer. But most certainly, the news of the last white rock to the north where no country was sovereign, where no government could enforce the debts it claimed a citizen owed to society, where no company complained except the gulls, this news sent Gog out on his final voyage.

He smashed all his lobster-pots before he left. Something about the wooden cages offended him for the first time. He picked up a sledge-hammer and went down to the water's edge. He hauled in the lines that attached the pots to the tarred posts by the sea. If there were lobsters in any of the pots, Gog pulled them out, ignoring their pinches that bloodied his fingers. He threw the armoured creatures back into the sea, then broke the pots with his hammer. He was sailing wild into the deep. He would leave all free behind him.

When he hoisted the white sail of the dinghy *Blake*, Gog felt a tremor run through him that would have meant love when he was young, success to his middle age, and release now that he was setting out to die. In the old radiance ahead lay a quest. Purposeless and pure as any grail, the rock, limed with birdshit, tempted the last adventurer in search of a place where no writ ran ahead of him. Gog moved back to the tiller.

The calm of the North Sea lasted until the sun dipped and Gog had sailed past the headland. Then a swell rose, the waves grew white combs, the combs blew into manes, the manes into sleet-flurries into choppy hillocks higher than the little sail of the *Blake*. In the darkling light, Gog saw the small peak of his own boat pitch and shudder among the taller peaks of the great breakers. And the spray stung and blinded his eyes into a blur of vision until he was sliding among the white wide wet shifting rocks that were shaking and rising out of the sea, he was spewing up at the birth of the white island, Albion, Albion, each man shall be an island unto himself, each man shall be a white island unto himself, no man shall leave his island to do harm unto the island of another, Albion, Albion, born in the time before time when the land came in surf and sorrow out of the legs of the Atlantic, never bloody and bruising until the iron ships of Mammon and Moloch and Magog made Albion brawl into Britain and paint the globe red, but in the time before time when Albion was born white and still in her druid mists, the reliquary of things past and lost and gone from the moiling world except in the chalk of Albion, in the white berries of the mistletoe on the sacred oaks, in the white horses on the green hills of Albion that was shifting and sighing and rising and roaring its birth-pain about Gog, until he was sudden-sitting on a cold wash of sea and the salt was his cradle and the foam his swaddling-band and brine his first-last choke of breath and the blind caul of the deep Gog's sleep at the new birth of Albion . . .

'Gog's drowned once before and come back,' Maire said. 'At the end of the war. Perhaps he'll do it again.'

'That kipper we saw,' Magog said, 'wouldn't ever come out of his box.'

'You couldn't tell it was Gog. It was all swollen. And the fish had eaten him.'

'It had to be. One boat sunk, one body found. One and one makes Gog gone.'

These remarks were not meant to be particularly heartless. They were meant to reassure Maire and Magog that Gog's death did not really matter, although it certainly left a vacuum in the imagination. They had both got very drunk in the Caithness Hotel after the funeral, but sober-drunk. Melancholy took the kick out of the whisky.

'You are always too logical, Magog. Gog has a strange habit of being washed up again.'

'Only at the Resurrection,' Magog said. 'Until then, we may be spared. Oh, I sent a telegram to Arthur.'

'That was very considerate. Not quite you. But Arthur was never really Gog's son, was he?'

'He may be. Who knows? Surely Gog was capable of it.'

Maire shrugged. Magog continued.

'I heard Arthur had an accident. One of those industrial ones he is always claiming his members are having. He lost a hand in a printing press. And then he flew to Prague to have it put on again. You remember Prague, Maire, when we were there before the war. All illusion.'

'And Russian tanks now.'

'Another illusion. But the Czechs do understand mechanics. You remember that play *R.U.R.*? And the Golem? They're very good at robots. Artificial men and spare parts.'

'But Arthur always hated Gog and you. He's the radical reaction. The alternative society.'

'Still, if he knows his reason for reaction is gone, perhaps he will end by joining us. Nearly everybody does. I would rather be a press baron than a Luddite print worker. It is perfectly natural, my dear Maire, that every son has to try and kill his own father before he can take over his role.'

'Lud,' Maire said. 'Gog told me of him. A Celtic god. He was very clever and had a silver hand.'

'Not the same as the Luddites. They are very stupid and try to wreck the new technology, which is inevitable.'

'Gog always fought you,' Maire said. 'And this Arthur always fought him. Perhaps he was right. There always has to be a fight. Gog versus Magog versus the Luddites. Always a big fight.'

'Gog was always paranoiac,' Magog said. 'I was his chief enemy in fantasy and mythology. If he's dead, then I'm the victor at last. Technology and the city and the factory have won. Magog lives. Gog and the people are dead. But the funny thing is, I haven't thought about politics or power all year long. I don't think I even know where Vietnam is.'

'You've been screwing my daughter instead,' Maire said.

'Not very often,' Magog said. 'And I wish I hadn't screwed her at all.'

'So do I,' Maire said. 'But what does a woman have daughters for, except to become a madam for them and pass them on to her lovers?'

'Rosa's taught me to yield,' Magog said. 'I could never surrender to you. I enjoyed the fight too much.'

'You never won,' Maire said. She patted the one white streak in her black hair down into her chignon and took another sip of whisky. 'No man ever beat me.'

'And with all your victims, Maire, aren't you tired of triumph? Wouldn't a defeat be a diversion?'

'I've never met my match,' Maire said. 'Give me time. At forty-nine . . .'

Magog raised his eyebrows at Maire, who smiled back at him, still smooth-cheeked, her white hair streak an artifice to contradict the ageless opulence of her youthful skin.

'At forty-nine,' Maire went on, 'I find that I have only just begun to learn how to deal with men. I think I may meet my master before I die. I have spent a long time preparing for the battle by practising with his understudies.'

'Nobody will ever beat you, Maire. While you make your body conditional on your victory, you must win. Rosa told me that she had met one of the top Black Power people and he'd confessed that Black Power was useless in front of Pussy Power.'

'But when that ultimate trap for men no longer lures,' Maire said. 'What then?'

'You will have to become a very wise woman to win.'

'You say you are becoming a wiser man. Perhaps you will learn to be my Armageddon.'

'At the moment, Maire, I think losing may be more important for me than winning.'

'You're rationalizing your defeats, Magog. Just like England *giving* up its Empire when it could no longer afford to keep it up, and then claiming the forced gift was really goodness of heart.'

'The action counts. Motives are meaningless.'

'The action doesn't count. Motives are fascinating. Tell me,

Magog darling, did you just want revenge against me when you seduced my daughter?'

'You would think like that. You always think from inside your skin.'

'I have no other. Then what was your reason to bang Rosa?'

'It would take too much time to explain.'

'Time?' Maire laughed. 'Don't count on too much of that. It's rationed now for all of us.' She looked wickedly at Magog. 'I suppose you'll bang little Mary Griffin too, when you're a dirty old man and she's too young to know better. You'll have to educate your grand-daughter too.'

Magog felt a stab at his heart. Was it fear or premonition or that most alien prick – remorse?

'Don't joke like that, Maire. I love little Mary just as much as I loved Josepha. I did bring her back to you from Cuba. I've left her with you to bring up. Through her, you're a young mother again. You're lucky. Grandmothers are young twice at the cradle, while men just stoop more to each new child.'

'You'll stoop so low over Mary, you'll lay on her. But next time, over my dead body.'

'She's only one year old, and even I . . .' Magog paused. 'You know, we did come to bury Gog, not talk about our own sins.'

'Well, we're still here, aren't we?'

1970

'The good thing about being old and unemployed,' Sir George Germain said, 'is that one can be subversive. On the edge of the grave, one joins the guerrillas. At last, there is nothing to lose.'

Magog looked at the white-haired death-mask which had a certain likeness to his former chief in the Civil Service, and wondered if old age had not sabotaged Germain's mind. He had lost contact with Germain for a decade. Now, Learlike on the brink of reason and oblivion, Germain had come to Magog's house to share his mania with his underling.

'Most former civil servants,' Magog said, 'age by doing good work in county councils.'

'It's too serious for that,' Germain said. 'What we did after the war is rising to haunt us. I know the sins of the fathers are visited on the children. But the bombs, the gases too?'

'You're worried over that nerve gas you said should be dumped off Ireland?'

'I have a tendency to thrombosis controlled by drugs. I also have a cancer arrested by cobalt rays as well as a plastic bladder. Radiation and chemicals have left me a sort of Lazarus recalled from the dead. I'm not as bad as Baldwin the Fourth, the leper King of Jerusalem, who went on fighting with his hands and feet rotted off, and his stench so offensive that his barons couldn't stand getting near their King. But I'm pretty well a walking mass of pollution. I don't want it to spread.'

Magog found himself instinctively flinching away from Germain, who was sitting on the double-headed sofa beside him. He was ashamed of his reactions. But it was human. Nobody wanted to get too close to the plague.

'Don't worry,' Germain said. 'I'm not contagious.'

'I didn't mean . . .' Magog said, ashamed.

'You couldn't help it,' Germain said. 'Who wants contact with the unclean? That's what I'm here about. Have you a copy of that minute you wrote for me? About the nerve-gas?'

'It's confidential, George.'

'Nothing is as confiding, Magnus, as death whispering in your ear that you may only have a few days left to atone. Have you still got a copy? You always used to keep everything in case you needed to produce it later to prove you were right and we were wrong.'

'I'm sure to have it in my papers,' Magog said. 'I'll send you a copy.'

'Is there any way of getting those rusty gas-containers out from the sea?'

'None. They're too dangerous. No diver would do it.'

'What have we done, Magnus? What have we done?'

'Nothing. We've allowed one or two things without protesting. We shut up then, perhaps we should shut up now.'

'No!' The old man spat at Magog, so that Magog had to wipe his hand across his face. The saliva might be poisonous after all. Doctors could be wrong. 'We must confess the horrors we have done.' Germain's face was full of agony. 'How else can we say to the new ones, "Don't you do it, don't you do it, don't you be as careless as we were!" God knows, it's the greatest crime, to be careless. We just took the easy way, the cheapest way, the way that caused least trouble – not for everybody, but for ourselves. But there's a terrible cost, a terrible responsibility we wouldn't face. We're responsible to the whole earth. It'll accept even my rotten flesh. It has no choice. But did I ever accept the earth? I had no choice either. I lived on it. Do you know, the Mayans, when they went hunting and found some deer, they would kill only one, however hungry they were. The deer also had a right to live. Then the Mayans would kneel by the dead deer and ask its forgiveness, saying, "We had to eat. We spared your brothers. Forgive us for our hunger." That's all I can say, Magnus, to the people who are now young. I ruled and I did not know how to rule. I did not spare my brothers nor the unborn. Forgive me, for I will tell you the wrongs I have done so that you shall not do them again to the new unborn.'

Old age had evidently driven Sir George Germain crazy. He was not being rational. He had never had enough power to feel so responsible for what had been done. He was not as guilty as he claimed to be. Nobody was ever that guilty in a bureaucracy, because there were no men who had the power of complete decision. Germain was mad.

'They'll prosecute you,' Magog said. 'You can't publicize official secrets.'

'I'll keep you out of it,' Germain said. 'What can they do to an old man like me? I'd die on their hands. I'd embarrass them, and governments hate embarrassment. They'd rather murder somebody in a war than be embarrassed by him. They'll look silly trying to prosecute a man on the point of death.'

'The gas will poison the Atlantic anyway,' Magog said. 'The ocean's big enough to absorb it. Go home and live in peace.'

'I want to die in peace,' Germain said. 'I am writing about how we fouled the earth and how people can begin to clean it up. There are uncontaminated people now, who won't just shift anything difficult or dirty on to the shoulders of the next government or the next generation. People who think of their life as a lease, not a right to plunder the planet. You should pass on the earth a little bit cleaner and better than you found it. We've used it as a piss-place, a rat-hole, a dump. It has to stop, or we will.'

'It'll last our time,' Magog said.

'Give me your minute on the gas,' Germain said.

'I will,' Magog said. 'If you insist.'

That year, the seas began to stink.

Off Devon, a trawler winched in a heavy catch. Then the sea began to boil and bubbles a yard wide exploded and the air burned and the sailors coughed and their tongues swelled and their mouths blistered and the Captain cut the trawl free with a hacksaw and the gases boiled down beneath the waves and the trawler went back to port.

In the North Sea, the crab-legged drilling platforms walked out to the middle of the grey waters and dropped their drills and took out of the depths natural gas and oil to pipe to the mainland. But not all the tapped juices of the earth would stay in the pipes. Some began to spread over the surface of the waves. The spokesman of the companies of exploration said: 'The North Sea is beginning to change its colour.'

On the beaches, the towels were full of tar and the oil slicks came floating in, dropped off the tankers, and Dunkirk fleets of small boats went out to blanket the oil with detergents and to soak it up with straw, and still the oil came floating in with the dying gulls screaming their clogged deaths in its wake.

Down the rivers that flow into the sea came the wastes of industries and cities, arsenic, mercury, copper, piss, acid, ammonia, nitrates. The fish died and the waterfowl. Only the rats thrived and the noble swans which, like Mithridates, ate poisons to become immune and to prolong their white-winged glory.

In a brook near a nuclear-power station, school children found three-headed tadpoles, frogs with seven legs, newts with thirteen, and other deformed pond life. They showed their teacher who showed the atomic energy people who took away the evidence and stopped the leak and went on making the mess that altered life itself.

The great red salmon that leapt the rocks and rapids of the Scots and Irish rivers began to die of a wasting disease, and the young salmon were trapped in their shoals by nets off Greenland, and their numbers fell until they were hardly seen, and people said the red salmon would never be found again in three years or so.

The land also had its blight.

Vietnam came to the hedgerows with defoliants called weed-killers that made mice bear legless babies, and, if mice, what of men?

The animals and fowls penned in the batteries and breeding factories began to suffer like those who ate them and who chose to herd themselves into cities. Cows, maddened by artificial insemination, took to leaping on one another like bulls. Rams, prisoned together, learnt the art of buggery. Calves in wooden cages grew soft hooves, as they did not need to walk; their keepers provided them with shoes. The meat of hens which never moved from their cages became white and tasted of chemicals and sponge cake. Old farmers did not like these new habits of the animals in their concentration camps; but the young farmers did not care and the people in the cities did not mind where their food came from as long as it was cheap enough.

At Porton Down, a scientist touched his lip with a rubber glove that had touched a toxic compound he had been making as a deterrent against biological warfare. When he was alive, he believed that Britain should make diseases so horrible that nobody else would dare to attack it with their man-made diseases. When he was dead within two minutes after the glove touched his lips, one of his colleagues said: 'If he had sneezed, there went Birmingham.'

The sky had its vapours.

Lead fell on Millwall from the chimneys and the few trees that reminded people in the docks of the old forests all wilted and perished.

Thunder cracked the clear air in Wales. It came from the high Concorde, flying faster than the sound that lagged behind it to rattle the glass in Saint David's Cathedral and to lay to rest God's palms. For why should He bother to clap up storms, now men could make their own?

When the wind dropped, smog filled the High Streets from the car exhausts and the lungs of the old people gave way and none called it murder except for a mad barrister who filed a suit for massacre against Henry Ford, forgetting that Ford was dead.

Magog knew of these things by looking at the newspapers during the months after Sir George Germain's visit. The old man had died, leaving the undoing of his life's work undone. Noting the creeping tide of poison that was licking at the feet of the human race, Magog began to admire the old man's last effort, but he did not feel inspired enough to carry on the fight himself. Nothing could stop the spread of the global cancer except a turning back to the old ways of earth, and even the young liked new things too much to stop the making of more and more things, which would mess up the land still further. And there was no time for Magog to do much. Rosa was ill. Better to care for one person than for mankind. The love was greater.

The love was too great to bear when Magog found out what was wrong with Rosa. The cause of the infection was never established. It could have been picked up anywhere. Her chances were not good. The doctors cut her open with a wide wound and took out the growths and swabbed her clean and stitched her together again below the bikini line, for she did not want her scar to show on the beach. And she lay, green and dying, on the hospital bed with the tubes running into her nostrils and her wrist and her stomach and even into her foot. And Magog knelt by her bed until his knees set like bones, and he held her burning hand, and he gave her ice-cubes to suck for her fever. She begged to swallow them, but this was not allowed.

Her stomach stopped working for three days and nights, and Magog knew she must die.

Her stomach started working again on the fourth day, and Magog hoped she might live.

On the fifteenth day, she was feeling better, and Magog saw she would live for some time.

She seemed grateful for his love and for his visits to her every morning and evening. What she asked him to bring, he searched out and brought. It was the best time of his love for her. He could show her all that was in his heart, and she could accept it in her need. Only she forbade him to come to the hospital at certain times of the day, when others visited her. He did not see her then. He was greedy to be alone with her.

'I love you, Magog,' she said. 'Your love is the first thing in my life. I can't really live without knowing you love me.'

He had planned to take her away to Morocco to grow brown and strong in the sun. He made the arrangements for them both, fussing endlessly at the travel agents. He had spoken to the Ponsonbys about having her son Simon for the school holidays when they got back, and Rosa seemed pleased to play mother at last. Then the day before she was due to leave with Magog, she discharged herself from hospital and disappeared, leaving no address.

The following weeks were the hardest. Magog was desperate. He hardly noticed that the fall of the stock market had wiped out half his fortune. Then Rosa wrote to him, saying that she was happy and getting well. She left him neither apology nor telephone number.

Two months later, she walked into the house, using her key. She gave no warning.

'I've come home,' she said.

He could not accept her. He had to cover her with reproaches. After all his love for her, how could she?

She replied that she could not bear that much love. The burden was too great. She had to run away with casual people, who loved her less. Nobody who had died and come alive again wanted the full weight of love. They wanted to live in the day.

'Why come back at all?' he said.

'Because I love you,' she said. 'Don't ask why.'

To keep her with him, Magog did everything that he had totally despised in other people. He lied, he wept, he begged. He caused rows over trifles, he blackmailed, he bullied, he bribed. He pretended illness, insomnia, breakdowns. He sometimes struck Rosa, threatened her with kitchen knives. He opened her letters if he got to the box first, and he destroyed any letter that might tempt her away. He even stole all her clothes for twenty-four hours, until she escaped in his overcoat. He saw himself reduced to a contemptible whining thing. He could not stop himself, even when he knew that every act of his made the situation worse, and that Rosa would leave him the moment she felt strong enough to find an alternative way of life.

Then one summer day she was gone. And Magog knew that, this time, she would never return. Although love always has a last time after the last time, this was final. She pitied him too much, she felt trapped by his weakness and his dependence. There was a sort of justice in it all. The man of power, Magog, had become powerless. The strong had become the suppliant, the arrogant had begun to crawl, the proud to be humble. Each man, Magog knew, contained his own opposites. Every virtue was the reverse image of a vice. Yet it took the beggary of obsession and the bankruptcy of the heart to reveal to a man that there was nothing vile he could not do, if need be. And need was.

So Magog did everything he had judged and condemned in others. And so doing, he began to understand that a man must suffer and commit everything against his own nature before he might start to comprehend the failings and natures of other men. Rosa stripped Magog of his power, his pride, his righeousness, his hypocrisy, his view of himself. She left him naked to the alien, open to the unknown. He had nothing left, no dream of glory, empire, might. He was ready for any chance the charity of the future might drop at his feet. He had hardly noticed that a man called Heath had led the Tories back to power in England, pledged to restore freedom and opportunity to the small island. The only opportunity Magog wanted was to see Rosa.

Dear Josepha, *Magog wrote*, I am sorry to tell you that Fidel didn't get his ten million tons of sugar. He only got eight and a half million tons. He offered to resign as leader of the Revolution, but the Cuban people would not let him go. The greatest power is to offer to leave power. Nobody can stand the prospect of a vacuum in power, which is against nature. So Fidel stayed on. I know you worked hard for that ten million tons and that your body stays in Havana for that ten million tons and the fact that Fidel didn't get it is no failure of yours. It is better to hope for too much than not to hope at all.

I do not hope at all at the moment. Rosa nearly died, and then she came back to me, but I could not keep her. Rosa always needed you, Josepha, because you gave her the one love she always wanted, love without any criticism or qualifications. When you stayed in Havana, she had nowhere to turn except to me, and I had nowhere to turn except to her, because we both needed you to love us. But I have failed her and she is gone away. So I have had to discover like Fidel that finally we are powerless to do even what we have promised to do, and that we must accept our weakness as the price of living on earth.

There is even talk of peace in Israel with the Jews going back to their old frontiers and Jerusalem becoming a holy city for everyone, an international zone of faith. But there is always talk of peace when we talk of Jerusalem, but we never seem to get there.

Josepha, my darling, I don't think you would know me now. I seem to be starting on a long journey to find out things about people that I should have known since I was born, only my life somehow got in the way and stopped me finding out. I shall set off soon . . .

So Magog went to the Isle of Wight. He had never meant to go. Everything about the pop festival there sounded repulsive. Two hundred and fifty thousand people in a small space on a Bank Holiday week-end. Rosa would be invisible in that mob, if she was there at all. Three-hour queues for buses and lavatories, food running short, a mass frenzy of freaking out as though death were tomorrow, air raids of detonating sound on amplifiers louder than sirens. Really, the Blitz had sounded more fun and better music.

Yet the young were on the move towards the Isle, along the roads, huddled in the corridors of trains, jammed in the buses, on foot, cushioned in hovercraft, the young of the world were going on a new Children's Crusade to hear their priests chant their liturgies and lead them in a holy war of innocence against the heathen, against the pigs, the fuzz, the blue meanies, the set-up, the straights, the squares, against the ordinary people of the world who wanted some law, some order and were

frightened by the coming of the vagabonds and troubadours with
coloured trousers and lusty beggars and bold molls and Tom
O'Bedlams of these new Middle Ages. For the wandering and
ageing children were looking for a third Jerusalem on the Isle of
Wight, island of man, white isle, the ancient first Jerusalem in
the wild mind of William Blake, beloved of Gog, before the
Druids' sin had driven it from Albion in wailing and woe, and a
second Jerusalem had been built in Israel. Jerusalem was no
place, as the children knew, but a state of bliss on earth. It
might come to England again by a mass act of belief.

Dear Josepha, *Magog wrote on his knee in the limousine that the
chauffeur was piloting past the trudging and lemming young,* I
am on a new Children's Crusade. It must be my second childhood. Do you know about the first Children's Crusade? In 1212,
a shepherd boy called Stephen was suddenly infected with inner
vision. He said that he would lead a crusade of children to the
rescue of the Holy Land from the heathen. The Mediterranean
and the Red Sea would dry up before their feet. When he told
this to the wise King of France, the King told him to go back to
his sheep. But the children of France and Germany listened to
Stephen. Thirty thousand of them, girls among the boys, gathered round him as he sang his siren song of heaven to the East.
Their parents wept, but the children always found enough priests
to bless them for their faith. Stephen rode on the crusade in a
painted cart under a golden canopy, surrounded by a bodyguard
of noble boys on horses. The poorer children walked through
the hot summer towards Marseilles, as they are walking now
towards the Isle of Wight . . .

When the children reached the sea, they stopped, expecting
the water to divide before them. It did not. Brine can be
bloody-minded. After a few days two local merchants called
William the Pig and Hugh the Iron offered to ship the children
for free to the Holy Land. Stephen gladly accepted this miracle
of human charity. The children set sail. Nothing was heard of
them for eighteen years. Then one returned home. William the
Pig and Hugh the Iron had taken the children to the slave-
markets of Algeria and Alexandria. If any child reached the Holy
Land, it was as a eunuch, a harlot, a servant or hand-maid. The

trouble with crusades is that the crusaders must pay dearly for their journey.

There was another sadder Children's Crusade, Josepha. Or at least Brecht thought so. These children didn't even have a dream like Jerusalem, they didn't choose to leave their homes. It was several hundred years later in the Second World War in Poland, at a time of famine and winter. Brecht says there were fifty-five children, Poles, Germans, even a Jew. They wandered through ruined farms, looking for food, running from tanks and soldiers, seeking the south and the sun, finally straying off into the falling snow . . . Only a hungry dog was found. Round its neck, a childish scrawl. The message said the dog would lead anyone who could bring help to the children.

> *WENN IHR NICHT KOMMEN KÖNNT*
> *JAGT IHN WEG!*
> *SCHIESST NICHT AUF IHN*
> *NUR ER WEISS DEN FLECK . . .*

I've never forgotten the words, though my German's not too good. Roughly they mean,

> *IF YOU CAN'T COME TO US*
> *PLEASE DRIVE THE DOG AWAY!*
> *DON'T SHOOT HIM AS NOBODY ELSE*
> *CAN FIND OUR PLACE.*

Then the poem ends, I can't remember the rest . . .

> *SEITDEM SIND EINEINHALB JAHRE UM.*
> *DER HUND IST VERHUNGERT GEWESEN.*

That means,

> *SINCE THEN TWO YEARS HAVE PASSED*
> *THE STARVING DOG IS DEAD.*

I can't explain this sort of Children's Crusade to the children tramping along the Isle of Wight. You see, they only put up with poverty and cold and hunger and sleeping out, because it's a brief experience, not a forced march just to exist day after day after day. They play at hard times like they play at innocence and togetherness. They don't know what real war is, real famine, real hunger, real violence, real horror. You're not like this, Josepha. You went to Cuba to help solve these real things. But if I say this to Rosa, she thinks I'm a sort of Methuselah playing Cassandra. I'm just too old to see what's going on. The kids will turn on everyone to love, peace, charity, togetherness with good vibrations. But what they're doing is already turning on the human race, to tear it apart. They turn on kids who don't want to go to the Isle of Wight because they have other work to do. They turn on the middle-aged and the old and condemn them to isolation from the young until death. They have excluded, just like the original Crusaders, anyone who will not join the Crusade. But when the first Crusaders took over the Jerusalem they found in Israel, they slew every man and woman and child and dog, because these were not the same as them.

Josepha, you are alive to me. I write this letter which I shall never post because I shall give it to you soon. I have a strong and sudden feeling that I am not going to the Isle of Wight for the reason I thought I was. I said to myself, I am going to look for Rosa. And perhaps I will find out why the children are on a Crusade again, leaving empty broken homes behind them because of a mad dream by their prophets that they can bring peace and innocence back to the earth. The truth is, I am going to the Isle of Wight because I feel I may have a vision there (the children claim to have visions all the time in these mass rituals). And in my vision, I shall talk to you and Gog again. How stupid we are, not to know how much we really love people until they are dead. Dead? Not you, Josepha, nor dear Gog. Dead? No, of course not. I am writing to you . . .

'Stop,' Magog said to the chauffeur. 'We'll pick up those three.'

The three wandering children by the limousine all had the weary, pouched faces of tramps. The two child-men wore beads

and amulets against the wrath of heaven, headbands to corral
their wild hair, painted anoraks and purple velvet trousers; one
wore flying-boots, the other sandals. The child-woman had the
fevered washed eyes of the lost who never find themselves.
She wore a granny dress and a coat made from a Persian carpet;
round her neck, silver and gold and greenstone beads; bare thin
feet. All three humped their bed-rolls inside the car without a
word and sat on the leather seats, looking at Magog fiercely,
trapped as animals.

'Going to Portsmouth?' one child-man asked.

Magog nodded.

'All the way,' he said, then added. 'Say nothing. I have nothing
to say to you either.'

So the travellers fell asleep in the limousine. And sleep
softened their faces and changed them into two young men and
a girl, no longer old pilgrims in search of childhood. One of them
had a Festival Funbook. Its cover showed a zany youth from
The Who wearing coloured clothes in a surround of stars and
flowers jumping over Rupert the Bear. Back to the land of dream
where there was always somebody to keep you safe and warm
in the cold world.

Magog wrote:

How can they expect us always to help them, Josepha?
They set off to Katmandhu, Utopia, the Isle of Wight. They
have the appetites of adults, yet they expect like children that
all will be given to them for the asking, all will be done for
them without return. Supposing I were to say, Why should I
help you? Why me, why you? They would say, Don't help us,
we'll still get to the Isle of Wight. And they would. For they
would find others to help them. Do we get our expectations,
then? All the lessons of living would say, No, no, no, we
never get our expectations, except if we are very beautiful
or very lucky or so wise that we expect very little. Yet these
aged children on their Crusade are often ugly and offer nothing
back. Or perhaps they offer the greatest gift of all, the
opportunity for us to do something for somebody without the
least wish for gratitude. I hope the Middle Ages are back.
The possibility of true charity for the love of God and man.

And for the fear that, but for the grace of age, I would be as the least of them . . .

'Portsmouth,' Magog said and woke the children. He let them go bleary away, before he himself went to the ferry to the white island.

The isle was green, of course. The whiteness had been brought by the people. The tents covered the fields in pale stooks, the harvest of the pure in heart. The armies of the young had met to feel by the mass of their being that each was not alone, to commune together by the passing of the joints from hand to hand, to crowd together for recognition and to escape from that crowd by drugs, to worship by contact with strangers and conversation without tongues. For all was a quiet hearing of the sounds of the rock bands and the blues, the groups and the single singers, the funky and the easy, all was communion with the priests on the altars, the knights at the lists, as they came on swinging their incense-burning guitars, chasubles of gongs, pennants flying high on their sitars like lances, organs pawing as warhorses, drums as the mouths of cannon. Hear their names called, the champions of the young people!

> *Judas Jump*
> *Mighty Baby*
> *Supertramp*
> *Howl*
> *Procul Harum*
> *Cat Mother*
> *Ten Years After*
> *Sly and the Family Stone*
> *Moody Blues*
> *Pentangle*
> *Good News*
> *Tiny Tim*
> *Heaven*

They ride out to the tournaments, raise their maces and their voices. The sounds of the battle are caught and whirled high low loud about the sitting lying squatting armies of the young, then boomed out from the great shields of the amplifiers closing in the hosts between the batteries of percussion, the charges of guitars, the trenches of organ music, the stone keeps of total noise.

There were other barriers about the armies.

The first moat was the sea round the Isle of Wight. And none shall pass over who cannot pay the fare.

The second barrier was the wooden palisade round the whole encampment. And nobody could enter without his sixty shillings, and when the free and the wild tried to break through to what they believed their birthright – the liberty of rock – the organizing brothers misnamed Fiery Creations called for the blue fuzz to keep out the hordes, which they had summoned with the blazing cross of gold.

The third wall lay ahead round the enclosure of the exploiters. There the feudal lords of the pop aristocracy sat, the producers and the merchandizers, the lawyers and the camp-followers, the grasping and the groupies, the fixers and the fat cats, the newsmen and the cameramen, ready to record what people paid to see so that people could pay to see it again. The lords in their enclosure were getting their tithes and their rack-rents, their bread-tax and their salt-tax. Few soldiers of the feudal young did not pay for the privilege of believing that they were ending the exploitation of the world by being fleeced by their own.

The last citadel was the stage, where the leaders of the kids sang their songs of innocence and mirth, of revolt and protest, of blood and liberty, of gods and the spirit, the wild calls to their people to take the world in their hands and remake it into the Eden that would some day come. Yet round themselves the leaders had built pillars of crystal, glass armouries, so that nobody could touch them, all should worship from afar, godhead should pass through the self-anointed kings to the hushed masses by the laying on of voices. And for this privilege of majesties that came and went on the dais, the pedestals, the thrones, the *imperium in imperio*, all must give even what they did not have. So it always was and so it always is, the leaders shall rise up from the people and the people shall pay to be led by the nose or the ears.

'I don't believe in gate-crashing,' said the hard rock harder lady hardest singer of them all. 'The people aren't up there when I'm sweating on a stage at a festival, breaking my ass. You can get the money, man. Sell your old lady, sell your dope. Look at me, man, I'm selling my heart.'

The labourer is worthy of his hire, but are the work of the king and the passion of the queen worthy of their palace?

Magog passed through the crowds as in a trance. The people seemed to make way in front of him. A strange weakness was water in his knees, water in his eyes. He moved slowly over the fields strewn with limbs, shoulders, heads, the relaxed carriage of the young. He was walking to the high places and the sound was growing louder about him.

'Make way for the zombie,' a voice said and put a joint in his hand. 'He's spaced out.'

Magog inhaled deeply from the joint and stood, looking into the sun. The joint was taken from his hand.

'Pass it on,' the voice said.

The light of the sun seemed to lead Magog forwards again. Kindly hands were his guides, touching him on his way, putting smokes in his mouth, passing him from finger to finger along to the front of the mass.

The barrier of the enclosure blocked him. On the other side, the seats of the almighty. Beyond them was heaven, the places where the cherubim and the seraphim serenaded their makers and fixers.

Magog turned back towards the crowd. Faces and arms covered the fields in white clouds with the clothes on their bodies brightening the grasses like flowers. All about, the tents were floes of ice that stretched to the sky and to the outer barricades that fenced in the four corners of the earth.

The dreams beat louder than the hammers of the blood before a stroke. Guitar strings were wired to Magog's nerves as in the tortures of Hieronymus Bosch, the devils plucking at harps strung from the intestines of the damned. Cymbals were shears to his ears, singers moaned the agony of the dying, the rhythmic croak of last breaths.

Then there was silence. And the still waves of the faces and the arms moved and murmured, then crashed into breakers of roaring and rolling noise, until the sea of the people rose into a storm of crumbling crests of surf that spilled forward to Magog, hurling him back against the wire barriers that separated him from the music makers. And Magog threw out his arms along the wires to keep himself from falling into the great wash of the applause. And the wires held and supported him, and he did not drown.

So it was throughout the afternoon and into the night. Magog on his wire breakwater, caught between the seats of power and the sprawling masses on the grass, his ear-drums split by the raging angels of light on the platform or sucked under by the onrushing tides of praise that hurled themselves against the breakwater at every pause in the chants.

Then the queen of the earth came forward, holding her guitar with bent outstretched elbow to make the mysterious initial of power to the crowd, the M of her majesty traced in shadow against the light traced between her swelling belly and her instrument and the crook of her arm. Her voice was so clear that it made water seem a marsh, the fall of rain as the whine of engines, the salt desert as a scum of oil. Her sound was a blade so keen it flayed the fat away in each man and woman and took out the buried heart of a child spitted on its point, warm and smoking in the faith that all might be peace and joy where no sin was.

When the queen of the earth stopped singing, there was a great sigh as if the ground had opened. The long roaring from the armies in the night was reverent, as if the sea of the people was glad in the fullness of its communion. This was the end of the festival in the Isle of Wight, the last act before the going home.

The children rose in the darkness and the crusade began to drift away, shriven ghosts sliding back towards the black and waiting north. Magog hung on to the wires with swimming eyes, the slow tides edging back in front of him. A figure suddenly held him in the night, large, looming ungainly.

'Gog,' Magog said. 'I knew you would come.'

'Man,' an unknown voice said, 'are you on a bad trip?'

'Good,' Magog said. 'Good.'

Magog woke later in the cold night to find himself fallen from the wires. A body lay at his back, he was covered by a blanket, he was safe in the warm of an arm. On his shoulder-blade he felt the soft press of two breasts. He stirred and said softly, 'Josepha.'

Then again he said, 'Josepha.'

'Sleep,' a girl said. The voice was a stranger's. She had taken him in.

In the dawn, Magog found himself alone, stiff and chilled below the wire, the seats of power empty, the glory gone from the bare platform. He looked out over the fields that had held the white faces and the white tents of the young worshippers on their crusade to the new Jerusalem. And the whiteness still lay on the fields now the crusaders were departing, the whiteness of paper, packages, wrappings, napkins, trash. Down the harvest of litter, the hired scavengers were already advancing, in one hand a brown sack, in the other a short lance to stab at each piece of waste.

Sighing, Magog got to his feet. Groaning, he eased the cramps from his knees. Yawning, he ground his knuckles in his eyes. Learning, he stooped and picked a bit of litter from the grass. Beginning to put the place right.

ANDREW SINCLAIR

KING LUDD

'The land's history seen by flashes of lightning'
William Golding

'Sure to prove a lasting monument on the landscape of modern British literature'
Ian Rankin in Scotland on Sunday

'With KING LUDD Andrew Sinclair completes his impressive Albion triptych – a fictional fantasy come of age, a sustained feat of myth-mongering, and more. He has fashioned and elaborately decked out a time-dissolving pageant, carrying us back to legendary rulers and forward beyond computers until we are in an Eliotesque trance where past and future are one. A kind of Prophetic History of Britain, you might say'
Norman Shrapnel in The Guardian

'Cannot fail to have a crucial impact . . . Andrew Sinclair uses poetry, prose, language influenced by bawdy medieval tales, fables, the Bible, Swift, nursery rhymes and ditties to communicate his message . . . It is beautifully written'
Hampstead and Highgate Express

'KING LUDD has much to say about loyalty and betrayal, love, friendship and patriotism, and Sinclair says it with force and elegance'
London Magazine

'Sinclair's technique and approach have affinities with the writings of David Jones, James Joyce and John Cowper Powys'
Country Life

Current and forthcoming titles from Sceptre

ANDREW SINCLAIR

GOG
KING LUDD

PAUL SAYER

THE COMFORTS OF MADNESS

WILLIAM McILVANNEY

WALKING WOUNDED

AIDAN MATHEWS

ADVENTURES IN A BATHYSCOPE

ANTONY SHER

MIDDLEPOST

BOOKS OF DISTINCTION